SATURN RUN

SATURN RUN

JOHN SANDFORD AND CTEIN

G. P. PUTNAM'S SONS | NEW YORK

G. P. PUTNAM'S SONS
Publishers Since 1838
An imprint of Penguin Random House LLC
375 Hudson Street
New York, New York 10014

Library of Congress Cataloging-in-Publication Data

Sandford, John, date.
Saturn run / John Sandford, Ctein.
p.   cm.
ISBN 978-0-399-17695-1
1. Space ships—Fiction.   2. Quests (Expeditions)—Fiction.
I. Ctein, photographer.   II. Title.
PS3569.A516S28   2015   2015024637
813'.54—dc23

Printed in the United States of America
1   3   5   7   9   10   8   6   4   2

Book design by Gretchen Achilles

CTEIN DEDICATES THIS NOVEL TO PAULA BUTLER

SANDFORD DEDICATES IT TO BEN, DAN, AND
GABRIEL CURTIS, HIS GRANDSONS

SATURN RUN

1.

FEBRUARY 9, 2066

From ten kilometers out, the Sky Survey Observatory looked like an oversized beer can. Yellow-white sunlight glittered from the can's outward side, while the other half was a shifting fun house reflection of the pale blues and pearly cloud streaks of the earth, a thousand kilometers below.

The can was not quite alone: an egg-shaped service module, human-sized, encrusted with insectile appendages, ports, windows, and cameras, was closing in on it. Storage lockers and canisters surrounded the base of the egg. Had there been any air around it, and anything with ears, the faint twang of country music might have been heard vibrating through its ice-white walls: "Oh, my ATV is a hustlin' on down the line, and them tofu critters are looking mighty fine. . . ."

The handyman was making a house call.

The Sky Survey Observatory carried four telescopes: the Big Eye, the Medium Eye, the Small Eye, and Chuck's Eye, the latter unofficially named after a congressman who slipped the funding into a veto-proof Social Security bill. The scopes stared outward, assisted by particle and radiation detectors, looking for interesting stuff.

All of the SSO's remotely operable telescopes, radio dishes, and particle sensors, all the digital cameras and computers, all the storage systems and fuel tanks and solar cells, lived at the command of astronomers sitting comfortably in climate-controlled offices back on the ground.

Until the observatory broke. Then somebody had to go there with the metaphorical equivalent of a screwdriver.

One of the groundhuggers called, "Can you see it?"

Joe Martinez said into his chin mike, "Yeah, I can. Holy cow. Something really whacked that motherfucker."

"What! What? Joe, what—"

"Just messin' with you, Bob."

"Hey, Joe? I'm pushing the button that cuts off your air."

"Didn't know you had one of those."

"You don't mess with astronomers, Joe. Cutting the air in three-two-one . . ."

Martinez was a handyman; his official title was chief of station operations, which meant that he kept the place running.

He hadn't had much to do except drink coffee and read the current *Guitar Riffs* for the last couple of hours, waiting to make the approach to the SSO. Barring some weird million-to-one mishap, his trajectory was fixed by the laws of physics and the impulse from the low-velocity rail-gun at the station; the computer said he was exactly on track. He sucked down some more of the decaf, his fingers unconsciously tapping out a counterpoint to the Blue Ridge Bitches, the band he currently favored.

Martinez wasn't a scientist. He did mechanics and electronics, a little welding, a lot of gluing, the occasional piece of plumbing, and still more gluing. He had a degree in electromechanical engineering, but there were days when he thought he should've gotten one in adhesives. His engineering and academic background, combined with an instinctive love of machine tools, made him a quick study, but he didn't have much interest in building new machines.

On the ground, he messed around with electric guitars, video games, propeller-driven airplanes and wooden speedboats. He loved real hardware even more than he loved his computer, and he *did* love his computer. If he could build it, fix it, refurbish it, or just plain tinker with it, he was happy.

But he was happiest up in the sky, where he did a little of everything; he was the world's best-paid handyman.

Bob Anderson came back: "What do you think?"

"I can't see anything," Martinez said. "I mean, nothing unusual."

"Good. You going manual?"

"As manual as I can, anyway. And that would be . . . now."

He flipped the arming switch on the thruster joystick. Checking the intercept lidar—less than five meters a second of residual velocity, very good—he played the cradle's thrusters. Practice born of hundreds of runs made his actions nearly unconscious, like riding a bicycle. His eyes took in the instrument readings while his fingers responded with bursts of thrust. It was safer, he'd told Amelia, his third ex-wife, than driving to work.

"What happens," she'd asked, "if everything fails? I mean, if everything fails down here, when you're driving to work, you go in a ditch. What if everything fails out there?"

Well, then, he'd said, he'd get a free tour of the universe and would still be on tour when the sun finally died, a few billion years from now. She hadn't laughed. Then or later.

Martinez had. As the shrinks had noted, isolation didn't worry him.

"Radar says you're there," said Anderson.

"Close. Just a bit further."

The egg's attitude matched that of the SSO—there wasn't any particular "upright" in space, but there had been when the can was put together on Earth, and the lettering on the side of it appeared in the proper orientation to Martinez's eyes. There'd been few visitors to read the lettering—in the eleven years that the observatory had been functioning, there'd been thirty visits, by fewer than a half-dozen different people, one egg at a time.

Of those thirty visits, Martinez had made eighteen. Most of the instruments and scopes were modular, boosted up into space as self-contained operational units, ready for deployment.

Some assembly was required. The instruments had to be fitted into the can, periodically serviced, and upgraded as new and better cameras, computers, and memories were invented. The SSO was the finest piece of astronomical machinery ever produced, and Americans—or the astronomical fraction of them—were committed to making sure it was equipped with the best the taxpayers could afford.

On this trip, Chuck's Eye was getting an eye exam along with a new camera: Chuck had developed a tic. The vibration could have come from one of the servos inside the camera housing. It could have come from a wire that had worked free from its housing because of the heat-cold cycles. It could have come from any number of things, but whatever the cause, it had to be stopped. The cost of stopping it could vary from nothing at all, to a million bucks or so. The people on the ground were praying for "nothing at all," since Congress was in one of its semi-decadal spasms of cost-cutting.

Martinez's right hand played on the sensor panel, bringing up his work tools and assists. At the index finger's command, power flowed to the servos on the manipulator arms and energized the tactile gloves. The thumb flipped a switch and dozens of tiny directional spotlights flicked on all over the exterior of the egg, banishing the darkness between the egg and the can—in space, flashlights were almost as vital as oxygen.

His right little finger swiveled the lights, bringing them to bear. Years of misspent youth at game consoles had given him reflexes and manual dexterity that a jazz saxophonist might have envied. As his right hand continued to play the instruments, his left worked the joystick, bringing the egg in close and slow. He circled the can one time, making a vid, then eased the egg to a stop relative to the observatory.

Slowly, slowly, a mere millimeter a second, that was the trick. There wasn't any danger to the observatory; the SSO's own navigation computers could easily compensate for a bump, firing the observatory's thrusters and running its orientation gyros to bring it back on point. But why waste the can's limited fuel supply on a sloppy docking?

With the very faintest snick, the grappler on the egg latched onto one of the docking sockets that were all over the can's skin. This particular socket was adjacent to the Chuck's Eye instrument hatch. Once tied in, Martinez ran a last confirming test on the safety and security cameras. Everything inside and out was recorded during one of these house calls, because you never knew when a detail you missed might just save the job . . . or your life.

"We show you docked," Bob said. "Good job. Barely a jiggle."

"That's why you hired a pro," Martinez said. "You looking at the vid?"

"Yeah, we're running it against the last scan, and so far we see no changes, no anomalies," Bob said. Three seconds of silence. "Okay, the scan is finished, we see nothing at all on the exterior."

"Good. Go ahead and cut the juice."

"Cutting the juice: juice is cut. You're clear."

Killing the SSO's power was a safety precaution, not for Martinez, who was well isolated and insulated in his egg, but for Chuck's Eye: an accidental short or surge during servicing could result in one of those million-dollar repairs the groundhuggers were praying to avoid.

A moment later, a ground-based scope specialist named Diana Pike, whom Joe had never met, but with whom he often worked, called back and said in her familiar southern accent, "We're good, Joe. Want to look for that tic, first?"

"Hey, Di. Yeah, I'm putting some pucks out now." Martinez used a spidery remote arm to drop a few micro-seismometer pucks on the can's skin and the outer case of Chuck's Eye. The bottom of the pucks had a layer of an electro-phosphoprotein adhesive, a synthetic based on the natural adhesive used by barnacles. With a tiny electrical current running through the adhesive, it would stick to almost anything; when the current shut off, the adhesive effect vanished. They were called Post-its. What that had to do with yellow pop-up reminders on a workslate screen was anybody's guess.

"Okay, Di, we're set up here," Martinez called. "Give me a rattle."

"Here y'all go," Pike said. "Three-two-one. Now."

Two opposing thrusters fired on the can, each for just a tenth of a second and so closely spaced that a human eye couldn't have told them apart. The can shuddered.

"Okay. We're cycled. You see that?"

Martinez said, "Yeah, yeah, I see it."

Martinez was watching his monitor readouts—the people on the ground were seeing the same thing—where the reports from the micros were popping up, giving him a directional reading on the vibration. It was near the surface of the superstructure, which was good, but outside the seismo array. "I'm gonna have to juggle some pucks," Martinez said. "Wait one."

He moved his micros, and called back to Pike: "Give me another cycle."

"Cycling, three-two-one. Now. Cycled."

Martinez looked at his monitor and called back, "It's right near the surface. I'd say it's between walls. I'm repositioning the pucks and moving a scope out to take a look."

"It's the insulating foam." Pike was hopeful.

"Probably. I'm moving the pucks . . ."

Another shot and the micros gave him a precise location, within a half centimeter of the source of the vibration. He moved a macro lens in and looked at the surface of the observatory. "There's no external defect," he said.

"Good," Anderson said. If it had been a micrometeorite, the repairs could have been a bigger problem. They'd never had one penetrate both skins, but the possibility was always there.

"Gonna cut a hole," Martinez said.

The process took an hour. Martinez drilled a three-millimeter hole in the meteorite barrier, then peeked inside with a fiber optic. As they'd suspected, some of the foam used as insulation between the two walls had shaken loose on Chuck's Eye. There'd probably been a fracture during construction, or one created when the can was boosted into space; years of heat-cold cycles had finally shaken it loose. Martinez gave it a new shot of foam, specially formulated for this precise repair—they'd done three others just like it—sealed it with a carbon-fiber patch, and was done.

That had been the tricky bit. The next part, a monkey could do:
"Breaking out the camera package," Martinez said.
"Okay. Got you down for the package extraction."

The new package for Chuck's Eye was less a single instrument than a spider's-head complex of primary and secondary eyes, operating at all wavelengths from the mid-infrared to the far ultraviolet. Chuck's Eye was like the scout that ran ahead of an expedition in the Old West, taking in a wide field of view and maintaining a lookout for unusual objects and events. The bigger, more impressive Eyes would do the research that mattered, but Chuck's Eye would be the first to catch a new supernova or gamma ray burst, or whatever else might show up.

The cameras were modular and self-contained, and the new camera module looked exactly like the old one. Joe yanked the old one, slipped the new one into the rack, flipped the locking clamps, and pinged Anderson:

"I got the old camera package out of the rack and the new one seated. It looks fine. Bob, you can power up again. Everything looks good here."

"Looks good here, too. Powering up."

And it was good. The repairs fell into the "nothing-at-all" category. Another of the mission scientists came on and said, "That's nice work, Joe. We've run fifty cycles, got no vibes, and the new camera is online. You can go on home."

"I'm gone," Martinez said.

On the way back, he grabbed a bulb of proper caffeinated brew and pulled the heat tab, ate a few crumb-proof peanut-butter-and-cheese crackers, and contemplated the prospects of a proper meal. He'd been invited to dine with the station commander, Captain Naomi Fang-Castro, and her fiancée, Llorena whose-name-he-couldn't-remember. Better look that up before I commit a major faux pas, he thought. The captain and her first wife had divorced two years prior. The ex and their two college-age kids were on Earth; the ex hadn't been much for space.

Fang-Castro was committed to the sky. Probably why he and the commander got along so well, Martinez mused . . . and probably why they were both divorced.

He took a call from the station, where Elroy Gorey, whom the groundhuggers called a farmer, was feeding the plants, or monitoring the nutrient cycles on the biotech program, depending on your need for long words.

Gorey had a Ph.D. in botany and did a little plumbing and programming on the side, and was good with circuit boards. "That honey from Starbucks called," he said. "She wants to know if you forgot about your coffee."

"Nah, I've got a bulb here, but it'd be nice to have a fresh espresso waiting for me."

"I'll tell her," Gorey said. "I think she wants to know me better."

"I beg your pardon, there, Elroy, you're more of a wingman type."

The honey worked in Seattle, and hooked up to the station via an audio/video link that allowed her to make coffee for station personnel through an automated coffee machine. The face-to-face chatter was supposed to improve morale, and mostly did. Station personnel suspected that the baristas, male and female alike, had been chosen more for their good looks than their coffee-making abilities.

Back behind Martinez, at the can, Chuck's Eye ran through its preprogrammed diagnostic sequence, firing off a series of wide-field photographs and forwarding them to the ground station at Caltech, in Pasadena, California. Once they'd been vetted, by an intern, for their utter routineness, Chuck's Eye would be handed back to real astronomers for real work.

That was the plan, anyway.

2.

He was running late.

Severely late, though he didn't much care. The warm, soupy aroma of marijuana hung about his shoulder-length blond Jesus hair. The van found an approved space, parked itself, and he climbed out, grabbed his pack, threw it over one shoulder, and ambled toward Astro, taking his time.

He was a large young man, barefoot, wearing damp burnt-orange board shorts and an olive drab T-shirt. When he came out of the ramp, he flinched: movement on the roof of a building down and to his right. A microsecond after the flinch, he recognized it as a Pasadena parrot, rather than a sniper. That was good. He moved on, detouring around the traditional Caltech drying-lumps-of-dogshit in the middle of the sidewalk outside Astro, sighed, and went through the door.

He no longer had implants and so wore a wrist-wrap, which cleared him through Astro's security gate. Inside the lobby, he took the fire stairs instead of the elevator.

At the fifth floor, he peeked through the window on the fire door, to make sure that Fletcher wasn't standing in the hallway. He'd been through a lot of trauma in his short life, and trauma, he thought, he could handle. And he'd thought he could handle Fletcher's pomposity, but he was no longer sure of that. Sometimes, he thought, bullshit was worse than bullets.

Fletcher was not in sight, and he went on through the door and trotted down the hall toward his cubbyhole at the far end of the building, also known as the ass end, where the lowest-status people worked.

The main thing that everybody knew about Sanders Heacock Darlington—besides the fact that he had three last names, no first names, and showed remarkably little ambition—was that in two years, when he turned thirty, he would inherit money. Lots of money. More money than anyone in the Caltech Astrophysics Working Group had any chance of making in a lifetime.

And he was hot. His eyes were the same deep blue as the Hope Diamond, he had big white teeth, and a dimple in his chin, all original. He had that Jesus hair, a terrific surfer's physique, and an easy way with women.

In the Astro context, that made him extraordinarily annoying.

But he had, said the women who got to know him—there were a steadily increasing number of them in Astro—an absolutely black side that never showed at work.

Where *that* came from, they didn't know. Drugs, they said, may have been involved. There were hints of violence, that whole untoward incident at the Santa Monica Pier, and some odd scars on his otherwise flawless chest, back, and buttocks. When they probed, they were politely put down. But there was something dark and werewolf-ish behind those perfect teeth. . . .

Best not to pry, they agreed.

As he turned the last corner, he nearly ran over Sarah McGill.

Sandy hadn't tried to hustle McGill, though she'd been more pleasant than most of the people in the working group. She wasn't a beauty—he tended to favor beauties—but she was prodigiously smart, and she didn't treat him entirely like dog excrement. He'd lately noticed a certain languor about her, and the languor was sending signals to his hormones.

McGill dodged him, said, with a thin rime of sarcasm, "Right on time," and was about to continue on her way, and he called, "Hey, you got a minute?"

"About ten seconds, Sandy," she said. She had a full set of implants and he saw her eyes narrow as she checked the time. "Group meeting in nineteen." She had a turned-up nose with freckles, and kinky dishwater-blond hair, cut short. She'd bagged Samsung as a sponsor and had a dime-sized Samsung logo on her collarbone, along with smaller and slightly less prestigious tags from ATL and Google, as fractional sponsors.

Sandy nodded. "I was wondering . . . you wanna get a steak and salad some night? Catch a show?"

"Stop there."

"Hey, I'm just being human," he said.

"Right. Thanks, Sandy, but I've got—"

"Listen, you've been nicer than most of these assholes. I kinda owe you. I've got tickets to Kid Little at the Beckman."

Kid Little. She was tempted, he could see it in her eyes.

"Sandy . . ."

"I just want to go out and shake it a little," he lied.

"Let me think about it," she said. "I gotta go."

"Yeah, the group meeting. Say hello for me."

She twiddled her fingers at him and disappeared down the hall. Sandy was satisfied. One small step, he thought, as he continued on to his cubbyhole.

A janitor was coming down the hall with a push broom and they slapped hands as they passed, and the janitor said, "Tomorrow at dawn."

"If I can," Sandy said.

The janitor was a semipro surfer. Semipro surfing paid mostly in free burgers and beer.

Sandy was popular enough with janitors and maintenance men. His problem was with the academics. His status hadn't been helped by the fact that his father had purchased the job for him. The senior Darlington had hinted to Caltech's president that he would be extremely grateful if one of the working group professors would take his son under his wing. His son, he said delicately, was troubled: but not in some fractious, embarrassing way. He simply . . . didn't do much.

Dr. Edward Fletcher, respected and thoroughly tenured astrophysicist, had been happy to fall on that sword. Darlington Senior had already given Caltech not one, but two research buildings, and was a major financial backer of Chuck, the congressman who got the money for Chuck's Eye.

Fletcher could use a new building. Hungered for one. Preferably one called Fletcher Hall.

And it wasn't as though Sandy was an idiot. He had a perfectly good degree, his father pointed out. In American Arts, from Harvard. He'd even taken the non-required science elective, called Calculus and Physics for Poets, by those who took it, and had gotten a B. That didn't score any points among the astrophysicists.

"American Arts" was also known informally as the "College of Dilettantery," and those who left with degrees could reliably identify both a Masaccio and a Picasso, manually expose a photograph, make a short film, discuss both Italian and Scandinavian furniture, dance, make him/herself understood in French, Italian, and Spanish, and play the guitar and piano. Orbital calculations, not so much.

As one of the Real Scientists put it, "He couldn't change a fuckin' tire," which, in Caltech terms, didn't literally mean he couldn't change a tire, it simply meant he couldn't reliably explain the difference between a Schwarzschild radius and Schrödinger's cat.

There had been a stir of interest when the Astro group realized how much money was about to arrive in the shape of an intern, but a few minutes of research on the Internet revealed that Sandy had been through a number of career changes since leaving Harvard, and none of the jobs would have interested anyone in Astro.

He'd worked for Federal Mail for a while, but had apparently been unable to deliver, and had been fired. He'd been a vid-reporter with a marginally respectable independent news-and-porn blog, but that had ended badly, when Sandy threw an unclothed producer off the Santa Monica Pier, at low tide.

Lately, he'd been a surf bum and rhythm guitarist with a mostly girl-group called the LA Dicks. When asked by a leading Young Astro Star what he was going to do when he grew up, Sandy told him after he got Grandpa's money, he planned to become a philanthropist, or a philatelist, or a philanderer, or perhaps a flautist?

"It's one of those things," he said, with a toothy grin. "I've never been, you know, a big vocabulary head." The Young Star left with the feeling that Sandy had been pulling his weenie, which wasn't supposed to happen to Stars; he'd had to look up "philatelist."

Six months into the job, Sandy's insouciance had begun to seriously wear on Fletcher, just as Fletcher's pomposity wore on Sandy. Sandy

couldn't be fired—there was all that Darlington money out there.
Fletcher did the next best thing: gave him make-work.

Sandy recognized the job for what it was, and so went surfing.

When he wasn't surfing, and partly in revenge for the treatment he got from the Real Scientists, he was screwing his way through the department. So far, he'd had hasty relationships with seven of the seventeen single women in the research group. (One of the Young Astro Stars, holding court in the cafeteria, pointed out that both seven and seventeen were prime numbers, and if Sanders wanted to stay on course, and yet maintain that kind of fine arithmetical symmetry, he'd have to screw four more women, since eight, nine, and ten were not prime. A woman who overheard the comment said the Star's erratic sense of humor was part of the reason that Sandy had managed to sleep with seven out of seventeen, while the Star was striking out. She added, before picking up her lunch tray, "You fuckin' dweeb.")

And the women who'd slept with young Sanders confessed to each other, over hushed lunches, that while it was possibly true that Sandy might not match their knowledge of advanced physics and astronomy, sex was one area in which young Darlington definitely knew how to change a tire. Even, on occasion, multiple tires.

So virtually all his male colleagues, and a considerable (but shrinking) fraction of the female contingent, loathed him. Not that their loathing amounted to much: rudeness, mostly. They cut him out of grad student meetings.

Which made what happened all that much worse.

The interns' room was a windowless hall, a nearly perfect cube of yellow limestone, divided into sixteen tiny cubicles; it had once been a storage room.

There were four interns present when Sandy ambled through the door. Three of them were peering at computer screens, and the fourth had her head down on her desk. She snored.

"Man, you smell like pachuca weed," one of the interns, Ravi Chandrakar, said, as Sandy passed.

"Yeah, well, you smell like chili-cheese wieners. Given a choice, I'd rather smell like dope," Sandy said.

"That's the goddamn truth," said another of the interns. "You keep eating those fuckin' chili-cheese wieners, I'm gonna drag you to a window and throw you the fuck out."

"Yeah, right, like where are you gonna find a window?"

The sleeping woman stirred, but didn't awaken; the hostility had been simulated.

Sandy took his desk, touched the ID pad with his index finger, and the screen popped up.

He had been assigned to nursemaid Chuck's Eye. The work was not hard. Or, maybe it was, but the computers did it. Sandy was the human eye that double-checked the results, to make sure the computers hadn't missed anything unusual enough that it fell outside their analysis parameters. And the computers would tell him if that happened, so he could alert a Real Scientist.

The current program didn't even hold the possibility of uncovering an event of astronomical interest: it was a calibration run on a new camera module. The idea was to take a well-known, and therefore uninteresting, part of the sky and make simultaneous exposures with all the different-wavelength cameras. Superimpose them and make sure that all the little points of light aligned properly and that the spectra looked more or less normal.

Repeat that three times, at half-hour intervals, and make sure that those later stacks of images matched the first, so you knew that the tracking was good. Nothing in deep space changed rapidly, unless you were so amazingly lucky as to catch a supernova or gamma-ray burst, and the computers would recognize those things. Absent such a rarity, the four sets of stacked images should match up pixel for pixel.

It was a job made for a computer. But Chuck's Eye was a seriously valuable resource, and the Real Scientists felt the same way about their time, so it fell upon Sandy to babysit it. It seemed the perfect place to park a guy who'd written a senior thesis on "Movement Art as Planetary Drive."

To do his job, Sandy was required to push three keys on a computer keyboard to bring up a string of associated photos, then put his finger on the screen and drag them together, and then pinch them, and the computer would compare the images to see if anything untoward might be happening.

All this, in revenge for being a rich, good-looking, unemployable arts major. And, of course, that whole serial womanizer thing . . . to say nothing of the way he ran his mouth.

So he brought up his computer, put his feet on the desk, pulled open a drawer, unfolded a practice-guitar neck, and began running scales; it was a mindless activity that allowed him to maintain his left-hand calluses while he formulated his next move on McGill. He'd been doing that for twelve seconds when the computer pinged and produced a line of type:

CRITICAL ANOMALY.

That hadn't happened before. Dating rituals forgotten for the moment, Sandy put the guitar-neck aside and frowned. "Hi-ho, Watson, the game's afoot." He touched a menu that had popped up on the side of the screen, selecting the word "Describe."

The computer said:

OBJECT DECELERATING.

Sandy dropped his bare feet to the floor and said to the computer, "It's not just afoot, Holmes, it's a whole fucking leg."

"What's that?" Chandrakar asked over a cubicle wall.

"Talking to myself. It's the pachuca weed."

"Told ja."

Celestial objects do not decelerate, not even for Harvard graduates.

Sandy touched another menu item—Report—and the computer prepared a short report. The computer said:

THE OBJECT IS REAL ~ 99%.

THE OBJECT IS BETWEEN ONE AND 10 KM IN LENGTH.

THE OBJECT IS BETWEEN ONE AND FOUR KM IN WIDTH.

THE OBJECT IS EMITTING MOST STRONGLY IN THE DEEP
ULTRAVIOLET.

THE OBJECT IS EMITTING HYDROGEN GAS AT UNKNOWN VOLUME.

THE OBJECT IS DECELERATING.

What the holy hell? When had the test series been photographed? He checked: okay, mid-morning, about three hours earlier. About the time he should have gotten to work. Sandy tapped a few more keys, and the computer ran its virtual clock forward to the present time, extrapolating where the object would be if its behavior remained unchanged.

He checked the status board for all the SSO's scopes and saw that none of them were in use at the moment. The various researchers had held off on scheduling observations in case the servicing of the SSO took longer than expected. Good. He walked down the hall and looked in Fletcher's office, which was empty, along with most of the others.

Ah, he thought. The group meeting, to which he wasn't invited. Okay, no witnesses.

Sandy punched in Fletcher's authorization—he paid more attention to computer use than his coworkers suspected—and told Chuck's Eye to grab another set of comparison frames. The anomaly was probably a camera failure in that new module, he thought. Really couldn't be anything else.

He thought about it for another moment, checked down the hall again, and then retargeted the Medium Eye, which had never given them any trouble, to the extrapolated coordinates. He instructed the Medium

Eye to send down three short-exposure images separated by five-minute intervals. That should confirm that nothing was at the target site: both cameras wouldn't be wrong, at least not the same way.

But what was that thing the computer said, about "the object is real ~ 99%"?

Real? And decelerating?

Ten minutes to kill. He went and made fresh coffee, one of his assigned tasks. Anything that kept him from watching the clock. There must be a glitch. A major glitch. Because if it wasn't, he'd found an impossibility. "The object is decelerating?"

Time's up.

Sandy downloaded the files and ran them through the comparator. The new Chuck's Eye image showed the same anomaly, same weird-ass spectra, not quite where the computer had projected it would be, but close enough for the Medium Eye to catch it. He pulled up those frames, superimposed them, centered on the anomaly at maximum magnification, and,

There. It. Fucking. Was.

Three little dots in a row. If this was an instrumentation glitch, then both telescopes were hallucinating exactly the same way.

Sandy punched in a new group of commands: calculate the current deceleration rate and position, combine it with those from three hours earlier, extrapolate an orbit.

EXTRAPOLATION: THE OBJECT WILL ACHIEVE SATURN ORBIT IN 13 HOURS.

The supervisory working group was meeting to argue about targeting priorities, when Sandy knocked on the door and stuck his head in. McGill was up at the whiteboard, writing down lines of mathematical symbols. He caught the words "synchrotron radiation" and "anomalous jets." Whatever that meant—whatever it was, it seemed to impress the working group. As they turned from the whiteboard to look at Sandy,

Fletcher rolled his eyes back into his skull. Then, with an effort, he controlled the reaction and said, with poorly concealed impatience, "What is it, Sanders?"

Sandy, knowing precisely how much he'd begun to irritate Fletcher, put on his best toothy smile and asked, "How's it going, big guy?"

Fletcher ground his teeth. "I'm in a meeting here, Sanders, as you can see. If you could come back in an hour, or maybe tomorrow . . ."

"The computer found a critical anomaly in Chuck's Eye and Medium Eye images," Sandy said. "I thought I should tell you before I called the *LA Times*."

In the momentary silence, one of the postdocs said to Fletcher, "He's looking at the test images from the vibe fix."

Fletcher muttered something to himself, which might have included the word "prick," and asked Sandy, "Well, Sanders . . . did you get a report?"

Sandy peered at the piece of paper in his hand, as if he were having trouble reading it, and said, "The computer said there's a critical anomaly. It says there is an object approaching Saturn, that it is real, that it is kilometers long and across, that its spectra is UV-rich-hot, and that it is emitting hydrogen."

Slight pause for effect; Sandy knew he was now the center of attention and didn't mind milking it for another fraction of a second.

"Oh yeah, it's decelerating, and it will achieve Saturn orbit in thirteen hours."

The Real Scientists all looked at each other, and then Fletcher said, "Give me that paper."

A minute later, he said, "We need to run a confirming series."

"Done that," Sandy said, holding up a second sheet.

Fletcher looked even more annoyed, started to snap out something, and thought better of it. He took a deep breath. "Okay, and what did that tell us?"

Sandy handed him the second sheet of paper.

The working group stampeded down the length of the table to crowd behind Fletcher's rounded shoulders, as they all read the paper together. After a minute, somebody said, "Sweet bleedin' Jesus."

Fifteen hours later, Fletcher, exhausted from hyperactivity and lack of sleep, scrubbed his balding pate with his fingernails, looked around at the others in the room—the working group plus a couple of Astro Ultra Stars, plus a thin, dark-eyed man from Washington who had managed to scare the shit out of everybody in Astro—and said, "So, what we're saying is . . . Sanders Heacock Darlington made the most important scientific discovery in history? That asshole?"

"He couldn't change a fuckin' tire," somebody said.

"Maybe not," said the man from Washington, who scared them all. "But he found an alien starship."

3.

President Amanda Santeros tapped her pen, rapidly and unconsciously, against her teeth, as she skimmed the executive summary. She was a thin woman, narrow-shouldered with expertly coiffed dark brown hair. She wore a blue suit and a gold necklace with small turquoise cabochons, a gesture toward her home state of New Mexico. A hint of Chanel No. 5 hung about her, barely discernible through the odors of the waxes and cleaners that kept the Oval Office spotless, sanitary, and bug-free.

There were eight people with her: Senator Anson Sweet, the Senate Majority Leader; Representative Frances Cline, the Speaker of the House; Admiral Paula White and General Richard Emery, the chairwoman and vice chairman of the Joint Chiefs of Staff; Gene Lossness, director of DARPA; Jacob Vintner, her chief science adviser; and Ed Fletcher, of the Caltech Astrophysics Working Group, who'd arrived in Washington from Pasadena an hour earlier on a private hopjet, accompanied by the thin, dark-eyed man.

The man was named Crow. He didn't sit next to Fletcher. He didn't sit next to anybody. The President looked at her science adviser and said, "Jacob: an alien starship? I mean, really?"

Vintner, a fat man with a shiny bald head and small blue eyes, was more than a little nervous. He'd known Santeros since she was in college, had mentored her since graduate school, had been her official science adviser and unofficial confidante throughout her political ascent. It had all been interesting and some of it had been crucially important. None of it had been like this: he felt like a bit player in a bad sci-fi movie.

"We can't think of what else it could be," he said. "Once we had a trajectory for it, we looked at the Large Synoptic Survey database and tracked it back a few weeks. It's gotta be from interstellar space. Our oldest photographs showed it already decelerating, with a residual velocity above one percent of c."

"A little bit more in English?" That was White, the chairwoman. Good military mind, not so strong in physics.

"One percent of the speed of light. It was already slowing down two weeks ago," Vintner said, "but was still traveling in excess of three thousand kilometers a second."

White nodded: "So, basically, moving a hundred times faster than anything we've ever built. That doesn't make it alien. I mean, we could build something that fast, right? Somebody could." She meant China.

Lossness, the DARPA director, chimed in. "Yeah, but we couldn't make anything very big. Takes a lot of energy to go that fast. This thing is kilometers in size. It's like, ahh, a million times more massive than the biggest rocket we've ever built. It's hundreds of times the size of an aircraft carrier."

The President: "Nobody on Earth built that. We'd know about an industrial base that large."

Lossness said, "That's correct."

Santeros turned to Fletcher: "You're the guy who found this thing, right? What else do we know about it?"

Fletcher, both exhausted and ebullient, fidgeted a moment, rubbed his bald spot for good luck, and said, "My group of researchers discovered it. Actually, one of the grad students brought it to my attention. He was the one who found it first in some test photos from the Sky Survey Observatory."

"Why isn't he here?" Santeros asked. "Too busy for me?"

Fletcher shook his head. "No, ma'am. To be frank, he's a kid who looks at a monitor and matches photos. He doesn't know much about anything. He's scientifically incompetent, personally irresponsible, and only got the job because his family is enormously rich—his father's given Caltech a couple of buildings, and we'd like to get a couple more. The kid's got a degree in art or something, and spends most of his time surfing and playing guitars. He wouldn't have anything to contribute."

Crow stirred, as if about to say something, but then he didn't.

"But not so incompetent that he couldn't recognize a starship when he saw it," Santeros said. "And not so irresponsible that he didn't know enough to bring it to you, am I right?"

"The computer did most of that," Fletcher said. "What he did was, he walked down the hall with a piece of paper in his hand."

Santeros: "Okay, so what is it doing right now? This starship?"

"We don't know. Not in detail. The best we can determine, it's settled into orbit within Saturn's rings. We think it may have rendezvoused with something. There's a moonlet about there, embedded in one of the rings. Whatever that is, it's too small for us to make out any details. We see a few flickers in the images, just pixels in size, which make us think that maybe there's some activity going on there."

"What about the moon it rendezvoused with?"

"We don't know much about that, either," Fletcher said. "The Saturn ring system is lousy with these little moonlets. There are hundreds of them, maybe thousands. Most of them we've never looked at in detail. This is a pretty typical one, dim and not perturbing the ring system too much, so it's pretty small and low mass, not something particularly interesting that we'd be paying attention to."

"Either that, or it's something big, hollow, and painted black," Emery mused.

"And that's what you got?" A wrinkle appeared in Santeros's forehead, which was not usually a good thing for people speaking with her.

Lossness spoke up. "Madam President, we're looking across more than a billion kilometers of space and we just can't see details that small. This thing is huge by human engineering standards, but on the astronomical scale of things it's almost insignificant. If we hadn't accidentally caught it in a calibration run, we'd never have even noticed it."

Santeros nodded: "Which means that nobody else knows about it?"

"Very likely not," said Lossness. "We know how big and how good the best telescopes in the world are, and what they can see. We still put more money into astronomical research than anybody else, we have the best instruments, and we got very, very lucky. There's always a chance somebody else got lucky, but the odds are a thousand to one against."

Santeros turned to Crow and asked, "What's our security status?"

Crow said, "We're off to a decent start. Dr. Fletcher told his working group that if any of them spoke a word of this to anyone, including husbands, wives, significant others, or any one-night stands they were trying to impress, he'd run them out of the astrophysics community," Crow said. "He apparently succeeded in shutting them down until I got there. I rounded up the same bunch, told them we'd given this the highest military and civilian classifications, and if they talked about it, they would be charged with treason and executed. I was not funny about it."

"Were they impressed by the threat?" Santeros asked Fletcher. "Shutting up academics is like trying to herd cats."

"They were . . . quite impressed," said Fletcher. "Mr. Crow scared the shit out of them."

"Good. That's one of the reasons he works here," the President said.

Crow said, "I have to tell you, ma'am—it's gonna leak. It's too big. There are lots of Chinese working at Caltech and they are patriots. Chinese patriots. They are far beyond smart. Sooner or later, one of them'll get a whiff of this and it'll wind up in Beijing. We've got some time, but not an unlimited amount."

"Give me an estimate," Santeros said.

Crow looked down at his hands for a moment, calculating, then said, "Anything between tomorrow and a year from now. Unless something unusual happens, I don't believe it'll be close to either end of that line. If we put our smartest security people on it—guys who won't go out there waving their guns around trying to shut everybody down and drawing a lot of attention because of that—I'd give you either side of a bet on seven months. Assuming that the aliens don't call us up."

"Huh. That . . . uh . . . ." The President turned to Emery, the vice chairman of the Joint Chiefs. He was a mild-looking man wearing old-fashioned glasses, with short, sandy hair. He looked more like a college professor than a man who'd directed the early glory days of the Argentine Incursion. "Richard, what's the military's assessment?"

"Gene and I ran this past a couple guys at the think tanks, and, amazingly, people have already considered scenarios like this and looked into their implications."

"Which are?"

"They're pretty scary, ma'am."

"Ray guns?"

"No. Bad movies notwithstanding, they wouldn't need them. The geniuses aren't scared by ray guns, they're scared by the ship itself."

Fletcher started, and muttered to himself, "Oh my, yes." Vintner nodded and, surprisingly, so did Crow.

Santeros glanced around the room, settled her gaze on her science adviser, and asked, "Jacob, what's making all of you twitch?"

"Ma'am, what I said earlier about how big this thing was and how fast it could go . . . If it ran into something, it would pack a monstrous wallop. You remember about that asteroid that hit the earth sixty-five million years ago, down by the Yucatàn, and wiped out all the dinosaurs? If that starship were to hit us at the speed we know it's capable of, intentionally or accidentally, it would be like that. Worse than that."

Santeros's eyebrows went up: "You're serious. That thing could wipe out all life on Earth? Just by running into us?"

"Well, no, it probably wouldn't wipe out all life on Earth. Just the majority of all living organisms, and about 99.9 percent of all individual land animals. Most land species would go entirely extinct. We might be one of them. The best we could hope for is that we'd only be bombed back into the Bronze Age. That's all assuming that the mass is what we think it is. If the mass is radically different—if it turns out to be a big hollow shell—then the impact would be much different. But we don't think it's a big hollow shell."

"We couldn't deflect it or blow it up?"

"We might be able to figure something out if we had a lot of time . . . but we probably wouldn't have a lot of time, if it was aimed at us deliberately. We can barely see this thing at Saturn. If we got lucky enough to detect it right at that range . . . and that would be saying something . . . we'd have a little less than four days to figure out what it was doing, and to get ready for it. That's if it never went faster than what we've seen. But we don't really know how fast it can go—we've only seen it decelerating. So, if it could go, say, four percent of c, we'd only have a day to get ready. If it can reach twenty percent of c, we'd only have a few hours."

They all thought about that for a moment, then Santeros said, "So, to sum up, the simple existence of a starship constitutes an essentially unstoppable threat to human survival. We don't know how real or how likely that threat is. Is that correct?"

Everybody nodded.

"We need to find out," she said.

White, the chairwoman, interjected, "Let's not forget for a moment that whoever these aliens are, they've got some tech that we don't."

Lossness, the head of DARPA, said, "We don't have it, but we can see it from here. A hundred years out, we could build that ship if we had the funding."

Emery said, "That's fine, Gene, but we don't have it now, and that's the trouble." He turned to the President. "The problem isn't with the aliens. The big problem is, if the Chinese get there first, they may wind up in possession of hard technology that's a hundred years ahead of ours. In terms of soft tech, biology, chemistry, who knows? They could be a thousand years ahead or ten thousand years. That would not be good. You get advanced-enough technology, and there's always a way to turn that to a strategic advantage. Always. Imagine the situation if the Chinese had our current computers, and we were stuck with a bunch of old Microsoft Inquirers."

Santeros: "So now we've got two reasons to get out there. To get our hands on next century's technology before the Chinese do, and to find out if the aliens plan to ram us." She turned to Vintner, her science adviser: "Is that even possible, Jacob? For us to get out there?"

"I've been talking to Janetta Jojohowitz, and Gene's been talking to his people. They've pulled in their smartest guys, made it entirely clear this is at the absolute highest level of classification, fed them a cock-and-bull story about wanting to one-up China's Mars mission, and then asked them if they had any ideas for getting a mission to Saturn really fast. What they've brainstormed at the moment are broad concepts, half-baked ideas. But, yeah, they say it's doable . . . given the highest priority and a year or so to prepare."

Fletcher jumped in. "Ma'am, I'm no intelligence operative, but are we sure that the Chinese ship is going to Mars? Is there any possibility that they spotted one of these aliens five years ago, and are on their way to Saturn? I mean, are we really, really sure it's going to Mars?"

White said, "Yes. We've seen their specs and their engines and we're watching the work in great detail. This is all . . . secret . . . so keep your mouths shut, but yeah: it's going to Mars. In fact, the mission's purpose is to establish a permanent colony there. Which is the reason they are being so secretive about it."

Fletcher leaned back: "And they don't know about this, this thing out at Saturn?"

Emery: "Apparently not."

Crow reminded them, "Not yet. They will."

Santeros turned back to White. "So, from our perspective the immediate problem is the Chinese, not the aliens."

"As we see it," said the chairwoman. "But really, it's all guesswork. We assume that any race that could build a ship like this, is at least rational. You'd almost have to be, to do the work involved in building the ship. What isn't guesswork is that we have this competition going with the Chinese. Japan, Russia, and Brazil are on the fence . . . and boy, it'd sure be nice that if somebody gets a hundred years of new tech, it'd be us. At least, you know, until we transit into the post-conflict world."

Lossness nodded. "As Crow said, it's gonna leak. The Chinese are just over a year away from launching their Mars mission. Their ship could be re-routed to Saturn without much work. Basically, they were already planning a long-duration mission to Mars, what with all the equipment and personnel needed to establish a permanent facility there, so they've got the supplies and the crew. If they rerouted, well, they'd be nearly ready to go. Offload a bunch of colony equipment, throw in a bunch more mission-relevant supplies, that'd be most of it."

"That'd be a hell of a long mission," Fletcher said. "Mars is a fifty-million-kilometer run. Saturn is a billion and a half. Two, three months to Mars'd become, ummm, five years or so to Saturn."

Santeros said, "That would give us some time, right, Gene?"

Lossness said, "Well, my guys were tossing around trip durations of under a year. The thing is, if the Chinese find out what's happening before they launch, they can soup up their ship. They'd need a longer initial burn, so they'd need a lot more reaction mass. But they'd be offloading weight by not taking the colony along. Strapping on additional mass-tanks in space isn't as big a job as it is here on Earth."

Fletcher said, "We're a little unlucky about the launch window here, if Mr. Crow is correct. If we could keep this secret until the Chinese launch for Mars, then it would be too late for them to recover. We could take our time building a ship, and there's nothing they could do about it."

"Except shoot it down," Emery said.

Santeros said, "Based on Mr. Crow's best guess, we can't assume they won't find out. And we can't afford a gamble. We have to win this one. Jacob? Those half-baked ideas? I want them fully baked by this evening's meeting. I don't care what kind of carrots or sticks you have to wave to get the answers, I want to know exactly what we can do and how fast we can do it. Clear?"

Nobody said anything for a long moment, then Santeros looked over at the politicians, Sweet and Cline, who'd been listening carefully, but carefully not making notes. "If we build a ship on a crash basis, can we get the funding through on the black budget?"

Sweet said, "Yes," and Cline nodded.

Sweet said, "Francie and I had a word before the meeting started. You can have as much as you want. We should talk to McCord over at the Treasury and Henry at the Fed. It may be possible to do it completely off-budget, though we might have to do a little . . . creative book-keeping."

"The security circle's getting pretty large," Crow said.

Santeros: "You see any way to avoid that?"

Crow thought a moment. "No. I'm just sayin.' I need to create a security group, right now. I need the authority to pull anybody I need out of the security establishment. I think I know enough smart guys to do this—at least, I know enough smart guys who know enough smart guys. But I need a budget and I need a letter from you. I need the authority to kick whatever ass needs it, and I mean up to Cabinet secretary, four-star rank."

The President tapped out a note on her pad: "I'll get the letter to you within the hour. We'll want to launch your group no later than tomorrow."

Crow nodded: "Yes, ma'am. No later than."

Santeros stared down at a briefing paper on the desk in front of her, then said, "Ladies and gentlemen, this is the biggest thing since the atomic bomb, in terms of turning the world around. We need to stay all over this, all the time. This becomes the number one national priority, and you eight are my working group. We'll bring in more people as we need them. I'm going to ask Jacob to act as the chief of staff for the group, at least for now. Everything should go to him, and he'll talk to me. I'm going to clear my schedule for tonight, and I need all of you to come up with outlines of what you can contribute to this project, and I need to be briefed again, then. That includes exactly how we're going to get to Saturn before the Chinese. We need that settled. Not tomorrow. Tonight.

"As I see it, Dr. Fletcher, you'll be in charge of monitoring the Saturn site with your telescopes. You military people will build the ship: work out your system. Paula and Richard, work with Gene on this. Senator Sweet and Representative Cline will take care of the money. Crow will handle security. Is everybody good?"

Fletcher lifted a hand and she nodded at him.

"There is one tiny problem with my group. The intern who spotted this . . . object. He could be a security issue."

"The incompetent one."

"Scientifically incompetent," Fletcher said. "Unfortunately, he's not

simply dim. He seems to be quite knowledgeable about the media and
he's somewhat irresponsible, in my view. I don't think he was as impressed with Mr. Crow as the others were."

"He's a loose cannon," Santeros said. "Mr. Crow specializes in loose
cannons."

"With all due respect, ma'am, Sanders Heacock Darlington—"

"Are you shitting me?" Santeros said, showing surprise for the first
time. "Barron Darlington's kid?"

"I'm afraid so," Fletcher said. "He's got an ocean of money, he's about
to inherit a lot more, and nobody has ever taught him that he has to be
responsible about anything. You can't scare him, because he's apparently
never encountered anything that he needs to be scared of. And his father, as you know, is heavily wired into Washington."

The President asked, "What does he want? The kid?"

"I don't know," Fletcher said. "Fame? Notoriety? I mean, he used to
shoot vid for a news-and-porn blog."

"Which one?"

"Naked Nancy . . ."

"Goddamnit," Santeros said. "Last time I looked, she had an eight
share worldwide."

"I wouldn't know about that," Fletcher said. "But she's big. Can you
imagine what the revelation of an alien ship would mean in terms of
ratings?"

Crow cleared his throat and said, "I need to say something here. Dr.
Fletcher's view of Mr. Darlington is not entirely correct. I've been trying
to herd these particular cats and I've put together some dossiers. Dr.
Fletcher, I saw on a note from you that Darlington worked for Federal
Mail?"

"Yes. Not very successfully, either. I understand he was fired for lack
of performance."

"He never worked for Federal Mail," Crow said. "He was actually a
first lieutenant with an army organization called the Strategic Studies
Group in the Tri-Border area."

Emery, the vice chairman, looked up and said, "Well, that's a horse of an extremely different color. The only messages they delivered were thirty-caliber or larger."

"He left there with a price on his head," Crow said. "The Guapos were offering ten million for it and they didn't care if a body was attached. The whole Federal Mail business is part of a cover story. Mr. Darlington's . . . attitude . . . if that's what you might call it . . . is also referred to by the Veterans Administration as post-traumatic stress syndrome."

Fletcher was astonished. "Darlington? Was in the military?"

"If what Crow is saying is accurate, he wasn't just in the military," Emery said. "The SSG was way out there. They didn't have a lot of survivors."

Crow looked at the President: "The point being, behind the surfer-boy attitude that seems to disturb Dr. Fletcher so much, there's not only a lot of money, but an extremely hard nose. From a review of his records, I would go so far as to say one of the hardest noses in the Western Hemisphere."

"I don't see it as much of a problem," Santeros said.

"It's not?" Crow asked, but with a smile. He didn't know what was coming, but he knew Santeros.

"Read the small print in the Universal Service Law sometime," Santeros said. "I've done that. If the former Lieutenant Darlington gives us any trouble, I'll draft his ass right back into the army."

Fletcher said, "Draft him? Into the military? Even with Darlington, that seems kind of . . . immoral."

Everybody looked at him for a moment, and then the group dissolved in laughter; except for Fletcher, who flushed, and Crow, who only grinned.

Santeros tapped her computer again. "I've got to go. Dr. Fletcher, thanks for your time, but now you should be heading back to California to make sure your group stays in line, at least until Crow's people can get out there. I'll see all the rest of you tonight. We won't be having a little tea party like this. Tonight, we get serious."

As the group rose to leave, Santeros said, "Mr. Crow, would you stay behind for a moment?"

When they were alone, the President asked him, "Is Darlington going to be a problem? I really could draft him . . . but we're talking about one of the biggest buttloads of money in America. If either he or his old man went off the rails, the whole thing could go up in smoke."

"I don't believe that will happen," Crow said. "Two things about Darlington: for all the surfer-boy bullshit, he started out as what you'd call . . . a patriot. I know it's unfashionable, but that's the only word that fits. He enlisted right after the Houston Flash, and was in the thick of things down at the Tri-Border. I think that fundamental impulse is still alive. The other thing is, I looked at his VA psych files, and I suspect Darlington does want something. Desperately. And we can give it to him."

"What's that?"

"He wants something to do," Crow said. "Something serious."

4.

A thousand kilometers above the Washington machinations, Captain Naomi Fang-Castro wrapped up the last meeting of the day, a report on the ongoing repairs to backup electrical storage units. The repair work was fine, but there was a shortage of critical parts, caused by a continuing army inspector general's examination of the Earth-bound support bases.

The bases wanted to show that they were fully stocked and ready to go for any emergency, and if they drew down stock lists to support U.S. Space Station Three, then they wouldn't be at one hundred percent. Since Fang-Castro was in the navy, she didn't have the clout she might have had if the support bases had been run by the navy.

"I'm going to be begging again," she said to her executive officer, Salvatore Francisco. "I've got to find somebody in the Pentagon who can squeeze Arnie Young."

Brigadier General Arnie Young was the commander of the support bases.

"Talk to Admiral Clayton. He's a sneaky prick," Francisco said.

"That's a thought. The problem is, he always wants some payback. I don't want to become one of his *girls*."

They'd make another round of calls in the morning, they decided, and gave it up for the day.

Fang-Castro headed home, carrying her briefcase. She was quiet, serious, short, and slight; the first impression she conveyed was that of the quintessential forty-something Chinese woman, despite being fourth-generation American. Her parents had brought her up with a traditional, antiquated propriety.

She was nowhere near as frightening as the name "Captain Fang" led some to believe, before meeting her . . . as long as you weren't standing between her and her objective, as long as you didn't ignore one of her suggestions.

The captain's "suggestions" were not optional. Very few made the
mistake of thinking so, a second time. The space station was a comfortable and safe environment, entirely surrounded by near-instant death.
Nobody had yet died under her command, and everyone agreed that as
unpleasant as her wrath could be, it beat the alternative.

Fang-Castro's home was in Habitat 1, Deck 1 of USSS3, known as
the Resort. The Resort had simulated gravity, equivalent to a tenth of
Earth's, created by the rotation of the habitats, and real private quarters
instead of dorms and sleep-cubbyholes. A select few of the quarters even
had two rooms. One even had a window.

Fang-Castro loved her window. After a long command shift, she'd sit
in her easy chair, raise the vid screen and the stainless steel shade behind
it, dim the room lights, and let her mind drift with the stars, and sometimes the dime-sized sun, and at other times the massive soft expanse of
the earth, as they all slowly swept past the window once a minute, the
markings of a cosmic clock.

It was a near-daily ritual, and she joked that that window was her
one addiction.

Her fiancée didn't like it. The window made Llorena Tomaselli
queasy. She'd logged seven months in space as a computer maintenance
tech, and she was fine in confined spaces like cable tunnels, but having
the whole universe rotate about her, like she was some lesser goddess,
gave her mild vertigo. Fang-Castro knew that while she was at work and
Tomaselli was home, the shade stayed tightly closed and projected a
pleasant Earth scene, someplace in Italy's Campania. When Fang-Castro
was home alone, the stars were always there. When they were both home,
they negotiated.

Tomaselli was cooking. As Fang-Castro entered the suite, she smelled
stir-fry for dinner—sprouts, jerked mock duck, ginger, hot peppers,
and platanos—with rice and red beans on the side. Her stomach rumbled impatiently. She wasn't an obligate vegetarian, and vegetarianism
wasn't obligatory in space, especially not if you were the station commander. Meat was hard enough to come by, though, that it was easier
just to put it out of one's mind.

"Tough day?" Tomaselli asked, when Fang-Castro dumped her briefcase.

"Too long, too messy. It was a nibbled-to-death-by-ducks day." She yawned, stretched, and said, "Smells terrific."

"It is terrific," Tomaselli said. "Want a drink?"

"I'll get it—maybe a margarita. You want one?"

"Sure, but take it easy on the salt. The last time—"

The security phone in the bedroom pinged; that almost always meant trouble. "Ah, really . . . ?"

"Go get it, I've got some work to do here yet," Tomaselli said. "Won't be ready for ten minutes, anyway."

"I'm sorry, dear, I'll make it quick."

"What if the station's ass just fell off?"

"Then it'll be even quicker."

Fang-Castro stepped into the bedroom and called up the screen, expecting to see the watch commander and the control deck. Instead, she saw the Oval Office, Jacob Vintner, and Gene Lossness. The President was there, too, in the background, reading something. Before they could ask, she hit the door-close and privacy firewall buttons on her slate.

"Captain Fang-Castro, Gene and I need to talk to you about a new assignment," Lossness said. "The President is here, too."

The President lifted a hand in the direction of the camera, without looking up from what she was reading.

Fang-Castro was careful: "Okay." Something serious was up. She did not travel in this bureaucratic stratum.

"We're about to ask you some big questions. We're on a tight dead-line, and we're going to need an answer right now. And when I say 'now,' I mean, this minute."

"Quickly, then. Dinner's waiting."

Vintner looked momentarily nonplussed and then plunged in. "We need to repurpose the station for interplanetary flight. Rework the habi-tats, strip off the physical plant, add engines and reaction-mass tanks and a new command section. We'd like your opinion on the feasibility of doing this in the next twenty-two months. We'd also like you to take on the assignment of mission commander."

"Can I give a quick call to my chief engineer?"

"Absolutely not. We need your assessment, and only yours, right now."

Fang-Castro looked down at her hands, thinking. "Okay," she said again. Stalling, as her mind ran through the possibilities and implication. "Engineering could probably cope, but life support won't handle a long-duration mission."

"This won't be long. A year at most, and your life support'll be beefed up along with everything else."

Fang-Castro said, "I can see where this is going. You want to beat the Chinese to Mars. But we'll need to do this in a lot less than twenty-two months, and we'll need some kind of landing craft, not to mention . . ."

In the background, the President reached away from her reading, touched something, and her face suddenly dominated the view screen: she was looking straight at Fang-Castro.

"Captain, this isn't a Mars mission. You'll be going to Saturn."

"What? Excuse me, ma'am, but that's . . . What happened?"

The camera's view angle slipped back and focused on Vintner, who filled her in on the previous day's events.

Fang-Castro gaped: "A starship?"

"Exactly," Vintner said. "Will you take the assignment? You know the station, you know how to work with both military and civilians. This will not be a military operation. There'll be a modest complement of military on board, but fundamentally this is a science mission and Gene says you're very good with scientists."

"I need to discuss this with my fiancée."

"Sorry, but this is most secret. You can't discuss it with anyone."

"Then I have to say this: if I can't tell her what's up, I'd have to decline. We're planning to get married two months from now. We don't keep secrets from each other, and we don't lie to each other."

Vintner looked at Lossness, who shrugged, and suddenly the

President's face was back. "What if it was me who told the lie? You'd only have to . . . prevaricate. All married people do that, as you must know— I see you were married once before."

"I'm not sure I understand . . ."

"What if you told her that I was going to make a big speech tomorrow—about how we were going to Mars, to assist the Chinese in their Mars mission, if needed, and to do our own orbital surveys."

"But we're not . . ."

"No, but that's what I'm going to say tomorrow. To everybody on the planet. Eventually, the secret will leak, and then . . . you'll have to deal with it when it happens. But there's not much difference between a long, slow trip to Mars and a long, fast one to Saturn. And your little prevarication wouldn't look like much, next to my big one."

"That seems pretty technical, I mean, on an emotional level."

"Screw a bunch of emotions. If your relationship can't survive a little white lie, then it probably can't survive, anyway," Santeros said. "Might as well get it over with."

Fang-Castro had a snappy comeback to that, but suppressed it. Santeros's husband was known as Happy Frank, as was his penis, which had reportedly traveled to places it shouldn't have. Instead, Fang-Castro said, "Listen . . . I, uh . . ." She put a finger to her lips, thought for a few seconds, realized that she desperately wanted to go. She said, "I'll take it. I'll go."

The President smiled and said, "Excellent. We want you pretty badly." And she was gone again.

Vintner said, "I apologize if I seemed a little . . . pushy, but we've been under a lot of pressure with very little sleep for the past couple days."

"Apology accepted," Fang-Castro said. "Let's get down to it. What kinds of mods are we talking about? What's our propulsion system going to be? Who is handling recruiting of the ship's complement and scientists? I have some current personnel I'd like to have vetted for this, particularly my Number Two . . ."

Ninety minutes later—it seemed like ten—Fang-Castro closed the screen, raised the security firewall, and took a deep breath. Ruined din-

ners were a point of discord in their relationship and there was some
making-nice to be done: Tomaselli took her cooking seriously, and this
wouldn't be their first ruined dinner.

Back in the common room, Tomaselli was immersed in a book. She
didn't look up. The window shade was drawn. Not good signs.

Fang-Castro said, "I need to tell you something that falls under your
top secret clearance. It comes with a warning from the President: you'll
be prosecuted if you say a word about this to anyone but me, before tomorrow at one o'clock."

Tomaselli was pissed, but she wasn't stupid: some things were more
important than dinner. "What?"

"The President says we're going to Mars," Fang-Castro said. "I made
them agree that I could tell you, before the announcement. They want
me to take the job, and I accepted. I'd never dictate to you, Llorena, and
I know this will be a long separation . . . but it wouldn't start for a couple
of years. I would be desperately sad to . . . leave you behind."

"Mars? You made who agree?"

"Santeros . . . and a couple of high-level bureaucrats," Fang-Castro
said. "That's who I was talking to." And, "Listen, I'm really sorry about
your dinner."

"Oh, fuck the beans, Naomi," Tomaselli said. "What in God's name
just happened?"

Fang-Castro said, "I don't have the details, because nobody does. All
I got was a lot of engineering questions. Maybe we'll get some details
tomorrow, when Santeros makes her big speech."

Little white lies.

5.

Sandy let the van's nav take him home; it was quicker that way, locking into fast-lane traffic across town to Pasadena. Zuma Beach had been a bust, with too many people, too few decent waves. And he'd been distracted: couldn't be thinking about alien starships when your board was trying to kick your ass into the deep.

He'd left Argentina in a medevac chopper, spent the next six months at the San Francisco Army Hospital. When he got out, physically rehabbed and mentally stable, give or take a med or two, he'd started looking for a job that might engage him. He hadn't found it. He was addicted to the rush of combat, but that was hard to find in civilian life. You could find jobs that were simply dangerous, but as dangerous as they might be, they were usually boring as well, until everything went sideways and you got killed.

He'd gotten a taste of the rush, running around L.A. with a news team and a camera, but after a while, it all seemed pointless: with nine billion people on Earth, anything that you could conceive of people doing to each other was being done. All the time. Taking pictures of it didn't change anything.

His father, though a rich and conservative plutocrat, was a nice-enough guy. He worried that Sandy was drifting, and, when he inherited his grandfather's money, would become another too-rich dilettante, wasting his life with sex, drugs, AR, and RhythmTech. He'd call every morning with suggestions, and finally had suggested a job that might engage Sandy's intellect: "I think I found you something different over at Caltech."

That hadn't worked out, and Sandy started drifting again. He stayed away from the Alternate Reality games, as too stupid and too addictive. His VA medical monitor suggested more drugs, something that might chemically re-create the spark.

The Benz parked itself, and the phone component of Sandy's wrist-wrap told the front door that he'd arrived. The door unlocked itself and disarmed the alarm. One step inside, he stripped off his damp T-shirt and dropped it on the floor, as the door closed itself. Another three steps and he stopped, then backed up to the door, passed his wrist-wrap over a faux-but-good Impressionist painting. The painting swung silently away from the wall, revealing a niche.

Sandy took the HK double-stack automatic out of the niche, turned it on, and selected the hard stuff without thinking, and asked, aloud, "Who's here?"

"Crow."

Crow. Sandy could smell him. Nothing offensive—mostly peanut butter—but not right for an empty apartment. Sandy followed the muzzle of the pistol into the kitchen, where Crow was sitting at the breakfast bar, handling the partly disassembled RED XV vid camera that Sandy had been refurbishing. A half-eaten peanut-butter sandwich sat an arm's length away.

"Careful with the camera," Sandy said. He dropped the gun on the kitchen counter with a metallic clank and pulled open the refrigerator. "I've been realigning the sensor and it's not tightened down yet."

"I can see that—I've worked with one of these before," Crow said. "Looks like a full hardware alignment."

"Yeah, it is. The actuators were screwed. And for Christ's sakes, don't get peanut butter on anything."

"Sorry. I haven't had much time to eat."

Sandy nodded. "You want a Dos Equis? And, uh, I got a couple splits of champagne if you're feeling girlie."

"Dos Equis is good. So: I talked to Larry McGovern last night."

"Yeah? I heard he got his birds." Sandy handed Crow a bottle of beer, picked up the HK and turned it off, and leaned against the refrigerator door.

"Yes, he did. He'll get a star in a couple of years, if he doesn't send the wrong memo to the wrong guy."

"He's not really a memo guy," Sandy said. "At least, he didn't used to be, when he was a light colonel."

"Still not. He says 'hello.' He doesn't call you 'Sandy,' or 'Lieutenant Darlington,' by the way. He calls you 'The X.' Not 'X,' but 'The X.'"

"Army bullshit," Sandy said. "Anyway, what's up with you? I assume this isn't a practice burglary. Especially with the security they've got in this place."

"No. We need to talk to you, about keeping your mouth shut. About not trying to blackmail us into letting you go on the mission."

"What mission?"

"To Saturn. Leaves in a year or two."

Sandy took his beer around to the couch that faced the breakfast bar, dropped into it, and said, "You're really going?"

"Yeah."

"Man, I gotta tell you—I want to go, and bad," Sandy said. "What do I have to do to talk you into it? Or bribe you? How about a huge fuckin' campaign contribution to Santeros? I could . . ."

Crow shook his head: "Nothing. You want to sign up, we'll take you."

Sandy thought about it for a minute, then asked, "Why?"

"Well, oddly enough, you precisely fit a slot on the ship. You're a decent videographer, bordering on good, and you'll be better than good by the time we leave. We need to document every millimeter of this thing. We'll want it in the highest resolution. And we want it done by somebody who has demonstrated some guts—somebody who won't cut and run because he's about to be flamed by a bug—and somebody who has shown that he can keep his mouth shut. That's one thing."

"One thing? There's another?"

"Yeah. There'll be a few guns on board," Crow said. "I'll have one. You'll have access to another one, if need be. Some weird shit could happen on this trip. There'll be a lot of stress, probably a lot of argument, given the kind of people who'll be aboard. Could have some psych problems. We think it'd be a good idea to have a hard-nosed security guy to back me up, if I need it."

"I'm really not interested in killing anybody," Sandy said. He took a hit of Dos Equis. "Not anymore."

"If you got to the point where you had to kill someone, you'd most likely be saving the whole crew, as well as your own ass," Crow said.

Sandy said, "Okay. That, I could do."

"So. You wanna go?"

"Absolutely. The only thing is . . ."

Crow: "What?"

"I'm afraid that you're setting me up," Sandy said. "Fletcher's told you that I'm entirely unreliable, that I couldn't change a fuckin' tire, and all that. That I smoke too much dope, that I screw my way through the Group . . ."

Crow waved it off: "We know what Fletcher's going to say, and I know what Larry McGovern told me yesterday. Larry said that if I ever needed a backup, and I didn't choose you when I had the chance, I was a fool. I'm not a fool. You couldn't take any dope aboard the ship, for obvious reasons, but—"

"I don't need it," Sandy said. "I'm still worried that you'll just lead me along, and then, at the last minute, after word about the mission has leaked . . . you'll kick me off the mission. Like totally fuck me."

"We considered that," Crow said. "But, given the fact that you rather neatly fit a slot we need, and all your money, and the potential for fucking us back . . . we decided it'd be easier to play it straight."

Sandy grinned at him: "I would have liked to have seen that decision get made. 'Playing it straight'? That's gotta be a first for Santeros."

"We're not that bad," Crow said.

"Of course you are," Sandy said.

Crow asked, "Why'd you drop the HK when you saw who it was? What if I'd come here to take care of our potential publicity problem?"

"You really do that?" Sandy asked.

"I'll ignore that question," Crow said. Then, a half second later, "Wait—I won't ignore it. Of course I don't do that. We don't go around killing innocent people."

Sandy nodded and said, "I keep the gun in case there's somebody who might try to collect the blood money. When it turned out to be you, I knew that the gun wouldn't help. If you were here to kill me, it was a done deal. Though, when I think some more about it, you wouldn't be here if I was going to be killed. There'd be an unfortunate surfing accident, or a semi-trailer's nav would go crazy and cross the centerline . . ."

"Paranoid fantasy . . . science fiction." Crow took a final pull on his beer, put down the bottle, and asked, "Would you be willing to go back under military discipline?"

"You mean reenlist?"

"You'd be reactivated. You're still technically—very technically—in the reserve."

"Could I be a major?"

"No, but you could be a captain," Crow said.

"Would I have to wear a uniform?"

"Actually, we don't want you to," Crow said. "The only reason we want you under discipline is so that if . . . mmm . . . there were some difficult orders, the consequences would be more severe if you didn't follow them. Orders from the President. Court-martial, instead of a bunch of surf rats on a jury from Venice Beach."

"I could—"

"There's a little more," Crow interrupted. "We'd want you to stay under cover. Keep your current persona. The rich and flaky vid guy whose father probably bought him a job on the ship. In other words, we wouldn't want people to know you're actually Superman, until it's time to leap over the building."

"Let me think about that a second," Sandy said. He thought one second, then brought out his toothy grin. "Okay. I'm in."

"And you'll do what we want." A statement, not a question.

"I'll tell you what, Crow," Sandy said, the smile slipping away. "I'll not only do what you want, I'll do what you need."

6.

Jiang, the ambassador from the People's Republic of China to the United States, grumbled over the morning briefings. Today's minor crisis involved a glitch in mining and trade negotiations, and he'd probably have to smooth a few ruffled feathers. What the hell was rhenium used for, anyway?

Chen poked his head in the door without knocking: "Boss? Hate to interrupt, but I got a call from my little birdie. He says we need to watch the President's speech. More than that: he's sending a messenger with an advance copy. He said you should read it . . . for your own good."

"My own good? Your little birdie is presumptuous," Jiang said. "What else did he say? Is this going to be ugly? Everything seems smooth right now. Haven't heard anything from home . . ."

"That's why I stuck my head in—my contact is very, very close to Santeros. He hinted that we're getting an advance look because they basically like us, and don't want you to look bad, back home. You'll be able to tip them off."

"It's already ten o'clock. The announcement said she's speaking at one o'clock. What good will three hours do us?"

"Better than no hours, if she's about to drop a bomb." Chen looked at his watch. "And it'll be less than three hours—I got the impression that the messenger wasn't on his way, yet. The messenger, by the way, will arrive in a Secret Service car. I suspect his arrival will be very closely calculated to give you just enough time to tip off the minister, but not enough time to shoot down whatever balloon Santeros is planning to float."

Jiang pulled on an ear, thinking, then said, "Tell Chong if he takes more than nine seconds to get from the street to my office, I'll have him hanged in the basement."

"Boss, that would be cruel. You know how serious . . ."

Jiang waved him off. "Okay. Tell him he'll be flogged in the basement."

A Secret Service agent, in the middle car of a three-car caravan, delivered a sealed package to Chong at 11:45. Chong made it to the ambassador's door in 7.5 seconds, handed it off to Chen, who stuck his head in again: "Boss, the package is here."

"They took their time with it," Jiang said, as Chen crossed the long Oriental carpet to his desk.

Chen handed him the package and asked, "Do you want me to . . ." He tipped his head toward the door.

"No. I prefer to have a witness," Jiang said. "Sit down."

He ripped off the top of the envelope, using the dangling ribbon that protruded from one end.

Chen nodded, and sat. He'd been Jiang's right-hand man since Jiang had joined the diplomatic service. Jiang wasn't entirely sure what the slight and shy man had done before joining the corps, but he was well-connected in Beijing and had excellent intuition. Chen seemed to possess certain kinds of information before other people even knew it existed.

Inside the package, Jiang found a thin sheaf of papers, cheap stuff available at any office supply store. There was no identification on the papers, and they'd apparently been produced on a routine office printer.

"This is serious," Jiang said, before he started reading. "The paper . . . we could never prove where it came from . . . who leaked it."

Chen nodded.

Jiang began skimming: Routine opening salutations, announcing a great new American initiative that would foster international cooperation, with our friends and allies the Chinese . . .

Allies?

. . . have decided to accompany them on their Mars mission . . .

"What the hell?" Jiang blurted, frowning at the papers in his hand. He looked up at Chen: "We need to get to the communications shell right now."

"What is it, boss?"

"Santeros is sending a mission to Mars . . . with us."

They were both moving, Jiang a half step ahead of Chen. "You're sure about your birdie?"

"As sure as you can get with Americans. They do seem to enjoy treachery for its own sake. On the other hand, I can think of no reason at all that they'd ever set us up, you and I, on something like this. No: it's real."

Jiang stopped: "I wonder if the sly boys have anything on this?" He was talking about the Chinese intelligence unit headquartered in the embassy.

Chen shook his head: "I would have heard . . . one way or another. I do know that they're asking about the speech, but I haven't heard that they've gotten much back."

Jiang said, "Then if these papers are correct"—he shook them at Chen—"not only will we be first in Beijing, we will stick a poker up Yang's ass, will we not?"

Yang was the head of the intelligence unit. Chen showed just a sliver of a smile: "I think, yes, we will. Now that you mention it, I suspect my little birdie knows that, too."

"It's a worthwhile thing, anytime, for all of us," Jiang said.

Jiang read more of the speech as they walked to the elevator that went down to the communications unit, buried deep in the soil of Washington, D.C. Some of it he read aloud to Chen, as the smaller man hurried to keep pace:

We all agree that space is the common heritage of humanity, and it is our future and our promise. Any effort to expand the human spirit enhances us all. We also know that space is still a very dangerous place. Anytime we push the frontiers and boundaries outward we are at risk.

Accordingly, after long-term and extensive consultation with members of Congress, the USSA, and other experts in the field, I am making it our highest priority to join China in their venture to send an expedition to Mars. We commend them for the bravery and spirit they've shown in initiating this magnificent undertaking, but our experts have concluded that, despite the Chinese's brilliant planning and engineering, the risks are too great for a single ship, alone. Failure cannot be considered an acceptable option; it would be a loss for us all. So, we will accompany them, in a ship of our own. Two ships, each self-sufficient, accompanying each other on this grand undertaking greatly improve the chances of success.

The Chinese are well along on building their vessel, and we have no desire to delay their mission. Our best people have come up with a plan to meet their timetable. Accordingly, I have ordered the repurposing of U.S. Space Station Three, to convert it for travel to Mars. Its two habitat modules can handle the personnel and life support needs for a long-duration mission, and they will become the core of the new ship. The addition of tanks, engines, and a new command and instrumentation module to turn it into an interplanetary vessel can be accomplished quickly and efficiently.

In recognition of the President who first brought the Americans and Chinese into ongoing cooperation in the modern era, breaking down the barriers that had separated our people for many decades, almost a century ago, we will rename the USSS3 as the Richard M. Nixon.

A century ago, it was only Americans who set foot on the moon. They gave lip service to "for all mankind" but nothing more. We've moved beyond that. We're not out to steal China's glory nor beat them to Mars. We fully intend to give them the honor of placing the first footsteps on Martian soil. They have earned it. Then we can proceed together, as humanity expands into the solar system.

I expect, not too many months from now, to be congratulating our Chinese and American pioneers as they stand side by side under the rust-colored skies of Mars. Godspeed to them all.

Chen shook his head, said, "What is this? What can it be?"

The elevator door opened in the communications unit, where two armed guards were waiting with submachine guns, which they promptly pointed elsewhere.

Jiang paused, and said quietly, "I can tell you what it is. It's bullshit, Chen. The Americans are fucking with us. I don't know why, but I want you to find out."

"They must know that we're sending a colony ship," Chen said. "They're afraid that we're going to use that to lay claim to Mars. They're making sure to let us know that that is not an acceptable outcome, and they're taking steps to prevent it."

Jiang asked, "Are we doing that?"

"Boss, that would be a complete violation of the International Space Treaty that has served both sides very well for the past thirty years. No, we are not doing that. Even if we did, everybody would just laugh us off. It'd be like . . . claiming the moon."

"You're sure?"

"I'm sure, boss. There are probably a few idiots in Beijing who've tried to bring it up, but it'd never fly."

"So we let the big brains figure this out," Jiang said. "I'd give a lot of money to see the chairman's face when this pops up on his screen."

"A lot of money," Chen said, "but preferably from a safe distance."

7.

Dr. Rebecca Johansson hurried past her workstation, grabbed her coat, let her implants turn her computer off—*do not look at the waiting e-mails.* The implants were already talking to the door and clicked the rems app. The radiation monitor flashed green, which meant she wasn't noticeably radioactive this evening, and that was a good thing.

She indicated the "out" app and the door popped open after registering her ID. In the hall she clicked on the elevator app, waited impatiently for the car, said, "Station," when it arrived, and dropped six floors to the Northfield nuke's underground shuttle station.

The ten o'clock train arrived three minutes after she walked onto the platform. She scampered aboard, sank into a seat, and sighed. She was twenty minutes from downtown Minneapolis, not much to see on the way but endless tracts of suburban houses. Way too late for sanity's sake, and Senior Star power engineers didn't get overtime. *If only,* she thought. With double and triple time on her usual hours, she'd be retired in five years.

But then what? She actually liked the work. Liked the action.

Two minutes out from the Nuke, too tired to read, Becca stared into the window at her own ghostly reflection. A door opened between her car and the second car and a young man moved up and took a seat across from her. A doctor, she thought, a surgeon, heading north to the Cities from the Mayo Clinic in Rochester, where the shuttle tracks ended. He glanced up briefly and she quickly flicked her eyes away, hoping he hadn't seen her seeing him.

People were always trying to chat her up. It wasn't always a half-baked mating ritual. People simply found her approachable: Partly it was that pure Minnesota-Scandinavian look, and a plump, finely featured face with a fresh-scrubbed pale pink complexion. She was, she sometimes thought in despair, "cute," like a doll you won at the state fair. Combine that with being both short and . . . plumpish . . . and the whole ensemble screamed, "I am sweet and I am inoffensive, and I am no

threat, and so I don't have to be taken seriously because no one this cute
and plump ever is."

Becca did not like being dismissed. She did not like to be thought of
as inconsequential. She'd worked too hard to get where she was, through
a grueling Ph.D. program at MIT, and now was known as one of the
best-trained and cleverest high-density power engineers ever to come
down the pike.

The young man was still there, sitting across from her, a pleasant
smile fixed on his face, and she thought, *Enough! Time for a positive
thought or two.*

Work was going well. The hours were way too long, but the intellectual challenges were irresistibly seductive. Designing power flows
for a reactor core that had one-quarter the volume and ten times
the power density of anything previously used in a commercial plant
was . . . exciting.

She was doing great and novel work; better still it was *conservative*
work. Power utilities liked conservative thinking. Their job was to reliably deliver electricity twenty-four hours a day, not get Nobel prizes for
innovation.

There were no new tricks in her flow designs. The cleverness lay in
how well she'd been able to optimize and integrate so many different
techniques. Massive-scale heat pipes with fractal fluidic passages to
pump the energy from the fissioning fuel into the boiling superheated
fluids that drove the generator turbines. Thermomagnetic liquids and
magnetic pumps and transformers to siphon the waste heat. Micro-
evaporative heat exchangers to dump it into convective radiators and,
ultimately, the air.

That was just a fraction of what she'd thrown at the problem. No one
technology, not even two or three, could manage so many gigawatts of
thermal energy in a confined space. The core would've melted down in
minutes. Put them all together, get them all tuned up, and get them all
working in concert. It was the difference between an instrumental solo
and a full symphony orchestra, engineering-wise.

Her mood was lightening as the train rolled through the old airport site, now a condominium complex, made a quick stop, and then out the other side and on toward the downtown towers where Becca lived.

The doctor—or maybe he was a nurse, or a technician—was still sitting across from her. Glancing at her from time to time.

He would, she thought, wait until they got off the train, then he'd hit on her. But her mood had lightened, and her stop was always busy, so there'd be no threat. She'd be nice to him, she thought, and maybe—he was good-looking, although, come to think of it, his neck was a little thick—hold out some hope. A cup of coffee in the morning? But she had to be to work at six . . .

Maybe she should find just a sliver of life outside work? Time for coffee with a good-looking surgeon?

Twenty minutes and twenty seconds after leaving the Nuke, the train rolled into the Hennepin Avenue station under downtown Minneapolis. Becca got to her feet and headed for the door. The surgeon—yeah, right—shuffled off after her.

On the platform, she half turned, expecting him to be there, with an approach. And he was. He smiled and held up an ID pack. He said, "I'm Robert Klipish with the FBI. We didn't want to startle you or attract attention, but we have some people who need to talk with you."

She felt her mouth hanging open as she winked her implant at the ID. A green light ticked in a corner of her eye: the ID was real. "Some people?"

He gestured across the platform, where two men and a woman were moving toward them, in a V formation, the woman at the point. She was neither chubby nor cute. She was athletic, and the three moved in a way that you might expect a school of sharks to move. As the woman came up, Becca noticed that sometime in the recent past, she'd had her nose broken.

"What did I do?" Becca blurted. She grasped for something, anything.

"You didn't do anything, as far as I know," Klipish said. "I was told to make sure that nothing happened to you, after you left work. I was told that if you got a hangnail, I'd be reassigned to Texas." He twinkled at her.

"Not that," Becca said, putting a hand on his sleeve.

The woman who was coming up said, "Bob, stop twinkling at her." The woman held up her phone and flashed her ID. "Dr. Johansson, my name is Marla Clark. Pleased to meet you. You have a meeting."

"A meeting? Right now?"

"Not exactly right now, but first thing in the morning, in Washington, D.C.," Clark said. "By the way, we assume you'll need a moving company, though you don't really have all that much. We've contacted two that have been approved by Homeland Security."

Becca: "A moving company?" *And how did they know she didn't have that much?*

The next morning, Becca was fifteen hundred kilometers from home. She'd been snatched, politely but firmly, and shoved into a private hopjet that had delivered her to the D.C. airport barely an hour later, a little after one o'clock in the morning, EST. Her "entourage"—she decided to think of them that way, instead of as her "handlers" or, worse, "captors"—had been pleasant, solicitous of her comfort, and entirely uninformative.

They'd hustled her off to a terrific hotel, where she was deposited in a luxury suite that contained a fresh change of clothes, which were her size and even her style, which struck her as efficient, considerate, and creepy. Clark had come with her. She recommended a hot shower before going to bed. "I've put in a seven o'clock wake-up call for you, so you won't be late for the meeting."

"What meeting?"

"The meeting," Clark said with a shrug.

Nine hours after getting on the train in Northfield, Minnesota, she was sitting in a White House waiting room decorated with paintings of former First Ladies. Clark was no longer with her, but another woman, this one named Marsden, from the same tribe as Clark, handed her a cup of coffee and said, "Relax."

"If you were in my shoes, would you relax?" Becca asked.

"I don't know exactly what shoes you're wearing," Marsden said. A navy officer was walking across the room toward them, and she added, in a low voice, "But if this guy is coming for you, my answer would be, 'No.'"

The officer was coming for her. His name was Rob, he was a lieutenant commander, and he shook her hand pleasantly and said, "You're up, you can bring your coffee," and to the escort, "I'm told she'll be half an hour or so."

Santeros was on her feet, talking to a fat man, when Becca was ushered into the Oval Office. Santeros smiled at her and waded across the carpet, extending a hand.

"Dr. Johansson, Rebecca," she said. "Good of you to come, on such short notice."

"Happy to," Becca said, biting back a less polite reply: *Did I have a choice?*

Santeros gestured to the fat man. "This is Jacob Vintner, my science adviser. We're going to have to make this quick. I brought you here because the United States needs your skills. We want you to design the power management system for a twenty-thermal-gigawatt reactor, and we need it rather quickly. Might you be interested? We want you badly enough to have rushed you here like this, but you're free to decline. We do have other candidates."

"I'm currently committed to a project with Minnesota Power—"

"We've already talked to your employer and they're happy to give you an indefinite leave of absence, with no loss of position or seniority, in the national interest," Santeros said.

"What kind of power plant is this?"

Vintner said, "We can't really go into the details because of national security. All I can—"

"Wait a minute," Becca said, jabbing her finger at Vintner. "This has got to be for the Mars mission! You need a big honkin' reactor, I bet. Hot damn. Okay, I'm in, on one condition."

Santeros asked Vintner, "Why do all these people have conditions?"

Vintner said, "Because they're important enough to have them, I guess."

Santeros was amused. She turned back to Becca and asked, "What's yours, Rebecca?"

"If I build your power plant, I get to go along."

Santeros nodded: "Okay."

Vintner, the bureaucrat: "Before we give you any more details or address your speculations, which we cannot confirm at this moment, we're going to need you to sign some documents." He handed her a slate.

"If this is about clearance, I'm already cleared for nuclear work," Becca said.

"We know that. This is a higher level of clearance. You were vetted for it last night," Vintner said.

Santeros walked around behind her desk, sat down, looked at a screen, tapped it a couple of times, and said to Becca, "Sit and read it."

Becca sat and gave it a quick scan. Boiled down to a few words, it said that if she talked out of turn, she was going to jail. She signed it, touched the ID square with her thumb, and handed it back to Vintner.

Santeros offered up the barest of smiles. "So we can give you a detail—and please remember what you just signed. We're not going to Mars—we're going to Saturn."

"Saturn?" Becca was dumbfounded. "Why Saturn? You can't just be one-upping the Chinese. Jupiter'd be closer. What's at Saturn?"

Santeros said to Vintner, "You're right. She is pretty smart." And to Becca: "More by accident than anything else, one of our astronomical observatories saw what we believe to be an alien starship going into Saturn—and we believe there's something else there, possibly a station."

"Holy shit!"

"Exactly. I'm sure you can work out the implications."

"But . . ." Becca rubbed her forehead with a knuckle, thinking, then said, "It'll take us years to get out there."

"Not with the power plant you're going to design," Vintner said.

8.

Crow had never allowed himself to get tired, when he didn't have to. Other people could get tired, but not him: he'd taught himself to sleep, anytime, anyplace. He'd slept on helicopters on combat missions, he'd slept in fighter planes, he'd deliberately put himself to sleep in the President's private office, waiting for her to return from a meeting.

His wrist-wrap tapped him, and his eyes popped open. The limo was easing through the narrow, rotting streets of the Ninth Ward, reading the address sensors buried in the street. Crow popped a piece of breath-cleaning gum, poured a palmful of water from a bottle, wiped it across his eyes, checked the time: he'd gotten a solid forty-five minutes rolling in from Louis Armstrong International.

A minute later, the limo eased to a stop outside a dilapidated faux-Restoration house. Crow picked up his slate, stuck it in his jacket pocket, got out, walked up the badly cracked sidewalk, pushed the doorbell, and stood back to look at the moss.

Moss everywhere, including fine tendrils advancing across the windows. The Restoration style became popular after Hurricane Clarence flooded the city in 2044. New Orleans had been submerged three times in the first half of the century, and each time, the levees were built higher, the pumps made bigger, and the city fathers swore that once and for all they'd solved the problems born of rising seas and eroding deltas.

The residents hadn't believed them in 2044, any more than they had the two previous times, but that hadn't stopped them from rebuilding. Now, with almost a quarter century gone since the last wipeout, houses that had been new in 2045 were beginning to sink into the landscape.

There was no response to the doorbell. Crow leaned on it again, and this time, heard a muffled bellow from inside; unintelligible, but not panicked or in pain. Crow tried the doorknob, which was unlocked, and as the door swung open he heard a more intelligible bellow: ". . . open, let yourself in!"

"Mr. Clover?"

"I'm in the kitchen. Come on back. Don't kick the cat."

Crow stepped inside, closed the door, stepped over an old, scruffy gray cat sleeping on the floor next to an ottoman, and threaded his way through a mass of paper—books, magazines, journals, legal pads—that occupied all visible surfaces but one: an easy chair.

The kitchen was at the rear of the house, and the man in the kitchen, his wide back to Crow, called, "Who is it?"

Crow found the question interesting: first, "Come in," followed by "Who is it?"—he'd never in his life done things in that order. The man hadn't even turned to check him out: he was stirring something on a stove, and whatever it was, smelled wonderful.

"My name is Crow," Crow said. "I work for the President. We've been trying to get in touch with you."

Now Clover turned, a wooden spoon in his hand. He was a heavy-set man, but not overly fat. He'd played pro football for a couple of years, a tackle, and had stayed in okay but not great shape. He had a beard and was wearing eyeglasses; the combination suggested a taste for anachronism.

He looked at Crow for a few seconds, then said, "Sonofabitch, you're real? I thought you were a spammer."

Crow began, "Maybe you should have—"

"Give me a minute. I just started sautéing the tomatoes and I don't want them to burn. Take that green wooden chair there—not the red one, that's for the cat."

The air was faintly blue with smoke, and smelled of cumin, pepper, oregano, and marijuana. Crow picked up a copy of *Nature* that was sitting on the green chair, sat down, looked for a place to put the magazine, and finally put it on the cat's chair. Crow's stomach rumbled; he hadn't had a decent meal since Darlington had taken him to a Mexican restaurant in Pasadena.

He said, "So . . . do you usually assume the Office of the President of the United States is a spammer?"

"Well, wouldn't you?" Clover asked. "You're sitting in a restaurant in the French Quarter, your mouth is open, you're about to stick the most delicate cream puff into it, with the flakiest butter crust, your computer dings, and it says, 'Greetings from the President of the United States.' What would you do? I deleted it and ate the bun."

"I see a certain logic in that," Crow admitted, "which is why we have authentication certificates."

"Yeah, well, my neighbor boy could produce one of those in about five minutes."

"Anyway, Mr. Clover—"

"Call me John."

"We'd like you to go to Mars with us."

Clover didn't say anything, but turned and gave Crow a long, steady look, then said, "Bullshit." And, "One more comment like that, I'll kick you out of here and eat by myself. So don't lie to me anymore. Just tell me the truth about what you want, and we'll work from there."

Crow crossed his legs and said, "That was the truth."

"Bullshit . . . well, hmm. Give me a minute. What you're telling me is, the reason the Chinese are going to Mars is that you've all found out that Deimos is a hollow shell left there by the LGMs, and so the race is on."

"What's Deimos? What're LGMs?"

"Deimos is the smaller of Mars's two moons and has some oddities. LGMs are Little Green Men. If you really don't know what Deimos is, then you were lying to me. Actually, you're lying to me either way—either you know about Deimos, or you don't want me to go to Mars."

"You're confusing me here."

"You don't look confused. By the way, do you have a badge?"

"Sure." Crow took an ID out of his pocket, held it up. Clover had a wrist-wrap on the kitchen counter and picked it up, waved it toward the ID, and a line in the wrap turned green. The ID was real.

"Okay, you're something," Clover said.

"Tell me why I'm lying," Crow said.

"Because there are two things I'm known for. The first is my studies of ancient Mayan hydraulic technology. It's brilliant work, if I do say so myself—and I often do. But it wouldn't be of much interest to the President of the United States." Clover took another sip of the jambalaya, swirled it in his mouth, swallowed, and continued. "The second is my entirely hypothetical work on how technologies and cultures might develop in alternate ways from ours, especially given different starting points, culturally, psychologically, and even physically. In other words, how alien civilizations might turn out. Mars has no LGMs. Mars doesn't even have living bacteria, as far as we know. We've mapped everything on the surface bigger than a baseball, and there are no hatches, doors, portals, ducts, or discarded pizza boxes. So there's no reason for an anthropologist to go there."

"All right."

Clover picked up the remnants of a joint, touched it to a flame from a burner, took a drag, adding to the mix of aromas in the room. "So what do you want, Mr. Crow?"

"We want you to sign a bunch of security regs that say you'll go to prison if you talk about what we tell you. Believe me, if you talk, you go to prison. If you don't talk, you become, in due time, the richest and best-known anthropologist on Earth."

"Wait: something popped out of the ice in Antarctica . . ."

"No. Nothing popped out of any ice."

"You found something on the sea floor?"

"No."

"Shit. I don't need the money—I mean, what could be better than this place?—but I wouldn't mind being famous," Clover said.

"That could happen," Crow said.

"You want some jambalaya?"

"Yes." Crow did; his meal schedule was leaning heavily on McDonald's.

"You want a hit on the joint?"

"No."

Clover carefully stubbed out the joint, saving the best for last. "Although Louisiana is one of only six states that outlaws weed for anything but medicinal purposes, I want you to know, I don't use weed for medicinal purposes. I use it strictly to get stoned."

"That confirms our research in choosing you for the Mars trip," Crow said. "We've got a specific slot for a weeder. Without that qualification, we'd have approached Jeb Rouser."

Clover bristled. "That charlatan? Let me tell you about Mr. Rouser, Mr. Crow. Anthropologically speaking, Rouser couldn't find his own asshole with both hands and a searchlight. He thinks—"

"He's the Morton K. Brigham Professor of Anthropological Research at Yale University."

"Fuck Morton K. Brigham and Yale University," Clover said. "You ever been to that place? You have to have a pole stuck up your ass before you're allowed to walk on campus. Seriously, they have a booth with poles. Before they hire you for a job, they stick a second pole up there."

"We were told you were perhaps the better choice, but there was an argument—"

"I'm better by a very wide margin, especially if this involves LGMs," Clover said. "But enough about me." The jambalaya smelled so good that Crow thought he might faint. "Give me what I need to sign, and fill me in."

Crow reached into his inside jacket pocket, extracted a mini-slate, and pushed it across the table to Clover.

"You can read them if you want, but I gotta tell you, they're pretty boring."

Clover was already flipping pages, dating and thumbing them. "Doesn't matter. I want to hear the whole story, and you know I want to hear the whole story, and if I don't sign our little tea party never happened and you don't exist. Anything else important?"

"Nope. That's about it."

"It'll be a while before the jambalaya is just right," Clover said. "I've got some chairs in there, somewhere." They moved into the other room, where Clover made another overstuffed chair appear out of the clutter. "So what's up?"

They sat down and Crow laid it out. Fifteen minutes later, Clover

pushed himself out of his chair and asked, "You want a large bowl or a
gigantic bowl?"

"Gigantic."

"Good man."

Clover came back two minutes later with the jambalaya and two bottles
of beer, and said, "If I didn't miss anything, the short version goes like
this: something you think is a starship came and stopped in Saturn's
rings and rendezvoused with some kind of 'whatever.' You haven't had
any evidence of communication between your starship and the 'whatever.' Neither of these artifacts has made an attempt to contact or communicate with us—"

"We don't know that," Crow interrupted. "We don't know if we'd
recognize an attempt to communicate."

"They haven't. At their level of tech, they could if they wanted to. In
any case, you don't have an indication that there are any alien beings at
Saturn, all you know is that the visitor's apparently extra-solar and artificial. You want my considered opinions? Of course you do, that's why
you're here."

"And I'm listening closely," Crow said. The jambalaya was really
good. Clover might be goofy, but he could cook.

In the other chair, Clover fired up the remnant of the joint, took a
drag, and said, "My first opinion is that if there actually are aliens there,
they don't want to talk to us. Showing up on their doorstep might not go
over real well. I mean that as understatement. What little information
you've got—the fact that there was already a station at Saturn—suggests
that they are not new to this game, which means they've probably got
good reasons, from their perspective, for what they're not doing. Like
communicating with us."

He continued: "My second opinion is that there probably aren't
aliens there, that it's just a space probe. No LGMs, no 'take-me-to-your-
leader.'"

Crow was getting a contact high from the dope; either that, or from the jambalaya. "Okay. Our problem is, sooner or later, this cat is going to get out of the bag. We know for sure that these . . . beings . . . are more technologically advanced than we are. We don't know by how much, but we do know that we don't want that tech falling into the hands of the Chinese before we get it."

"Ahh . . ." Clover blew smoke toward the ceiling. "I'm beginning to see."

"And it's probably not a probe. We've had some people thinking about that, and the ship's simply too big to be a probe, for beings that advanced. Right now, we could build a computer and sensory package not much bigger than a soccer ball, stick it in a probe, run out to the Centauri system in a couple of decades, and the computer would radio back everything we need to know about the system. No need to build a starship the size of an asteroid."

Clover shrugged. "Well, I've told you what I can, at this point. If you get more information, I'll be happy to advise—and I'll think about what you've told me so far, and get back to you with some ideas. If you get out there, and get more information, I will look forward to hearing about it. With more information, I can probably give you better opinions and better evaluations of what your options are. Leastwise, I can probably keep you from making boneheaded mistakes."

"John, I didn't actually want to throw this out there before I heard your opinions. . . . The President would like you to join the crew on the Saturn run."

Crow took some small pleasure in the surprise on Clover's face.

"You mean . . . go out in space?"

"Well, yeah."

"Jesus, Crow, who'd take care of my cat?"

It took Crow a moment to realize that Clover was serious.

"John, we've got bigger problems than your cat."

"Maybe you do, but I don't. Mr. Snuffles is sixteen years old. He's been my best friend all that time. I mean, we've dug in Mayan ruins together. We've fought snakes, mano a mano. No way in hell I'm going to leave him now. He's only got a couple of years left."

Crow took a second to rub his forehead. "Let me check to see if the cat could go."

Clover leaned back: "That would put a different complexion on it. If the cat could go, well, yeah, I could see making the trip. It's still a crappy idea. I don't trust aliens."

"You don't know any aliens."

"Yeah, and they don't know me. Seems like a hell of a good reason for not trusting them." He took a hit on the joint. "What are the chances of getting back?"

"Don't know. Assuming the aliens don't turn out to be hostile, probably ninety-nine percent. The other one percent, everybody dies."

"You mean, some massive failure."

"Yeah." Crow leaned forward. "John, the last thing we want to do is get anyone killed. That would defeat the whole purpose of going out there. As far as the aliens go, our Pentagon people don't think there's any reason that they might be hostile."

Clover shook his head. "Your Pentagon people are piss-ignorant. They don't know anything about the aliens, if there are any aliens. And that cuts both ways. The aliens might not know anything about us. Or maybe they only know the big stuff: Hiroshima, Vietnam, the Oil Wars, 9/11, the Tri-Border Fight, the Houston Flash. You think that might worry them? Crazy people, coming to visit? First contact—it's gonna be dangerous no matter how you cut it."

"All right."

"And then, we could get out there, find that they are a bunch of beautiful spiritual Zen people, ready to give us the secret to eternal life, and the Chinese show up and throw a nuke at us."

They sat staring at each other for a moment, then Crow said, "If you can take the cat?"

Clover waved a heavy hand at him: "I'll think about it. Probably say no. But I'll think about it." He inhaled, held it. "I don't believe my pot would be a good idea, given a recirculating ventilation system, but I'd want to take a few gallons of Old Horseshoe to get me through it."

"Let me know soon as you can, or we'll have to talk to somebody else," Crow said. "We'll stick you on a large retainer, until you say no, anyway. We'll want to see you in D.C. in a week to meet with our study group. Bring every idea you've got on this."

"I can do that," Clover said, as Crow got up to leave.

Clover watched Crow as he walked down the crooked sidewalk to a waiting car. When he was gone, Clover looked at his cat: "Tell you what, Snuff: I've got a feeling that I might say 'yes.' But it's possible that we should stick with the Mayans, and let the aliens go."

9.

Three weeks after the alien ship was spotted, Sandy was going up.

He'd been allowed two packs—a big one for equipment, a small one for clothing and personal effects. At eight in the morning, he popped the door on his condo, hauled the bags outside, sealed the door, jacked the alarms to the highest settings, and carried his bags and a paper cup of coffee through the complex gates and out to the curb, to an empty bus bench.

The sky was light gray: the marine layer hadn't burned off yet, so the L.A. basin hadn't had a chance to heat up. Sandy sipped his coffee and kicked back a bit. Might as well relax and enjoy the moment.

He lived in a condo complex built around an enormous swimming pool, and populated by affluent, good-looking people. Most affluent people were good-looking, not because they inherited the right genes, but because the surgery was so good and painless and safe.

From outside, the apartment complex might have been a tropical jungle: something painted by Winslow Homer on one of his Caribbean trips, he thought. The complex also had tight security, another benefit: he'd once been dropped off by a drunk friend, drunk himself and mostly naked, and when he'd tried to cross the wall, he found himself surrounded by armed guards in about six seconds.

They hadn't been fooling around; they'd run a DNA check on him before they let him back in his apartment. He didn't live in a place where you just dropped in.

Sandy hadn't had that many moments to relax in the two previous weeks. After making his deal with Crow, he was flown to Maryland, to the Defense Information School at Fort Meade, where he was turned over to a harsh, hawk-nosed marine gunnery sergeant named Cletus Smith, who didn't care for Jesus hair or burnt-orange GnarlyBrand pants or RhythmTech overshirts.

The gunny was not happy: "I don't know exactly what's up, Dingleberry . . ."

"That would be Darlington . . ."

". . . Darlington, but I don't like it. It wasn't done right. I got some freshly made West Point asshole shoving security papers down my throat, I got the sergeant major yapping at me, my schedule's screwed for the next six months, I was supposed to start an advanced vid class . . ."

The gunnery sergeant was wearing the usual uptight marine camo uniform, which had some kind of special marine name that Sandy didn't remember, and as ex-army, really didn't care about. He reached forward and slipped two fingers inside the placket on the sergeant's shirt, and gave it a tug.

"Gunny, gunny, gunny," he said, leaning toward the sergeant until their noses were only six inches apart. "Nobody gives a shit what you think or how inconvenient it is, or what Mrs. Cletus or the Cletus rug rats think. But you should give a shit what I think—because if you don't have me up to Ultra Star vid status in two weeks, Major General Harrington will be down here with a fuckin' power mower. Guess whose ass gonna be grass?"

Few marines had ever had their placket tugged; Smith was not one of them, and his nose turned white. "Get your fingers the fuck outa my . . ."

Sandy broke in: ". . . and if you ever give me any serious shit, I will personally take your skinny, ignorant peckerwood Marine Corps ass outside and stomp a new mudhole in it, to replace the mudhole you already got."

Smith stared at him for a moment, then showed a very tight grin: "They didn't tell me you'd been in the service, and the hair fooled me. Argentina?"

"The whole cruise," Sandy said. The whole cruise was insider code for those who had been shot up.

"I was on that boat," Smith said. He took a step back. "All right. You can call me Clete. Let's take a look at your gear. . . ."

Ten straight days of hard work—and a Marine Corps haircut: Jesus hair didn't work all that well in weightless conditions.

Maybe he wasn't Ultra Star when he finished, but Sandy was two thousand percent better than he had been, and he hadn't been bad to begin with. Cletus Smith had been a combat videographer, and had actually filmed himself being shot down in a Marine Blackfoot IV helicopter; he rode the vid right into the ground, with commentary, although the commentary had been suppressed for the good of the Corps. Smith said, at the end of their last day, "Y'all come back: I got more."

"Clete, I wish I could take you with me," Sandy said, as they slapped hands. "Once I get some space under my feet, I'll be looking for ideas."

"Bring the vid. And boy, I'd love to go to Mars. If you can find me a slot . . ."

Sitting outside his condo, Sandy's wrist-wrap told him that his ride had been held up on the 110, because some underclassman had dropped a bowling ball off a bridge. Traffic had resumed, and the underclassman was being pursued through the Avenues, where he wouldn't be caught. Sandy hoped the cops were watching all available bowling balls. Having a sixteen-pound Brunswick blow through your windshield could seriously screw up your trip to Disneyland.

Eight or ten minutes later, his wrist-wrap told him his ride was turning the corner, and he got to his feet. A black limo, unmarked. The car hummed to a stop, and a driver got out of the front. A rear door slipped open, and the truck lid popped. Sandy said, "I got it," threw his bags in the back, kept the coffee, and climbed inside.

The driver got back in, the door slid shut. Sandy nodded at the woman who sat opposite him, and put the coffee cup in a cup holder.

The woman was a redhead, a spectacular example of the species, and it took only a moment for her name to register: Cassandra Fiorella, chief science editor for the *Los Angeles Times*, and the daily on-air science correspondent and producer for the biggest netcast on the West Coast.

She was stunning: red hair, green eyes, and the rest of the package wrapped in a slippery green-black jumpsuit. Her face showed none of the stress lines of plastic surgery; she was wearing a charm necklace with gold endorsement charms from Apple, IBM, MIT, Stanford, Mitsubishi Heavy Industries, and EuroBank, and in the center, a big fat green diamond that matched her eyes. Crow had not told him that she was on board.

She didn't introduce herself—you'd have to be an idiot not to know who she was—but gave him a low-wattage smile and said, "You're Sanders Darlington."

"Yup."

"Where have you worked? Crow didn't tell me much about you. Except for an assistant videographer's stint on *Naked Nancy*, I couldn't find your professional résumé."

"Well, that's about it," Sandy said.

She frowned: "I don't believe it. For this trip? There must be something else."

Sandy had been outrageously rich since childhood, living in L.A. Some of the most beautiful women in the world had made the effort to say 'hello' to him. While he'd taken advantage of that, from time to time, he'd also learned that behind a certain percentage of great beauty, there lurked a wicked witch of the west. He got that vibration from Fiorella.

He said, "Well, I won the 2064 Oscar for the best manual projection of a naked producer into the Pacific Ocean."

"I saw that, too." Fiorella nibbled a little lip gloss from her lower lip, then shook her head. "You bought your way on."

Sandy shrugged.

"This is absurd," she said. "I will tell the President that. I'm supposed to be on-camera, recording this for the whole future of mankind, and I've got to work with an inexperienced daddy's boy who'll inevitably mess it up, and not only that, has a history of violence—"

"Hey, Cassie?" Sandy smiled at her and said, "Go fuck yourself."

She blanched. Nobody talked to her like that. "What did you say?"

"I said, 'Go fuck yourself.' I don't need any ego rages from the talent. You just get the makeup right, sweetheart, and practice reading without crossing your eyes, and I'll see that you're looking good. But I gotta tell you, this little rant just took you a step down from 'looking great.'"

With her face bright red with anger, Fiorella crossed her arms and looked away from him. Sandy knew this wasn't over. There'd be consequences. Someone with Fiorella's creds wouldn't take that lying down. Well, tough shit. As they headed up the 210, Sandy closed his eyes and dozed off.

The Mojave Spaceport was unseasonably cool: at 10 A.M., the thermometer was only slowly climbing past ninety-four. The sun, though, was starting to burn. Sandy let Fiorella haul her case out of the back of the limo—she wasn't talking to him—and then threw his personal duffel on one shoulder and rolled the bigger equipment case along behind.

They'd been dropped at the far end of the terminal. Inside the doors, Sandy found himself in a private waiting room. Through glass doors on the far wall, he could see a larger waiting room, with more people in it.

Crow was sitting on a bench, looking at a tablet: he glanced up when they walked in, and raised a hand to them. Fiorella made a beeline for him and Sandy heard her say, "Mr. Crow, we've got to talk . . ."

The two other people included a short, round blonde, who hadn't looked up when they walked in, probably the power engineer, Rebecca something, and a large black man with white hair, who was clutching a nylon travel case, and had to be the anthropologist. The blonde was pounding on a tablet; the big man looked like he needed somebody to talk to. Sandy went that way, stuck out a hand, and said, "You're John Clover, you're more important than I am, so how about if I suck up for a while?"

"I could use some good suckin' up," Clover said, as they shook hands. "You must be the rich kid."

"Not only that, but I'm good-looking, have a terrific singing voice, and women find me irresistible," Sandy said, as he dropped into the chair next to Clover. "For the most part, anyway. I've already pissed off half the women on this flight."

Now the blonde looked up at him, glanced over at Fiorella, back to Sandy, and said, "If you keep talking over my work, here, you'll have pissed off all of them."

Clover said to the blonde, "Let me tell you something, honey—"

"I'm not a honey," Becca snapped.

"Of course you are, and I'm a southerner, so I get to call you that,"

Clover said. "What I'm gonna say is that they are about to strap a twenty-megaton nuclear weapon to our asses and blast them into orbit. Y'all ought to be sweating it out. Like me."

Sandy smiled at that and said, "A twenty-megaton nuke?"

"Might as well be, as far as we're concerned, you know, if it blows," Clover said.

"Ah, it's not going to blow," Sandy said. "A fortune-teller in Venice told me that I'd suffer a long, lingering, painful death."

"Good, good," Clover said. "I'm reassured."

He had a case by his feet; the contents meowed. Becca looked at it and asked, "You're taking a cat?"

"Only way I'd go," Clover said. "You got a problem with that?"

"No. Actually, I don't," Becca said.

Sandy shrugged. "Neither do I. Long as it doesn't shit in my shoes."

"I can't promise anything," Clover said.

Crow strode toward Sandy, typing on his handslate, not looking at it. He bent over and said, quietly, "Don't fuck with her."

"She started it. I'm tired of people assuming that I'm incompetent because I'm rich. I—"

"*Don't . . . fuck . . . with . . . her.*"

"All right, all right. I'll go easy," Sandy said.

"Good answer."

Sandy muttered, "I just gotta remember, journalism school grads can be touchy about their lack of intelligence."

Crow said, "Actually, it's a double major in economics and general science. From Stanford."

"Jesus. Is everybody on this trip a genius?"

"Pretty much," Crow said. "Except maybe you and me."

"But we'll have guns."

Crow brightened. "Yes. Yes, we will."

A woman in a Virgin-SpaceX sky-blue flight attendant's uniform walked into the waiting room and said, swinging her face between the two groups, Crow-Fiorella and Sandy-Becca-Clover, "Mr. Crow, everybody, the crew has completed their preflight check. You're free to board the shuttle."

They did.

Five humans and one cat went out the back of the terminal to a canopied, air-conditioned people-mover that hauled them out to the shuttle, followed by another shuttle with people from the other waiting room.

The Virgin-SpaceX shuttle was called *Galahad*, and featured horizontal takeoff and a maximum pull of 2.2 gees. Seating twenty-four, not including the flight crew of five, it wasn't much different in overall size than a commercial hopjet. What caught the eye were the retractable wings, now just stubs on the fuselage, the unusually large and long engine nacelles, and the broadened belly, the better to hold more fuel and evenly distribute the heat on reentry.

The shuttle rested in its launch stage, a less conventional-appearing aircraft. A pilotless drone, not much bigger than the shuttle, it was essentially a cradle slung between two large engine and fuel tank cylinders with oversized air intakes. Four stubby fore and aft wings projected outward from the cradle. Heavy on the muscle and light on the brains, the launcher was commanded by the flight crew during the first stage of ascent and by ground control after it separated from the shuttle.

The *Galahad* ferried people from Mojave into low Earth orbit. That was the hardest part, energy-wise, but also the shortest part of the trip. Takeoff to orbit took half an hour. The shuttle couldn't take them all the way to the station in its thousand-kilometer-high orbit, though; not enough fuel. Once in orbit, *Galahad* would dock with an orbital tug that would take it the rest of the way to the station, an energetically easier jaunt but one that would take another four hours. Not much different than the flight from L.A. to Sydney.

Crow and Fiorella had been up before, hitching rides on space-available seats. Fiorella had spent two weeks at the station, while Crow had only been up two days. The other three had never been.

They boarded the shuttle on a mobile escalator; inside, the space was a little cramped, but the seats were large and extraordinarily comfortable. Smartfoam cushions, supported by a powered carbon-fiber skeleton, monitored a hundred pressure points and molded themselves to their backs and butts.

Clover was looking nervous; the flight attendant came and smiled at him, whispered something. Clover nodded, and she gave him a bottle of water and something else. Pills, Sandy thought. Clover popped them, and two minutes later, said something funny to Fiorella, who was sitting across the narrow aisle from him, and the TV lady laughed.

Good pills.

When everybody was seated, the flight attendant said, "I know some of you haven't been up. In front of you, there's an oxygen mask capsule. They have been sanitized since the last flight. The slightly astringent odor you may smell is actually a sealer, should you need to press your face into the mask. When we reach maximum acceleration, you'll feel as though you weigh twice as much as you do now—we'll be pulling two gravities, or two gees, as we say. There may be a sensation of suffocation. You won't be suffocating, but you may feel that kind of pressure. Simply press the tab under your right thumb and a mask will extrude. Don't worry about moving toward it—the face-recognition system will find you. Breathe normally. Don't try to remove your safety harness—that won't help. If any of you are feeling even the slightest bit nervous, we have some excellent calming medications available. Feel free to ask."

She went on for a while, and when she finished, Sandy asked her, "How about Mr. Snuffles?"

"Mr. Snuffles is asleep," she said.

"Snoring like a chain saw," Clover said over his shoulder. And, said the man who moments before had been sweating like a Miami sneak-thief, "let's light this motherfucker up."

Really good pills.

10.

Becca was annoyed with herself. She was about to take a trip that maybe one person in a million got to make, that every techie dreamed of, and she couldn't stop thinking about heat flow integrals. A symptom, she thought, of her obsessiveness. On the job, it worked to her advantage. At times, though, it got in the way.

Like now. Intellectually, she'd love to get the full launch experience. But the heat problem . . . it nagged, and nagged, and nagged.

She'd been running herself ragged. The government had tried to make her life as easy as possible. The transfer from Minneapolis to Georgetown had been seamless. Her new condo was a slightly scary demonstration of the government's ability to read a single individual's habits and tastes, purely through available databases.

Because it was perfect, right down to the smart door.

The door read her implants, unlocked and opened itself, and closed itself behind her. She could mumble out a shopping list—for anything, from food to clothing—and the door would arrange for it to be delivered, and then would keep an eye on the delivery cart. It was like having a perfect invisible doorman, whom she never had to be nice to or remember on holidays.

The government apparently also got her a housekeeper, although she'd never met that person: the only reason she knew of his/her existence was that when she got home, her clothes had been washed and ironed, and the apartment was spotless. If she dropped a crumb from the always-available crumb cake, and left it on the counter, the crumb would be gone the next time she got home.

The only thing the door, and the government, couldn't get her was the one thing she most desperately needed: time. There was plenty of money—she'd told Vintner that she needed a better workslate, and six hours later, she got the best one that she'd ever heard of. He just couldn't get her another three hours in the day, or an extension on the flight deadline.

Planetary alignments defined the launch window. The shortest and fastest trip meant launching in November, only eight months away, or December of the next year. Santeros wanted to go this year, but every engineer involved had told her that was impossible. Doing it in twenty-one months would be hard enough.

What was causing her sleepless nights, and obsession with integrals, was that she wasn't convinced that twenty-one months was enough time. Pushed by presidential imperative, the DARPA engineers were proposing what at first glance seemed like a harebrained scheme: take the two habitat modules from U.S. Space Station Three, build it a new back end with a nuclear power plant and some heavy-duty electric-ion rockets called VASIMRs, strap on several thousand tons of water to provide oxygen and hydrogen for the VASIMRs, and off they went to Saturn.

Except that they wanted to get this all built in less than two years and they wanted the trip to take less than five months. And that was mildly insane.

No laws of physics were broken, it was simply an impossibly tight deadline and an unreasonably large amount of power. If they'd told her she had three years to get the ship built, and two years to get to Saturn, no sweat.

That's what she told them.

In turn, they fed her details of the Chinese Mars mission, and just how good the Chinese were at large-scale orbital spaceship construction, and how long they thought they had before the Chinese might find out that something was up at Saturn, and how fast the Chinese might be able to get there once they did.

With an ETA of a little over two years, the DARPA brains were pretty confident they could beat the Chinese. Five years? Might as well not even try.

Rock and a hard place.

The amount of power involved *was* unreasonable. Not impossible, just unreasonable, comparable to the amount used by the entire Twin Cities.

The reactors themselves weren't a problem. There were designs dating back to the twentieth century that could generate enough heat in a space not much bigger than her kitchenette. She knew how to get that heat out of the reactor with a pressurized liquid sodium cycle; that was also well-understood tech. Getting the turbines and generators down to a workable size was a bit of a do, but Vintner had people working on that and they claimed they had the matter in hand.

But what came after the turbines?

There are some laws of nature that can't be ignored: thermal electric power plants generate lots of waste heat. Gigawatts of it have to go somewhere out of the system, and Becca didn't have the luxury of building some honking big cooling towers to dissipate it. Size and weight were at a premium, and you couldn't carry along all that cooling water to boil off. The water alone would weigh millions of tons.

So now she was using the super-slate to run simulations for increasingly unlikely and experimental cooling systems and getting more and more frustrated with it. She heard the flight attendant talking about the flight schedule, but paid no attention. What to do with the fucking heat? How do you get it out?

The possibilities were looking thinner and thinner: she almost didn't notice that she was being spoken to, until the flight attendant touched her arm. "Everything okay, Dr. Johansson? You all set for takeoff? You look uncomfortable. Is the seat adjusting correctly for you?"

"It's fine. I was running some engineering stuff in my head."

"Most people don't do their best thinking under two-plus gees. Maybe you should just relax and enjoy the flight up. You'll have plenty of time once we make orbit to do work."

Not really, Becca thought, as the flight attendant moved away.

Time!

The intercom pinged a two-minute warning. The cabin attendant took her station at the front of the cabin, looking back at them. A backward-facing seat, pulling negative gees? That had to hurt, Becca thought. The flight attendant must be tougher than she looked.

The thirty-second warning sounded. Becca took a last look around and saw green lights blink on over every seat in the cabin: smartcams scanned each seat and verified that there were no loose objects lying about and that each passenger was safely positioned and properly strapped in. The last preflight check complete, the computer system unlocked and armed the engines. The pilot started the cradle's engines and the cabin filled with the throaty two-tone note of turbine whine and exhaust thunder.

Takeoff was a lot like that of any commercial jet. The *Galahad* accelerated a little harder and lifted off the runway sooner, but then the shuttle reared back and started on a thirty-degree climb as the hybrid engines throttled up. They passed the ten-kilometer altitude mark at better than Mach 1, a minute and a half into the flight. The acceleration picked up, and the monitor over the flight attendant's head said 2.2 gees of force were pushing Becca back into her chair.

A little more than a minute later, they hit Mach 3 as they slammed through thirty kilometers. The smartfoam that cradled Becca's head and neck prevented her from turning her head, but the high-res 3-D display in front of her gave her a clearer view than the thick-paned window to her left. Becca thought she could make out the curvature of the hazy powder-blue horizon under a sky that was rapidly transitioning from deep indigo to black.

In even less time, they reached Mach 5 and sixty kilometers. The cradle's hybrid engines had given up the increasingly futile task of trying to suck in oxygen from an almost nonexistent atmosphere, and were now running in pure rocket mode, gulping down their tanks of liquid oxygen and hydrogen.

Five minutes into the flight, the *Galahad* reached an altitude of a hundred kilometers and a velocity of 3.5 kilometers per second, running hot in essentially airless space, so the speed of sound no longer meant much. The cradle's fuel was exhausted, save for that needed to safely return to the Mojave Spaceport, and the pilot hit the disconnect. The cradle dropped away with a *thunk*, turning for its return to Mojave. *Galahad* proceeded under its own engine power, steadily gaining altitude and velocity. Becca gratefully noted it was a less grueling procession; she no longer felt like she was trying to bench-press her own weight.

In the next quarter-hour, the *Galahad* added another four kilometers per second to its velocity, and three hundred kilometers to its altitude. The pilot cut the shuttle's engines; they were in stable low Earth orbit and they could stay there almost indefinitely without engine power. Eventually, the minute but unceasing drag of the thermosphere would slow them enough that they'd fall back to Earth . . . but they'd be gone before then.

Looking out the window, Becca could see the curved, pale bluish-white horizon that rimmed an immense swath of white clouds over the dusky icy-green hues of the Atlantic Ocean. She was in space, and it was glorious, and best of all, she wasn't vomiting! No weight, nothing to hold her breakfast down, but it was staying there of its own accord: the space sickness patch really worked.

Crow had told her it would, but she'd heard it wasn't foolproof.

Maybe it wasn't, but it was working for her.

"Hell of a thing," said the guy across the aisle from her. Darlington? Too good-looking, notch in chin. Big white teeth . . . like the big bad wolf.

He was right, though, and she nodded: hell of a thing.

The pilot came up and said that they were closing with the orbital tug, so they might feel a slight bump. In truth, the nudge was almost unnoticeable.

Becca couldn't see it, but she knew the tug was similar in design to the shuttle's launch cradle. Since the tug operated solely in space, it didn't need wings or streamlining or air intakes or the robust framework of the launch stage, but like the launch cradle, it was unpiloted and remotely controlled.

Right now it was under the command of the shuttle crew. As they approached the space station, it would come under station control. *Galahad*'s pilot brought the tug up under the shuttle and the shuttle docked into the tug's rigid carbon-composite mesh hammock. Twin sets of engines and fuel tanks flanked the craft, much smaller than the ones that had lifted them from Earth.

There was no announcement from the pilot or any bright flare of exhaust from the engines firing in space, but Becca could tell when they were on their way out of low Earth orbit. Her weightless state disappeared, as the thrust of the tug's engines pushed her back into her seat with a few tenths of a gee. It wasn't uncomfortable, but, already, she was missing the experience of weightlessness. She was actually relieved by the feeling: she'd be spending a good part of the Saturn trip in zero-gee and the rest of it in low-gee accommodations, and secretly she'd been worried it might not suit her.

One more of the many things that she fretted about that she could scratch off her list of worries.

The pilot came on and said, "Folks, there's not much to do now except sit back and enjoy the ride up to the station. Since we're passing over the terminator line, I'm going to dim the cabin lights so you can get a taste of what night in space is like. Enjoy the view."

Becca pressed her face as close to the window as she could and looked back. The broad arc of the horizon was aglow with a thin rainbow band of light, a sunset scene from orbit. The sunset faded rapidly as the spaceship passed over to the night side of the earth, and the stars popped out. Clear and untwinkling, they were set in a true-black sky that she'd never seen at night on Earth, even hiking in the Rockies. The effect was so intense it felt unreal, like a movie special effect. Below her she could see an occasional flicker of lightning in the clouds and, through the gaps in the clouds, she could see the lights of the modern metropolises of northern Africa and southern Asia.

Then dawn started to break ahead of the ship, and Becca pulled out of her reverie. She checked the time; she'd lost an hour enraptured by space. She sighed and went back to her workslate. She needed some kind of plan, even a quarter-baked one, to present when she got to the station.

"Okay, deep breath," she murmured to herself. "What do I know that I can't change?"

The good-looking guy asked, "Did you say something?"

"Nothing," she said.

Becca ran through the big picture in her head. In space, there was only one way to get rid of heat, and that was by radiation. At room temperature, it would take roughly a square kilometer of radiator to get rid of a gigawatt of heat.

She needed to get rid of several. So that approach wouldn't fly, because the radiator would simply weigh too much. *So let's run hotter and to hell with efficiency.*

She punched numbers into the slate to check her mental arithmetic. At five hundred degrees Celsius, she could dump forty times as much heat per square meter of radiator; six hundred degrees Celsius would be even better, at more than sixty times.

That should get the radiator down to areas that might be manageable. *Let's make believe that works. How do I get the heat to the radiator?*

She scanned through her tables of heat properties of materials.

If I'm running that hot, the best thing for sucking up heat is probably melting metal. It's hundreds of times better than heating up a radiator fluid. Man, gotta love those phase changes.

Becca closed her eyes and began running design possibilities. How long she was down, she didn't know. As she worked, unseeing, Space Station Three appeared on the monitor, three white tubes side by side. The central axis tube was longer and thinner than its flanking partners, the two living modules, which the station personnel called "habitats." At one end of the axis was a smallish cluster of stocky modules, at the other a much larger cluster, with solar panels extending from it like petals on a daisy.

The habitats rotated about the axis tube at one revolution per minute, attached by hundred-meter-long elevator shafts at both ends. It created the illusion that the whole station was rotating lazily in space.

The *Galahad* began its delicate rendezvous maneuvers. Becca was oblivious, the excitement of space travel completely driven from her mind. This was her real element—the space between her ears. She'd taken an impossible engineering problem, run it to ground, and was now bludgeoning it into submission. She couldn't have been happier; in some ways, an emerging solution to an impossible problem resembled an orgasm in the pleasure it created.

Yeah, melts just above 600°C, great heat of fusion, decent emissivity . . .

She opened her eyes and punched in a new set of heat flow parameters and watched the plots come up.

Oh, sweet. I can pull this off, I think . . . the power boys won't be pleased.

She grinned to herself; let them deal with intractable problems for a change, see how they like it.

The shuttle jerked beneath her butt: ever so slightly, but definitely. The pilot came up: "Ladies and gentlemen, welcome to USSS3. Thank you for flying Virgin-SpaceX. We hope to serve you again soon."

11.

Three of them hadn't been up.

Sandy, Becca, and John Clover were fine when they were strapped down—weightlessness had been more or less meaningless in the comfortable flight chairs, more like a science experiment than anything—but walking on their own was disconcerting: the combination of weightless limbs and shoes that stuck to the floor was odd. They shuffled off the *Galahad*, moving slowly; a group of cheerful station employees kept an eye on them, and pointed them off to their various destinations.

"Don't worry about it," Crow said to the three of them. Having been up before, he more or less knew what he was doing, and Fiorella had already disappeared. "When we get out to the habitats, we'll get some weight back, and you'll be fine."

"I need someplace that I can work, right quick," Becca said. "And I need just a few minutes' access to the Big J before I talk to Fang-Castro." The Big J was a government supercomputer.

"We can get you that. Figure something out?"

"I think so," she said. She felt ungainly and floppy, and kept having to remember to put the next foot down.

A tall, thin woman in a jumpsuit said to Clover, "Dr. Clover? I'm Sandra Chapman. I've read your 'Possible Aspects of Alien Cultures' about two hundred times and I have a lot of questions for you. Here, let me take the cat. Put your foot down. Now the next one, down. You'll get it."

Becca, Clover, and their guides got on an electric cart, which whirred away, leaving Sandy behind with a heavyset, middle-aged balding fellow, who introduced himself as Joe Martinez.

"I'm a handyman up here. I'm going to show you around. We need to get your camera gear," he said. "The other folks are going to take the lift out to one of the habitats, where they'll have some 'gravity.' You and I'll head over to Engineering. It's down the axle where the solar arrays and physical plant are. It'll be zero-gee the whole way, which will give you a chance to practice your movement skills."

They found his camera case—Martinez said his personal effects would be delivered to his cabin and tied it into another cart. "You don't actually sit down on these things so much as just hang on," Martinez said, as they started down the central tube.

The inside of the axle looked like the inside of some . . . well . . . science fiction movie tunnel, Sandy decided. An ice-white rectangular tube lined with pipes ranging in size from five or six centimeters to thirty centimeters, all neatly labeled and color-coded.

Sandy held on and asked, "What are we doing?"

"I was told that you're going to be the primary cinematographer, as well as the documentarian on this mission with Ms. Fiorella. You'll have to do a lot of EVAs, so, we thought as long as you're up here, we'd check you out on an egg, and let you figure out how to shoot from one."

"Sort of like a test, to see if I *can* shoot from one," Sandy said.

"I wasn't going to say that," Martinez said. "Some people find eggs to be pretty intuitive, but I've had Ultra Stars up here who froze the first time we put them in one. We sort of need to find out where you're at."

"Gotcha," Sandy said.

Sandy thought they might have been pulled a hundred meters down the axle when they arrived at what Martinez called the egg crate. A dozen eggs hung from overhead mechanical arms, each in a separate cubicle, much like a series of garages. Each cubicle was an air lock, with an elevator-sized area between two inner doors, and an outer door that opened to space.

"There are interlocks that prevent the space door from being open when either of the inner doors is open," Martinez said. "We have two inner doors . . . just in case. In fact, everything has a just-in-case safety factor built in."

He pointed at an egg: "This one is yours."

They cycled through the air lock, and Martinez showed Sandy how to climb into the pilot's seat, how to strap himself down. "You fly it in shirtsleeves—anything that would wreck an egg wouldn't be salvaged by wearing a pressure suit. An egg sort of is a pressure suit—it's just bigger, heavier, and more capable."

"I was in one once," Sandy told him. "At Disneyland."

"Yeah, that's a pretty good one," Martinez said. "Not nearly as much fun, though—you still get dragged down by gravity. With these babies, you fly."

Martinez spent an hour running him through the egg's controls. At the basic level, there wasn't much to it. The joystick and some push buttons controlled the low-power thrusters. Grips on either side controlled the manipulator arms. "Looks like an old-fashioned video game," Sandy observed.

"You play those?" Martinez's face lit up.

"When I was a kid, I was obsessed with them. Played 'em, took 'em apart, put them back together again. Sometimes they still worked when I got done with them."

"What was your best old game?" Martinez asked.

"Jeez . . . if you put a gun to my head, I'd say, *Hi-Speed Ass-Teroids.*" Martinez: "No! You got one?"

"Somewhere. There's something fundamentally wrong with the left-hand wiper, though."

"Oh, man. You gotta get that up here."

When Sandy had the major controls down, Martinez asked, "You wanna go out and play in the yard?"

"Can we?"

"That's why we're here."

Martinez slaved Sandy's egg to his own, so that he could override Sandy's controls if he needed to. "That's not likely unless you get really disoriented. The thing is equipped with safeties up the wazoo. You can't spin it too fast or ram it into anything. Proximity and acceleration sensors and overrides won't allow it. You can't blow yourself out of orbit. And if you think of some other way to wreck it . . . don't do it."

"Gotta take my cameras," Sandy said.

"Yeah. There's an equipment rack just to the left of your seat," Martinez said. "I'll take us free of the dock. Once we're well clear of the station, I'll let you mess around for a while and then I'll hand the controls over to you and you can try it for real."

When Sandy was set, Martinez moved to the next air lock over and strapped himself into another egg: Sandy could watch him through a hardened glass window that separated the two compartments.

A few seconds later, Martinez spoke to him through a speaker set into the bulkhead behind his head: "You ready?"

"All set."

"Opening the air locks."

The outer doors rolled back, and the overhead mechanical arm pushed them out of the station, then retracted. They were floating free, and Martinez said, "I'll take us out to the playground."

They slowly jetted away from the station, and Sandy had his first good, long look at the Resort.

The living modules, the habitats, rotated about the main axle at a leisurely one revolution per minute, attached by hundred-meter-long elevator shafts at both ends, which conveyed personnel and cargo to and from the center axle. Computer-controlled counterweights piggybacked on the shafts, a few tons of dead weight that slid in and out to keep everything in balance as equipment and personnel moved around the modules.

The one RPM rotation of the habitats produced enough centrifugal force to simulate one-tenth of Earth gravity in the living quarters. Because of the distance between the tubes and the axle, the rotation actually looked quite swift from Sandy's viewpoint outside the ship. An egg that was motionless relative to the center axis, if struck by a moving tube, would be batted away like a tennis ball. The egg's proximity alerts would not permit that, and it had never happened, but it was a theoretical possibility, given a dead egg.

The habitats themselves were squarish tubes, ten meters on a side and a hundred meters long, with meter-thick walls. The walls were slabs of self-healing structured foam that was less dense than air. The foam was inter-layered with ceramic-composite and carbon fiber fabric, designed to be resistant to micrometeorite impacts. Anything smaller than a millimeter or so shattered against the fabric layers in the wall.

A centimeter-sized rock could punch its way entirely through and exit the far side, but that wasn't a fatal accident as long as it didn't hit anyone on its way through. The foam could fill in a several-centimeter-diameter hole in seconds. In the thirty years the station had been operational, an impact like that had happened only once. A researcher's quarters had been trashed as it went through, but she'd been working, so all she suffered was considerable aggravation and the irrevocable loss of a childhood teddy bear that had been unlucky enough to be in the meteorite's path.

When they were a few hundred meters out, Martinez said, "I'm giving you your controls. Try not to screw it up, but if you do, I've still got you."

"Got it." Sandy sat there for a minute, looking around. Strapped into the egg's chair, he was as comfortable as he had been on the shuttle. Not even his subconscious had to think about what to do with body parts and zero-gee. All that surfing: sometimes you'd get driven under by a big wave, and you needed to relax, and let it happen, but always remain aware of where "up" was. Where the air was.

And the view here was much better than anything he'd had in the Pacific: his own personal window into the universe.

"You just gonna sit there?" Martinez called.

"Just soaking in the view. You've got one hell of a backyard," Sandy said. He started to laugh, and didn't stop for a moment, his first good laugh since the day he left for Argentina. He felt like somebody had just taken two hundred pounds of lead off his back.

Martinez laughed with him, the pure joy of being outside.

They worked it for an hour, Martinez pushing Sandy to react more and more quickly to weird, unnatural commands. He fumbled a few times, but got it right more often than not. As they worked, station personnel would sometimes pause at a nearby view window and watch them play.

For some reason that Sandy didn't know at the time, the station wall behind the port was painted black. He found out later that the paint job cut down internal reflections, so if you were contemplating, say, the Milky Way, you could really see the Milky Way. What he saw with his art history eye, though, was that when the station personnel paused by the window, framed in a rectangle slightly wider than it was high, they looked like paintings by Caravaggio.

Sandy unhitched the lid of his camera case and pulled out a Red. He pressed it up against the egg's window, using the front-edge electro-adhesive grips to hold it in place. Then he nudged the controller and sent the egg into a very slow spin, doing a fifteen-second pan of Habitat 1, the earth, and the black, starry space surrounding it all.

He killed his rotation with the window facing the station and did a slow zoom-in on the viewing port. He moved closer, and closer, until he was hovering just outside, and his proximity alarm beeped.

Martinez said, "You're getting pretty tight there."

"I know," Sandy said. "Give me a second." Sandy unstuck the Red, selected a 100mm zoom setting. A crewman walked past the window, paused to look at the egg hovering outside, then went on, but Sandy had time to do a basic reading on the light coming off his face.

"Hey, Joe, how much of a hassle would it be to get Fiorella over by that observation window?"

"Depends on what she's doing," Martinez said. "We've got links to all you new guys, let me try her."

"Thanks."

Joe came back a moment later. "She's at Starbucks, probably fifty meters away. What's up?"

"Can you link me to her?"

"Sure. Hold one . . ."

Fiorella came up: "What?"

"I need you to walk fifty meters down the hall, or whatever, to the viewport. I'm outside in an egg. I want to look at the light on your face. Do an establishing shot."

After a second of silence, probably calculating exactly how much she hated him, Sandy thought, Fiorella said, "Okay."

A minute later, she appeared at the window. The reflected sunlight off her hair was spectacular, maybe too spectacular.

"What do you want me to do?" she asked.

"Let me get a read . . ." Sandy thumbed down the red-gain, just a bit, because he wanted to keep the play of light off her hair, added a touch of color to her face, brought up her cheekbones, deepened a few shadows, then said, "Look sort of pensively off to your left, as though you're watching construction work. . . . Tip your head just a millimeter or so to the right, I need to get that reflection off your nose. . . . Step five centimeters back. . . . Okay, hold that . . . one, two, three. Now slowly, slowly turn back to your right, turn your shoulder as you survey the scene. . . . Shit, I'm losing your hair. Let's do that again. I need to make the background a little denser, and I need you to do all that over again, and talk, tell people what you're seeing out there."

They worked it for five minutes, then Sandy said, "Okay, I got it."

"Send it to me," Fiorella said.

"Don't have your phone number."

He could see her sub-vocalizing, talking to her implants, and then she said aloud, "You should have it."

Sandy checked his wrist-wrap, saved the number, and sent the vid file. "You've got the file. I'll talk to you when I get back inside."

Martinez called: "You ready to go back in?"

"I'm ready, but I don't want to."

"I'm getting hungry out here."

"Then let's go. I've got some vid to look at."

Inside the air lock, Sandy popped the egg's door, then relaxed back in the seat, pulled the monitor out of the Red, and skipped through his survey footage to the shots of Fiorella. Martinez cycled through the double doors to look over his shoulder.

When the last of the shots ran out, Sandy asked, "What do you think?"

"You're a natural on the egg. You could get a job up here. And if Fiorella doesn't like that vid, she's nuts. She's a redheaded Venus."

"Thank you. Listen, how hard is it to alter the canopy on the egg?"

"What do you need?"

"I need to inset some ports. I need to take out a few chunks of standard glass and replace it with optical glass. Shooting through the standard canopy glass degrades the image. That's okay for the propaganda vid, but if we want the highest level of detail on the documentary stuff, I'll need optical glass."

"I can do the insets if you can get the glass, and if it can pass the stress tests," Martinez said.

"We'd probably need some clip-on covers—lens caps—when we're not actually using the glass, protect it from scratches."

"We've got a good fabrication shop up here, shouldn't be a problem," Martinez said. "Shoot me some specs on size and I'll print them for you."

"I'll talk to Leica, see what they can get us," Sandy said. "I'll try to get the specs to you soon as I hear from them." He thought for a moment. "Is your stuff sophisticated enough to print a guitar?"

"You gotta be kidding me—you play?"

"Yeah. You too?"

"I've printed maybe twenty guitars since I've been here," Martinez said. "Shoved all but two of them into the recycling, but I've got a Les Paul replica that's so sweet you won't believe it. Right now, me and another guy are about halfway done printing a piano—like a whole fucking grand piano with strings—but making pianists happy is a lot harder than getting a guitar right."

"We could start a band," Sandy said, with his toothy grin.

"We got a band—in fact, there are five or six bands, if string quartets count as bands," Martinez said. "Music is big up here. Everybody's a specialist in something, with not a lot of overlap. Music is one thing you can do in low gravity without complications, and it's a good way for people to get together."

They headed back down the corridor to the lift that would take them to Habitat 1, talking about cameras, video games, and guitars—a friendship being formed. On the way, Sandy's wrist-wrap tingled: Crow.

"Yeah, what's up?"

"What'd you do?" Crow asked.

"I was getting checked out on an egg," Sandy said.

"I mean, what did you do with Fiorella?"

"Took some pictures of her. Why?"

"She mentioned that it's barely possible that she might be able to work with you, after all."

12.

Captain Fang-Castro looked from the visitor sitting across the desk, to the screen on the wall opposite. The screen was divided into chunks, the chunks growing or shrinking depending on who was speaking. The occupants of the screen's real estate were scattered across the U.S., the best and brightest geeks that DARPA money could buy. Which was pretty damn good, she'd found out back when she was a DARPA liaison.

They were the reigning heavyweight champions of design, putting together a system that would kick her station across 1.5 billion kilometers of empty space, to a rendezvous with who-knows-what.

The geeks were not happy.

Their unhappiness was focused on the challenger, a short, round blonde who was part of a team ferried up by Crow, who'd told Fang-Castro that the blonde, Rebecca Johansson, was probably the best in the world at what she did, which was designing power and heat flow management systems.

Fang-Castro was still getting a read on the engineer; she mixed the soft-spoken style of a well-raised Midwestern woman with the social graces of an engineer, which was to say, not all that many.

She was quiet, pleasant, and blunt.

Johansson was wrapping up her spiel. "That's about the size of it. Literally. If we try to run ordinary low-temperature heat radiators, they will be so many kilometers in size that the mass will kill us—they'll be larger than the mass budget for the entire ship. We need to go to high-temperature radiators, I'm thinking around six hundred Celsius, with molten metal heat exchangers. Then I can pump the heat from the reactors fast enough, and get the waste heat into the radiators fast enough, to dump all of that waste heat into space with a radiator that's a few percent of the size we'd need otherwise."

One of the earth engineers started to jump in, but Johansson cut him off. "I know the reactors are up to it, don't tell me they're not. You can get a lot better than a gigawatt out of a ton of core, and I can siphon it off with pressurized liquid sodium at around two thousand Celsius. You can either boil that directly or run a secondary boiling sodium cycle to run the primary turbines at nineteen hundred Celsius and a downstream supercritical water vapor turbine to get the exhaust down to six hundred and fifty Celsius, and I can take it from there."

The face of one of the earthbound engineers, Harry Lomax, ballooned in size on the view screen, as he waved his hands in frustration. "Are we really supposed to consider this? It's nuts. There's no possible way."

From the corner of her eye, Fang-Castro saw Johansson about to jab back. Without taking her eyes from the monitor and the engineer, she waved one hand at the blonde in a way that said, *Wait. I'm the referee. Let me ref.*

"Harry," Fang-Castro said, "you're saying it's literally impossible? Because if it is, if this is simply a dreadful mistake on Ms. Johansson's part, I'll be happy to dismiss our new engineer and request someone better suited to the task."

The blonde opened her mouth, Fang-Castro waved again, and the blonde closed her mouth.

Lomax paused a moment, disconcerted by the opening he'd been handed. Fang-Castro waited patiently.

"Okay, maybe the wrong choice of words," Lomax said. "It's not physically impossible: it doesn't violate any known physical laws and it doesn't require materials we haven't invented yet. But it's completely and utterly unrealistic."

"So what you're saying is, it's a possible solution in a terribly difficult situation, you just don't have the wherewithal to do your part of the required design."

"That's not *exactly* what I was saying . . ."

Fang-Castro pointed to Becca, who said, "I agree with Dr. Lomax that the whole mission timetable is ridiculous and unrealistic, but it is what it is. Dr. Lomax, you can design all the reactors you want, but if they melt, they ain't going to Saturn. We gotta get rid of the heat. That's not optional. Run the numbers yourself. If you've got a better suggestion than mine, I'd be delighted to hear it."

Fang-Castro jumped in: "Harry, I agree with Dr. Johansson here. We've got to get rid of the heat. I also agree with you: this solution does strike me as unrealistic. Come back to me with a better idea. Quickly, if you please. Orders need to be cut."

Lomax wasn't ready to let it go. "Dr. Johansson's scheme wastes huge amounts of energy. We'll need to scale up the entire power plant by fifty percent to compensate, and we still have to stay within our weight budget. I don't see how."

"That's why I'm giving you options," Fang-Castro said. "You can come up with a different way to handle the heat management, or figure out how to upscale the power plant. Give me a call when you get that figured out. Tomorrow would be good."

Fang-Castro shut down the conference window and turned back to her guest.

"So, Becca: Will they come up with a better idea? And if not, can they build the power train you need?"

Becca chewed the end of a stylus for a few seconds, then her eyes flicked up to Fang-Castro's. "I don't believe there is a better idea. The DARPA guys are really smart, and maybe I've overlooked something, but I don't think so. I want to be clear: I'm not saying my solution is optimal, but there is some basic thermodynamics at work here, and my solution is as good as it gets, with the timetable that's been imposed on us. I'm pretty sure I can handle my side of the engineering. As for them handling theirs, I don't know. I've seen refractory ceramic composite turbines demonstrated that ought to do the job, but that's not really my expertise. Maybe they'll find they can't do it. I'm not sure there's anything else. So, no: they won't find a better idea."

"Good enough, Becca." Fang-Castro sighed. The whole mission was right on the bleeding edge of insanity. "I'll get someone to take you down to Engineering so you can get a feel for our current environment."

John Clover didn't have to take pictures of the station, or set up news reports about it; he didn't have to worry about anything but his brain. And the cat.

Chapman, the tall, thin woman, led him to the elevator-equivalent that took them to Habitat 1. "We're having a get-together in the Commons in fifteen minutes," she told him "An informal affair, open to anyone who wants to come, but there were already quite a few there before you arrived."

"The Commons. That sounds a trifle ominous," Clover said. "Like the place where the aliens touch their heads together while they're getting Roto-Rootered by the Leader."

"Okay. Call it the cafeteria," Chapman said. "It's that, too, at mealtimes. Anyway, we can drop your stuff and the cat at your cabin—the cat should sleep for a while yet, and we've already set up a cat pan and so on—and let you wash your face or whatever."

"I do have to whatever," Clover said. "But I don't want to hold people up. I hope Mr. Snuffles is okay."

"I'm sure he is. We've had a couple of cats up here before, you know. They were subjects of various experiments. They adapt quite well."

"Good. I'm a little worried."

Clover took a leak and washed his face, and Chapman escorted him to the Commons, where twenty-five or thirty people were waiting. They stood and applauded, which made Clover smile, and Chapman led him to a lectern, gave a brief introduction, and Clover said, "I have no prepared comments. I didn't know they might be needed. The main reason I'm up here is to see if I can stand it . . . being up here. So far, so good. I just keep saying to myself, 'Put your foot down, John.' Anyway, maybe I'll give a talk some other time, but right now, I'll put it on you-all. Ask me questions: ask me anything."

They did. They asked about the probability that Earth-like evolution would be working on an alien planet. Clover said, "High. Unless the beings were created instantaneously by their own biblical God, they probably proceeded from simple organisms to complex ones. I also suspect it's probable that they grew up in a gaseous atmosphere rather than a liquid environment, and that they have sight, that they hear sound. All of those things have been invented several times on Earth, and are critical to an evolved tech state, in my opinion. Note that I don't say their eyes are necessarily like ours—they could be like insect eyes—but they can see. Note that I also don't specify that they see the same wavelengths as we do, only that they can see. In my opinion."

They asked about the possibility that aliens would be so culturally unlike Earth people that communication would be impossible. Clover said, "Depends on what kind of aliens you're talking about. Exo-bacteria would fit the definition of alien, and we can't communicate with our own bacteria. But if you're talking about technological beings, we should be able to communicate because communication involves the manipulation of symbols, and we should be able to build a dictionary starting with basics. For example, no matter how alien the aliens might be, hydrogen is hydrogen, and iron is iron, and light travels at the same speed for both cultures. With a highly evolved species, we should be able to create the equivalents of *The Physics Handbook*, and compare them, and that in itself would provide leads to sophisticated symbol manipulation—or language. The place where we might have problems would be understanding highly evolved cultural tastes based on physical differences. For example, we have rather inane performances called 'light shows' on Earth. Given an alien species with different eyes, that respond to much wider wavelengths than ours, they may have evolved a terrifically sophisticated 'music' based on vision, rather than hearing. We might never understand that. On the other hand, there are millions of people on Earth who don't understand jazz—so those kinds of differences can be dealt with.

"But that doesn't mean we'd be compatible. They sure wouldn't look like us, they sure wouldn't think just like us. Think about how many wars have been started on Earth over misunderstandings, and we're all the same species, evolved on the same planet. Would we have lots in common with aliens? I expect so. But we'd probably have lots of ways to piss each other off without even knowing it, so if and when we meet the little green guys it'll be 'step lightly, people.'"

They talked for two hours, the questions ranging from high-school basics to postdoc details. Chapman called a halt when the food service started opening up at a shift change.

"Lot of smart people here," Clover said, as Chapman took him back to his cabin.

"Yes. And that was probably less than a third of the people who actually wanted to come, but couldn't because of work assignments or sleep period. The fact is, half of us are up here because we got interested in space and aliens when we were kids. . . . But I have a question for you. I didn't want to ask it during the meeting, though I thought it might come up."

"Go ahead," Clover said.

"Why are they sending an anthropologist to Mars? There aren't any aliens on Mars."

Clover smiled and said, "I asked the same thing. Promise you won't tell?"

"I won't."

"Because the President wanted me to go," Clover said. "She's a fan, she's read my books. She was one of those kids who wanted to know about space and aliens. She sent me a note and said she hoped that actually living in a space environment would inspire me to new insights."

"Really," Chapman said. "Well, she's the President, I guess she can do that."

Clover suspected that Chapman suspected that something was up.

When Clover shut the cabin door behind him, Mr. Snuffles meowed before he had a chance to sit on his bunk and look around. The cat was still in its nylon carrying case, and Clover put the nylon case on the bed, sat beside it, and unzipped it.

Mr. Snuffles stuck his head out, tentatively, looked around, and then hopped out onto the cabin floor. That was odd enough. Five minutes later, the cat launched himself halfway up the fabric-covered wall, dug in with his claws, and hung there, turned and looked at Clover, and meowed, something beyond a standard meow. More like a meow combined with a purr.

Five minutes, and the cat had gone through a rebirth. His weight was one-tenth of what it had been in New Orleans; his heart didn't have to work as hard, his arthritis didn't hurt as much when it landed. He could jump again. In fact, he was jumping all over the place.

After a while, Clover stretched out for a nap, and the cat snuggled on his chest. The cat, Clover thought, was thanking him, and that made him want to cry, although former WFL tackles didn't do that.

Hardly ever.

Crow spent two hours with Fang-Castro, locked in her bedroom with all the security measures up. "We're going deep on all your crew members. I'm sure you've noticed that you've had a few unexpected transfers down. Those were obvious security problems. I'm not saying they are guilty of anything, I'm just saying that we're not going to take any chances at all."

"I understand. I've been told that you'll be the security chief on the trip."

"That's not quite right. I'll be *your* security chief. You're the boss, I'm the underling. I'll make that work: I've been employed by two presidents, both of whom are assholes of a magnitude you can't even begin to imagine. But. I need you to pay attention to me. When it comes to security issues, I am rarely wrong."

"And if we have two conflicting issues, one involving security, the other the safety of the ship . . ."

"Just like a ship's captain to come up with the immovable-object problem," Crow said with a grin. "If that should happen, I'll give you my best advice and even urge it on you. But you're the captain. I'm paid to give advice, you're paid to make decisions."

Fang-Castro said, "Then we agree."

DAY TWO:

Fiorella took Sandy aside, as they geared up for the first recording session. "I have to tell you, if we're going to work together, that I probably will never like you very much. I grew up in the underclass and there's something about rich people that causes me to itch."

"What are you talking about?" Sandy said. "You gotta be rich yourself."

"I'm affluent—now—but I don't work with the assumptions of the people who are born rich. People like you. But: I can work with people I don't like. I do it all the time. I just don't know if you can handle that kind of relationship, without cutting me up. I don't want to be cut up: this is my career. This is my life."

"No problem, then," Sandy said. "I don't watch much screen, but I've been told you're very good at this. As long as you're good, and you pay attention when I'm telling you camera stuff, we can do it. I'll pay attention to what you say about your reporting requirements. You take care of the talk, I'll take care of the pictures."

Fiorella nodded. "Fine. Now. How did you make that shot of me, at the window? I've never seen anything quite like it. My camera guys all have Reds, the same equipment you have."

Sandy shrugged. "I was an arts major and I've looked at a lot of paintings, and I actually did quite a bit of painting and color studies myself in the studio courses. When I saw that dark window, and the light on the people walking by, I saw a painting, a Caravaggio, that deep, dramatic lighting," Sandy said. "The other thing is, most photographers want sharpness. That's most of what they think about: sharp, sharp, sharp. But people can look too sharp—a little softness can really pop with a naturally sensuous face. The thing is, I was shooting you through the glass on the egg, and then through the view-port glass, and that degraded the sharpness enough to give you the glow. Instead of re-sharpening in-camera, I left it that way."

"You're saying I look better if I'm fuzzy?"

"I'm saying you look better if you can't see every single pore," Sandy said.

She nodded: "Did you learn that with Naked Nancy?"

Sandy smiled and said, "Did you know Naked Nancy once had an emergency appendectomy?"

"No, I didn't."

"None of her viewers know, either. It's a very fine scar, like a white hair, but thinner than a hair, a half centimeter long. Anytime you get a full body shot of her, it's done with a special soft-focus lens. It softens her imperceptibly, so that she looks perfect. Which she almost is. You see everything else, but you won't see that scar, or any little skin blemishes."

"Why doesn't she just go with makeup? On the scar?"

"That would be sort of . . . anti–Naked Nancy. The word would leak. Her viewers have an aesthetic, you know. They want her naked. That's why she doesn't have any hair."

Fiorella said, "I gotta tell you, that never occurred to me. The aesthetic thing."

Fiorella was acting as a pool reporter. Her own services got an hour head start, but after that, it was on to three dozen networks—if the networks wanted it. "That's why I was so worried about you screwing it up," Fiorella said. "Right now, if you were to make a list of news stars, I'd be a Senior Star—maybe—but nothing like an Ultra. When I get done with this, I want to be an Ultra. I've got a shot at it."

Sandy rubbed his nose. "How bad do you want it?"

"Real bad," Fiorella said.

The first broadcast was to be twenty-two minutes long, leaving eight minutes for commercials at each end and the middle. With an Earth-side recording, there'd usually be three cameras, but Sandy would have to work it with two, one stationary, one on his StabileArm.

The whole production took six hours on their second day in the station, squeezing out the twenty-two minutes of airtime.

Fiorella had written a script before she left Earth, had edited it the night before, to take into account actual conditions, and then they cut it up into shooting segments.

And they argued about costuming, they looked at colors against her skin and against the colors of the pipes and ducts inside the axis tube, against the blackness of space, against the white/beige colors of the eggs.

They settled on her green-black jumpsuit with a gold-chain belt for the "reporting" shots, and a pale army-green blouse with a narrow V neck for her "commentary" shots. She wore a simple gold necklace that showed off her endorsement charms, and gold earrings, with both sets of clothing.

She had to do her own makeup, though they found a crewwoman who could help with her hair. When they were ready, she took an egg out, slaved to Joe Martinez's egg, while Sandy orbited around her.

And they shot the first five hours.

At the very end, sitting in a conference room looking at the vid on big high-res screens, Fiorella said, "We got most of it: we really did. The editors down there will turn it into gold. But: we need to reshoot the window."

"What? The window shot is perfect," Sandy said.

"Perfect Caravaggio—I looked him up," Fiorella said. "Then I looked up a whole bunch of other pictures from the Renaissance, and you know what? I think we go for Sandro Botticelli. I'd like to make a costume change for the window shot . . . just for the window shot. We leave the green blouse for the other commentary."

"What costume change?"

Fiorella said, "I got a blouse from Caroline. . . ." Caroline was the hair helper. Fiorella dipped into a gear bag and produced the blouse and handed it to him.

Sandy shook it out and said, "I don't think so. It does have a nice casual look, but it's so sheer that you'd see the brassiere lines under it and . . ."

Fiorella was shaking her head. "No brassiere."

"No brassiere? You're going to Naked Nancy?" Sandy was as shocked as a neo-Victorian. "You're *not* Naked Nancy."

"No, I'm not. But. I've looked at all the vid, and it's very, very cool. I'm very, very cool. I've always been that way and I need to heat it up a little. Everything in pop culture is about sensuousness now. That's worldwide. Sex. Food. Perfume. AR games. MassageSilk. RhythmTech. I don't want porn, or anything like it, but I need to add some heat. I'm looking for the hot librarian. We don't have to send it—we can dump it, if it's too much."

Sandy looked at her for a moment, then said, "You wanted Ultra Star."

"I do."

"Okay. But you're walking on a scary edge here. Go too far . . ."

"We won't." Fiorella went to change, came back a few minutes later. Sandy checked her out and said, "You'll need some double-sided tape: you'll need to stick the edges of the neckline to your skin, or you're gonna show off a little more than you want. Not that that'd be a tragedy."

"Maybe not from your perspective, but like you said . . . I'm walking on an edge. I'll get some tape."

When she'd taped the blouse down, she asked, "What do you think?"

Sandy said, "Uh, Fiorella . . . you know, redheads, in my experience . . ."

"Which I suspect is extensive . . ."

". . . may tend to have somewhat pale nipples." He put up his hands to fend off objections, then continued. "If you have in your makeup kit something with a touch of rose to it . . ."

"Go get in the fuckin' egg," she snapped.

They worked for another hour, a windup shot that would last perhaps two minutes on the broadcast vid. Sandy didn't want to quit, but Fiorella started to lose her voice, even with saltwater sprays. Back inside, they reviewed the footage.

"You are so . . . venal," Fiorella said, as she watched herself at the window. The gauzy blouse showed the finest, subtlest flashes of rose, almost as though they were part of the viewer's imagination. "You are fundamentally an immoral, manipulative snake."

"So you like it," Sandy said. "I had to kick up the red channel, and believe me, after I did that, it was hard to keep your red hair under control."

"We'll send it down, see what my exec thinks," she said.

The exec called her the next morning and said, "Unbelievable. Unbelievable. You're a fuckin' ice cream cone, Fiorella. They're gonna eat you up all over the world tomorrow night. Uh, the guy who shot this . . . is he around?"

Fiorella looked at Sandy: "He's standing right here. We were going to see if you needed another shot or two."

"Won't be necessary. We're good. Ask Randy . . ."

"Sandy . . ."

"Ask Sandy how much they're paying him to take this trip . . ."

DAY THREE:

Becca was called into Fang-Castro's suite on the morning of the third day: "They couldn't find a better solution," Fang-Castro told her. "They're going with your idea, they think they can do something with the reactors that I don't entirely understand . . . you'll have to talk to them."

"I've been thinking about it ever since we talked the first time," Becca said. "I've got a lot of work to do. Boy, do I have a lot of work. I've got to get back down. Like right now. Fabrication is gonna be a bitch. Gonna make 3-D carbon-printer heads look like a kid's crayons. I've been having nightmares, thinking about it."

"But it's not impossible."

"No—but right there with the hardest things anybody's ever built."

Five plus a cat went up, four came back down.

Clover asked for, and got, permission to stay up, with Mr. Snuffles. "I wasn't doing anything down there, anyway, that I can't link into from up here. If somebody can throw out the garbage, lock up my house good, and send me up the rest of my clothes and some culinary supplies . . ."

"We'll see that it gets taken care of," Crow told him.

Crow talked to the President: "Fang-Castro and I spent six or eight hours talking about it, all told. It's coming together: I think we're good. And she's better than good. Now we just have to screw down the security. If we can get six months, it's a done deal."

13.

Fiorella's broadcast on the first night got a six-share nationally, and a two-share worldwide, as the first comprehensive on-site vid from what would become America's first interplanetary ship. For her blog, a six-share was terrific. A worldwide two-share was even better.

From there, it should have dropped off fairly sharply. But at midnight, Pacific time, she was running a twelve-share worldwide, meaning that twelve percent of the people in the world who were watching television were watching her.

Vid Ultra Stars were lucky to get an eight. An analysis by Public Analytics implied that it was the cross-breeding of Serious Science News with the sensuality of the photography that kept people looking. A hack collective had blown the images to one thousand percent in an attempt to isolate actual nipple pigmentation, and had reported that it may have been some kind of chemical composition overlaid on Fiorella's epidermis. It wasn't clear whether the hackers had ever heard of makeup.

Becca didn't notice any of that. She got back to Georgetown and took up residence at the National Center for Mathematics. Somehow, the designs would go better, she thought, if the supercomputer were in the next room, so she could yell at the support techs if necessary.

Clover learned that there was a twenty-two-pound underage on the next Virgin-SpaceX flight up, and got Crow to send up a cold case with a giant sack of raw medium shrimp, an uncooked chicken, a bag of rice, a box of smoked pork sausage, bottles of olive oil, Worcestershire sauce and New Mexican red sauce, onions, garlic, a couple of green bell peppers, celery, tomatoes and bay leaves, some chicken stock, sea salt and three kinds of pepper and a variety of other spices. Fang-Castro and Tomaselli were invited to the Midnight Special, as Clover called it, a secret dinner out of sight in the back of the cafeteria, and when they were done, Fang-Castro said, "Okay, we're going to need some extra freezer room for specialty cooking . . . what would you call it? Can't say, 'Jambalaya for Important People.'"

"Rations," Clover said. "Special rations for morale purposes."

"Exactly. Rations," Fang-Castro said. "God, this could kill my waistline."

Sandy bought two more Reds on his own, and had a long talk with Leica about optical glass for the new vid ports on the egg. Leica could produce the glass over the next six months or so and guarantee that it would meet stress requirements. They also offered an endorsement. Sandy turned it down; not that he wasn't flattered, but he didn't like the idea of wearing labels, and didn't need the money. After being turned down, Leica offered the loan of a half-million-dollar ultra-zoom, which he took. He called Martinez with the glass specs. Martinez said, "Yeah, I can do that, but they're quite a bit bigger than I'd expected."

"Believe me, it's been thoroughly worked out by some of the top guys in the vid field," Sandy said.

By that, he meant Gunnery Sergeant Cletus Smith, who told him, "As a rule of thumb, figure out how big you need them. Then double that. Then double that again. You'll wind up using all of it."

Outside the eggs, in space, he would carry his Reds in a special housing, adopted from dive housings. He got in touch with a French dive manufacturer and made arrangements to pay for three housings, to include battery-driven heaters and Leica glass. The housings would cost him forty thousand dollars each, but Sandy didn't care: it was faster if he paid himself, rather than wait for government approval.

The dive manufacturer offered an endorsement. Sandy almost turned it down, but then thought of his surfer friend pushing brooms in Caltech's Astro building. "Listen, if you endorse a friend of mine—he's big in the surf world—I'll talk about your dive gear when we get back and maybe we could do a vid on the equipment we use up there."

The deal was done; Sandy was walking down the hall the next morning when the surfer/janitor exploded from a machine room, off a crowded corridor, and wrapped him up in a hug and kissed him on the cheek. "Man . . ."

"They're looking at us strangely," Sandy said.

Sandy also needed every picture he could get, and every analysis he could find, of the environment in Saturn space. What was the light like? Would there be dust problems?

His best secure access to the information on Saturn's environment was through the Astro center, and Fletcher, with Crow's encouragement, unhappily gave him a closet-sized office with nothing but a shaky wooden table, an uncomfortable chair, and a computer port.

"The thing is, he's got to look at this stuff, since he'll be spending so much time out in the environment," Crow told Fletcher. "We can't have a guy who's going to Mars being caught doing in-depth research on Saturn. He needs a computer with your security shield on it."

Sandy left the crappy furniture in the hall and brought in his own. He was working there late one night when he heard people running in the hallway, and looked out and saw an Astro Senior Star go by—a fat guy, running like an Olympian, really pumping his knees—and out of simple curiosity, followed.

The fat guy knew Sandy was cleared for Saturn work, and so didn't shoo him away as he called Fletcher, and sputtered into the secure phone.

Crow's wrist-wrap had a nasty urgent alert that sounded like a frog in agony: "*BREET BREET BREET* . . . You have an urgent phone message. Do you wish to hear it? *BREET BREET BREET*. You have an urgent phone message. Do you wish to hear it? *BREET* . . ."

"Okay, okay, goddamnit, I'm awake. Shut up. Who is it? What time is it?"

"Five o'clock in the morning, March twenty-sixth. Call from Sanders Darlington listed Most Urgent no details . . ."

Two in the morning on the West Coast. Whatever was happening there, Sandy didn't think it could wait until later.

"Answer."

Sandy came up: "Crow?"

"This had better be good."

"Sorry to bust you at this time of the morning, and you would have heard in the next couple hours anyway, I think, but I thought since I had the direct line—"

"What the hell is it?"

"The starship's leaving."

"Shit!" Crow fumbled for the bottle of stim pills on the nightstand. "You mean it's gone?"

"It's going. It fired up its engines about twenty minutes ago. It's already got enough velocity to break orbit, and it's looking like it's vectoring well out of the plane of the solar system. The smart boys think it's leaving for good."

"And now everybody and their cousin can see the goddamned thing?" Crow popped three stim pills, one more than the max.

"That's what they're saying. Well, not exactly that. They're saying that at Saturn's distance it'd only look like about a twentieth-magnitude star. You'd need several meters' worth of telescope to detect it."

"So maybe we're going to get lucky, again?" Crow didn't much believe in luck, not the good kind, anyway.

"No. Listen, I don't know the details about this stuff, but they're saying that it's burning a lot hotter than when it came in. It's putting out a load of 511 keV gamma rays. I asked one of the other grad students. That means—"

"Shut up, kid, let me think for a sec."

"But 511 keV—"

"SHUT UP!" Crow took a breath; sleep deprivation and stim pills weren't conducive to clear thinking. Calm down.

Sandy kept his mouth shut.

After a moment Crow said, "Sorry I yelled at you. We've got gamma ray satellites and detectors up the wazoo to ferret out any evidence of folks playing with Bad Things. So does every other major power. Some of those systems will see this. At first they'll just think it's another false alarm from some gamma ray burster out in another galaxy, but they're going to figure out pretty fast it isn't. Five hundred and eleven keV, that's the signature of electron-positron annihilation, and you bet we look hard for that. We do not want anyone screwing around with measurable amounts of antimatter on Earth."

"So, what?"

"So no change in what we're doing. We still need to find out what the hell the little green men have been doing at Saturn, and what they rendezvoused with and what they left behind."

"And how they're making a whole lotta antimatter, apparently."

"Yeah, and how they're storing it. Hey: thanks for the call. Keep your ear to the ground out there. I gotta call Santeros and a few other people."

Crow disconnected and thought for ten seconds, then put in an urgent call to Fang-Castro. USSS3 kept to the same time as Washington, D.C. She was unlikely to be happy to hear from him.

The moment her bleary-eyed face appeared on the screen, he said, "Sorry about the early hour, Captain, but there's been a sudden change of plans. The starship has departed Saturn, and if the entire world doesn't know that already, it very soon will. Accordingly, I'm upping the security level at USSS3. I need to take some immediate steps."

While he was talking, he was thumbing instructions into his phone.

Fang-Castro was now fully alert. "I imagine so, Mr. Crow. What exactly are you planning?"

"Within the next few minutes, we'll be locking down your computer systems and Earth links. Everyone except you will need a new password, which we'll provide as we finish vetting your personnel. In order to keep essential station functions running, nobody currently logged in will be kicked off yet, but they will be in thirty minutes. You will have admin status and can assign new 6V passwords to personnel you deem necessary and absolutely trustworthy, to keep the station running. Please keep it to a minimum. Any passwords you assign will also have to be updated every twenty-four hours, until we get the personnel completely vetted and permanent new passwords assigned."

"Are you expecting trouble, Mr. Crow?" She was tapping the pad by the phone. "I'm rousing our security detail, such as it is, right now."

"I don't know about trouble," Crow said. "I mean that literally: I don't know. That's why I'm casting such a broad net. We need to isolate and remove all foreign nationals and non-citizens from the station. I have a list of those personnel . . . sending it to you . . . now. Until we can ferry them off the station, make sure that these people are always in their quarters or under the visual supervision of your security people or mine. Under no circumstances are they to be allowed access to the computer systems, not even for personal business. If they have personal or research files on the computer, I'll see that they get forwarded to them promptly and in full once they're groundside. Nobody in particular is under suspicion. Anyone I had doubts about was reassigned off the station weeks ago. This is purely precautionary."

Fang-Castro gave him an appraising look. "So noted, Mr. Crow. I appreciate getting the heads-up before you shut down my station."

Crow was not oblivious. "I hear you, Captain. The station remains under your authority. I apologize if I implied otherwise, but this is a bit of an emergency. Now I gotta talk to Santeros. I'll be in touch again, soon as I can."

Crow checked the time: 5:20. The President normally rose at 5:45. Good. He thumbed her private direct access number. It was a necessity of the job, rousting the high and mighty out of bed.

Nothing would ever get him to admit that he enjoyed it.

By the time Crow made his prediction that everybody would soon know about the aliens, that fact was already history. Near-Earth space was filled with an assortment of civilian radiation telescopes and a multinational network of radiation-detecting arms-control satellites.

Simultaneous with the Sky Survey Observatory seeing the starship engine's ignition, the arms control array had picked up a faint but statistically significant increase in the 511 keV background. Near-instantaneous analysis by security computers did not point to a terrestrial origin so, following a tradition that went back the better part of a century, the data was passed on to the astronomers' computers.

Some of those instruments were already on top of it. Their "first alert" radiation scopes talked directly to a slew of fast-response telescopes that covered everything in the electromagnetic spectrum from ultra-high-energy gamma rays to long band radio wavelengths. The new gamma ray source was identified and localized in less than a minute.

In less than five, phones started ringing in the offices and by the bedsides of any astronomers who had the faintest interest in this kind of astronomy. The telescopes were looking at something new. This source wasn't showing anything like a normal time vs. brightness curve in any wavelengths. It was unlike a gamma ray burster or supernova or any other known astronomical object.

It took only a few more minutes for the position of the new source to be refined enough to be able to tell that it was moving and that it had obvious parallax—telescopes on different parts of the earth and in different parts of the sky were seeing it in slightly different locations relative to the background of stars.

The difference was a lot bigger than experimental error. Though the source might be extraterrestrial, that meant it was damn close by astronomical standards. It not only *looked* like it was close to Saturn, it *was* close to Saturn. It took even less time to determine that the motion was changing. The source was accelerating.

The ball finished dropping twenty minutes after first detection. By then, no fewer than five different astronomers' working groups had back-extrapolated the trajectory, which is what they were already calling it, having stopped thinking of it as a natural object. The source had departed from a specific point in Saturn's rings.

The International Astronomical Union had clear protocols for how to handle detection of extraterrestrial intelligence (DETI). Everyone with enough brains to call themselves an astronomer agreed that if this didn't qualify as a plausible detection, then nothing would, until they were shaking hands with the little green men themselves.

All of that instantly became the worst-kept secret in scientific history.

In another hour, a dozen different astronomy departments at a dozen top universities had figured out that what was going up must have previously come down. The data-mining began in earnest. There was a lot to be mined; the assortment of sky survey and space watch telescopes generated zettabytes of new imagery across a wide swath of the electromagnetic spectrum every day. It was exactly like looking for a needle in a haystack.

The thing about that: once you knew you were looking for a needle, metaphorically speaking, the looking got a lot easier. You could toss out anything that was too long, or too broad, or too heavy, or that wasn't made of metal, and so on. The astronomers had some idea of what this needle would look like. It would only be a matter of time, working their way back from the present through the archived data, before they found it.

It took less time than anyone would've guessed. Knowledge of the discovery hadn't just gone viral, it was pandemic. An enterprising grad student at UC Berkeley whipped out a new code module for the BOINC-XV crowd-sourcing research network.

The download demands for it crashed the UC servers in short order, but before that happened it was already mirrored on seven thousand sites around the world. By the middle of the morning, millions of amateur astronomers were meticulously combing through the fodder. In Cedar Rapids, Iowa, 12:23 P.M. local time, a bedridden comet- and asteroid-hunter named Jenny Wright found the needle in an astronomical haystack dated February 9.

So much for the DETI protocols. The news blogs carried every known detail of the historic discovery. Real information being nowhere sufficient to satisfy the insatiable monster, the news conduits were replete with every imaginable speculation and hypothesis about the significance of all of this. Most of it, of course, was ignorant nonsense, but that didn't stop every crackpot from trying to claim his fifteen minutes of fame nor inhibit some willing journalist from giving it to him. It was all that everyone, everywhere, wanted to hear about.

The interest was so intense and universal there was even talk of canceling a World Cup soccer match. Just talk, as it turned out.

The official statements that evening from every major government around the world were both terse and vague. The one-paragraph press release from Washington summed them up: "The President is consulting with top experts and advisers on this unprecedented and momentous discovery. It is engaging her fullest attention. As soon as we have a fuller grasp of the situation, we will keep you fully informed."

It was bullshit, but the public didn't know that and the press couldn't be sure.

Until the following morning, anyway.

It didn't take a rocket scientist—or even an astronomer—to figure out that the surprise U.S. announcement on February 11, just two days after the arrival of the mysterious starship, about joining the Chinese on their mission to Mars and repurposing U.S. Space Station Three for interplanetary travel hadn't been a coincidence.

Nor, for that matter, the least bit honest.

It was all over the AM news coverage. The White House had no comment. The more hysterical pundits talked of a major diplomatic rift between the United States and China, maybe even the possibility of a war.

Their apocalyptic anticipations were dashed by the Chinese government's press release. It merely expressed deep disappointment that the U.S. had acted in such bad faith and that given that behavior, they most sorrowfully had to withdraw from any cooperative efforts to explore Mars, as if there had been any in the first place.

Private diplomatic communiqués were more heated, but what they really boiled down to, once the oblique language and the political posturing were stripped away, was this: "You had a big secret and you didn't tell us."

"You would have done exactly the same thing in our shoes."

"Fuck you."

That was the end of it.

The other world political blocs had more predictable responses. The European Union, the Russian Confederacy, the Conclave of African States, India, Brazil, even the United Central American States, a staunch U.S. ally, condemned China and the United States for "attempting to monopolize alien technology." They decried their exclusion from the planned missions and demanded to be allowed some measure of participation.

The United States and China had identical responses to these challenges. They ignored them.

Space watchers noted that activity around USSS3 abruptly increased,
while construction efforts on the Chinese Mars ship just as abruptly
ceased. Presumably Mars was off the table for the Chinese—hardly sur-
prising when they might find aliens, and alien technology, at Saturn.

Within two weeks, construction activity resumed at the Chinese
ship, but it appeared to be operating in reverse. Based on the boost and
flight profiles of the Chinese cargo ships and orbital tugs, they were
stripping their ship.

Anything related to colonizing Mars—hardware, landing and
ground supplies, living quarters, and support for a decent-sized coloni-
zation party—all of it was going, stuck in an orbital dump several kilometers off the ship. Security had tightened up massively around both
countries' missions, so good firsthand information was impossible to
come by, but this much was obvious to any observer with a decent
telescope.

The Chinese were adding extra tankage both internally and externally to their ship. More reaction mass for their nuclear thermal rocket
engines. That meant more velocity and a shorter trip to Saturn. How
much shorter was still anybody's guess.

Externally, the ship would not wind up looking a lot different. A bit
beefier, a bit stockier with the additional tanks, but still pretty much the
same deep space cargo hauler, refitted for speed rather than capacity. A
smaller crew, but with longer-duration life support. Nothing radical or
unpredictable there.

USSS3 was another matter. It was undergoing a major makeover.
Beams and spars hundreds of meters long were being constructed in
near-station space. The main axle of the station was being extended two
hundred meters and there were several major construction sites along
the length of it. The Americans were assembling new modules and adding reaction-mass tanks. Unlike the Chinese mission, the station had
never been designed for space flight; it was a lot harder to guess what all
these changes would mean.

Nobody outside the highest circles of the U.S. and Chinese governments was entirely sure what was going on. The activities were taking place in total public view and complete public silence.

All anyone could be sure of, and again, it didn't take a genius to figure it out, was that the U.S. and the Chinese were in a race to Saturn and hell-bent on making sure the other didn't get there first.

The Chinese launched first.

14.

On the day before Halloween, the image of the Chinese ship filled the wall display in the Oval Office, as Santeros, Vintner, Lossness, and Crow watched the broadcast. The ship was impressively large, massing an estimated ten thousand tons. Originally called *Martian Odyssey*, it had been rechristened *Celestial Odyssey* for its new mission—to beat the U.S. to Saturn's rings and to whatever the alien starship had rendezvoused with.

The *Odyssey* had been designed to be a cargo hauler, intended for routine runs to establish and support a Chinese colony on Mars. The ship could haul nearly three thousand tons of payload and deliver it to Mars in less than four months, with round-trips happening at year-and-a-half intervals when the Earth-Mars alignment was most favorable.

The Chinese plan had been to run it to Mars, unload the first colonists and colony supplies, stick around for a bit to make sure everything was working, and then make a slower run back to Earth. After six months in Earth orbit being maintained, refurbished, and resupplied, the *Odyssey* would be ready for another trip out. As dramatic and history-making as the first trip would be, *Odyssey* would then settle into a routine of unglamorous but vitally important cargo runs for the nascent colony.

Plans had changed.

The ship looked much the same, externally, as it always had: chunky and solid. American intelligence said the Chinese engineers had stripped every bit of unnecessary weight and filled most of the cargo bays with water and liquid hydrogen tanks, which would make up additional reaction mass for the lightbulb reactors.

The reactors would heat the reaction mass to nine thousand degrees Celsius exhaust plasma. Ten of those reactors collectively provided over ten million newtons of thrust. As big as that was, it was only one-third the size of the historic rockets that had landed humans on the moon nearly a century before; even so, they were by far the most powerful engines flying in space in 2066.

All in all, the reaction mass and reactors provided enough power and water to get the *Odyssey* to Saturn—but they weren't enough to get the ship there and back, not quickly. The expectation was that the Chinese would harvest water from the moons and rings of Saturn.

The audience in the Oval Office was mirrored by seven billion other human beings, planet-wide. With all pretense of secret missions gone, the whole world was watching the final launch preparations for China's Saturn mission. Someone in the Politburo with an excellent sense of Chinese history decided his nation's thrust into an uncertain future needed solid traditional roots.

There were fireworks.

Earth had never seen a show like the one the Chinese put on. State-of-the-art hypergolic engineering was married to pyrotechnic expertise that stretched back fifteen hundred years. A thousand kilometers above the earth, a round of chrysanthemum bursts three kilometers wide blossomed in gold, pink, and white.

People didn't need vid feeds. Everybody on Earth within line of sight of the ship got a clear view of the display of Chinese history, culture, and power. Even with unaided eyes, earthbound humans on the night side of the planet could see multicolored pinpricks and puffballs of light as the ship passed overhead. With simple binoculars, they could see intricate starbursts, fountains, and sculptural fireballs. The show went on for nine orbits of the earth. Nine times, as the ship passed into sunlight, the fireworks ceased; nine times, as the ship passed into Earth's shadow, they resumed. Over eighteen hours, seven billion people saw a show of glorious and unprecedented scale.

In the President's office, Crow conferred quietly with the others.

"Ten minutes," somebody said.

American intel had projected the likely ignition time. Intelligence had been right about the launch date, and they were pretty sure of the tech, but nothing else was certain. Until the Chinese actually launched,

nobody in the U.S. had a solid handle on the Chinese's target arrival date
at Saturn. The best guess was two years and change.

Whatever they had planned, the Chinese were confident enough to be broadcasting live from orbit. Not that it would have done them much good to try to keep the launch secret, but usually they maintained a polite fiction of silence until after a launch. This time, the Chinese had a full professional broadcast crew in orbit, not far from the *Odyssey*, and they were letting the whole world watch from fifty-yard-line seats.

The *Odyssey* was roughly over Beijing, bathed in midday sun. The running commentary from the announcer on board the broadcast ship was interrupted by another voice: subtitles on the Oval Office display identified it as that of the *Odyssey*'s commander, Captain Zhang Ming-Hoa. He reported to Beijing that all final checks were complete and launch would commence in 10 . . . 9 . . . 8 . . .

Seven seconds later, the monitor flared white for a fraction of a second until the cameras could compensate. For a fleeting millisecond, Crow wondered if the ship had exploded, even half hoped it had. That would solve a lot of problems. But, no, it was those ten massive nuclear engines coming online, their fiery blue-white exhaust much more brilliant than the surface of the sun. The ship started to move away, steadily picking up speed. Within a minute, it was nearly two kilometers away from the cameras, receding at two hundred kilometers an hour. By space travel standards, it was a snail's pace, but it looked impressive on the big screen.

The status display from U.S. tracking reported that the *Celestial Odyssey* was accelerating at a tenth of a gee, adding one meter per second of velocity each and every second. That was pretty much what DARPA had expected, or at least hoped. The Chinese hadn't souped up their engines. They seemed to be more or less the same as they had been for the Mars mission. The big question was, how long would they keep firing?

"All right, everybody out," Santeros said to the watchers in her office. "I'll stop down at the situation room every once in a while."

Crow, Lossness, Vintner, and top military and congressional personnel shuffled out of the office, and walked down to the situation room for the waiting game. In an hour, the *Odyssey*, now on the night side of the earth, had reached escape velocity.

"No surprise there," a general said. "Christ, I could use a drink."

The Chinese engines needed to burn for at least two hours to send the ship to Saturn. The tracking status predicted that if the Chinese cut their engines after two hours, it would take them over seven years to reach Saturn. No one in the situation room expected that to happen, and no one was disappointed.

Three and a half hours after launch, the engines were still firing. Vintner and Lossness looked at each other and then at Crow, who shrugged. Trajectory status reported a velocity of nearly twenty kilometers per second and a transit time to Saturn of under two years. This was shorter than what the ostensibly knowledgeable experts had predicted.

Santeros walked in, talking on a handset, spotted Crow, and her eyebrows went up. Crow nodded toward a monitor. The ship was too far away to be anything but a searing blue-white pinpoint of light, but there was no sign of an engine shutdown. The *Odyssey* continued to accelerate away from the earth.

"Where are we at?" Santeros asked when she got off the handset.

"Still moving," Lossness said. "They're gonna get there in a hurry."

"How big a hurry?"

"Can't tell yet, but they've already exceeded our projections."

Santeros lingered, watching the screen, then, after two minutes, said to Crow, "Call me."

With every passing minute, the *Odyssey*'s ETA to Saturn dropped. The five-hour mark passed. Suddenly, the blue-white speck disappeared; it took the cameras a second to adjust, but then, distantly and dimly, a tiny image of the ship could be made out on the monitor. The *Odyssey* had completed its ejection burn and was free-falling toward Saturn. Status numbers completed their final update. The Chinese nuclear thermal engines had imparted an extraordinary twenty-kilometers-per-second delta-vee to the *Odyssey*. The projected transit time to Saturn was a year and a half, with an ETA in late April of 2068.

Crow pulled up the timeline for the *Nixon*. If they stayed on schedule, they'd be launching by the end of 2067, which would have them to Saturn just about the same time as the Chinese. Not good. He called Santeros, and five minutes later he, Vintner, and Lossness were back in the Oval Office.

"This isn't acceptable," Santeros said. "Best case, we and the Chinese are there at the same time, and that's a powder keg waiting to blow up in our faces. Worst case, our schedule slips and they beat us to whatever's out there. We need to get there faster. I don't care how you make it happen, but make it happen."

She looked up into thin air and said, "Gladys, tell the kitchen to send fresh pots of coffee to Vintner's office, then meals for Crow, Vintner, and Lossness." The White House computer pinged acknowledgment. "Jacob, Gene, figure this out. Call in whatever resources you need. Crow, I want you in on this so you can report back to me and in case any of their ideas have security implications we need to be on top of. By the morning briefing, I want to know how we're going to beat the Chinese to Saturn."

Crow had been running on catnaps for two days, trying to stay on top of last-minute intelligence about the Chinese launch. More stim pills.

Two hours later, in Vintner's office, the three of them were well-caffeinated and fed, but they weren't any happier. Crow massaged his forehead. "So, really, there's no way to speed up the trip? Neither of you geniuses can come up with anything?"

Lossness grimaced. "Not enough to matter. Constant-boost trajectories eat up energy like a son of a bitch. If we could figure out how to up the ship's power by fifty percent, it wouldn't trim more than a month off the travel time, and that's still too close for comfort. And, anyway, we can't do it."

Vintner looked up from his third cheeseburger—Crow marveled, where did the man put it all?—"Gene, any chance your guys didn't optimize the trajectory for the shortest trip?"

"You're kidding, right? Fastest is what we asked for—fastest is what we got. But if it will make you happier . . ." Lossness checked the time.

"It's the middle of the night in California . . . he should be home. I could call our orbit maven at JPL."

"Do it," Crow said.

A few minutes later, a sleepy-looking David Howardson peered at them from a vid screen. "This is Dave. Hey, Gene . . . Ah, let me guess. The timetable's shot."

"In spades. Any chance in hell that you didn't pull together the fastest trajectory for our ship?"

Howardson gave him a look.

"I didn't think so," Lossness said.

"I take it there's no possibility of making the ship significantly faster, right?" Howardson asked. He was pulling up ship's specs and orbital simulations on his slate while he talked.

"Not in the time we have left," Lossness said. "Sorry to wake you. We need to get back to brainstorming before Santeros has us dismembered."

"Hold on a sec." Howardson was reading through his logs. "I'm looking at the simulation optimization you requested six months back. It's the right answer—it gets you there fastest, which is what you asked for. You wanted the fastest trip because it reduces the expenditure of life-support supplies."

"Yeah?"

"But now you've changed the question. Implicitly, anyway. You don't want to get there fastest, you want to get there soonest. Right?"

Crow interjected, "What's the difference?"

Dave was dragging orbital curves around on his screen, fiddling with launch dates and noting arrival times. "The difference is that you've got so much delta-vee in this ship that you've got a huge launch window. It's like the better part of five months. The fastest trip is at the end of that launch window, sometime in December of next year. But you could launch as early as, mmm, July? I'll have to do some numbers to nail it down. You'll still get to Saturn. It's just that the trip takes longer. But let me see . . . mmm, it'd only take about a month longer. If you're able to launch in July, that'd buy you four months on the ETA. You get to Saturn for Christmas—that's a rough guess, of course. I'd need to run a finer-grained simulation."

Gene said, "Get on it."

Howardson grinned. "There is one catch, though."

Crow asked, "What?" in a tone that suggested he didn't want to hear about catches.

The grin disappeared. "The ship'll be doing a flyby of the sun. If you launch in late July, Saturn will be on the far side of the sun. You don't launch out, you launch in, right toward the sun, swing past it and let its gravity bend the ship's trajectory so that it's on target for Saturn on the far side."

"How close are we talking?" Lossness asked.

"Couldn't say quite yet. Looking at my pictures here, I'd say somewhere inside the orbit of Mercury, maybe as little as 0.2 AU."

"Thanks. Get back to me when you've got the refined model." Lossness logged off the connection.

Vintner looked at Lossness. "Can we advance the schedule that much? Launch in nine months instead of fourteen?"

Lossness nodded. "Pretty much got to, pending Dave's finished simulation. And we'll need a design mod for close solar operations."

Crow: "I'm guessing your engineers are gonna love that."

Becca got a call from Vintner just before dinnertime. From the background, she could tell he was in his private office, which was little more than a cubbyhole. He used it for private conversations.

"Hey, Becca. Is this a good break point?"

"Hiya, Jacob. As good a time as any," Becca said. "We finished another control simulation. We're doing good here."

"You may not feel that way in a minute. I've got news you're not gonna like."

"Santeros scrubbed the mission?"

"That'd make life simpler, not harder. She's advanced the launch date by five months. You've got nine months to get ready."

Becca responded, and when she ran out of breath, Vintner asked cheerfully, "All done? 'Cause, you know, you were repeating yourself there at the end. I think you said 'bitch' at least four times and 'mother-fucker' five or six."

"Funny. What in the hell is she doing?" Becca asked. She could feel the heat in her face: she must be glowing red on Vintner's screen.

Vintner filled her in on the Chinese mission status and the planning session on the night before. "So that's the size of it. I'm sending you Howardson's new trajectory model right now."

Becca blinked up the plots and the time markers, read through them. "Okay, that's clever. Cutting it a little close to the sun, aren't we?"

"Yeah, the ship design guys'll have to rig up a heat shield for the close approach, so we don't overload our cooling systems. Shouldn't be a big deal. We'll deploy an aluminized plastic film parasol that will reflect ninety percent of the extra sunlight. We'll jettison the parasol on the way outbound. And speaking of heat, how will this impact your cooling system?"

Becca hummed for a minute. "Well, absent any clever tricks, it'll diminish my thermal outflux by, I'm guessing, maybe twenty-five percent for about two weeks. Only while we're within about a quarter AU of the sun. We'll have to cut back on thrust, but that shouldn't cost us more than a couple of days and we're picking up, what, four months, after we add back in the extra flight time? Couple days one way or another won't make a difference."

Vintner nodded. "I'll leave it to you to coordinate with the propulsion engineers and get a modified thrust profile to Howardson to plug into his model."

"Jacob, do we need all five months? I mean, do we really have to launch at the beginning of the launch window?"

Vintner sighed. "Honestly, I don't know. Probably not. But this is turning into more of a race than we had planned, and we don't know what we're going to find out there or how long we're going to have to stick around investigating it before heading back to Earth. We don't want to collide with the Chinese—that's a party Santeros wants to avoid."

"Okay."

"Which leaves the big question. Can you complete your part of the project in nine months?"

Becca asked, "What happens if I say no?"

"Santeros doesn't like to be told no. If I have to tell her you're not up to it, she'll send me off hunting for a replacement," Vintner said. "If I hunt long enough, eventually I'll come across someone who'll say yes, just for the opportunity."

Becca sighed. "No doubt. But they won't be able to do it. There's not enough time for them to come up to speed on my design and not enough time for them to come up with one of their own."

Vintner nodded. "That's pretty much my take on it. Even if you don't think you can do it, the odds are still better if you do it than if someone else tries. So, what the hell. Say yes."

Becca fidgeted. Buying into a schedule she didn't believe in was a plausible path to professional suicide. On the other hand, quitting in midstream would also trash her reputation. *Game theory,* she thought. *If I quit now, I keep my professional integrity and it's a sure loss. If I stick it out, there's a chance I might be able to pull it off and no one will know that I was blowing smoke. A guaranteed loss vs. a possible win.*

"I'll give it a try."

"Thanks. I'd love to be able to tell you that nobody will hold it against you if you can't pull it off, but we both know that'd be a lie. If we don't beat China to Saturn, we'll all be pilloried. The President will tank and she'll make sure we're all in the handbasket with her. Talk to you later."

Vintner hung up.

Becca threw her coffee cup across the room where, unsatisfactorily, it bounced without shattering off a whiteboard and landed in a corner of the carpeted floor. Fuck it, she was done for the night. She shut down her workslate, pushed back her chair, and walked out of the office. Tomorrow was going to begin an unrelenting hell. Tonight she was going to study some margaritas.

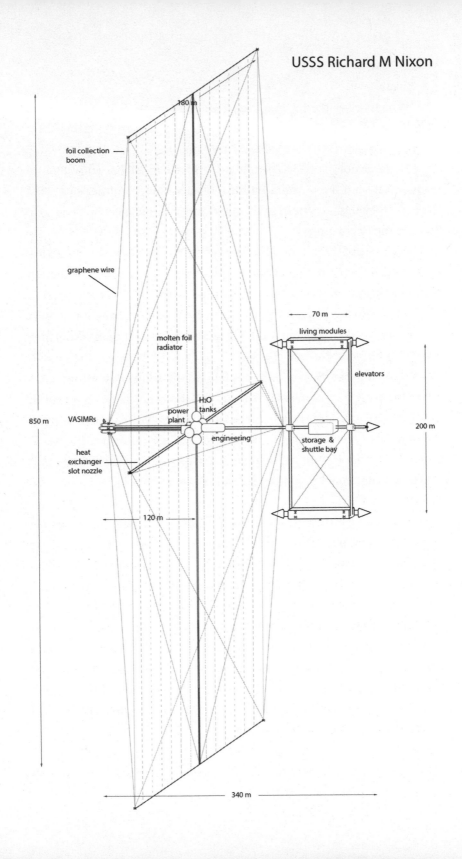

USSS Richard M Nixon

foil collection boom

graphene wire

molten foil radiator

850 m

VASIMRs

heat exchanger slot nozzle

power plant

H₂O tanks

engineering

120 m

180 m

70 m

living modules

elevators

storage & shuttle bay

200 m

340 m

15.

Sandy had spent a week working on the vid for the first test of the *Nixon*'s power plant. In fact, he'd worked right through New Year's Eve, three days earlier. Fiorella, as it turned out, was a genius at explaining complicated technical matters in terms that anyone could understand, and occasionally even laugh at.

As with Becca Johansson's solution for dissipating waste heat from the reactors . . .

Sandy launched his egg from the central axle and took it a kilometer out. In the past year, the metamorphosis of USSS3 station into the *Richard M. Nixon* had come a long way. He'd documented all of the major construction activities, the vid instantly relayed groundside. If anything went wrong, if there were any problems, analysis of the vid might give clues for possible fixes.

The *Nixon* was obviously a reworked USSS3. It still had three parallel tubes, side by side and spaced a hundred meters apart. The two outer tubes, each a hundred meters long, still contained the ship's living quarters and were still known as Habitats 1 and 2. The center tube, the axle, contained storage and the shuttle bay.

The axle, instead of stopping where it intersected the rear connecting elevator tubes, continued back for another two hundred and seventy meters. About halfway back on the extended axle—all of it still zero-gee—were the engineering section and the twin reactors of the nuclear power plant. At the aft end, another hundred meters away from the reactors, the VASIMRs were still under construction. Between the reactors and the engineering system were a cluster of spherical tanks that would hold the thousands of tons of water that would make up the reaction mass for the VASIMRs.

And then there was Becca's answer to the waste heat problem. In the nine weeks since the Chinese had launched, she'd moved heaven, Earth, and no small number of recalcitrant engineers. Between Engineering and the reactor modules, two four-hundred-meter-long masts projected out from the center axle, from Sandy's viewpoint, one "up," one "down." At the end of each mast was what Sandy, who had done some sailing, thought of as a spar—but which also looked like the crossbar on a capital letter T.

Two more beams, the same length as the top spars on the T, projected out "horizontally" for a hundred meters on both sides of the axle. They held the extrusion nozzles for the molten radiator alloy that Becca Johansson would use to cool the reactors. The "T" spars would re-collect the now-frozen alloy, effectively thin sheets of foil, and send it back to the reactor.

Dozens of nearly invisible guy wires ran from the booms and masts to the axle. The guy wires were made of graphene composites that tied all the pieces into a rigid structure, far more inflexible and lightweight than any equivalent scaffold of metal. It reminded Sandy of an unfinished box kite, all balsa wood struts and string. At this moment, the struts were bare.

Shortly, there would be sails.

The engineers and design teams had fallen in line behind Becca Johansson's scheme for handling the *Nixon*'s prodigious power demands. Not because they were happy with it; they just couldn't think of anything else that would let them beat the Chinese to Saturn.

Grumbling, they designed a ceramic core reactor that ran at a glowing-yellow temperature and heated the primary coolant—pressurized liquid sodium—to over nineteen hundred degrees Celsius. The superheated liquid sodium ran through a heat exchanger where it boiled more sodium. That vapor drove the primary ceramic composite turbines at two hundred atmospheres and nineteen hundred degrees Celsius.

The sodium vapor condensed downstream of the turbine, in a secondary heat exchanger, where it heated steam to a supercritical eight hundred and eighty degrees. That drove the next set of turbines. Extreme as all of this was, it didn't justify an epithet like harebrained.

The final stage was another matter.

Downstream of the secondary turbines, the steam, cooled to six hundred and fifty degrees Celsius, entered the heat exchanger for the ship's radiators. It melted radiator alloy, a eutectic blend of aluminum, magnesium, and beryllium that liquefied at six hundred degrees Celsius. In doing so, it absorbed nearly two hundred watt-hours of heat per kilogram of melt. All Becca had to do was get rid of the heat in the molten alloy, and that was what merited the epithet.

Her heat exchanger extruded the alloy into space in molten ribbons a meter wide and a tenth of a millimeter thick. Cold rollers in the extrusion nozzles clad the ribbons in a skin of frozen and roughened alloy, just microns thick.

The rough skin improved the ribbons' heat radiation properties and kept the thin, wide bands of liquid alloy from breaking apart into a spray of droplets. As they sped toward the spars four hundred meters away, the ribbons cooled and froze, radiating tremendous amounts of energy into space.

It was a brutally efficient scheme for dumping the vast amounts of heat, but it was tricky.

The nearly liquid ribbons of metal had to be guided electromagnetically as they squirted out from both sides of an extrusion boom, and then led to the spars over four hundred meters out. There, the solidified ribbon was fed by rollers mounted on the spars to the central masts and back down into the melting pot. Managing one ribbon was a technically challenging feat. For Becca's system to get the *Nixon* to Saturn, it had to extrude and control hundreds of them, all at the same time.

Thus, sails—or, for the more poetic, a moth with huge wings and a tiny body.

Each of the sails comprised almost a hundred ribbons, running side by side from the boom that extruded them to the spars, across the spars and back to the heat exchanger reservoir. The alloy circulated perpetually, hundreds of semi-molten ribbons in constant motion, safely disposing of the reactors' waste heat. When the ship was under full power, 150,000 square meters of the dull silvery metal—the equivalent of twenty-eight

American football fields—would radiate nine gigawatts of heat into space. So said the theory.

As for the practice, the first full-scale test would give them a good idea of what worked, and what might not.

The power engineers had to bring the reactors online to produce enough heat and power to test out the turbines and the boilers and melt the alloy reservoir of the heat exchanger. But they couldn't go too far, too quickly, because the relatively puny auxiliary cooling system had to handle the thermal load until the main heat exchanger was fully operational. It was a delicate matter. Reactors of this design didn't really like being run at less than one percent of their rated output. If an instability got out of hand it could result in a core meltdown, and that would be the end of the mission, and possibly the space station.

From a cinematographer's point of view, the first days were mind-blowingly boring. When you've photographed one status display being monitored by a furrow-browed engineer, you've photographed them all.

But after a week, life got interesting again. The reactors were as happy as they were ever going to be; the heat exchanger reservoir was stable at its operating temperature of just over six hundred degrees Celsius; and all the guidance sensors were nominal. Becca had taken a deep breath and given the instruction to open one slot nozzle, at minimum operating pressure.

Slowly, slowly a tenth-millimeter-thick, meter-wide ribbon of metal crawled out of the boom toward one of the spars. It wavered for a moment, wobbled, and then the guidance sensors and control magnets latched onto it. Dedicated supercomputers analyzed the ribbon's hesitant path and issued instructions to guidance magnets to induce precisely formulated eddy currents into the ribbon. Electromagnetism did its part; the ribbon was forced back onto the straight and narrow toward the waiting spar.

After two minutes, the leading end of the ribbon reached the recovery spar, was picked up by the rollers, and fed across the spar and back down the mast.

Engineering broke out in cheers. Sandy was happy; it was dramatic.

That languorous silver band creeping across four hundred meters of space was great for building tension, and Sandy planned to include every second of that footage in the final cut. Make the audience sweat the same way the engineers had.

The engineers opened the second nozzle and extruded a second meter-wide ribbon. It behaved much like the first. There were three hundred and fifty more of these to go. Allowing for pauses for status checks, the engineers would be at it for eighteen hours before all four sails were fully deployed. Sandy stuck a camera on a station-keeping pod to record the repetitive affair in real-time mode, and left for the day.

Back in the ship, he headed into a ladies' restroom, where he found Martinez gluing a toilet-paper holder in one of the booths, while Fiorella, standing outside, was getting her hair done. She said, "You're late."

"But not too late," Sandy said. "I was here earlier, I worked out the lighting."

The Reds he was using didn't need much light, but Sandy needed shadows—the light in the restroom was simply too flat and indirect to be interesting. He rolled his equipment case into the restroom and began sticking LED-light panels to the walls.

When they were ready, Fiorella sat on the toilet seat. On either side of her, at chest height, were two toilet paper rollers, one with a roll of toilet paper on it, the other bare; Martinez had installed the second one, and moved the first one to the right height for the shot.

They were about to start shooting when Fang-Castro stuck her head in the door and said, "I really didn't want to know about things like this, but then somebody had to tell me. Why did they do that? Why do people tell me about things like this?"

She shook her head and disappeared again.

"Heckled from the cheap seats," Martinez said.

Sandy had stuck his Reds to the restroom walls, controlling them from his slate, and said, "We're on."

Fiorella said to the cameras, "The problem was getting rid of the heat. The only feasible way to do that was to extrude extremely thin bands of molten metal into space, where, after they froze—thus getting rid of all the heat—they'd be gathered up and recycled into the ship's reactor, where they'd be remelted. . . .

"Think of it as working like this toilet paper roll." She took a tab of toilet paper between her fingers and began pulling it across in front of her, toward the bare roller. "The molten metal is extruded into space, in a ribbon, like this paper. It then crosses to the other side, where it is picked up by a roller."

Martinez had put a thin line of adhesive on the top of the roller, and Fiorella carefully stuck the paper to it, then began turning the empty roller, taking up the toilet paper.

They did it seven times before they had enough fragments of good vid that the editors could make it into one continuous segment; and it ended with Martinez on his back, under the toilet and between Fiorella's legs, providing invisible drag on the feed roller with his fingers, while Sandy focused on bringing up the gold flecks in Fiorella's eyes.

When they were done, and Fiorella and Martinez were back on their feet, Martinez said, "That was really pretty easy, except when the toilet paper broke."

"That's why we have editors," Sandy said. "The paper won't break on screen."

The next morning, back in his egg, Sandy watched as four giant frosted-pewter rectangles of metal, hundreds of meters in size, ran from the spars to the booms, like square-rigged sails. The alignment was so perfect that from a distance the sails looked like single sheets instead of hundreds of parallel ribbons of radiator alloy.

He recovered his automated camera and moved it, reset it, changed memory modules: the cameras had both internal memory and simultaneous remote recording capability that went straight into a dedicated memory core in the station. Some videographers thought the equipment was now so good that no backup was really needed. Sandy had never believed that: he backed up everything.

He was outside that morning because Becca Johansson and the other engineers were finding out if their baby could walk. The reactor managers would take their plants up to twenty-five percent of rated output, the first field test of the reactors under anything close to normal operating conditions. For the time being, they'd be bypassing the turbine-generator stage. Dumping all the power into the heat exchanger would test its capabilities to over fifty percent of full capacity.

Ramping up the heat exchanger-radiator system was simple enough in concept; it just required speeding up the extruders. The faster the metal got fed into space, the faster they could dump waste heat. Currently the extruders were streaming ribbons at a leisurely three meters per second, but in full operation the ribbon velocity would be over a hundred and sixty meters per second. The plan for the day would be to take the ribbons to ninety meters per second. If that worked, the system would be taken down while Sandy and the other engineers went over every bit of data produced by the dozens of recorders watching the event.

Even at the slower ninety meters per second, everything needed to work hand in hand perfectly. The heat exchanger needed sufficient heat coming in from the reactors to keep the alloy reservoir molten. If the extruders ran too fast for the reactors, the exchanger would dump too much heat into space and the reservoir would cool down. If the temperature dropped below the six-hundred-degree melting point of the radiator alloy, the reservoir would freeze up and the engineers would have to shut it down. So the reactors depended upon the heat exchanger to keep from melting down, and the heat exchanger depended upon the reactors to keep from freezing up.

Sandy, waiting for the test to begin, focused on giving Fiorella as many different views of the station as he could, using a variety of imaging techniques. He would switch from normal real-color imaging to thermal imaging, and the sails would go to a brilliant white, set in a framework of dim, dark gray masts and booms and other station components, with a dull gray Earth in the background. When he had enough of that, he thumbed through a variety of alternative modes, doing false-color mapping, which showed sail temperatures in a rainbow of hues. Fodder for the editing session later; anything to jazz up the presentation.

When the test began, it looked like nothing. Nothing changed.

Sandy slowly panned back and forth over the station, muttering notes to himself into his throat mike, the Red dutifully capturing all that as well as multiple channels of audio from Engineering.

In fifteen minutes, he had more vid than Fiorella would ever be able to use, so he picked the best spot, a kilometer out, set two cameras at different focal lengths, picked up his slate, and went back to a novel he'd been reading.

In an hour, the reactors were up to five percent, dumping nearly a gigawatt of heat into the exchanger and radiators. Ribbons streamed out at twenty meters a second. The reactor managers sounded happy. The heat exchanger engineers sounded happy. Dr. Johansson sounded slightly less stressed than usual. Sandy went back to his novel, a bit of undemanding popular science-fictional fluff about the first space mission to Jupiter. Set ten years in the future, he thought. How quaint: this mission would blow Jupiter's doors off.

Each time he scrolled the tab's screen, Sandy glanced up at the sails. The Reds would run fine on their own, unattended, he was just spot-checking. As the station moved in its orbit about the earth, the sun's light constantly changed angles and intensity. There was the especially dramatic transition from lightside to darkside and vice versa on the earth. Sure, it was repeated every two hours, but audiences lapped it up. More eye candy he could edit into the footage so that viewers wouldn't notice that nothing interesting was happening. Occasionally he panned across the earth to capture the sunset/sunrise terminator and its delicate rainbow, or the lights from humanity's bigger and brighter megaplexes.

Two and a half hours into the test, Fiorella and Martinez came out in separate eggs, Fiorella's egg slaved to Martinez's. Sandy spent an hour doing close-up shots of Fiorella in her egg, commenting on the sails in the background. Martinez hovered behind Sandy, out of camera range.

When they were satisfied with the vid, Martinez and Fiorella looped over to the far side of the test ribbons, so that Sandy could shoot them with the ribbons in the foreground, the earth in the background.

The reactors were up to twenty percent. The heat exchanger was happily dissipating 3.5 gigawatts, its ribbons zipping along at seventy meters off one of the sails. Something different.

He said, "I'm seeing something different out there, what's . . . Hey! You guys! Joe! Cassie! Back up! Back up! Get out of there, get away!"

He started to zoom in on that section of that sail with Camera 1, his longest lens, when he saw more glimmers, then ripples of light starting to flicker across the sail. He zoomed Camera 2, catching the ripples, but carefully kept Fiorella's and Martinez's eggs in the shot, then thumbed over to object-lock, locking Fiorella's egg onto Camera 2. It would track her wherever she went, within the limitations of his egg's attitude and the Red's gimbals. Martinez was backing them off, as the ripples and flickers extended over all four sails.

A second later, the sails exploded.

That's what it looked like, anyway, from Sandy's vantage point.

The three hundred and fifty-two silvery metal ribbons making up the sails broke free of their lock-step, straight-as-arrow paths and went flying wildly into space, thin silver streamers spewing out in all directions like Christmas tinsel.

He'd dealt with any number of explosions in the Tri-Border area, and one of the things that he had learned was that if the explosion didn't kill you outright, you could get killed by the stuff coming down. Like bricks. He'd trained himself to look up after something blew: a flying brick was like a softball lofted into the outfield, and you could easily dodge it, if you could see it. Your mind would automatically scope out the vectors of the various flying pieces of rubble.

As the cloud of silvery threads grew, Sandy saw a hole forming in the expanding ball of chaff, and his explosion-trained brain told him the various object vectors wouldn't be passing through the hole. He jammed the egg into it, careful to keep the egg oriented toward Fiorella's and Martinez's eggs, so Camera 2 could track them. He put Camera 1, with the half-million-dollar lens, on the corner of the extruder where the ripples had started and thumbed the constant focus setting, and closed in on it, at the same time selecting both real-color and thermal settings, and the highest recording speed.

As he dove in on the extruders, Martinez started screaming at him: "Get out of there, you crazy motherfucker. Go north, go north. Get out . . ."

Fang-Castro's cool voice interrupted: "Mr. Darlington, do what you think best. Those vids will be valuable. Mr. Martinez, try not to distract Mr. Darlington any more than is necessary to warn him of a problem he may not be able to see."

Then another woman's voice, as cool as Fang-Castro's: "This is Johansson. Darlington, we're monitoring your vid. We could use a full scan of the extruder bar at your best resolution in both real color and thermal—"

"Doing that, real color and thermal, I'll need to close a bit more to get the best resolution."

Although he was focused on the technical video going into Camera 1, he made sure that Camera 2 stayed locked on Fiorella. He was shooting her through the expanding ball of silvery chaff, and though he knew at the back of his mind that the chaff represented a disaster, it was also one of the most beautiful things he'd ever seen, the metallic strands writhing in the sunlight, with the blue-marbled Earth far below: and Fiorella's egg right in the center of the shot.

As an honorary techie, he was appalled. Something had gone badly wrong. The test was clearly a failure. Was it a fatal one, in terms of either the mission or the people? He switched his headset over to the engineering channels the Red had been recording and caught the stream of reports coming into the chief reactor manager and Becca Johansson and quickly caught up on the status.

No permanent damage done to the station or to the mission, no human injuries of any kind, though Johansson sounded mightily pissed off. From what he could tell, the ribbon guidance system had cratered. As the speed of the ribbons increased, an instability appeared. From what he could hear over the audio links, the engineers didn't know if it was vibration in the extruders or some sort of feedback loop between the ribbons and the sensors and the control magnets, or if the computer controls hadn't been up to the task.

Whatever, those fast-flying ribbons had developed wobbles and the wobbles had grown uncontrollably until finally the whole control system collapsed under impossible demands and the ribbons started flying off in all directions.

He'd reached the end of the extruder bar and he clicked over to the engineering channel and asked, "You need another run on the extruder bar?"

Johansson came back almost immediately.

"If you can, give me a thermal image of the end of the bar where the instability started. Just leave it there for a while. Two minutes, anyway."

"Doing that now," Sandy said.

Fiorella called, "I don't want to seem crass," she began.

"Never bothered you in the past," Sandy said.

"I'm laughing inside," she said. "Tell me that you got at least a few seconds of our eggs floating in the background, when the thing blew."

"Camera two was locked on you the whole way, and still is. The chaff is clearing out. If you want to motor over this way, we could do a tracking shot of you coming in, right up to your face. Dodge around a few pieces of the metal—that should look pretty spectacular."

Fiorella asked, "Joe, can we do that?"

"Yeah, we can do it, but I still say he's a crazy motherfucker."

Crazy motherfucker I might be, Sandy thought, *and it was all chaos theory in motion and one hell of a screwup: but, ohmigawd, that's* entertainment!

16.

Becca ran all night on coffee, junk food, and stims. If the spectacular radiator failure, recorded for all posterity by that goddamn videographer, turned out to be an unsolvable fatal flaw in her engineering . . . guess who'd be America's chosen dumbass for the next hundred years?

The vid of the heat exchange extruder bar had given them some clues to the problems, but not the details. The vid had been valuable—but she hadn't been aware that the videographer had also been doing news vid, even as he was recording the technical stuff.

All Becca had to do was close her eyes, and she'd see that gorgeous redheaded creature on the screen, gold flecks in her eyes, as she sat in her egg, unnaturally calm. "We've had a disaster here. The first trial of the critical heat exchangers in America's Saturn ship . . ."

And the vid flew backwards in time to show the ribbons of super-heated metal exploding into space. It was, Becca had been told, the single most-watched vid of the current century except for those of the 9/11 Twin Towers attacks and the Houston Flash.

The logs on her work screens wandered in and out of focus. She rubbed her eyes; no sleep for the wicked. She'd eliminated the control sensors and magnets as the source of the problem. The data said they were up to the task, they just hadn't been provided proper control. The problem still might turn out to be an oscillation in the ejection nozzles for the heat exchanger, but she was betting on the supercomputer array.

At high ribbon run speeds, it was probably getting swamped with data and the granularity of the modeling just wasn't fine enough to deal with it. Which meant more supercomputers—easy enough to come by with an unlimited budget—and better, finer-grained control code. None of it would come with a snap of her fingers, but later today, she'd meet with the code monkeys and rake them over the coals.

She pulled up the logs for the nozzles. Even if it turned out that they weren't misbehaving, the cleaner they operated the easier it would be for the supercomputers to control the ribbons. She'd started looking for a signal in the noise, when she got beeped for a priority call that overrode her privacy block.

"Yeah, who? I'm busy and I'm not happy, so don't be wasting my time."

"Dr. Johansson, President Santeros here. I'm even less happy than you are. Yesterday's fiasco looked bad. You need to—"

Becca cut her off. "That was not a fiasco. It was an experiment, a test. The first one on an untried system. The system failed. The data will tell me why it failed."

"Dr. Johansson, don't interrupt me again! Not unless you want to be looking for a new job."

Becca had heard about Santeros's temper; this was a small sample of it. But, ever since she'd been the fat little blond kid, she'd hated being pushed around. Now that she was a fat little blond adult, she didn't like it much better. It got her Midwest backbone up. She knew the smart thing would be to smile, apologize, and kowtow.

"Good luck with that," she snapped. "You want to find a replacement for me, you're welcome to try. At this late date, it's only gonna push your launch back by a year."

Santeros was turning red.

"One more thing," Becca said. "You're not my boss. You want me fired, call my boss. Right now, YOU are wasting MY time. Stop trying to bully me and let me do my job."

She hung up. *Not my best career move. I should probably start packing my stuff. Or keep working on these logs until they come and kick me out. Eh, screw it. I need a break.*

Becca kicked out of her chair and headed to the commissary. Reflexively she tried to shove the door behind her as she left, but it just slid closed with a soft hydraulic snick. *Can't even slam a goddamned door in this place,* she fumed.

A thousand kilometers down, Santeros looked at her science adviser.

"That little bitch just hung up on me! She's history, Jacob. Get a replacement on board and get rid of her."

Vintner glanced over at Crow, who raised one thin, dark eyebrow. Otherwise his face remained a carefully composed blank. Vintner suppressed a smile. "Madam President, I say this with all due respect . . . Uh, no."

"That wasn't a request, Jacob."

"Planning to fire me, too? I'm your adviser—let me advise. First, she's right. The only thing replacing her will do is to set us back by more time than we can afford. You replace her, the Chinese get to Saturn first."

"Meaning I'm supposed to put up with that?"

"Yes. That's what I mean. You were elected President, not the Red Queen. You chop off her head, you'll be cutting off your own at the same time. Let it go."

Santeros looked like steam might start flowing off her forehead, but then she slowly cooled off, and finally smiled. "All right."

Crow raised a finger.

Santeros asked, "What?"

Crow said, "I don't think we should rule out sabotage as an explanation."

"Do you have any evidence to support that, Mr. Crow?"

He shook his head. "Nothing. Barely even a feeling. But there are so many holes a saboteur could slip something through, so many moving parts. And God help us, how many times have we proven in the past that it's impossible to vet everyone perfectly? Plus, everything—the hardware, the software, even the procedures and protocols, are prototypes that are getting tested and debugged in the field. So many places for things to go wrong, for an unwanted modification to be snuck in."

Santeros said, "Jesus. This radiator thing hurts. This really hurts. I don't see what we can do here."

"I don't know that I'll ever have more than a hunch, but in the meantime I'd be a lot happier, from a security point of view, keeping the devils I know," Crow said. "Minimize personnel changes. Like Johansson."

After talking with Santeros, Becca was bouncing off the walls.

Literally.

In 0.1 gee, it wasn't hard to go careening about unless she paid a lot of attention to controlling her actions, and right now she wasn't feeling much like controlling anything. She was pissed. She wasn't really hitting the walls hard enough to hurt, but it felt good to be slamming something. The corridor was empty of other crew members, so all that got bludgeoned were the walls.

She lurched into the commissary and ran full tilt into a large male figure. They both bounced back in low-gee arcs, as their sticky boots lost their grips on the floor, like two cartoon characters. A lidded zero-gee coffee mug traversed its own lazy trajectory across the room.

"Oh, God, I'm sorry . . ." the guy said.

"Damnit, look where you're . . ." She landed, regained her footing, and looked at the human obstacle she'd just bounced off of. It was the Hollywood pretty-boy videographer guy. Oh, lovely.

"Uh . . . Are you okay?" Sandy asked her. "You don't look okay."

"I'm fine. I just got myself fired, that's all," Becca snapped.

"Over the accident? That's . . . I didn't think—"

"No, I'm gonna be fired because I just told the President to go fuck herself."

Sandy stared at her, agape, for a second, then started laughing. "You told Santeros to go fuck herself? Oh, I like that."

Becca could feel her face getting even hotter.

Sandy put up his hands. "Whoa. I'm not laughing at you. It's what you did. Man, I wish I could've seen her face. Hey, you wanna grab a mug and tell me about it?" And he laughed again, an infectious laugh.

Becca found herself smiling at him. Oh, what the hell. The day after she left, it would be all over the station, anyway. Screw discretion, there ain't any to be had. "All right. I can do that."

Sandy retrieved his coffee cup from the other side of the room and they eased into a table and belted down. She let her mug warm her hands and inhaled the steam. Her shoulders were starting to unknot, a little bit. She managed a smile. "So. That vid from yesterday wasn't terrible. The technical stuff, I mean, not the news stuff. The news stuff—"

"What do you mean not terrible? I'll tell you what, Johansson, that was about as close to perfect as—"

"Why don't you call me Becca? It's Sandy, right? Sanders? Sandy?"

"It's Sandy," he said. "About that vid . . ."

17.

Fang-Castro sat back in her easy chair, drank her morning tea, gazed at the curved horizon of the earth displayed on her giant wallscreen, and sighed. She'd moved to new, single-room quarters and no longer had the pleasure of her living room window.

As part of the weight-saving measures for the *Nixon*, the design teams had reworked the living modules for more efficient use of space, paring them from their original hundred-meter length down to seventy. Compared to what was being done in the power modules, this was unglamorous reengineering, but eliminating the excess living space would cut the dry mass of the ship by twelve percent. It wasn't a lot by itself, but it cut the requirements for power, heat disposal, and water for reaction mass, reducing the final size of the ship by a thousand tons.

For all that, it wasn't asking a lot to give up a window, and her new quarters did have a wall-sized high-resolution 3-D screen, totally state of the art. But it wasn't real, she thought sadly. It was like the sound system in her new quarters; recorded music sounded wonderful and was a delight to listen to, but nothing like a live performance. Unfortunately rank, along with its privileges, had to set a good example.

Fang-Castro had sent most of the crew ground-side, starting two weeks earlier at the end of January. After the non-essentials had departed the station, construction crews installed temporary bulkheads thirty meters inward of the front ends of the modules. They'd stripped the furnishings from the forward thirty meters and bled the air back into the station's reserves.

Then they'd fabricated and attached support pillars between the axle and the modules just rearward of the cutting line. In the final preparation for the trimming, each module's forward elevator shaft had been cut free and moved off to a safe distance. That final bit of prep had finished up yesterday, two days ahead of schedule, Fang-Castro noted. Everybody was working hard: no slackers allowed.

Her slate chimed: John Clover. "You called? I was in the bathroom."

"Are you close by my quarters?"

"Yeah, I'm in mine. Just got back."

"Stop in if you have a minute."

And a minute later, her door chimed, and she said, "Come in," which released the door.

Clover stepped in, with his cat sitting on his shoulder. He put the cat on the floor, and Fang-Castro got up, went to a drawer, took out a pack of salmon jerky, and gave a strip to the cat, who was expecting it.

Virtually everybody in the station was a technician of some kind: Clover wasn't, and didn't much care about tech. He was a thinker, and a conversationalist. Ever since their clandestine late-night dinner, they'd been meeting a couple of times a week, to chat. As might have been expected of a leading anthropologist, he was both intelligent and observant.

"Sit down," she said.

He took his usual chair and said, "So—do we have an agenda, or are we ruminating?"

"Ruminating—I'm waiting to give them the go-ahead to start cutting up the place," she said. "Let's assume there are aliens at the station—a resident crew. Do we need to take weapons with us? If we do, what kind?"

"I'm not a shrink," Clover said. "But we'll need a few weapons on board, not for the aliens, but for the humans. As we get further out, there'll be a lot of stress, and there'll be some personal conflict. There may even be some good old-fashioned mating-ritual violence . . . too few women, too many alpha males. We'll need some electrical stunners . . ."

Fang-Castro waved him down. "Let's stick with the aliens. We've got the crew problems covered, I think."

Clover nodded. "Okay. First—"

He was interrupted by a computer voice: "Incoming priority for Fang-Castro from Joe Martinez."

Fang-Castro held up a finger, and took the call: "Joe?"

"We're ready to go out here. We need you to give the order."

"Recording with time-note: I'm ordering you to commence the quarters trim."

"Thank you, ma'am. We're starting now."

Back to Clover: "So, do we need a weapons system to deal with the aliens?"

Clover said, "Basically, no. I've talked to Crow about this, and there are only a few ways to fight in space. Some of them are suicidal, so we rule those out. I haven't been able to think of a situation in which we'd destroy our own ship as a method of attacking the aliens. There are some movie scenarios out there—the aliens are an evil life-form that preys on humans. Or they take over our minds and turn us into zombies with some kind of infectious virus and the only way we can save Earth is to blow up our own ship. But if the aliens really want to do that, why haven't they done it? That's the critical question. Why haven't they done it? The fact is, we know they could have destroyed all life on Earth if they'd wanted to, long before this. Or even with this arrival—we only saw them by mistake. If they'd simply accelerated an asteroid into Earth, and we know they can do that, given the size of their ship, we probably wouldn't even see it coming until too late. From all of that, I'd deduce that they don't want to destroy us. Simply because they could have, anytime, and didn't. So, we ignore the movie scenarios."

"What if they don't actively want to destroy us, but want to keep us away from their station?"

"That's what I've been talking to Crow about. They're a century ahead of us, maybe more. I can't begin to guess what they'd have to stop us, but they'd sure have something! They might warn us off . . . or we might not even see it coming."

"Bottom line, we can't defend ourselves against them, if they get aggressive."

"No. We can't. That's my feeling. We anthros are very good at war—maybe even better than they are. The overriding fact, though, is there really isn't a very good way to fight in deep space. Fights would lead to annihilation, first of the fighters, and then later, of the warring ships or bases, or even the warring planets."

"Not desirable."

"For either side," Clover said. "Suppose we get out there and find a station. The existence of the station as a stopping point suggests that they really need the place. So what happens if we go out there, and they do something to piss us off? What happens when the next starship shows up, and the gas station has been burned down? They may represent a danger to us, but we also represent a danger to them. It seems to me, it behooves both sides to act with some . . . courtesy. Some rational approach to contact."

"You're suggesting we do nothing."

"Nah. That's not safe, either. They might be territorial and want to see how far they can push us. So, they give us a little whack. We give them a little whack back—but only once."

"The problem with that is, the little whack could be the end of us."

"I don't think so. Look, once a planetary civilization reaches a certain point—the generation of radio waves, say—a lot of other things just naturally fall into place. Radio waves suggest a command of electricity, of course, and everything that comes out of that—internal combustion engines, airplanes, and advanced understanding of practical physics. They know we're here. Even if they didn't before, they know now. They could have been watching our TV programs all the way in. So if they give us a little warning shot, it'll be small: I think. It's not likely to happen at all. I think. I don't really think they'd even take the chance. We could have detected these ships coming in fifty or a hundred years ago, but we didn't. Why not? Probably because their visits are extremely rare. If they destroyed us, or our ships, then the next time they show up, we could have a nuke waiting for them. A nuke they wouldn't even see until it would be too late to do anything about it. So there are reasons for them not to annoy us, just as there are reasons for us not to annoy them."

Fang-Castro nodded. "I buy most of that: the aliens probably don't want to kill us. You understand what our biggest problem could be . . ."

"The Chinese."

"Yes. It seems to me that we're getting in a bind here. They would have a problem with our getting exclusive use of an alien tech. That's something we've got to work through."

"Are you going to weaponize the *Nixon* to fight the Chinese?"

"I doubt it. We have to see what the big brains on Earth think. But if we did—and if the Chinese already have—I think what you'd have is mutual assured destruction. If we don't arm ourselves and the Chinese attacked us, I'm pretty sure Santeros would destroy their ship in retaliation. And vice versa. There wouldn't be a huge war, or anything, but nobody would be able to put anything out in space—or more to the point, get it back. At the same time, exclusive use is pretty tempting."

"Lot of ugly possibilities growing out of those fears," Clover said.

"Yes, there are." Fang-Castro glanced at her view screen and said, "They're cutting up the hulls. I've got to go check on things. Listen, John—we've got to talk more. Read some twentieth-century stuff on the way the Americans and Russians managed the Cold War. Tell me what you think about that—their management techniques."

"I will do that," Clover said. "I've got to tell you, though, you've got me a little puckered up here."

"I've been puckered up ever since I found out the Chinese were going to Saturn."

Trimming the living modules wasn't technically difficult; it just had to be done carefully and in a coordinated fashion so it wouldn't throw the station out of balance. Industrial lasers could cut through the frothy walls in minutes. After the cutters sliced off the excess thirty meters from each module, crews would build new proper front ends, reattach the front elevators, and remove the temporary supports.

Clover had just gone, with his cat, when the station computer pinged Fang-Castro to move to the command module. She relieved the officer on watch and checked the external monitors and status displays; the four industrial cutters were in position.

"Mr. Martinez, how's everything out there?"

"We're good. We're about through the first one, the tugs are positioned to get it out of the way."

In carefully coordinated action, the four laser operators had fired up their beams and begun simultaneously cutting through the inner and outer walls of the two living modules, just forward of the temporary bulkheads. Grooves had appeared in the four walls and deepened into narrow cuts; otherwise there was little to see besides a faint purplish glow.

The excimer laser cutters projected intense shortwave ultraviolet light, invisible to human eyes. The high-energy photons didn't burn their way through materials; they directly broke apart molecular bonds. Foam and fabric simply disintegrated into vapor where the beam hit, cold-cutting that the laser crews controlled with surgical precision.

It took most of an hour to cut through the first two pairs of walls. The job could have been done in half the time, but Martinez was being careful. He periodically called for work stoppages while status readings were checked. Were the station's stabilizing computers keeping everything in balance? Were the brackets doing their job of keeping the forward sections from breaking loose prematurely? Any stray debris flying around, something blown off by the lasers?

After January's failed radiator test, Fang-Castro was being super-careful about creating space junk. That hadn't just been embarrassing, it'd been expensive. Nobody had been prepared for such a spectacular failure, and the station personnel were only able to recover about three-quarters of the chaff created by the uncontrolled radiator ribbons.

Interops, the International Orbital Operating Commission, had levied a fine whose size was described as "astronomical" by almost every punster on the Internet. Space junk had made low Earth orbit space almost unusable by the mid-thirties, and it had taken a decade of concerted and costly international effort to clear out the big stuff. A lot of the small stuff was still circling the earth, and now the space nations were talking about who'd pay to clear that.

The cutting proceeded, carefully, until the forward thirty meters of modules were severed from the rear seventy. The cutters shut down the lasers, a final systems check came up green, and Martinez spoke an authorization into his workslate. The operations computer simultaneously released the locking clamps on the module sections and a millisecond later fired the engines on the pair of robotic tugs.

From the command module, Captain Fang-Castro watched as the now-superfluous forward sections were moved to a safe distance away from the station. Some of their materials would be recycled into the

Nixon, but most of it was scrap, possibly recyclable to a new station. She
checked the status reports: the station was stable and the temporary forward bulkheads on the truncated living modules were working perfectly. The whole operation had gone off with exemplary smoothness.

She realized she'd been tensely hunched over the console and consciously relaxed her shoulder blades. The rest of the reconstruction
wouldn't take more than the remainder of the day. Crews had pre-fabbed
new front ends for the modules with all the fittings, docking collars, and
brackets they needed to smoothly hook them up to the living modules
and reattach the free-floating front elevator shafts to them and the new
axle hubs.

"Mr. Martinez?"

"Yes, ma'am."

"Outstanding work. Pass that along to everyone who had a hand in
this. I just spoke to the President, and she is extremely impressed, and
she is not an easily impressed woman," Fang-Castro said.

"I will pass that along, ma'am. Thank you."

She hadn't spoken to Santeros in a week, at which time they'd agreed
on two possible statements: congratulations for a job well done, and a
second, "The responsibility for this problem is mine, not the men and
women who did the work."

"Mine," as in Fang-Castro's, not Santeros's.

Fortunately, she thought, as she headed back to her room, the second
statement wouldn't be needed.

As yet, anyway.

Sandy and Fiorella had stayed up, when most of the crew had gone
down, because they were documenting the reconstruction. Sandy had
been outside, and had just gotten back, when Fiorella pinged him.

"We need to talk to you. Privately."

"Uh, where are you?"

"My cabin."

"I just got in, I'm in Engineering. I could stop by . . ."

"Please do. Soon."

Was she now using the royal "we"? Sandy wondered, as he dropped down the shaft to the habitat. Or was there more than one person waiting for him? Whatever, Fiorella definitely sounded conspiratorial. Of course, she was of Italian heritage; the Medicis, and all that.

He got to her cabin, tapped the call bell, and the door popped open. "Come on in," Fiorella said. John Clover was sitting in the single chair, and nodded. Fiorella sat at one end of her bunk and patted the other end for Sandy.

"So what's up?" Clover asked.

Fiorella looked at Sandy. "Despite our personal differences, the people on this ship believe that you and I are destined to sleep together."

"Fools," Sandy said.

"I would agree," Fiorella said.

"Although you are not totally unattractive," Sandy allowed.

"I would have to say the same about you," Fiorella said.

Clover said, "Excuse me. I don't think I want to hear this conversation."

Fiorella said, "Yes, you do. Wait until I finish."

Clover subsided, and Sandy, curious, asked, "What happened?"

"I was sitting in an egg, not going anywhere, checking out a possible internal shot. That feature we were talking about, showing the ground-huggers how you control an egg. Anyway, your friend the handyman walked into the garage, with a tech, and they were talking about us. They were being sneaky about it. Joe kept glancing over at me, making sure I couldn't hear."

"You turned up the gain on the external mike," Sandy said. All the eggs had external microphones and speakers. They were useless in space, but convenient when two people were working on an egg repair, one inside and one out.

"Yes, I did," Fiorella said. "Anyway, it seems that the crew has a pool, on the day we fall into bed together. The pool is still open. The buy-in is one thousand dollars."

That didn't seem like much to Sandy, but Clover grunted. "There are what, ninety-plus people going on this trip? More or less? That's ninety grand, if everybody buys in. Nice. That's three months' salary for a poor man like me."

"Much nicer than that," Fiorella said. "Because these guys are a bunch of scientists, they all think they're statistical savants. They weren't happy with a simple, pick-your-day pool. They set up a market."

Sandy: "A market? You mean like a political market?"

"Exactly. You buy a date that you think it'll happen. If you start to feel your pick was weak or if your date goes by without any action, you can buy back in, any date you want—but you have to pay the market price, which is set by consensus. Everybody who already has that date won't want you to buy in at all—they'll want to keep all the money to themselves. But if you have the right to buy in, they'll want to jack up your reentry price as high as possible.

"On the other hand," she continued, "people who don't have that date, and don't believe it will happen, will want other people to buy in—because the money stays in the pot if it doesn't happen. So they want the buy-in price to be low enough to encourage people to buy in, but also high enough that the pot gets fatter downstream."

"Okay," Sandy said. "I got that."

"Once the market price is set, you can put your money in," Fiorella said. "Say that it looks like we're going to get together on Friday. Okay, the price to buy in on that Friday could be quite large. With a basic, say, hundred thousand dollars on the scale, you might have to kick in another five or ten thousand dollars, or even more, to buy back in, if the event looks likely. If we're all kissy in the corridors. The amount would depend on how many people already have that date . . . The market price for the gamble."

"I don't entirely understand that," Sandy said.

"Look. Say there's a hundred thousand in the pot, and only three people have that date," Fiorella said. "If you can buy back in for, say five thousand, the pot is then a hundred and five thousand. Split four ways, that would be"—her eyes rolled up as she worked it out—"twenty-six thousand, two hundred and fifty each, a profit of twenty-one thousand, two hundred and fifty dollars on the five-thousand-dollar buy-in. But only if we get together that day."

"Tell me again why the three original buyers let him buy in?" Clover asked.

"They don't have any choice—the buy-in is by consensus of all the bettors," Fiorella said. "And the people who don't think it's going to happen on one particular day, would always be a majority, and they can force the buy-in price down to an acceptable level. Because they *want* other people to buy in."

"Because the money stays in the pot if it doesn't happen, and they don't believe it will," Sandy said.

Fiorella: "Yes!"

Clover: "If Sandy doesn't nail you on that Friday—"

"Please, John," Fiorella said.

"If you and Sandy don't have coitus on Friday—"

"Coitus? That's even worse," Fiorella said. "Anyway, to get to the point, the money stays in the pot and the action moves to the next day."

Clover scratched his chin. "Hypothetically, if you and Sandy were to stretch this out, running hot and cold along the way, raising hopes, then disappointing them, the money could get . . . large."

"I wouldn't say large. I would say huge," Fiorella said. "Actually, as the retained pot gets larger and larger, the amount will tend to snowball. It could go to, who knows? A million? More? If Sandy and I had a really loud argument on the morning of the day it happened . . ."

"The buy-in on that date would be really low," Clover said.

"And if we picked a fight date that nobody had bought, and then jumped in bed later in the day, someone who bought in would keep it all," Sandy said, his eyes narrowing.

"You and Sandy couldn't bet on this, because then everybody would know that you could fix it," Clover said to Fiorella. "But if a third person were to know the actual date, you and the third person could move things around so . . ."

"We could make a fuckin' fortune," Fiorella said. "Excuse the pun."

Sandy said to Fiorella, "You have a criminal mind. I admire that in a woman."

"So do I," Clover said. He rubbed his hands together. "Who do I talk to about getting in the pool? The handyman?"

A few days later:

Becca said, "If this doesn't work, I'll kill you."

Mark Vaughn, a computer tech safely ensconced on Earth, said, "It would have stopped the last one, or anything like that. We won't have the same fault, I promise you that. Other faults—well, it's your design, sweetie."

"Call me sweetie again and I'll kill you."

"Anyway, Becca, ma'am, sir—you're good. That last batch of code looked great if you didn't look too hard, but basically, it was marginal, in my opinion, and you probably ought to burn down that code farm and switch all the contracts to us. This batch . . . this batch is the cleanest, most robust stuff in the world. I mean that literally. In the world."

"If this batch blows us up again . . ."

"I know, you'll kill me."

"That's correct."

"Let me know what happens," Vaughn said.

"Don't worry about that: it'll be all over your screen, one way or the other."

A few days after that:

The other marines all looked at Sergeant Margaret Pastor, who said, "I know. I'm the smallest."

"It's not much of a leak," said one of the guys.

"It's not 'how much.' It's what it is," Pastor said.

What it was, was human waste, a brown trickle that could be seen spattering the floor. What was happening was a leak in a pressurized sewer pipe, and the fastest way to get to the leak was to send somebody down a cable tunnel, not meant for human access, with a laser cutter. That person would cut a hole in the wall of the cable tunnel, and then reach up and seal the leak in the sewer pipe with an epoxy injector.

"A shit job," said one of the guys, and the rest of them, with the exception of Pastor, fell about laughing.

"I didn't join the Marine Corps to clean up somebody's poop," Pastor said.

"No, but you volunteered to be cross-trained in maintenance, and none of the rest of us can fit into that pipe."

"Give me the fuckin' cutter. And get a garbage bag. I'll wrap myself in the bag."

The job took an hour: fifteen minutes to carefully cut through the cable pipe, another fifteen to plug the leak, during which time Pastor got liberally spattered with the effluent, another fifteen minutes to vacuum the crap out of the cable tunnel.

When she finished, she scooted herself backwards, until her feet were sticking out of the tunnel, and then the guys grabbed her by the ankles and pulled her out.

She was still on the floor, unwrapping the plastic bag that hadn't done much to protect her from the waste, when Fang-Castro turned the corner and asked, "What's that smell?"

When the explanations were finished, Fang-Castro told Pastor, "We've got a seat going down on the shuttle tomorrow. You want it, it's yours."

Leave was getting scarcer, especially for the military people. Pastor said, "Ma'am, I'd really love to see my mom one last time, before we go."

"I'll fix it with Captain Barnes. And thank you for this."

A few days more:

Vintner was not quite asleep, his feet up on his desk, when he heard the heels snapping down the subbasement's concrete floor, coming fast.

Women's heels had different sounds. Most of the higher-ranked women in the White House wore chunky heels because they wanted to look dressy, but knew they'd inevitably spend a lot of time on their feet, and their days were long. Women of lesser rank tried to emulate the dressiness of those higher up, wearing the chunky heels some of the time, but many, on the days when they didn't expect to do anything important, took a step down and wore flats, or disguised flats. Those of still lesser rank, who generally were making deliveries—mail, policy statements, budget documents, and so on—usually wore running shoes.

The chunky heels went *clunk-clunk-clunk*; the flats went *clack-clack-clack*; the running shoes went *flap-flap-flap*.

The shoes coming down the hall toward Vintner's office were going *peck-peck-peck* on the concrete, which meant that they were high-heeled dress shoes, and very, very few women in the White House wore them, and those who did would not be coming to Vintner's subbasement office . . . with one exception that he could think of.

The President.

A really, really angry president.

Santeros didn't get angry when dealing with disaster, or plotting a disaster for somebody else—in those cases, anger was inefficient. But when she was pissed, usually about some stupidity, she tended to get physical.

Vintner kicked his feet off his desk, grabbed a bottle of water, poured some in his hands, rubbed the water across his face and up through his thinning hair, then wiped his face on his jacket sleeve. One second later, Santeros burst into his office.

She started by shouting, "Twibbit!"

Vintner popped to his feet. "Mr. President! I mean, Madam—"

"Grabaddibbit!"

"Ma'am, I can't understand . . ."

Santeros's face was a fiery red, but she slowed, took a deep breath, and when her voice came back, it was icy cold and totally comprehensible, which was worse.

"Jacob: your man Johnson Morton. Unless it's Morton Johnson . . ."

"Uh, I'm sorry, ma'am, I don't recognize the name."

The volume increased: "Do you recognize the name 'Center for Psychological Policy Studies'?"

"Well, uh, sure, it's a think tank, we contract out some policy studies to them when there might be a psychological component to whatever . . . the military sometimes . . . ma'am . . . what happened?"

"This happened!"

She fired a stapled wad of paper at his head. He managed to grab it, and unwadded and flattened it on his desk. The title said "Psychosexual Aspects of the Flight of the *Nixon*," and beneath that, the author's name, Johnson Morton.

Vintner's mouth dropped open: "Psycho what? I never heard of this."

She was shouting: "Morton! Or Johnson! Thinks we ought to put hookers on the *Nixon*, to take care of the crew's sexual problems."

"What?" Vintner would have laughed, if he hadn't feared for his life. And job.

"Two each, male and female, bisexual for efficiency, to haul the ashes of those unable to pair up!"

"What?"

"Honest to God, Jacob, if you say 'What?' one more time, I'll strangle you!"

"Ma'am, I know nothing about this. I'll track it down, we'll—"

Shouting some more: "Look at the bottom of the last page. The small print. What do you see there?"

Vintner looked and saw a typical block of small print, with some handwritten numbers. He looked more closely. The study had been sponsored and paid for by the federal government, under the handwritten grant number.

"Oh, shit. Well, ma'am . . . we can still bury it—"

"No, we can't! No, we can't! You know how I found out about this? I found out on PBS! I had Gladys download the doc, and they're right. You know how much we paid for the study? One-point-two million. Morton! Or Johnson! According to the doc, INTERVIEWED some candidates for the job. Did he fuck them, Jacob, with OUR one-point-two million? If he did, how many did he fuck? Look at page seven: he says . . . Give me that goddamn thing." She ripped through the pages, and then, "I quote: 'obviously would require sexually desirable physical characteristics . . .' What's that, Jacob? A big fat cock? Is that what we're talking about? Grabaddibbit, Twibbit . . ."

It would be difficult, in the best of circumstances, to tell a president that she sounded like a gerbil, and these were not the best of circumstances, and Vintner stood and took it until the spit stopped flying through the air, and she slowed down again.

"I swear to you, on my life, that I didn't know about this," he said. "I never heard about it. I never had a hint or a suggestion of it, and if I had, I would have stopped it and fired Johnson. Or Morton."

She stared at him for a moment, then said, "I'm gonna rip somebody's heart out."

"I believe you. Do you want me to ask around—"

"No. I've got people who can do that better than you can. I just wanted to make sure you weren't involved."

"I was not."

"Good. I really didn't want to can your ass. But somebody will die."

"Maybe nothing will happen . . ."

She snorted: "Jacob, this will be in history books. When they write the history of the Santeros Administration, this will be the third item. It will go viral, worldwide. They're already cracking up in Beijing and Moscow. If I handle it just right, it will cost me only one percent of the vote in the next election. One-point-two million dollars, and there are underclassmen who work all day for eighteen dollars an hour. Jesus H. Christ." She took a deep breath, then said, "Thank you for letting me scream at you, and not getting up in my face. I need to calm down."

"A little yoga . . ."

"Yoga? Yoga? Gzzibit! Magrabbit! . . ." And she was gone.

Vintner turned on his office vid screen, which was tuned to CBSNN. He'd intended to click over to PBS, but that was unnecessary. The talking head—actually it was more of a talking-head-and-body, a woman so beautiful that she must have come from a different planet, possibly with the aliens—was saying in the most somber tones, "So we asked Johnson

Morton what he meant by that, 'obviously would require sexually desirable physical characteristics,' and this is what he told us . . .'"

Cut to Johnson Morton, a fleshy young man with black hair combed straight back from his forehead, and eyebrows like woolly bear caterpillars; Morton knitted his fingers together and said, "We did a comprehensive study of the most desirable physical . . ."

From up and down the subbasement hallway, where the President's temper tantrum had been overheard, people started laughing. Roaring with laughter. Back-slapping belly laughs.

Vintner closed his eyes for a brief prayer, that Santeros was in fact gone.

Then he started laughing himself, laughing until the tears came.

If Morton hadn't gotten fucked in the course of his studies, he thought, that was about to change.

Early May.

Fiorella was in an EVA suit, floating next to a construction worker who was re-forming a wedge-shaped piece of the station's superstructure on the habitat side of the reactor; Sandy was in an egg, twenty meters away, working his cameras.

The worker, whose name was Everett, and who came from Tacoma, Washington, gave a ten-second explanation of what she was doing, and then Fiorella moved away from her, just a bit, so that Sandy could keep her working in the background, but also close on Fiorella's face.

"With two months to go until *Nixon*'s launch, this former space station is an around-the-clock hive of activity. With the whole world following the *Celestial Odyssey*—the Chinese ship has just passed the orbit of Jupiter—space has stopped being routine for a large fraction of humanity, for the first time in a century. Anyone with a pair of binoculars or even a small telescope can watch as dozens of construction workers like Everett finish the American ship."

"I don't like that sentence," Sandy said on his direct link to Fiorella.

"I think it should be, space has stopped being routine for the first time in a century."

They talked about that and Fiorella reworked it, and when it was done, they headed back inside.

The work outside was now so intense that getting egg time and suit time was becoming difficult; they wouldn't get it at all, if the President hadn't spoken directly to Fang-Castro about it. "This will either be a triumph or a disaster. If it's a disaster, there's nothing I can do about it. But if it's a triumph, I want the credit, goddamnit, and that means you put the news people out there anytime they want to go. I'll talk to them about keeping it to a necessary minimum, but if they think it's necessary, you put them out there."

The news links now had countdown clocks on their screens, and England's *Daily Mail* announced a new construction disaster at the top of every cycle, along with rumors of zero-gravity orgies, secret contacts with the aliens (with photographs of Santeros talking with a meter-tall large-eyed silvery alien in the Oval Office), and rumors that the whole trip was a fraud by the Americans and Chinese, just as all twenty moon landings had been.

For the general public, what Fletcher had characterized as "the most important scientific discovery in history"—Sandy's discovery of the starship—was increasingly lost in the noise: there wasn't any starship, not anymore, just some scientists announcing there'd been one. There were no little green men coming to visit, no "To Serve Man" landings on the White House lawn or in the plaza of the Forbidden City. The starship was an abstraction that fascinated folks for a few weeks and then got pushed out of consciousness by the humdrum minutiae of daily life.

But when you could look up in the sky and see a spaceship being built, *that* was real.

Back inside, Sandy tracked Fiorella as she floated down the length of the center shaft, through Engineering. Sandy was floating as well, but behind him, one of the engineers, who was off-shift, was standing on the "floor" with gripping pads on his shoes, holding Sandy upright and at the same time backing down the shaft, as Fiorella, given a shove by another volunteer, who had then slipped out of sight, floated toward them. Every minute or so, air resistance would start slowing Fiorella down, and they would start over.

"This all became very real for us with yesterday's one-hundred-percent burn, our first full-fledged engine tests," Fiorella said to the cameras. "The *Nixon* has four VASIMR engines, two coupled to each reactor/power subsystem. Each engine, full on, gobbles down over two and a half gigawatts of electricity. Combined, they suck up more juice than many major cities. What the *Nixon* gets for all that juice is thrust. For those of you with scientific minds, at launch, the VASIMRs will deliver over two hundred thousand newtons of thrust. That sounds like a lot, except each of the Chinese's ten nuclear thermal engines produces five times as much thrust as *Nixon*'s entire complement.

"The *Nixon* is not a sprinter. At launch, it won't even manage half a percent of a gee. The Chinese ship took off twenty times faster, the rabbit to the American tortoise. It couldn't keep that up. After a handful of hours of that, the *Odyssey* had exhausted its reaction mass and was coasting on its trajectory to Saturn—as it still is.

"The *Nixon* is a marathoner. The nuclear-electric VASIMR system won't shut down after a few hours or even a few days. It can run nonstop for months, accelerating the ship to the halfway point near Jupiter's orbit and then continuously decelerating it until it arrives at Saturn. The VASIMRs will only add a handful of centimeters-per-second velocity to the *Nixon* every second. But there are a lot of seconds—more than eighty thousand in a day, two and a half million in a month. That adds up to a lot of velocity."

"I think we might be getting too technical," Sandy said.

"Hey: let me do this, you just run the cameras," Fiorella said. "I've written in optional cuts. Some people will get the comic-book version, some of them will get the science."

"If you say so."

"I say so. How does my lipstick look?"

"It's okay so far, but stay away from that left corner." Fiorella had a tendency to chew the lipstick off her lower left lip. "Keep going."

"I will have to say," Fiorella said to the camera, "that as important as the tests were, they were spectacularly boring to look at. The engineers who were in charge of making the reactor play nice with the cooling vanes were successful, but once the sails were out, they didn't look like much of anything but sheets of tinfoil, and the plasma exhaust from a VASIMR engine produces only the faintest of glows. You can barely see it even on the nightside.

"But make no mistake: this was a critical test and the *Nixon* passed it with flying colors. This was our first real space flight. We only raised our orbit by a hundred kilometers or so, but it was our first step, if only a baby step, toward the mysterious moons of Saturn."

Sandy looked away from his cameras: "Moons of Saturn?"

"Well, we think we're going to a moon."

"But most people don't know that, they think we're going to the rings."

"Sandy . . ."

18.

Early June, six weeks before launch, and the new arrivals were becoming accustomed to their new world. More or less.

Barry Clark was a tall, thin, dark-haired biochemist, an associate professor at Ohio State. Chuck Freeman was a short, stocky, red-haired Marine Corps sergeant. Clark lived near the center of Habitat 2, and was walking down the hall to his room when he saw Freeman—who'd cross-trained as a maintenance tech—unloading a vending machine from a wheeled pallet.

There would be six vending machines in a small room in Habitat 2, so that those who lived there would not have to travel all the way to the Commons, in Habitat 1, to get a simple snack.

With the pallet in place just outside the vending room, Clark saw Freeman lift the heavy machine off the pallet and, taking backwards baby steps, maneuver it into place in the vending room.

"You work out, huh?" Clark asked, as he passed by. The vision of Freeman lifting the machine created a particular mental construct in Clark's mind. The machines weren't that heavy in space.

Freeman said, "Ah, it's four hundred kilos down on Earth. Up here, only forty. Forty kilos, I can handle."

"When will they be up and running?" he asked.

Freeman patted the machine. "Gotta plug them in and load them up. Four of snacks, two of drinks. If I'd had to carry this baby full of water, it would have been a different story. That'll add another twenty kilos. Anyway, should have them up in an hour or so."

"Terrific. Can't do it fast enough for me."

Clark went on to his room, where he spent some time reading papers from a seminar he'd continued to teach by vid while on the *Nixon*. An hour later, feeling peckish and a little thirsty, he stuck his head into the hallway and saw Sandy emerge from the vending room with a pack of crumbless crackers and a candy bar.

"Ah: it's in."

"About time," Sandy said. He was working in the fab shop at the end of the habitat, and continued on his way.

Clark went into the vending room to check out the offerings. He was a biochemist, not a physicist, and though he could have explained the difference between weight and mass had he been given a few seconds to think about it, the concept was not right at the top of his mind when he pushed the button on the drink vending machine.

A bottle of Diet Coke was mechanically pushed into the descent tube. It slowly slid down, in the one-tenth gravity, halfway. And stopped. It wasn't supposed to stop, not in a vending machine engineered for low-gee. Nonetheless, it stopped.

Clark said, "Goddamnit"—he really wanted the Diet Coke—and slapped the transparent plastic face of the vending machine. The bottle moved down perhaps a half centimeter. "Goddamnit . . ."

He slapped the machine a couple of times, then did what he'd done on other such occasions at Ohio State: he braced his feet, grabbed the top corner of the machine, and yanked it forward. But the machine weighed only one-tenth of what a similar machine weighed at Ohio State, and the whole thing lurched forward . . . with the same mass and momentum it'd have had on Earth. The mismatch between the real physics and Clark's expectations threw him completely off balance. He fell on his ass, directly beneath the machine.

Clark would've been fine, maybe bruised but not broken, if he'd been thinking. The vending machine was falling a lot more slowly than it would have on Earth. It'd hurt when it hit him, but if he'd taken it flat the forty-kilogram effective weight wouldn't have crushed him.

When you're looking at what experience has previously told you is a half ton of vending machine coming down on you, you don't think clearly. He tried to roll out of the way.

The machine was falling much more slowly than it would have on Earth, but it was still falling and Clark was still a little clumsy in tenth-gee.

He grabbed the side of the machine. It twisted. He twisted. He almost made it. Not good enough. Forty kilograms of vending machine crunched, edge-on, into his feet, from his ankles to his toes, breaking several bones in the arch of his foot and pinning his feet to the floor.

Clark screamed and fell backwards. Because the machine was no longer moving, he could have picked it up except that he was badly positioned to do that, his two feet pinned and pain surging through his feet.

He tried to pull a foot out, by gripping an ankle and pulling, but the pain was too great and when he let go, he found his hand smeared with blood.

He screamed, "Help! Help!"

Sandy had just unlocked the door to the fabrication shop when he heard the machine hit the floor and Clark scream. He dropped his snacks by the door and ran back up the hallway to the vending machine.

Where the delicacy of real-world mental constructs revealed itself again.

Clark had long hair, and brushed it back out of his face as he struggled with his pinned feet. When Sandy ran up, he looked down at a dark-haired man with blood on his face, his feet pinned . . .

. . . by a wall. Two important Guapo leaders had been meeting in a village just off Rio Tinto. American intel had picked up word of the meeting, and had sent in an SSG squad to hit the two enemy big shots. They'd approached the village at three o'clock on a moonless morning, had isolated the targets using laser mikes, and at first light, three shooters had gone into the house where the two leaders were sleeping with their wives. The rest of the squad had set up on two other houses where the leaders' bodyguards were asleep.

Somebody in the target house had gotten off a shot before they were wiped; the bodyguards came boiling out of the other two houses and were cut down by the waiting SSG members. Then somebody in one of the bodyguard houses had blown a satchel charge, suiciding, and a wall of splinters had punched through the dawn.

One of the splinters, longer than a hand and half as wide, had hit an SSG lieutenant named Roger Jackson in the throat. Jackson had been one of the designated shooters, and had been running out of the house he'd just helped wipe, when the charge went off. In addition to being hit in the throat, his legs were pinned by a falling wall.

Which was where Sandy found him, running around from the other side of the leaders' house. Jackson, a thin, dark-haired man, was pinned, blood on his face, looking up, trying to call out . . .

Jackson bled out in a little more than a minute, dying in the now-complete silence of the village. They had to leave him there, running ahead of the Guapo revenge squads, until they were picked up by gunships fifteen miles from the village.

The flashback lasted only a few seconds. Clark looked up at Sandy, crying, "Get it off me, get it off me," not understanding why Sandy was clutching at the wall. The flashback was absolutely real—Sandy was there, on the Tri-Border, all over again, in the heat and the dust, the smell of blood and raw bloody human meat and chicken shit—and then, just as quickly, the flashback flickered out, and he was back aboard the *Nixon*.

He asked, "It's going to hurt when I lift. Can you pull on your legs?"

Clark groaned, "I think so . . ."

Sandy lifted the machine; it didn't weigh much even loaded with bottles of liquid. When it was upright, he called for help, and sat next to Clark until help arrived, and after they'd explained what had happened, he wandered off to the fab shop while Clark was carried to the med station in Habitat 1.

The fab shop was empty—a number of people used the shop, but he, Martinez, and Elroy Gorey were the only regulars—and Sandy dragged a chair around to the printer he'd been using, and sat down and picked up a partly printed arch-top guitar body.

The flashback at the vending room had been utterly real, and now little flickers of that day at the Tri-Border began scratching at his mind, like a guttering flame, hot, then gone, then hot again.

A half hour later, he wandered over to Habitat 1, down to his room, dug a case of meds out of his personal kit, popped a blue pill. The pills worked well, but only by ironing out every little crack and fissure in his mind, leaving him feeling like a biscuit . . . a really bland, flour-and-water biscuit.

Can't have this, he thought, as he lay back on his bed. If the people running the *Nixon* understood his condition, they might unload him.

He needed the *Nixon*.

He really did.

19.

Like watching a bunch of troops getting ready to ship out, Crow thought: somber passengers with their bags, milling around the terminal, with a few dozen anxious and sometimes weeping family members to see them off. At this point, he didn't really expect anyone to back out. There had been a few dropouts on earlier flights, but—unknown to the passengers—they'd all been evaluated for the possibility that they might refuse to go at the last moment, and this bunch had been found to be the least likely to do that.

If somebody did, there'd be several more round-trips by the Virgin-SpaceX shuttles before the *Nixon* departed, which could take up an alternate crew member. Right now, Crow's major concern was baggage. All the passengers had been required to present their baggage the day before departure, and all of it had been minutely scanned for anything that could represent a security hazard, including electronics that could be used to attack onboard systems.

Two exceptions had been made: one passenger had a rare but treatable form of cancer, and his extremely expensive medication simply hadn't been ready because of a bureaucratic entanglement with Ameri-Med. The insurance system refused to provide a three-year supply of pills because of cost considerations, and had no way to change its mind without rewriting its software, which might cost a couple of billion dollars. Crow had called the pharmaceutical company that made the medication, and after carefully explaining the situation to the CEO, in which he pointed out the intense interest in his decision by both the President and the IRS, a batch of pills was put on a hopjet from Philadelphia and had arrived that morning.

The other exception was for a violin; the psychiatrist who owned it refused to allow an electronic scan. "If it gets ruined," he told Crow, "I'm out nine million."

"Couldn't you take a cheaper violin?"

"No. It wouldn't have the tone. I need the tone."

Now one of Crow's security officers, a woman named Carol, hurried up to him as he watched the crowd, and said, "We have a tiny problem. Roger Ang doesn't want his violin x-rayed, either. He says x-raying it could damage the tone by changing the varnish at a molecular level. It's like a rare"—she looked at a slip of paper in her hand—"Enrico Politi. He says we can x-ray the case, and has no problem with an internal fiber-optic check on the violin itself, if he can watch it to make sure we don't harm the instrument."

Crow nodded. "All the musical instruments will be loaded at the same time in the cargo hold. Do the fiber-optic check, tell him that I've decided that an X-ray isn't necessary. When the instruments are put on the cargo mover, pull the violin, x-ray it, and if it's clear, put it back on the cargo mover. Just a little sleight of hand, Carol."

"What if the tone is affected?" she asked.

"It won't be—but there's no arguing with that brand of asshole-dom. If he knows it's been x-rayed, he'll hear a difference and sue somebody. If he doesn't know, he won't. Okay?"

"Okay." She hurried off.

The crew of ninety-one would be taking along eighty-one musical instruments of all varieties. They were a brilliant, disciplined bunch, and people who were both brilliant and disciplined often played musical instruments.

"There's a clear connection there—people who learn a musical in-strument early in life are basically learning to discipline themselves, and that carries over to other intellectually demanding fields," said one of the shrinks who'd been hired to consult on possible shipboard prob-lems. He'd recommended sending along both personal musical instru-ments and a supply of loaner instruments, so that those who didn't actually play an instrument could learn en route.

"If you can get a bunch of bands going, there's no better way to build teamwork and tie people together," he told Crow. "It's also a great way to kill time, for people without a lot to do."

The manifest now included four electronic pianos.

Crow checked his implants: July 21, 2067, a hundred and forty-three hours to departure.

20.

Fang-Castro checked her implanted clock: 7:45 A.M. Universal time, which was about to become Ship's time. She went back to looking at her brief speech, which would be broadcast throughout the ship and linked with an Oval Office broadcast by President Santeros.

She would broadcast from the control deck. Sandy was there with his cameras, which were already linked with broadcast control on the ground. At 7:50, the news anchor for PBS appeared on the screen; he spoke for a little less than a minute, setting up the President's talk.

At 7:51, Santeros appeared on-screen. She looked almost . . . sweet, Fang-Castro thought. The power of digital makeup. Fang-Castro herself had only the old-fashioned kind, painstakingly applied by Fiorella. They were walking a narrow path: Fang-Castro wanted to look good, but by no means better than the President.

Santeros was saying . . . "a possible great step into the future for all of mankind. We have no idea exactly what our visitors have left behind out there, but we fully expect to benefit from the technology that we've already been witness to, as their ship arrived and then departed . . ."

Blah, blah, blah . . .

Fang-Castro checked the clock again, and saw Sandy holding up a fist. That meant that she was less than a minute away. Sandy flashed five fingers, twice: ten seconds . . .

Five fingers, four, and Santeros said, "From the command deck of the *Richard M. Nixon*, Naomi Fang-Castro, captain of the *Nixon*. Captain Fang-Castro."

She was on.

"This is Fang-Castro of the USSS *Richard M. Nixon*. In just under two minutes, we will start the engines and begin the voyage that will see us arriving at Saturn at Christmas. Initially we will be firing a twenty-five percent thrust while we run our in-flight checks. Assuming every-thing is nominal, and we expect it to be, after one orbit we'll bring the engines up to fifty percent power. At the end of the second orbit, we'll take them to full power. The status display on the wall here in the ship, and on our blog down on Earth, will keep everybody current on our progress."

This, she said, had already been a long journey. Hundreds of workers had visited the *Nixon*, to get the ship ready for the longest manned voy-age in human history.

Blah blah blah . . .

At the carefully timed end, she said, "Thank you for your support, Madam President. We could not have done this without you. Now it's time for me to say . . . three . . . two . . . one . . . and . . .

"Launch!"

In the ship, half the people in the Commons unconsciously braced themselves . . . for nothing.

The Chinese launch had been high drama. This was the exact op-posite, a non-event. There was nothing. No vibration; no new sound, no feeling of acceleration or indication of motion. The status display showed no change in speed or altitude.

Somebody asked, "Is there a problem?"

Somebody else pointed at the broadcast feed on the main monitor. They were on the nightside, and the steady bright glow from the engines proved that they were firing.

Fiorella smiled into the camera: "Yes, the *Nixon*'s doing just what it was supposed to do, which is to begin its spiral out of low Earth orbit. At twenty-five percent power, though, and fully laden, its acceleration in open space is undetectable to human senses—a thousandth of a gee. In the zero-gee environment of the axle modules, free-floating objects will have started drifting, but none of the crew has felt anything differ-ent at all. In the zero-point-one gee artificial gravity of the Commons, there isn't even a perceptible tilt to the floor."

The reality of the departure was even more peculiar than that. The engines that were trying to push the ship forward were actually causing it to slow down. Before the *Nixon* could go to Saturn, it had to claw its way out of Earth's gravitational well, and that took prodigious amounts of energy. The energy that was pouring out of the VASIMR engines as thrust all went into raising the ship's altitude ever so gradually. With the passage of each minute the *Nixon* climbed by about one kilometer under the push of four plasma exhaust streams.

Bit by bit, the ex–space station's orbit was expanding, and that's what made things seem weird—a normal state of affairs in orbital mechanics. Larger orbits were slower orbits. In its original thousand-kilometer orbit, the space station zipped along at over seven kilometers per second. A geostationary communications satellite, orbiting at thirty-six thousand kilometers, only traveled at about three kilometers per second, while the moon, three hundred and eighty thousand kilometers away, traversed its path at a stately one kilometer per second. The *Nixon* obeyed the same laws of orbital physics. As the *Nixon* climbed kilometer by kilometer, it slowed down, and it would continue to do so until it was finally on an escape trajectory.

By lunchtime the earth that slid past the window was shrunken, the curvature of the horizon more pronounced. The *Nixon* was on its third expanding spiral orbit about the earth and the status monitor showed that it had lost about a third of a kilometer per second of velocity, but picked up more than five hundred kilometers of altitude. By dinnertime, the view of Earth, now three thousand, six hundred kilometers below, was dramatically different.

Sandy and Fiorella were doing two-minute squirts of commentary, every half hour. In their cameras, which ran continuously, the earth looked much smaller than it had at the start.

"Man, a freaking year with no surf. I think I want off," Sandy said.

"I don't know, Earth might not be a safe place for us," Fiorella said.

"What?"

"We might have made Fang-Castro look a little too good."

"Ah, bullshit," Sandy said.

"Hell hath no fury like a president upstaged."

Sandy grinned. "You know, FC did look pretty good. And when I left the command deck, I thought she looked a little smug."

"It's funny now, but . . ."

By breakfast the next morning, the *Nixon* had completed seven ever-expanding circuits of the earth. The planet, nineteen thousand kilometers away, was fully visible as a ball. The *Nixon* had lost almost half its speed, but no one could doubt that it was leaving the earth behind. The day before, the crew had been jubilant, hyper. By the next morning, everyone was simply subdued. For the next year, for better or for worse, the *Nixon* would be their entire world.

They were stuck with each other. No chance for second thoughts, no opportunity to back out.

John Clover finished his usual breakfast of pancakes, tofu sausage, and orange juice, looked at Becca and asked, "What?"

"Nothing. I've been up here for weeks, never a thought about it—the separation. Now I'm thinking about it." She pushed an egg around her plate, nibbled at a piece of toast.

"Well, stop thinking about it."

"Not always that easy." She looked past him, at the shrinking Earth out the window, and at the altitude display, which was steadily clicking off kilometers like a second hand, each clock-tick marking their increasing separation from home.

"No, but you'll get used to it," Clover said.

"How do you know that? Maybe I'll fabricate a hatchet and run screaming through the ship . . ."

"First, don't let Crow hear you say that. Second, tens of thousands of people are sent to prison in the United States every year. Conditions are not good, but the vast majority manage to survive long periods inside when they are effectively as contained as we are. Many times, brutally contained, without access to any society at all. We, on the other hand, are all quite comfortable, well-tended, and engaged in one of the most prestigious adventures in the history of the world. We'll all be famous in our various professions. You already are."

"I couldn't handle prison, either," Becca said.

"Sure you could. In fact, if you were telling the truth about your last job, you were in a kind of prison—at least, a little green man from Mars couldn't have told the difference. You woke up in one building, went to another building, spent the entire day there, until late at night, then went back to the first building, where you went to sleep. Here, you wake up in one building, take an elevator to the engineering department, work all day, and come back here to sleep. Same exact thing that you had been doing."

"But back home, I could go out when I wanted to."

"But you didn't. Not often."

"But if I poked a hole in the wall of my apartment, or a hole in the wall of a prison, the world would be outside. Apple trees and birds. Poke a hole in one of our walls, and there's nothing out there but a giant void. Nothing but a black, airless hole and meaningless death."

Clover smiled and said, "Take a pill. No, wait—don't take a pill. Pull your shorts up and go back to work. You're in an office building. Don't worry about it."

After a little more chat, Becca checked the time and said, "I like talking to you, John. I'm in an office building. I'm going to work. Nothing to worry about. And now, I gotta go to work."

As she walked away, Clover leaned back in his chair and closed his eyes: poke a hole in one of our walls, and there's nothing out there but a giant void. Nothing but a black, airless hole and meaningless death.

Oh, Jesus Christ, he thought. *What have I done?*

By lunchtime, the *Nixon*'s altitude had almost doubled, by dinnertime, nearly tripled. The earth was more than fifty thousand kilometers away. Still the most impressive object in the sky, thirty times the size of the full moon, the big blue marble was diminishing with each hour.

The *Nixon* was more than halfway through its eighth outward-bound loop around the earth, but it would never complete the orbit. Shortly before eight o'clock, Sandy walked through the Commons room and found Clover staring at the earth as it swept past with the rotation of the spacecraft. He was not alone. Everyone who wasn't on duty seemed

mesmerized by the shrinking Earth, sliding past the window, hypnotic
as a stage magician's swinging watch.

The PA system pinged. "This is Captain Fang-Castro. Our altitude is
sixty-eight thousand kilometers and our velocity is three-point-three kilometers per second. We are now on an escape trajectory. Our next stop
is Saturn. This will be the last status report of the day. Everyone have a
good night."

Clover sighed and smiled at Sandy. "On our way. Thank God. Life
gets easier when there aren't any choices, you know what I mean?"

"Yeah, exactly."

"Less than a day and we'll be out past the moon," Clover said. "Hope
we don't hit it."

Sandy laughed and said, "That'd embarrass the shit out of the orbit
guys, huh?" He watched for another minute, then said, "I'm heading for
the gym. Stink the place up a little, so it's more like home."

Clover said, "Good idea. I'll catch you there."

Sandy left and Clover turned back to the view screen. Even if the
engines cut off this very second, they'd never return to Earth. They'd
just coast through the solar system forever. Gravity no longer bound
them to home and they were heading into deep space.

In an office building, Clover thought. In an office building with his
faithful cat.

21.

"Good morning, this is NPR and you're listening to a special edition of *Science Friday*. I'm Flora Lichtman and today we have a first: a live broadcast from an interplanetary mission. With us is Dr. Rebecca Johansson, who is the senior power engineer aboard the U.S.'s spaceship to Saturn, the *Richard M. Nixon*, which launched two days ago. The *Nixon* is already approaching the moon's orbit, so there'll be about a three-second light-speed delay between my questions and Dr. Johansson's replies.

"First, Becca, thanks for taking the time to talk to our listeners—we know you've a busy schedule."

BECCA: That's an understatement, but it's my pleasure to be here. I'm a big fan of the show.

FLORA: Becca, you're a nuclear power plant engineer, not a rocket scientist. Why are you part of this mission?

BECCA: The propulsion system for the *Nixon* isn't a conventional nuclear rocket like the Chinese are using—it is, in large part, an electric power plant. That's where my primary responsibilities lie.

FLORA: Can you explain the difference in the engines on the two ships?

BECCA: Sure, the Chinese are using a nuclear thermal rocket. Take a nuclear fission reactor, get it real hot, and pump hydrogen through it. The hydrogen heats up and jets out the back, and there's your rocket engine. The only difference between their engine and a chemical rocket is that they're heating the gas in a fission reactor instead of by combustion.

FLORA: Okay, and the U.S. mission is using . . . ?

BECCA: An engine that's never been used on a major space mission before, called a "va-si-meer" . . .

FLORA: You better spell that.

BECCA: V-A-S-I-M-R, which stands for "Variable Specific Impulse Magnetoplasma Rocket."

FLORA: Oh, well, that clears everything up!

BECCA: [laughter] Well, then, my work here is done. Okay, before everyone tunes out . . .

FLORA: It may be too late for that [more laughter] . . .

BECCA: What we have is a really big, fancy kind of ion engine. We take a gas and ionize it—knock an electron or two off of each atom so instead of being electrically neutral, each atom has a positive charge. We funnel those ions into a big particle gun. It uses magnetic and electric fields to grab those ions and accelerate them to very high velocities. We squirt them out the back, and there's your rocket exhaust.

FLORA: So where does the reactor come in?

BECCA: Reactors, actually. We have two. That way in case something goes wrong with one, the *Nixon* isn't dead in space. The reactors come in because our rocket engine uses electricity. It takes electric power to ionize the gas and it takes electric power to generate the magnetic and electric fields that accelerate the ions. We use the reactors to power an electric plant, just as we would on Earth.

FLORA: Then, the ship's power plant is a lot like the systems you're used to designing for electric utility companies?

BECCA: Yes, which is why they want my expertise. But there are some important differences. The ship's power plant is considerably bigger than any reactor complex in commercial use. It puts out nineteen gigawatts of thermal power. That's an awful lot of power in a small space, and make no mistake, it is a small space. The reactors themselves wouldn't fill up this room.

FLORA: Wow. Why are reactors in regular power plants so much larger?

BECCA: Partly because they don't have to be any smaller. It's a lot harder to manage that kind of power in a small volume than a large one. Also, the reactor on Earth is surrounded by tons and tons of shielding and containment vessels to protect people and the environment from its contents. In our spaceship, we dispense with most of that.

The reactors are all the way at one end of the ship and just need a small shielding cap to provide a radiation shadow for the occupied portions of the ship. We don't need a big, bulky containment vessel. If something goes wrong and the reactor fails catastrophically, that's gonna be the end of us, anyway. My job, along with the reactor designers, is to make sure that won't happen.

FLORA: Okay, then, what makes a VASIMR better than a tried-and-true nuclear thermal rocket?

BECCA: Two things—the first is that we can get a much higher exhaust velocity out of the VASIMR. That means we can go a lot faster using the same amount of reaction mass. I think I can explain how that works to your listeners.

FLORA: I certainly hope so.

BECCA: Imagine you're on a pair of roller skates and you're holding a bowling ball. If you throw the bowling ball away from you, you start rolling backwards. Action balances reaction, thank you, Newton. Now suppose instead of a bowling ball, you have a small pistol that you fire. What happens? The bullet goes forward and the recoil sends you rolling backwards. A very small mass, like that bullet, can push you just as hard as the bowling ball did, if it's going very fast. The VASIMR gives us a lot more push than a nuclear thermal rocket would, for the same amount of reaction mass.

FLORA: And the second thing?

BECCA: This part's a bit peculiar. The way rocket physics works, it takes a lot more energy to get the ship up to speed with a high-velocity exhaust than with low velocity. Our fast-moving ions are very efficient at using a small amount of reaction mass but very inefficient at using small amounts of energy.

To put it another way, if we want to use as little reaction mass as we can, we want to throw bullets. But if we want to get the most speed from our power plant, we want bowling balls.

In between those extremes is a happy medium. If we adjust the exhaust velocity as we go, we can get by with a ship that's about half as big as it would be with a fixed exhaust velocity. Rocket scientists call the exhaust velocity "specific impulse," which is where the first three words of the engine's name come from: "variable specific impulse."

FLORA: On to my next question. If VASIMRs are better than thermal nuclear rockets, why didn't the Chinese use them in their ship?

BECCA: VASIMRs have one big disadvantage—they're electric. A nuclear thermal rocket puts all its heat energy into the exhaust, it's essentially one hundred percent efficient. We have to convert the heat of the reactor into electricity and using every trick we know, we can only do that with fifty-five to sixty percent efficiency. The other forty-odd percent? It's waste heat, and if we don't get rid of it the ship'll fry. To give you an idea how much heat I have to deal with, it's as if you took all the power used by a city the size of, say, Minneapolis, and stuffed it inside our little bitty rocket. My job is to get rid of it!

Believe me, that's not easy. There's a lot of specialized plumbing, some humongous heat radiators, the whole thing is very complicated. Our early tests . . . well . . . we had some hiccups.

FLORA: That radiator test in orbit last January?

BECCA: Ummm, yeah, that didn't go so well. But cutting-edge engineering is like that. That's why we test instead of just flying off. Anyway, a gas core reactor with a hydrogen flow-through, like the Chinese use, is child's play compared to this. That's a lot more stable and we have a lot more experience with it. If we didn't need to be going really, really fast, we'd never be using VASIMRs. The Chinese were originally going to Mars. They didn't need to be going anywhere that fast. A simple nuclear thermal rocket would get them there in a few months with a very reasonable mass-to-payload ratio. To get that same ship to Saturn, though, they had to hot-rod the whole setup, add some truly monstrous hydrogen tanks for the additional reaction mass they need, and it's still going to take them a year and a half to get there. They are the tortoise and we're the hare. This time, though, the hare is going to win the race.

FLORA: Thank you very much for your time, Becca.

22.

As the *Nixon* passed the moon's orbit, it officially entered interplanetary space. The ship was finally starting to show what it was made for. By interplanetary standards, its velocity was still modest, at six kilometers per second relative to Earth, but now the *Nixon* was essentially free of Earth's gravity. The thrust of the VASIMRs produced a small but steady acceleration that piled another four kilometers per second onto the ship's velocity each and every day. It had taken about sixty hours to pass lunar orbit, but another sixty would see the *Nixon* some two million kilometers from Earth.

The *Nixon*'s nose was pointed directly sunward, so that the VASIMRs' thrust could push its orbit into a tighter and tighter ellipse, a trajectory that would skim the sun at a scorching thirty million kilometers.

That was well within the orbit of Mercury, and the sun's light would be twenty-five times as intense as it was on Earth. The small risk was worth it: the sun's gravity was equally fierce; they'd be whipping past the sun at better than a hundred kilometers per second but the gravity would still bend the spaceship's heading by forty degrees, putting the *Nixon* on track for a Saturn rendezvous. That was Howardson's "solar slingshot" trajectory, the one that would let them beat the Chinese to Saturn.

Martinez and the other handymen began prelim work on rigging the solar parasols to protect the ship. The parasols didn't need to be anything fancy: they weren't going to be there that long, and once the *Nixon* was past the sun, they'd be jettisoned. They would be large—hundreds of meters on a side, but that was nothing compared to building the *Nixon* in the first place. Deployment wasn't imminent, as perihelion was a month away. Still, it was something to do.

As the *Nixon* left Earth's orbit, the crew began self-consciously to develop daily routines.

There was a constant stream of information coming in from Earth, so the Internet and all the related research facilities were there for the academics; and the maintenance people always had work to do.

For most of them, the *Nixon*'s voyage was their first experience living in a low-gravity environment. One-tenth gee wasn't much in the way of artificial gravity, not enough to prevent loss of bone density, some atypical edema, and other signs of space deterioration.

Too many of the residents were out of shape, and for the first time in their lives, had to maintain a strict regimen of daily physical exercise. If they didn't, returning to Earth would be a nightmare, with elevated risks of broken bones or heart attacks.

Sandy found himself in demand as a physical trainer, and led two classes a day in core exercises, and spent an hour working out himself under the eye of Marine Captain George Barnes, a physical fitness nut. Sandy enjoyed the workouts, but never, in all his gym experience, had he heard so much bitching and moaning. Fang-Castro ordered monitoring of all physical activity, logging both cardiovascular exercise and resistance training for every crew member.

John Clover taught a weight class, with steel weights fabricated by Martinez from bits and pieces of space junk left behind at the *Nixon*'s former niche in Earth orbit. Clover had been out of shape for years, and now found himself slimming down and adding muscle at the same time.

Roger Ang, the violinist/psychiatrist who'd been worried about the tone of his rare instrument, turned out to have been a college wrestler, and taught a popular wrestling class, which combined both cardio and resistance. The first time they wrestled, he pinned Crow four times in less than two minutes, despite the low gravity, which made it more difficult to keep an opponent pinned to the floor.

As they headed for the showers, Sandy said to Crow, "He kicked your ass. A pencil-necked shrink. A fuckin' violinist. A snowflake. A delicate little flower . . ."

"In sports, the rules define outcomes," Crow said. "He won because I wasn't allowed to bite his nose off, knee him in the balls, or gouge his eyes out."

"There's gotta be some rules," Sandy said.

"Really? I hadn't heard that."

Seven bands, an orchestra, three string quartets, and two choirs popped up within days. Sandy and Martinez put together a Country/Rhythm-Tech trio, with Imani Stuyvesant, an exobiologist who played drums. Fiorella, as it turned out, having grown up in Bakersfield, California, was an expert two-stepper. She began giving dance lessons. Crow hadn't brought an instrument along, but admitted to Sandy that he'd once played an upright bass in high school and in the Naval Academy orchestra.

"If you played an upright bass, you could play an electric—it's all just ears," Sandy told him. "I'll start fabricating an electric one in the shop. We need a bass player."

Crow didn't say "no."

Because of the low gravity, activities took on a bit of a slow-motion quality, like living in a special-effects movie. The new crew members learned to act more deliberately, because an unthinking gesture or swipe of the hand could much more easily send objects flying across the room. Tossing a salad without scattering greens all over the table was a delicate art. Get careless reaching for a coffee cup and you'd knock it off your desk. It would take three times longer to hit the floor, but you'd still have to clean up the mess.

Consequently, most crew members found living in one-tenth gee a little surreal. Still, it was more familiar and comfortable for most of them than living in zero-gee, which they would pass through when moving from one habitat module to the other. A few liked it better than Earth gravity

Like Mr. Snuffles. His favorite space was the cafeteria/commons, where there was always an ailurophile or two or three to slip him treats—bits of tofu salmon, tofu beef, tofu chicken, engineered to the point where not even a cat's taste buds could tell the difference.

23.

Becca sat at her desk, pondering an uncompleted e-mail to home, one eye on the clock. Because of the security team's paranoia, she couldn't write much about the things she was most directly working with: the reactors.

Outgoing mail was computer-scanned for sensitive content, and if any were found, the computers triggered a look by humans. So, no shop-talk about the mission. She could mention that they were twelve days into their flight and sixteen million kilometers from Earth, accelerating toward the sun, but that was about it. Nor did she feel inclined to get very personal, with who knows who reading over her shoulder.

That left shipboard routine, which was both sensible and irritating.

Like the mandatory lights-out. The ship's computer, under the direction of the ship's doctor, would be killing the lights in her room in half an hour, at 23:00. Sleepy-bye time—it made her feel like she was nine years old again, on a school night.

In this case, though, the logic was unassailable. She had ultimate responsibility for the ship's power systems, and the docs had decided that her usual workaholic running-herself-ragged style was not conducive to the ship's safety. Fatigue could lead to errors in judgment; errors in judgment in space lead to death.

Consequently, she was required to spend eight hours in bed every night. She wasn't required to sleep. She could twiddle her thumbs, calculate cube roots in her head, or chant her mantra, as long as she was in bed with the lights out.

So, she slept. And, she had to admit, her working day seemed to go more smoothly and her attitude toward the world was brighter. She still resented the parental authority. Her mother and father found the irony to be vastly amusing.

She'd just finished the letter when something bumped the leg of her chair; she felt it in her still-plump butt, though the mandatory gym time seemed to be making it a bit less plump.

Uh . . . bump?

There was nothing in the room to bump the chair—it had come up through the floor. Which meant the whole ship had bumped. It was a pretty unimpressive bump; if she hadn't been sitting stock-still and relaxed at her desk, she wouldn't have even felt it. But there weren't supposed to be any bumps at all. The compensating actuators that coupled the propulsion modules to the rest of the ship ought to catch all of those.

A meteor strike?

She pulled up a comm window and called Engineering. "Talk to me."

Wendy Greenberg's face popped up: another MIT grad, thin, intense, vid specs linked to the major readouts. Before Becca could ask, Greenberg said, "I was about to call. Reactor 2 safed itself."

What? "How's Number 1?"

"Just fine. We're still running at fifty percent power. All the telltales are normal on both reactors."

"I'm on my way down," Becca said, her heart beginning to thump. Before she could move, a new comm window opened up on her screen: Captain Fang-Castro. "Becca, thrust just dropped by fifty percent. What's our status?"

"Reactor 2 has gone into safe mode. I'm on my way down. I'll call you as soon as I know something."

As Becca hurried down the corridor to Engineering, her pocket com chimed a priority call. Palming the screen, she saw Crow. Oh great, Mr. Stick Up His Ass Security. "Dr. Johansson, is something going on that I should know about?"

"Reactor 2 put itself into automatic safe mode. Reactor 1 is running fine. There's no danger, no security risk, and I expect I'll have Number 2 back online by morning." Crow looked dubious but only said, "Thank you, Doctor, I look forward to talking to you tomorrow."

Then that will make one of us, Becca thought. Here they were less than two weeks out and something had gone off.

Becca had to thread through the dual air locks into Engineering.

Normally one stayed closed, since Engineering and the forward part of the ship ran separate air systems as a routine safety precaution, but both had engaged when the reactor threw the fault. As she headed to Propulsion Control, she could hear a buzz of concerned conversation. A half-dozen techies were examining a status monitor. Greenberg was there with Martinez, the chief of station operations.

"What have you got?" she asked Greenberg.

Greenberg shook her head. "As far as we can tell, the reactor safed itself for no good reason. The process safety subsystem sent Number 2 into its shutdown routine because it detected a loss of pressure in the primary coolant path. The thing is, the coolant path subsystem logs show the sodium pressure entirely nominal, not even a quiver. Best as we can figure, the process safety subsystem got it wrong. Furthermore, it seems to have righted itself—currently it sees all cooling system parameters, in fact all system parameters, as being exactly where they should be."

Becca was looking at the status monitor: "So, we're a hundred and fifty percent sure that there is absolutely nothing wrong with the coolant system? That there's no physical reason this reactor shouldn't be online?"

"Joe is about to go pull data directly off of the pressure sensors, to be three hundred percent certain, but everything in all the logs in all the systems says we're good. The process safety subsystem momentarily hallucinated and hit the panic button for no good reason. As far as we can tell."

"Maybe for no good reason, but there's always a reason. Joe, make your readings. Wendy, if they check out, bring Number 2 back online at twenty-five percent for an hour and fifty percent for another hour. If everything looks perfect, take it up to full power."

"Okay. But I'm worried."

"So am I—but we're not going to blow anything up because a bad piece of data takes the reactor down," Becca said. "If it was the other way around, if a bad piece of data kept it up when it should be taken down . . . then we would have a problem."

Becca hung in Engineering until Joe began calling back: all the pressure sensors showed pressures were normal. No problem anywhere.

Walking back to her quarters, Becca thumbed up Fang-Castro. "Short version, the safety computer choked on a bad byte of data. We're checking out the hardware personally, but every indication is we'll be back to one hundred percent power by morning."

The medsystem computer woke Becca at 07:45, having allotted her an extra forty-five minutes to compensate for her delayed bedtime. This was a good sign. The absence of sleep-interrupting emergencies or fretful phone calls from Command meant that nothing untoward had happened during the night. That meant that the reactor was online and everything was nominal again.

Happily, her deductions were right. When she got to Engineering command at 09:00, things couldn't have been running more smoothly. The one-time glitch had, indeed, proven to be one time. Greenberg had pulled in a double shift for the morning so that a full complement of people could run hardware and software diagnostics without taking anyone off of normal operations. So far they'd found nothing but a textbook operation; everything was so on-spec that she could almost imagine it was a computer simulation.

The ship's engines were back up to full power, adding a good four kilometers per second every day to the ship's already impressive velocity. The VASIMRs' control systems continued tuning the mix of hydrogen and oxygen, ratcheting up the exhaust velocity past a hundred kilometers per second. Just as planned, they were sacrificing some of the thrust and some of the acceleration but saving a lot of reaction mass. Without these clever, clever engines, the ship would've been twice as big and, Becca thought, her headaches three times bigger.

She'd have to find some way to reward Greenberg and her team for doing such a good job of dealing with and dismissing what had proven to be nothing more than a minor irritation.

At 10:23:47, the Reactor 2 safety subsystem reported a drop in primary sodium coolant pressure and initiated a safe shutdown of the reactor.

It was the first shutdown, all over again, except the inquiries didn't
go as well.

"No, Captain, I can't tell you when I'll have Reactor 2 back online. I've got a double complement of people here and we're all over it, and, once again, it looks like a hiccup in the data. Which shouldn't have happened once, and definitely not twice. Until I track it down, we're at half power."

As they worked through the computer data, the last thing she needed right now was another call from Crow, but there it was. At least he was gracious enough not to look smug. In truth, he looked as noncommittal as ever; Becca wondered, a bit maliciously, what it would take to throw him off his guard.

"Dr. Johansson, we should have a conversation."

"I will be happy to do that, Mr. Crow, as soon as I've figured out what's causing the glitch in Reactor 2's safeties."

"You misunderstand me," Crow said. "We need to have a conversation, now."

"Really, I've got more pressing matters than indulging Security's paranoia."

"You don't have any choice, I'm afraid. We either talk now, or I have a marine come down and fetch you, and we'll talk in the captain's office. Pick one."

Becca nodded: "Okay, fine. What would you like to know?"

Crow looked down at his tablet. "I've made up a list of questions. Some are very simple, but bear with me. I want to make sure I'm not making any wrong assumptions. You've had two incidents with Reactor 2 in less than twelve hours, but Reactor 1 is one hundred percent operational?"

"Correct. Unit 1 is behaving perfectly. And, to clarify, there's no problem with the Reactor 2 or any of its related hardware, as far as we can tell. It's the safety subsystem that keeps registering a coolant problem and shutting the core down. Which is exactly what it is supposed to do, except there's no reason for it to be doing that."

"What's different about Units 1 and 2 and why hasn't Unit 1 also gone off-line?"

Becca had to grudgingly acknowledge Crow's talent for getting to the heart of the matter. "There's the rub—there is absolutely no difference between the two units. The reactors, heat exchangers, turbines, and generators and the computer systems are absolutely identical. Well, the hardware is as identical as we know how to make it, and the software is one hundred percent identical. So, we'd expect a purely software glitch to appear in both units."

"Meaning you think it's hardware?"

"No, we're nearly positive that it's software, we just don't understand why it's showing up in only one system."

"Is there any chance this subsystem malfunction is going to shut down both reactors?"

"No, absolutely not, not unless it replicates itself in Unit 1. The two power systems are completely separate. They run completely independently. They don't share any resources, they don't even swap data. We made them as perfectly firewalled, physically and virtually, as we could, so that any kind of failure in one could not trigger a failure for any reason in the other. It's like they exist on different planets."

"Got it," Crow continued, ticking points off on his fingers. "Two identical twins, separated at birth, identical in every imaginable way. Except they're not behaving identically. So they can't be identical." Crow paused for a moment. Then: "I see two possibilities. The first is that you guys didn't do your job right and you missed some critical difference between the two units."

Becca heated up: "I can tell you—"

"Shut up for a minute," Crow said. "The second possibility is that I didn't do my job right and you started out with two identical systems and somebody's compromised one of them. You should assume the former: that it's your screwup. Drill down until you find it. Then keep drilling. If you made one engineering mistake, you made more than one."

"Mr. Crow, my team is very, very good. I'm very, very good. We are entirely competent to do our job—"

"I know that, Doctor, but you're human and you're not perfect. The past twelve hours proves that something here is not perfect. It's got to have a presence, so find it," Crow said. "In the meantime, I'm going to assume it's my screwup. In truth, I think that's more likely. Security is not the reliable business that nuclear engineering is. You think it's a data glitch. I think it's sabotage. I think you're right about the 'what,' but I'll bet you I'm right about the 'why.'"

Becca nodded again. Crow's analysis was plausible.

"I've got everybody I can working on it," she said.

"Do it with the idea that it could also be sabotage. Don't assume that it's simply a data fault: think about how the fault could have been deliberately introduced."

"I will."

Crow disappeared from the screen.

Sabotage was outside Becca's work experience. She needed to work with what she knew. Okay, keep most of the people looking for ordinary hardware or software problems, any kind of anomaly. Put the best computer jocks on cross-checking data dumps between the two systems and thinking about where an error might be injected into the system. A Trojan? Something coded directly into the process control software?

Back at his desk, Crow's thoughts ran even darker. A casual computer cracker wouldn't be able to infiltrate a nuclear power computer system. Nuclear plants had long been considered targets for cyber warfare and the code monkeys had long had procedures in place to prevent some malcontent from inserting a back door or sabotaging a plant.

That, though, was for a normal level of civilian nuclear security, attacked by ordinary crackers. The stakes were a lot higher here, and Crow had no doubt that his own people could break one of Becca's nuclear plants if they really wanted to. Only the criminally stupid or naïve assumed the "other side" was less clever. And who would that be in this case?

The Chinese were the obvious possibility, but there were plenty of governments that would be happy to see neither the U.S. nor China get starship technology—and every major state or state-alliance had excellent crackers. Had the Chinese suffered sabotage? Was there any way he could find out?

If it were sabotage, indications so far were that whoever was behind it only wanted the American ship to lose the race, not to be destroyed. They'd only taken out one reactor, not both. Was that by intent, or lack of opportunity, given the system firewalls? Was the disabling of the reactor a warning shot across the bow, a polite attempt to dissuade, but one that could be followed by lethal force?

Another vagrant thought crossed his mind. *What if the aliens . . .*

No.

Crow launched a secure window request to Santeros's office and cross-conferenced it to the science adviser. At this distance, the round-trip time for a data packet was just shy of two minutes; it'd take a while for the security computers to complete their handshaking. While he waited for them to respond, he reviewed the ship's logs and status reports. Ten minutes later, he got the three-way alert and switched his attention to Santeros. He kept his report screens open. With a several-minute round-trip time at light speed, this was going to be a slow conversation. Santeros launched without preamble.

"Good morning, Mr. Crow. I presume you're calling with regards to last night's power problem on the *Nixon*. Jacob briefed me this morning. I was given to understand it was a singular event and under control."

"Unfortunately, no. Reactor 2 just safed itself again. Dr. Johansson is proceeding as if it is an engineering fault of some sort, but I don't think she really believes that. Nor do I."

Four minutes. Vintner spoke up. "Run us through your thinking on that."

"One failure could just be a bad byte of data, noise in the line," Crow said. "That's not supposed to get through, but it could. Two in twelve hours is statistically unbelievable. Hardware log checks didn't turn up the phantom pressure drop. It's a repeating problem that only appears in the control software's data. The two power systems are supposed to be identical. Physically, it's not possible to make them *exactly* the same, so there could be a hardware fault or construction error in one that isn't present in the other. The control code, though, is identical, exactly du-

plicated in both systems. There should be no fault in one, that doesn't
show up in the other. If it was a simple fault, we should be able to isolate
it and fix it. The engineers have not been able to do that."

Crow went back to reviewing logs for a bit less than four minutes.

Vintner said, "Got it. If the software's identical, one set can't be
throwing repeated faults when the other isn't. Ergo, they're not identical."

"Meaning we're looking at sabotage?" asked Santeros.

Vintner: "It's possible the two systems are running different software
builds. They're not supposed to be, but mistakes happen. That'll be easy
to check on. Gimme a moment," he said, as he launched a separate call
to the code farm that had written the control systems.

"Crow, short form: What was the objective, if it was sabotage?" asked
Santeros.

"There're several possibilities." Crow ticked off on his fingers. "On
its face value, it slows us down by forcing us to run at half power. The
thing is, it doesn't slow us down enough—we still beat the Chinese there.
But whoever is responsible for this may not know that. Or it could be a
warning shot across our bow—if we don't turn back, worse things will
happen. Or it could be the sabotage was only partially successful. Maybe
both reactors were supposed to go down and one hack didn't take, or
they didn't have time to finish hacking both systems.

"The problem is, there are so many who have the motive and means.
On a venture as ad hoc as this one, there'll always be opportunities. The
Chinese are almost too obvious a candidate. Doesn't mean they wouldn't,
especially if they were sure we couldn't trace it back. Then there's Brazil,
India, the United Central American States . . . Did you know most of our
code jockeys come from UCAS these days?"

Four minutes and Vintner was back. "The logs check. There's been
version coherency on board for at least two full generations of software.
The build uploads are done simultaneously to the ship's two power systems after they've passed QC on Earth."

"What does that mean?" Santeros asked.

"It means that if it is a software problem, either the version logs have been falsified to spoof coherency or an Easter egg was inserted outside the normal process. Either way, someone's messing with us," Crow said.

Minutes passed.

Santeros chewed her pen, an ancient and anxious reflex she kept well hidden from the public. "Okay, fellows. Anything else, Mr. Crow?"

Crow said, "One last point. The timing. If it's an Easter egg, the egg didn't go off until we were solidly past solar system escape velocity. If the intent was to shut down both reactors, and if we couldn't fix it, we wouldn't ever be coming back. We'd be on a one-way trip into interstellar space."

24.

Becca rubbed her eyes, clutched her coffee, and stared at her half-eaten bagel as though it were a life preserver. She could use a life preserver: she was drowning in data.

In this case, no news was bad news. She was no closer to figuring out why the reactor had shut itself down than she'd been twenty hours earlier. Looking around the conference room, she could see that everyone else looked as bad as she felt. No consolation that. Everyone there—Fang-Castro, Crow, Greenberg, a couple of code jockeys, and Darlington, the ever-present videographer, recording the conference for posterity.

Self-consciously, she brushed her fingers over her hair. She was still getting used to having it cropped really close, but with the three-minute shower limit it seemed the most practical thing to do. The blond buzz cut she saw in the mirror each morning still startled her. If the marines took short and fat women . . . heh . . . she yawned: it had been another all-nighter, running on coffee and stims. *Really, I'm too old for this all-nighter shit—that's grad student stuff,* she thought.

Fang-Castro rapped her glass and Becca forced herself to focus.

"Becca," Fang-Castro began, "any miracles?"

"No. I'm really sorry, ma'am, but I don't have anything new to report. I wish I could say we've found a flaw in design or in engineering or a bug in the code or something that we just plain did wrong. I can't say that. Everything looks perfect on Reactor 2, hardware and software. Since we know there's something wrong, I don't feel like I dare fire it up again until I understand what the problem is."

"I agree with Becca, on the hardware side," said an engineer, Larry Trout, who had her back. She felt upset, frustrated, and irrationally furious at the reactor that wasn't behaving itself, but she didn't feel alone. She had the best engineers to work with, ever. "There's no physical reason for the safeties to have gone off. Not once, definitely not twice. It's gotta be a software problem."

Becca nodded unhappily. "But we haven't found it. The diagnostics and the test simulations all come up nominal. Maybe they're faulty, too, but we get identical results from both reactors' computers, and their codes match down to the last bit."

Crow raised a finger. Fang-Castro said, "Yes, Mr. Crow?"

"I don't think you'll find any difference in the operating code," Crow said. "I chatted with some of my colleagues, yesterday, about ways we could sabotage the power system, if we'd wanted to. They had some ideas. Especially about hiding the Easter egg even if you went looking for it. Most of the sabotage isn't buried in the operating code, it's in the data logs."

Fang-Castro looked puzzled, but Becca immediately saw the possibilities, and they did not make her happy. "I know where you're heading with this, Mr. Crow. I don't like it. Go on . . ."

Crow nodded. "The operating code for both reactors is supposed to be identical and the build versions check. If someone had sabotaged only one of those, it would turn up in a byte-by-byte comparison of the systems. There are gigabytes of operating code, but that kind of comparison only takes seconds. Maybe a minute or so, if you're looking for something that isn't resident on the system but in the libraries."

"The data logs are another matter. These have to be substantial?"

Becca made a mental estimate, then said, "Oh yeah, we log every bit of sensor data we can about the reactor performance in real time. It's probably a hundred terabytes a day, maybe more."

"Right. What my colleagues pointed out is that the log records for the two power plants will not be identical, because this is real-time data collected on real physical systems, and they don't perform exactly the same. You can't do a simple byte-by-byte comparison of the data logs, because they shouldn't be the same. That's where you hide the Easter egg."

Fang-Castro said, "I'm not quite seeing it. Something has to put the bad data there, right? We should be able to find that."

Crow smiled. "Ah, that's the tricky part. The operating system is constantly checking the sensor readings and the data logs to make sure everything's running within normal parameters. Bad data can creep into such a system. In fact, it's almost guaranteed to."

Becca chimed in, "For example, the operating system rejects negative pressure values. A noisy bit might switch the sign on a pressure reading once in a blue moon. You don't want the system to respond to that and try to kick the pressure on the lines up. So there'll be a line of code in the software that says, 'If you see a negative value for pressure, ignore it and go look at the next value.' Actually the range and type checking is a lot more complicated than that, but that's the idea. It's to make sure the system can't get confused by obviously erroneous data."

"Just so," Crow said. "But suppose a small loophole were left in the variable checking. It would just take a few lines of code, but if it let the wrong kind of bad data through, that could trigger a fault or put the operating code into an unexpected state and open it up to all sorts of mischief. It might even be something as simple as a handful of code in the operating system that says something like, 'If you read a pressure value of exactly 0.1876, then jump to the following library module.'"

Becca jumped in again. "Oh, I could get a lot more devious than that. We played pranks like this back at MIT. If I were being really nasty, I'd trigger a fault that would load code that was buried in the data log itself. Here's how I'd do it in a couple of lines:

"When the attack code reads the trigger data, it loads the Easter egg code from the log. The Easter egg executes, and the first thing it does is erases its code from the log, along with the trigger data. Then it writes itself and new trigger data back into the log at a different point. That way the Easter egg is a moving target in memory and in time. That's a lot harder to pinpoint. Next it triggers the reactor shutdown. Once it's done that, it tells the operating system that it's finished with this task and it's relinquishing the block of memory it's sitting in so that the operating system can load a standard library component back into that chunk of memory. It's erased its footsteps—nothing to find.

"It's all just strings of binary. The computer treats what's in the operating system as programming instructions and what's in the logs as data values. But there's no reason it can't load data from the logs as a program to be run. Normally, that wouldn't make any sense, it would just crash the operating system and it would reboot. But if there really is code buried in there . . ."

Crow nodded approvingly. "Considerably simpler than what my colleagues had in mind, but it's a starting point. Have you ever thought of coming to work for me? I could find a place for you."

"I like my world fine, thank you very much," Becca retorted. "But I'll take the compliment."

Crow said, "If it is sabotage, we don't know this is what the saboteur did or exactly how they did it, what they're using as a trigger. Could be a specific data value, could be an untrapped out-of-bounds fault, there's a dozen ways to do this. And because it only takes a few lines of code to set it off, looking through the code factory's maintenance and revision records wouldn't tell you anything. If the Easter egg were resident in the operating system, there'd be thousands of lines of code, and you'd find the discrepancy in the records. But all that's in the operating system is the tripwire. A couple of lines of odd code? That gets written every day. It can be as simple as a few typographical errors getting corrected. Nobody reviews the quality control records for a couple of lines of code unless it misbehaves, and this is designed to never misbehave without the trigger."

Fang-Castro: "So why has this affected only one reactor and not the other?"

Becca responded, "I can think of several reasons. Maybe someone didn't have time to insert it into the logs on both systems. Or maybe it got inserted in and then flushed and scrubbed in one of the log modifications. The logs are just big repositories for the data that's collected from the two power plants. Essentially they're nothing more than storage bins, and beyond making sure that they're operating the way they're supposed to, we don't worry about them much. We don't treat them exactly the same way."

Fang-Castro ran her hand through her hair. "So you're saying we got lucky. Or half lucky, half unlucky."

Crow said, "I doubt that luck has anything to do with it."

"And we can't bring both reactors back online?"

"If I do, I'm pretty sure the second one is just going to shut down again," Becca said. "I don't see what we'd gain by it. Plus, these emergency shutdowns are hard on the system. That's not the way it's designed to be run. We keep this up and we're going to break something before the mission is done."

"How about wiping the data logs and starting from scratch?" Fang-Castro asked.

Becca started to say, "We could try that . . . ," but Crow cut her off in mid-sentence.

"That's such an obvious thing to do that if I were in charge of this little hack, it's the first thing I'd make sure wouldn't work," Crow said. "It'd be very easy to circumvent."

Fang-Castro sighed. "So we're stuck with half power indefinitely. Assuming that, and that things don't get worse, I had Navigation work up a revised trajectory for us." She pulled up an orbit plot on the wallscreen. "The dashed line is our old trajectory. The solid one our new course. You can see there isn't much difference." She zoomed in on the part of the trajectory near the sun. "The main difference is we don't need to come in quite as tight by the sun, because we won't be traveling as fast. A perihelion of thirty-five million kilometers will be close enough for the sun's gravity to swing us onto the right vector for Saturn. That should make you a little happier, Becca."

Becca smiled just a bit. "I'll take what good news I can get, Captain. It'll put a little less strain on the radiators. Plus, since we will be running at half power anyway, we won't need to throttle back when we're close to the sun, like we had to in our original plans. The radiators have more than enough capacity to shed the waste heat, even that close to the sun."

Fang-Castro continued. "That's good. Of course, the bad news is that with only half the thrust we had before, we're not going to get there as quickly. Fortunately we were already moving at a decent clip, fifty kilometers per second relative to the sun, when we lost Reactor 2. Consequently, the impact isn't as bad as it could've been. When all is said and done, we're going to arrive at Saturn about thirty days later than we'd originally planned. Our new ETA is January 23, 2068. That's still more than three months ahead of the Chinese."

She continued: "Mr. Crow, please have your colleagues put in some more thought on this problem and let me know if they come up with any ideas for eliminating the Easter egg from System 2. If there is one. In the meantime, Dr. Johansson, I suggest you reassign most of the System 2 personnel to System 1. Just keep as many people on 2 as you think you need to continue looking for the source of our problems there, but I want the priority to be pampering our one remaining power system and keeping it as happy as possible. So—let's go.

"Ahh, Dr. Johansson?" Becca looked at Fang-Castro, who was tapping her slate. "I'm reinstating your med computer regimen. No more all-nighters. In fact, as soon as you finish reassigning personnel, and I'm giving you exactly one half hour to do that, I'm ordering you to go shower and get at least two hours' sleep." Fang-Castro looked at Becca more closely. "No, make that three hours. We're out of crisis mode, and I need you in the best possible physical and mental shape to see that we don't slip back into it. That's all."

Becca started to protest, but the look in Fang-Castro's eye made it very clear that this was not a negotiating point. She closed her mouth, nodded, smiled a wan smile, and left the conference room.

25.

Even with one reactor shut down, the *Nixon* was by far the fastest ship humanity had ever built. By late August, less than a month into its flight, it was crossing the orbit of Mercury; six more days would see it at perihelion, thirty-five million kilometers from the surface of the sun. Its velocity was already ninety kilometers per second, more than twice as fast as the Chinese *Martian Odyssey*. The combined pull of the sun and the thrust of the VASIMRs would add another twenty kilometers per second to that before it crossed perihelion.

The earth had dwindled to a starlike pinpoint of light on the screen in the Commons, while the sun had visually swelled to two and a half times its normal size. It would nearly double that again before it started to dwindle on the outward leg of *Nixon*'s voyage.

Power management and waste heat disposal required some adjustment, but nothing Becca and her engineers couldn't handle. The closer they got to the sun, the less effective the radiator sails were at disposing of their burden of heat. At closest approach, the amount of solar energy hitting the sail, head-on, would have been almost half the amount it needed to radiate.

However, at closest approach, the radiators would be edge-on to the incandescent disk. They'd get minimal baking. Coming and going, the sails faced more toward the sun, but then the ship was farther away and solar heating less of a burden.

In the original mission plan, cutting back the power in response to the lower radiator efficiency would've cost them maybe two days of travel time, a small price to pay for trimming months off their ETA. Running on half power, though, the radiator system had capacity to spare. Their close pass by the sun wouldn't chew up any additional time.

Running at half power vexed the *Nixon*'s chief engineer. As Crow'd predicted, they'd had no luck in figuring out exactly what was wrong with the Reactor 2 software, so Becca had continued to veto any restart of the second reactor. Commander Fang-Castro could override that, but she didn't.

Becca was appreciative. Designing commercial power plant cooling systems meant dealing with company executives who felt the laws of engineering and even physics ought to be bent to improve the fiscal bottom line. Becca always won those disagreements, but she wasn't much for hiding how much they displeased her. Minnesota-nice vied with engineer-geek, and the geek usually won out. Her personnel evaluations suggested she might show a bit more understanding of the requirements of the business world.

Becca, in turn, wished the business types had more of an appreciation of the requirements of the real world. She was discovering, to her pleasure, that captains of spaceships entirely appreciated those requirements, probably far better than she did. Space was not tolerant of wishful thinking.

A reactor that failed to perform as designed, for reasons nobody could properly diagnose, was more than merely aggravating. It violated her sense of order. Unpredictable power systems were dangerous power systems. She worried that Reactor 1 would prove similarly unpredictable and possibly considerably more deadly. There was no evidence for this at all, but worrying about hypotheticals was a big part of Becca's design strategy. It cost her restful nights, but so far it had saved her ass more than once.

There was a more personal peeve. She was damned proud of having solved the propulsion system's seemingly impossible power dissipation problem, and her engineer's ego wanted to show it off. Simmering along at a mere half power made her feel like she'd designed the fastest race car on Earth and was limited to using it to commute to work.

Okay, not reasonable. It didn't stop her from being bugged. Still, it was a small silver lining. The reactor and generator crews wouldn't need to make any adjustments, and she'd just have to slow down the radiator ribbon velocity a bit to give the molten metal more time to dissipate its heat into space before it was collected by the far booms.

As for the rest of the ship . . .

Time to rig the sunshades.

The parasols were huge but thin, a mere half micron of metallized Kapton. Their total mass, including the struts to hold them as they swept through their close approach, was a few tonnes. An insignificant amount of extra weight at launch, considering the four thousand–plus-tonne ship it was designed to protect. Once the *Nixon* was safely distant from the sun again, the parasols would be jettisoned, off on their own unpowered escape trajectory from the solar system.

The parasols—there were two sets, in case there was some kind of failure to deploy the first one—were stowed on the outside of the axle. Each shade assembly came in two sections.

Martinez and the other handymen would be deploying them; the procedure was only semiautomatic.

Six of them went out in eggs, Sandy running his cameras, Fiorella broadcasting from another egg. In theory, one large parasol could have done the job, moving it during the course of solar flyby to keep it positioned between the ship and the sun.

In practice, that would've required either bulky external control equipment to move the parasols around, as the angle to the sun changed, or more EVAs much closer to the sun to manually reposition the screen. The latter was vetoed on pure safety grounds; it would stress the service eggs' cooling systems enough having them operate at sixty million kilometers from the sun. They could not be used safely at forty million, not for very long periods of time, anyway.

Two separate sections that would not have to be moved were both simpler and safer.

The first of the two parasol sections was simply a disk three hundred meters in diameter that would be mounted at the forward end of the axle, about the nose cone that protected the module from micro-meteor impacts.

The gossamer-thin disk would shield all the forward modules— engineering, storage and shuttle bay, living and command—as they approached the sun nearly head-on.

All the egg crews had to do was detach a parasol package from the exterior of the ship, move it to prefabbed attachment points, clamp them in place, pull back to a safe distance, and let Martinez send the triggering signal to activate the packages.

Fang-Castro: "Mr. Martinez?"

"Yes, ma'am. Ready here."

"Then you are instructed to continue. Mr. Darlington, if you please, we will want at least one camera fully dedicated to documentation, rather than journalism. We will be watching that feed from Engineering and from here in Command and Control."

"Yes, ma'am."

Martinez: "Jerry, Lou, slip the buttons and back the pack away."

"Got that," one of the crewmen said. Their two separate eggs were already in position, and they simply reached out with mechanical arms and disconnected the first of the parasol packs from the side of the axle.

Martinez and the third crewman, Phil Jakes, in their own eggs, were near the front of the ship, waiting as the first two slowly towed the pack toward them. Fiorella backed away—she was now actually in front of the *Nixon*, temporarily leading the way toward Saturn; Sandy had her position-locked in his number two camera, while the number one fed the documentation to Command and Control.

When the first two eggs had reached the attachment points, the other two moved up and began jockeying it into place. Before the clamps would fire, each external connection had to be grounded in the base of the clamp, which meant maneuvering the bulky package in three dimensions.

That took five minutes: when all were in place, Martinez said, "Engaging clamps."

He pushed the "execute" button on the clamps app, and the clamps snapped shut.

"We're engaged," he said. "Everybody back off. Cassie, I'm going to bring you around closer to Sandy. I don't want you out in front of this thing where I can't see you."

"All right."

When everyone was in place, Martinez made a last check, and said, "Popping the clamshell."

He hit the "execute" on the clamshell app, and the two halves of the package cover folded back, precisely as they'd been designed to.

The final phase of the deployment was the automatic part, and also the most nerve-racking. The parasol had been intricately folded into the clamshell, along with the memory-metal hoop that would support its edge. If it had been folded correctly, and if nothing went wrong, then the parasol should unfold like a flower blossom. If something did go wrong, then, because of the delicate nature of the film shield, it'd probably wind up looking like a box kite that somebody had worked over with a shotgun.

Martinez maneuvered his egg around the open clamshell, inspecting each connection point, a theoretically unnecessary operation, since the monitors showed everything proceeding as expected; but he took no chances.

When he was done with his inspection, he called Command: "Captain, we're ready to deploy. On your command."

Purely a courtesy. Fang-Castro: "You may proceed, Mr. Martinez."

Martinez made one last check to make sure all the personnel were clear, and then said, "Deploying the shade. Three-two-one-fire."

He pressed a button, the package unzipped, and the parasol unfolded exactly like a metallic flower, and for the first time ever, the *Nixon* was in the shade.

A minute inspection of the shade showed no tears; a tear could be fixed, but it would be a pain in the ass. No such pain would be experienced.

The second section was larger than the first, a huge rectangle of metallized Kapton to be stretched broadside to the ship on the side that would be facing the sun at closest approach. At four hundred meters in length, it was longer than the entire ship.

Temporary memory-metal support booms were attached to key mount points on the axle, booms, and mast of the *Nixon* and triggered to unroll. The unpacked parasol would be attached to a rectangular x-frame, whose double handful of sockets would mate with mounting points on the ends of those booms. The process wasn't fundamentally different from the deployment of the front-end disk. The shell containing the shade was towed into place and attached to one of the support booms.

At Martinez's command, the package began to blossom, just as the first one had, until nearly half a square kilometer of shiny plastic film and its x-frame floated in space next to the *Nixon*. The servicing jockeys maneuvered the ungainly oblong into position close enough to the other booms that the mounting teams could drag the couplings on the parasol frame and mounting booms together.

By mid-afternoon, the crew had finished with the attachments, and the *Nixon* was ready for its close encounter with Sol.

The vid of the work, condensed to five minutes on that night's broadcast, was quite beautiful, Sandy thought. For one shot, using a digital sun filter on his longest lens, shooting from the far side of the ship, he had shown the shade eclipsing several minor sunspots as it was maneuvered into place. He'd locked on Fiorella's egg, holding it in a constant predetermined set of pixels, which did not have the digital filter, so her egg hung like a bright white star across the pumpkin-colored face of the sun.

Fiorella had narrated.

The ratings were down.

The earth was moving on, as the two ships were moving out.

26.

Time passed—for most of the people on the ship, it was business as usual. Although there was a growing time lag for radio-wave contact between the ship and the earth, it wasn't noticeable except in direct conversations. Professors who lectured continued to lecture; they might then have to wait for some minutes for blocks of questions from the audiences, and the audiences would have to wait a similar number of minutes for a block of answers, but they adapted to the delay.

As Clover said, "I can finish a lecture, walk down the hall, take a leak, and get back in time to answer the questions. Can't do that when you're there in person."

Sandy spent a lot of time in the shop, designing and printing a five-string bass guitar for Crow. There'd been carbon-composite guitars for most of a century, and though wood-bigots still ruled, most objective measures suggested that properly designed and printed carbon instruments now exceeded their wooden counterparts in the various parameters of tonality.

"Properly designed" being the stumbling point: nobody knew what that meant, just as nobody knew what "art" meant.

And Martinez and Sandy did not see precisely eye to eye on the matter: although the same pitches were involved, Martinez favored more of a country *whack* sound, while Sandy favored more of a RhythmTech *boom*.

Either sound could be simulated with software, of course, but sound-bigots still insisted that amplified native-wood resonance was clearly distinguishable from electronic sound. Both Martinez and Sandy subscribed to that view, although numerous blind tests had proven that even professional musicians couldn't tell the difference. But, carbon composites would have to do.

"Hey."

Sandy turned and found Becca standing behind him, dressed in her usual jeans and T-shirt. "Haven't started printing it yet?" she asked.

"Not yet. Still tweaking the sound, making some adjustments in shape."

"You know, with a perfect sound system, you guys probably couldn't tell the difference between the native resonance . . ."

"Yes, we could."

". . . and constructed sound, and after you finish running it through the leads and stompboxes and then through the preamp and power amp and out through a couple of speakers and then bounce it around the Commons . . . you're lucky you can even tell it's a guitar."

"Shut up."

After a moment of silence, she said, "So, not to abruptly change the subject, will you be sleeping with Fiorella tonight?"

That stopped him: "Jesus, where did that come from?"

She leaned against the printer bench and grinned at him. "From rumor central. And it's all over the ship."

Rumor central was a guy named Larry Wirt, who, in addition to being an excellent cook, knew more about who was doing what to whom than anyone else on the ship. And he talked about it. Incessantly.

"Ah, he saw Cassie and me talking down by Cassie's cabin . . . he's just making up bullshit."

"Don't wanna see my boy get hurt. That woman is a snake."

"Becca, I'm just thinking about guitars. That's it. Fiorella is a good-looking woman who doesn't do a lot for me." Sandy paused to think. Actually, Fiorella did do a lot for him, but then . . . This had to be handled carefully. "We started out hating each other and have improved that to active dislike."

"Ah, well. Say, don't basses have four strings?" She waved at the screen on Sandy's slate. "Yours seems to have five."

"Becca . . . Look, basses have as many as seven strings. . . ."

The following lecture on bass guitars was a cover, designed to con-

ceal a temptation to giggle. Sandy hadn't actually giggled since Harvard,
but now . . .

Earlier that day, John Clover had collected Wirt, supposedly to talk about a menu change for their joint cooking class, and had skillfully guided him past Sandy and Fiorella, who'd been waiting for them.

When Clover and Wirt appeared, Fiorella had her back to the corridor wall, while Sandy's hand was planted on the wall next to her head, their faces barely half a meter apart. Or, as Wirt put it later, in the cafeteria line, "He was practically drooling on her perky little breasts. Wait, did I say little? Anyway, she liked it."

That posture, that image, went viral. According to Clover, who talked to them later, eighteen thousand dollars had gone into what had become known as the Hump Pool: "We're at a hundred and forty-eight thousand and counting," Clover said, gloating.

"Gloating is unbecoming in a man of your stature," Fiorella said.

"If you'll excuse the language, my asshole is unbecoming of a man of my stature, but I got one anyway," Clover said. "Honest to God, one more day like this and we'll be at two hundred thousand. A month, if we manage it just right, we'll be at half a mil, and from there on out . . . snowball heaven."

After finishing the short lecture on bass guitars, Sandy asked, "You play an instrument?"

"I started playing a violin when I was five," Becca said. "My parents made me do it, for the discipline. I quit when I was ten. I hated it. I still hate it. I can't even stand to listen to violin music—and I mean classical, bluegrass, whatever."

"Ah, too bad," Sandy said. "But if you already know the theory, you could pick up something else, pretty quick."

"Nah. The fact is, I don't have music in my head," Becca said. "If you don't have music in your head, you can't really play—all you can do is reproduce what's on the page. No fun in that."

"Mmmm. So what do you have in your head?"

"Structures, mostly," Becca said. "Shapes. Next life, maybe I'll be an architect. I've got a whole town in there, that I put together building by building, and block by block. I can lie in bed and close my eyes, and walk through it. Move stores around, change apartment layouts, streets, you know . . . shuffle the whole deck."

"How big is the town?"

"About five thousand right now, but it's growing. I think I might get it to thirty thousand, someday, but that'd about be my intellectual limit. . . . Why are you pushing that edge out?" She was looking over his shoulder at the schematic on the screen.

"Because Crow's thin," Sandy said. "A heavy guy, I'd cut some off the basic pattern—you need the guitar to snuggle up to you, when you're standing up." She nodded, and Sandy pushed the edge out a bit more.

"Where are the frets?"

"No frets. He started by playing the upright bass," Sandy said.

"Huh. Who woulda thunk."

"What are you doing down here, anyway?" Sandy asked.

She shrugged. "Looking for something to do, I guess. I'm about burned out on pushing bytes . . . and I thought I might borrow one of the smaller printers and poop out a Go board and some stones."

"Yeah? I tried playing that, back in school," Sandy said. "The chess guys were such jerks about it that I gave up on chess and tried Go. It's like playing chess in a heavy fog . . . sort of."

"If you help me poop out my board, I'll teach you how to play," Becca said. "In a couple of months, you could fake being an intellectual."

"Yeah . . ." He laughed. "I can do that now. Set up the Go board and stare at it. Chuckle every once in a while. What more do you need?"

"Well, you need the board . . ."

"All right. You give me secret Go lessons, we'll print up a board and the stones. Then when I look like I might know what I'm doing, we'll go play in the Commons where we can impress people."

"Deal."

They chatted for a couple of minutes, then Becca wandered away and Sandy went back to his schematic. After a moment, he smiled, just for himself.

27.

Six days after parasol deployment and thirty-two days into their mission, the *Nixon* passed perihelion. This was the most uncertain part of the mission plan, next to visiting the alien whatsit.

There were a number of ways the ship could get into trouble. Parasol failure was only the most obvious and predictable one. That wouldn't kill the crew.

"Well, probably not," Fang-Castro told Clover. They were drinking tea in Fang-Castro's apartment. "The ship could take the heat, at least for a couple of weeks. We don't know if the heat pumps could shunt the thermal load from the living modules to the radiator system, but we think they could. Probably."

"I wasn't really thinking about the heat," Clover said. "We got the heat handled. But I was talking to Alfie, and he said we're near the solar maximum . . ."

"True . . ."

". . . and so we get these flares and coronal ejections and whatnot, and there's no really good way to model them. They can't really see forward for more than a few days or a week. After that, it's guesswork."

"Guesswork and statistics. Statistics say we'd have to be really unlucky to get hit."

"But if we did, it'd be all bad," Clover said.

"Yes, it would be." She smiled at him. "Since there's not much we can do about it, except have fire drills, it's best not to think about it."

A major flare would unleash a burst of X-rays, and at the *Nixon*'s distance, the hard radiation would hit them in a few minutes—most of the crew wouldn't get enough warning to reach the safety of aft Engineering, where they would be shielded by the huge water tanks that provided reaction mass for the VASIMR engines.

There were hidey-holes in each module of the ship, which, in a pinch, could accommodate the crew in a radiation-safe environment for the hour or so they might need protection—but it would be crowded and uncomfortable. Crowded and uncomfortable was better than dead.

Fang-Castro had insisted on drill after drill until every crew member showed they could make it to safety in less than ninety seconds, three times in a row. In the month leading up to perihelion, every crew member had come to hate the sound of the flare alarm.

After the X-rays, there'd be a proton storm. The flood of charged particles was immensely damaging, biologically, but it would also wreak havoc with electronics, inducing massive eddy currents in anything metallic.

The hidey-holes and the water tanks were enough to protect the crew but there was no way to electrically shield the entire ship. Shunts and circuit breakers would provide some protection, and the ship builders believed the craft would make it through without fatal damage. Nobody was quite sure, and there was no way to test for it.

The worst possibility was that they'd be hit by a coronal mass ejection. If that happened, they were toast. The massive plasma stream would overwhelm any imaginable safeguards on the ship's critical systems.

There really wasn't much to be done except prepare for what they reasonably could. Space weather could give them some advance warning, but the *Nixon* was not a maneuverable ship. The math was simple and irrefutable: the ship was barreling along at one hundred and fifteen kilometers per second deep in the sun's gravitational well. At best, its engines could alter its velocity by two kilometers per second in a day's time. Major course changes were out of the question. If the *Nixon* found itself on a collision course with a coronal mass ejection, then a collision was what was going to happen.

The anxiety was compounded by the boredom. There just wasn't much to do on the ship: eat, work, sleep, exercise, watch vids beaming in from Earth. Ten days on, it looked like they were going to luck out, as far as solar storms were concerned. No news was the best news. Still, it was no news.

Boring.

Well, not all the time.

28.

Francois Peneski, a biochemist known for research into the possibilities of non-carbon-based life-forms, finished dinner in the cafeteria/commons. He took his tray and empty dishes to the dirty-dishes corral, dumped the dishes, then carried the tray back to where Don Larson, a mathematician, was chatting with friends, and used the hard-plastic tray to smash Larson in the face, breaking several blood vessels in Larson's nose and knocking him off his chair.

Larson knew precisely why this had occurred, and though the nose pain was nearly blinding, and blood was running down his chin, he got up off the floor and swung wildly at Peneski, connecting, more by luck than anything else, with the other man's left eye.

Then it was on: flailing fists and feet, several bites, screaming crew members. A woman named Rosalind Aster, a mechanical engineer, ripped at Peneski's face with her fingernails. Peneski elbowed her in the mouth, and she fell backwards, hard, taking a table full of dishes down with her.

(After the fight, several of the numbers people and one of the physicists tried to work out the optimum tactics for a low-gravity fistfight. The problem proved to be surprisingly difficult, given the number of variables involved; the actual fight, however, was carried out with some efficiency.)

Francisco, the ship's executive officer, was in the cafeteria at the time, as was Ang, the wrestling, violin-playing shrink, and between the two of them, they managed to pry the fighters apart. There were three empty reinforced cabins designed to be used either as hospital rooms or as cells, as need be. The exec ordered the three fighters confined to the cells, and to be attended by a ship's doctor, while he talked with Fang-Castro about the next step.

The next step was to interview the fighters.

Fang-Castro appeared at Peneski's cell, with Francisco, Crow, and Ang in tow. Peneski was sitting on the floor—the room had no furniture—and when the door opened, he stood as Fang-Castro walked in.

Fang-Castro said, "Mr. Peneski: What in God's name was that about? My executive officer tells me that you launched an unprovoked attack on Mr. Larson. Mr. Larson has a bloody nose, and Ms. Aster has several loosened teeth, which will require braces. Your face looks like a raw steak. Can you give me a good reason why you shouldn't remain locked up?"

"I'm sorry," Peneski said. "It won't happen again. And it wasn't un-provoked."

"Then give me an explanation to consider."

"Roz and I had developed a . . . relationship," Peneski said.

"A sexual relationship," Fang-Castro said.

"Yes. She was . . . she was really a good thing for me. I have difficulty with relationships. But then, she joined Larson's orgy club and she didn't want to be with me anymore. I couldn't—"

Fang-Castro: "The *what* club?"

"The orgy club. Larson started an orgy club. There are six members, four men and two women. Roz invited me to get in, but I didn't want to, I wanted to be exclusive. She started avoiding me and finally I said I'd do it, but then she said it was too late, they'd recruited a fifth guy, and I couldn't get in until they got another woman, unless I was bi, and maybe not even then, because I was a stick-in-the-mud, and they didn't want any stick-in-the-muds."

The exec said, "Ah, Jesus."

By the time Peneski spoke with Fang-Castro, the well-lubricated rumor mill was already in overdrive. Not only was the reason for the fight well known, but the details of the Larson orgies were also revealed. Not only revealed, but extensively embroidered upon.

Larson was quoted as having said, "Women are basically recreational areas, with several separate facilities available at any given time."

The quotation was completely fabricated, but people were entirely unamused. And, of course, *then* the jokes started, often based on Peneski's occupation: "Is that a silicon-based life-form in your pocket, or are you just happy to see me?"

"What would you recommend?" Fang-Castro asked Francisco, Crow, and Ang, in the hallway outside the cell where Peneski remained confined.

Crow said, "There was a violent attack. It's not something you can ignore, even if there's no danger of another one. There has to be some kind of punishment. Since you're the captain, you have to decide on what it should be."

Ang said, "Peneski doesn't seem irrational—he managed to work himself into a momentary rage, watching them sit at their table, laughing. He says it won't happen again and I tend to believe him. Whatever the punishment is, I don't think we should shame him. He's already shamed enough. And Larson was provoked, beyond question. I'd suggest a monetary fine, a couple of weeks' pay, for both of them. I would also find out who the other members of the orgy club are, and I would peel the skin off them. It's not so much the group sex that worries me, it's the exclusionary attitude—Peneski couldn't qualify for membership."

The exec said, "Ah, Jesus."

Crow: "Ma'am, I would also recommend that you address the situation directly. Call a crew meeting and broadcast it. Be very clear about the limits of what you'll tolerate."

"I should say it's okay to have orgies, but you have to invite everybody? I don't think so," Fang-Castro said. "The President would be the teensiest bit annoyed."

Crow actually smiled at the thought. "That's not quite what I meant. You outline the damaging effects that this kind of thing has on ship morale, tell them that you won't put up with it. Tell them to behave like adults on a deadly serious mission, and that while sex is their own affair, morale is your affair. That if they do anything that will impair morale—and indiscreet sexual liaisons might well qualify—you will lock the offenders in the restraint cells with nothing but a TV set and three meals a day, for the duration of the mission. That you will not allow any behavior, even if legal on Earth, that will impair the mission: this ship is *not* a democracy, and you are the Queen."

"I can do that," Fang-Castro said. "I will also make it clear that assaults, for any reason, are not tolerable and no provocation will be considered an acceptable excuse. Don't look at me like that, Dr. Ang— regardless of the bizarre circumstances, shipboard discipline requires this."

Ang waved a finger. "If I may make a suggestion? Remind them that shipboard, libido is a privilege. A privilege that can be revoked. I have the necessary drugs. Would you support that?"

Crow interjected, "I can tell you the President would. Hell, she'd likely have them spaced."

"Which is why she doesn't get to command a spaceship," said Fang-Castro. To Ang, she said, "I'll mention the drugs."

The exec said, "Ah, Jesus."

29.

Crow was completely and intensely aware of the crew's opinion of him— the knot-headed security man, unfriendly, possibly psychopathic, certainly sociopathic, and perhaps even a semi-comic figure, in the Godot sense, unless he happened to be strangling you or pushing you out the air lock. Given the makeup of the rest of the crew, he was considered hardly anyone's intellectual equal, and was therefore treated with a thinly disguised disdain.

Crow hadn't graduated first in his class at the Naval Academy because he hadn't wanted to: something in his makeup insisted that he remain obscure, a man behind a curtain. Adjustments made to his academic record lowered him to the eleventh spot, high enough to be taken seriously, low enough that he wasn't a threat to anyone.

He'd gone directly from the academy into intelligence work as a Marine Corps officer. Given the nature of intelligence work in the last half of the twenty-first century, he had made himself expert in computer and communications technology, and in statistics. He could speak Mandarin as well as most Western academic China specialists—well enough to understand it and make himself understood—and was fluent in Russian and Portuguese.

His work in the intelligence world gave him a sixth sense about intelligence operations: he was certain the *Nixon* had been sabotaged. He'd remained publicly ambivalent, even with Fang-Castro, but in his heart, he knew, one hundred percent.

His cabin was heavily shielded. The best electronics security people he'd ever known had come up to the *Nixon* to make sure of that. After they vouched for its cleanliness, he brought up another group, to check the first. Then he checked it himself. From his cabin, he could talk to his ground support, completely outside normal communications channels.

If the *Nixon* had been sabotaged, as he believed, there could have been two ways to do that: with a timed action, or with a specific local signal to a prepared bomb of some kind, either virtual or physical, and probably not the latter—though he didn't entirely discount the possibility.

The timed action would be the most secure way to attack the ship. Once the sabotage was set, it would happen no matter what. There'd be no foul-ups caused by unreliable personnel, no last-minute changes of mind.

The specific local signal would require an agent on board, who could act either by his controller's demand, or, if he were trusted enough, act of his own volition.

When Reactor 2 went down, it appeared to be a time bomb, set to detonate the Easter egg at a certain point in the trip—after departure but not too far into it, probably triggered by a random, but practically certain, event in the data stream going into the reactor logs.

Crow believed that the Easter egg had probably been created on Earth, and that he could do nothing about it without pushing the ship's risk profile to an unacceptable level. The fact that there'd been an Easter egg, however, told him something else: that someone—probably China—was willing to take substantial risk to design and carry out sabotage right in the face of extraordinarily heavy security.

That suggested to him that the ship had been the target of a major and extremely intelligent espionage effort, and the effort probably would not have been one-dimensional, entirely dependent on the Easter egg in the software.

A heavy espionage operation would want an ear on the ship, and a way to talk.

A spy.

Crow worked the vid link, though the delay between transmission and reply was beginning to drive him crazy. Phaedra Mellis was on the link this morning, talking in long blocks for the simple efficiency of it:

"Hey, Crow, got an eye-opener for you. We got a call from Will Jackson. They won't tell us how they got the data, though it has to be human intelligence rather than something they pulled out of the ground.

Anyway, the key *Celestial Odyssey* strategists have been told that Becca Johansson says you might be able to kick up thrust on the remaining engine by no more than three percent and still remain within the 99.5 percent reliability status on the radiators, or, four percent thrust at ninety-seven percent reliability. Those numbers were precise and so was the attribution to Johansson. Jackson ran all the data traffic from you guys through Grendel, and he said that in no case, not even in the encrypted data downloads, were those specific numbers mentioned," Mellis said.

Will Jackson was the three-star general who ran the NSA, and Grendel was their fastest sorting computer.

Mellis continued: "Jackson checked with the orbit guys here. They hadn't heard those numbers, and were under the impression that Johansson and her people had to do more studies to come up with a precise number, and those studies might take a while—a week or two. Our question here is, did Johansson ever mention those precise numbers? The Grendel results show quite a bit of conversation with various people down here, including the President's circle, where an increase in velocity has been discussed, but only in terms of projected arrival dates. I'm told it's possible that the Chinese intercepted some of that data and extrapolated the power boost, but that's pretty unlikely. If they did get it here and extrapolate it, it'd mean that they've got a source pretty close to the President, which would also be . . . discomfiting. So that's where we're at, man. Over."

Crow said, "Johansson mentioned something like those numbers—I think those exact numbers, I'll check—in a meeting here a week or so ago. She was pulling the numbers out of her butt, more or less, nothing she'd want to go on the record with. I think we've got a Chinese asset on board. The meeting room has been heavily scanned for bugs, but just inner-ship chatter could have picked up the numbers. What's happening with the re-scan on the crew?"

He waited, and waited, and then Mellis was back:

"We are shredding the crew, but we're not seeing anything that we didn't already know. I'm telling you, we did a first-rate job the first time

through. The only thing new is that you've got a guy there, Cary Roth,
microbiologist, cross-trained as a medic and welder, degrees in biology
from Iowa State and Texas. Twenty-two years ago, somebody cracked a
safe in the controller's office at Iowa State and stole forty-eight thousand
dollars. Police thought it might have been Roth, more for proximity reasons than anything. He had a part-time job there—I'll ship you all the
details—but he was never arrested, charged, or even spoken to harshly.
If he did it, he got away with it. That's about it, it's nothing that the Chinese could use as a lever or even know about. I really think that if you've
got somebody up there, it's a paid asset, not an ideological one. Not
something we're going to find out by pushing their background.

"On the other hand, we're seeing nothing on the financial side. This
is one of the cleanest bunch of people I've ever seen. Maybe a little fooling around with income taxes, but nothing that would push a guy into
Beijing's lap. Almost all of them are salaried, and they get good salaries,
and the IRS knows what they get down to the penny, and they are living
within their means. We've traced them all the way back to their birth
dates, we've looked at their school yearbooks and their grade records,
we've talked to people who remember them from kindergarten, photos
from unrelated people, vids of Little League games. The original work
we did still looks good. So, uh . . . that's what we got, long files to follow
on the data links. We need ideas. Over."

Crow: "I'm burning out my brain here, Fay. If there's a spy on board,
they'll want him to have some access to communications. I kinda don't
think we'll find it, but if you guys develop any reasonable ideas, let me
know. Maybe they had to do something in a hurry, and they built a link
into our outgoing data streams. I doubt that they'd have any kind of a
regular schedule—if there's a schedule at all, it's randomized and linked
to a one-time pad that we won't find.

"Most likely there is no schedule: they've set up a link that can be
used anytime, but that they'll only use for something urgent. We've got
three big data links coming out of here, but I'd look particularly at the
low-bandwidth omni-directional antenna carrying the black-box data
from the ship. Nobody's going to look at the black-box signal unless we

blow up, so if they're going out through one of the antennas, I suspect that's the one they'd choose. We need to do an analysis of the black-box signal all the way from Earth orbit to here. If there's an encrypted message buried in the black-box signal, I suspect it'll be disguised as noise, so you need to tell the guys to look specifically at the noise. The optical link is a lot cleaner, so it'd be harder to hide a signal there, but there's also so much data that a full analysis might not be feasible. If it is feasible, then do it. But to tell the truth, I don't think we'll find anything. Over."

He waited a while for the reply, then Mellis came back:

"We can run the data screens, but we're gonna need more money. That's a lot of data to look at, and we're gonna need access to Grendel again, and you know how those guys get about that. Over."

"You'll get it. Jackson is aware of Santeros's interest. Over. And out, unless you've got something else."

Mellis had nothing more. Crow called Johansson, asked her to switch to encryption, and put the question to her. Had she mentioned those numbers anywhere outside the meeting room?

"Well, sure, here in Engineering," Becca said. "We've been trying to figure out what we might do, and if it makes any sense to do it. But we're sort of backing up on the numbers. I don't think four percent is at all feasible anymore. . . . But to go to your question, I mentioned those specific numbers only in that meeting. Here in Engineering, we're pretty aware that it's a range, not a specific number."

"Huh. Becca: thank you. You've been a help."

And she was gone.

30.

Elroy Gorey and Joe Martinez were sitting in the garden—a space dedicated to hydroponics, growing lettuce, cabbage, spinach, kale, arugula, tomatoes, cucumbers, and peas, all overlaid with the light stink of fertilizer—and working through a few country tunes, Martinez on guitar, Gorey on fiddle. Crow showed up with his bass, plugged in, and they rocked along for twenty minutes or so.

When they took a break, Martinez asked Crow, "You ever going to find that Easter egg?"

Crow shook his head: "I don't expect so. There's still some smart guys working on it, but the thing is, what we've found out is that there are a lot of undetectable ways of doing what was done. That we could scrape the computers clean, and there are ways they could still get at us."

Gorey: "So the other reactor . . . that could go out, too?"

Crow shook his head: "We don't think so. We're not entirely sure, but we suspect there may be some kind of physical component to this whole thing. That it might not be purely software. But we don't know."

"Wish you would," Martinez said. "I don't like running on one cylinder."

"Neither do I," Crow said.

"The thing is . . . the whole competition doesn't make any sense," Gorey said. "If we get out there first, or the Chinese get out there first, and one of us gets amazing tech, what's the winner going to do with it? If the Chinese build a time machine, our intelligence guys will have the specs in three weeks, anyway."

"Yeah? What if they go back through time to, like, 1200 A.D. and they discover North America, and when Columbus shows up, it's wall-to-wall Chinese?" Martinez asked.

"Won't be any time machines," Gorey said. "We're right at the end of physics. Everybody knows it. Not much left, and one of the things that's not left is time travel."

"Good thing, too," Crow said. "We've fucked up about everything else we've touched, we don't need to fuck up the time stream."

Sandy stuck his head in the door and asked, "Tomato?"

Gorey asked, "You got a note from Fang-Castro?"

Sandy wheedled: "Elroy, I've been talking to Fiorella about doing a feature on the garden, but I can sink that in one minute. I'm not saying I will, because I'm a good guy, but I'm telling you, she needs some convincing."

"I might be able to spare one tomato," Gorey said. "If nobody talks."

"He made my bass," Crow said. "I won't talk."

"Me neither," Martinez said.

"I want a big one, and juicy, but not overripe," Sandy said. "And maybe a couple of lettuce leaves."

"Picky, picky, picky . . ."

Sandy knocked on Becca's cabin door and she popped it open. She was sitting on her bunk. The Go board and two bowls of Go stones, half black, half white, took up most of the space on a small table.

Unlike the chess nuts at Harvard, Becca had proven to be cheerfully patient with his beginner status: he was even starting to improve. She'd gone from spotting him eight stones, to seven, though he suspected that he'd never be playing her even-up. It was that whole brain thing, he thought, and the differences in cerebral structure that probably went to early childhood or even to genetics. She visualized whole towns with buildings and apartments and bicycle racks, a useful ability in Go. He couldn't do that.

But she couldn't let go of that structure. She'd seen him drawing, freehand, different concepts for guitars that he was manufacturing with Martinez, and asked him to teach her a little drawing. As it turned out, she could draw neither a straight line nor an accurate curved one. She insisted on drawing what she knew, rather than what she saw, a tendency not easily curable.

They'd talked about those differences: he'd argued that a mind that could build and contain an entire town, right down to the wallpaper in the apartments, was a winner at Go. She'd said, "There's a part of Go, at a level higher than I'm at, that involves intellectual release. . . . I can't do that, but you can."

"Maybe," he said doubtfully.

In any case, he pushed through the door carrying two paper bags and a covered plate that smelled of hot buttered toast and tofu bacon, though the tofu bacon was indistinguishable from the pig kind.

"What's that?" Becca asked.

"Got a contraband tomato from Elroy," Sandy said.

He rolled the tomato out of the smaller sack and popped the lid on the covered plate. Four slices of hot buttered toast, six strips of crispy bacon.

"Oh my God, BLTs. Real ones," Becca said. "You should have gotten one for yourself."

"Yeah, you try to eat one bite more than your share, you're gonna be in a fistfight," Sandy said. "And . . . I got beer. I bought Wagner's ration." Jim Wagner, a navigation tech and Sandy's backup photographer, didn't drink. Didn't like the taste of alcohol, he said; but he had no difficulty in collecting his ration, and selling it to the highest bidder.

"If Fang-Castro finds out he's selling his ration, she'll kick his ass," Becca said. "Somebody could get enough beer together to get drunk."

"Yeah, but who's going to tell her? Besides, if you really wanted to get drunk, you could just save your own ration for a few days."

"When you're right, you're right. Pop me one of those babies."

Four days past perihelion and thirty-six days into their flight, the *Nixon* was now a safe fifty million kilometers from the sun, and shipboard life, despite the two-day furor over the orgy club, had resumed its previous level of boredom. Sandy would've thought that impossible.

The *Nixon* was still too close to the sun for extravehicular sorties, but the risk to the ship from solar misbehavior had diminished. The giant metal radiator sail protected the living and engineering modules from the killing heat of the receding sun; they'd also block the brunt of any soft radiation or charged particle winds that might blow their way. X-rays were still a risk, if there were major flare, but that was about it.

Sandy handed Becca the first of the four beers he had in the sack, and they ate the BLTs in companionable silence, and finally settled behind the Go board. Sandy had a seven-stone handicap. He'd thought about the game during the day, had reread part of a famous Go instruction book by Nicholai Hel that he'd downloaded from the Internet, and confidently began to lay out his handicap.

This time—and maybe because she drank three of the four beers—it took her almost an hour and a half to beat him.

When it was over, Becca pursed her lips thoughtfully and said, "You know, Sandy, I think you're actually getting the hang of this. Maybe you should move up to a six-stone handicap."

He grinned. "Or maybe I should stay with seven stones and get to win a game, for once."

"That's probably not going to happen, not yet," she said.

"You really like to win, don't you?"

"The business I'm in, when I'm right, you bet. Keeps power plants running, keeps people alive. And I'm just about always right. On the big points, anyway."

Sandy looked at her thoughtfully. "Isn't that kind of self-aggrandizing?"

Becca was taken aback for a second, by both the thought and the vocabulary. *Damn,* she thought. *I keep forgetting he's not stupid, just lazy. Harvard degree. Gotta remember that.*

"Sandy . . ." She paused for a moment, organizing her thoughts before responding. "I have to be. You are a rich, handsome, privileged, white guy. You get to play on the easy level. If you gave a crap, people would take you seriously, automatically, because guys like you get that

as a freebie. I'm a short, blond woman who was raised Minnesota Nice,
plus I have a cute face and I'm fat! How seriously do you think I'd get
taken in the world if I didn't regularly throw it in their faces?"

Sandy's gaze was fixed on her; it was a little unnerving when he focused like that. "But wouldn't people like you better if you weren't quite
so, um . . ." He fumbled for a word. Becca interrupted him.

"What? Assertive? Aggressive? Pushy? Do you really think people
will pay more attention to my technical advice, my expertise, if it comes
from a nice Minnesota girl? Really?"

Sandy held up his hands, palms outward. "Okay, okay. I get it."

Her eye ticked, which meant she was checking the time. "Speaking of
winning, we could probably squeeze in another game before lights-out."

Sandy didn't say anything, just looked at the board for several
seconds.

"Yoo-hoo, Sandy?"

"So . . . I've been thinking . . ." He paused.

She looked at him impatiently. "Aaaaaannnd? Tick tick tick . . ."

What the hell, he thought: she was the blunt sort: "Have you considered the possibility of the two of us having sex?"

Becca blinked and then she laughed, a real laugh. "Wow, so that's
how you smooth Harvard stud-muffins woo your women? Who knew!
Be still, my heart."

"Look, there didn't seem to be any . . . if this pisses you off . . . I'm
saying, I'm not real big on pressure, it's, uh . . . I don't think our friendship . . . or the Go, for that matter . . ."

"Hold it, hold it, hold it. Did I say no?"

Sandy relaxed just a trifle. "I thought you might be about to. Especially after the freak-out with the orgy club."

"Did fantasizing about the orgy club get you to this? Because if it
did . . ."

"No, no, no, nothing like that. You're a good-looking woman—"

"I'm fat . . ."

"So you're round. That's fine with me. Doesn't mean you aren't cute,
except when you're slicing me up for something. . . . Anyway . . ."

She looked him up and down, deadpan. "Tell you what. Take off those clothes and I'll decide if I like what I see. Then I'll let you know."

Sandy shrugged again. "See, what you probably don't know is, I'm the least body-shy person you've ever met." He sat back down and started to unzip his softboots.

"Wait, wait, that was kinda a joke. You really . . . want to do this?"

"You really want to play another game of Go?"

"Fuck no," she said, pulling her shirt over her head. "Hurry."

"What do you think?" she asked forty-five minutes later.

"About what?"

"About the fuckin' quality control, dumbass."

"I give us a B-plus."

She propped herself up on her elbow and said, looking down at him, "Excuse me? A B-plus? I'm pretty sure I haven't had as many partners as you have, so my statistical baseline is not as long—"

"B-plus is as good as it's ever been, for the first time," Sandy said. "This was most excellent. Check the time."

She did the blink thing: "Oh, yeah. We've got time for more . . ."

The ship's computer wasn't very smart. Under the captain's orders, it killed lights in Becca's cabin at 23:00. After checking to make sure that Becca was in her bed, it periodically checked to make sure that she mostly stayed in bed until it turned the lights back on at 7:00 each morning.

It didn't check to see if she was alone—it could have, but it hadn't been told to. Nor did it have any way to make sure she was actually asleep. That night, mostly, she wasn't. Neither was Sandy.

Early in the morning, Sandy woke, bumped around in the dark until he'd located his clothes, sat on his Go chair to tie his shoes.

Becca said, "That was pretty amazing." Then, "Okay, that's a cliché, what you're supposed to say the next morning so nobody's ego gets bruised. But, really, I mean it."

Sandy groped for her in the dark, kissed her. "What you said. It was amazing. You were amazing. We were both amazing. How come nobody ever told us low-gee sex would be that good?"

"Damned if I know. Maybe it's like a rite of passage. Or maybe they're just afraid that if they told us when we came on board, we wouldn't get any work done. We'd be too busy humping."

"I don't think they're that subtle," Sandy said. "If they'd actually thought about it, it'd have been included in our shipboard-life manual."

"So . . ."

"We need an encore, if you're up for it," Sandy said. "Maybe like, mm, a couple hundred encores."

"I'm definitely up for it, but we've got to be careful after what happened with the orgy group."

"We're not an orgy group," Sandy said.

"Still . . ."

"Gotcha. And you're right. Discretion. Nobody says nothin' about nothin'."

"I . . ." she began, then stopped.

"What?"

"I kind of want to tell you about something that involves you and Fiorella."

"Don't," Sandy said. He pressed a finger to her lips, happy that she couldn't see his face in the dark. The Hump Pool was up to a hundred and ninety thousand. "I don't want to hear her name again. Not from you."

"Well . . ."

"Please. Promise."

"Okay. Her name shall never pass my lips again."

"Excellent," Sandy said. "Now, I sneak out and creep down to the Commons, like I was up early, on my way to breakfast."

"Kiss me again."

Sandy arrived at the Commons two minutes later. There were few people in the room, and he got a tray, some heart-healthy cereal that tasted like cardboard, and some heart-healthy reconstituted simulated free-range chicken eggs, scrambled, that tasted like yellow stuff with salt on it, and looked around.

Crow was sitting by himself, as he usually was, but squinting in Sandy's direction. Sandy carried his tray over, put it on the table, and said, "How's it goin', big guy?"

Crow looked at Sandy's fresh, pink, relaxed face for another moment, then said, unconsciously mimicking the executive officer, "Ah, Jesus."

31.

Sixty-eight days after launch, five hundred million kilometers from Earth, and three hundred seventy million kilometers from the sun, Fang-Castro was methodically paging through her morning reports—boring morning reports—when her door pinged.

She had no appointments scheduled. On the other hand, the new open-door policy, instituted after the orgy fight, was her idea. "Come in," she said.

Crow stepped into the room carrying a slate. "Apologies for the interruption." He lifted the slate. "Vintner's calling. The President wants to chat. Now. With both of us."

"Bad news?"

"That's usually the case when they surprise me," Crow said. "Another alien coming in? I don't know."

"Let's get it over with."

"I'll set up the channel and secure the room." The presidential seal on Crow's slate display was replaced by a rapidly changing diagram, mostly in green, with orange highlights.

Fang-Castro's lips turned up at the corners, amused by his intensity. "You think my office might be bugged?"

Crow's eyes flicked up to hers, then back to the display. "Of course it is. I'm making sure that nobody else has bugged it."

Fang-Castro's slight smile disappeared.

"All right, we're ready at this end. Now we wait," Crow said. Earth was half a billion kilometers away. It would take most of an hour for Crow's go-ahead to reach the Oval Office and for them to respond. "I'll be in the Commons."

"I presume you have business to keep you occupied?" Fang-Castro said. "You're welcome to stay here, if you wish."

Crow nodded. "Thank you. I will, it's quieter than the Commons, and not as lonesome as my quarters." Fang-Castro poured herself another cup of tea, and poured one for Crow. She pushed it across her desk. "Indulge yourself, Mr. Crow. It's an especially good vintage."

The dark-eyed man looked up, came to some kind of decision, and leaned forward and picked up the delicate china cup. He sniffed, slurped, and held the brew for a moment in his mouth. Fang-Castro almost believed there was a momentary look of pleasure on his thin face.

"Very good," he said. "Yes, very, very good. Thank you." He returned his attention to his slate, cradling the cup in one hand.

They worked in an almost comfortable silence for an hour. The encrypted signal from the Oval Office was picked up by the ship, routed to Crow's slate, decrypted, and sent to Fang-Castro's office screen, and only to her office screen. Vintner was in the foreground of the vid image, with Santeros and DARPA director Lossness in the background.

"Good morning, Captain Fang-Castro, Mr. Crow," said the President's science adviser. "Not good news, I'm afraid. The Chinese did another midcourse correction burn, but this one was considerably longer than we expected or even knew that they were capable of. They've picked up three kilometers per second. JPL says it's advanced their Saturn ETA by over three weeks. They're now expected to arrive at Saturn near the first of April."

Lossness loomed on the screen. "The deep space network indicates that they also jettisoned some material or sections of their ship both before and after the burn. We don't know if this was planned from the beginning or is some sort of contingency plan, or if it's an act of desperation. If they had that much additional reaction mass in their original burn budget, we'd have expected them to use it on launch. It would've bought them a lot more time."

Vintner took over again. "We believe it's probably some combination of all those motives. Likely they jettisoned as much mass as they could before the burn to lighten the ship and take best advantage of the thrust, and then they threw away some extra tankage afterwards. Our guess is that they've burned into the reaction mass they need to decelerate. They need to drastically reduce their dead weight if they're going to have enough delta-vee to achieve Saturn rendezvous.

"We've developed several possible scenarios. The first is simply as described. In that case, they're going to be hampered on their return to Earth. They'll have less dry weight, but probably considerably less reaction mass, what with the jettisoned tankage. In that contingency, they've decided the crew can live with a several-year return trip, or they're planning a rescue mission to meet the returning spacecraft.

"The second possibility is that the *Celestial Odyssey* is an intentionally staged vehicle, and the return spacecraft was always planned to be much smaller than the outbound one. That seems unlikely, given the advanced state of construction on their ship when they decided to convert it from a Mars transport to a Saturn mission, but it's possible.

"A third possibility is that this was planned as a one-way mission from the beginning, that the Chinese didn't think they had enough time to prepare a round-trip ship. The Chinese are now well along on construction of their second Mars transport. Maybe it was also repurposed, as a follow-up mission to bring back whatever the first ship found."

Santeros barely moved a hand, but all attention turned to her. "There is an additional possibility that most concerns me and should concern both of you. The Chinese may have no contingency return plan, and they are now on what amounts to a one-way run. In that case, they may be planning on the kindness and generosity of the U.S. for a lift home." Santeros smiled without humor. "Or they may attempt to commandeer the *Nixon*. You obviously need to keep all of this in mind. I would like your reaction to all of the possibilities that we've mentioned, in the next day or two, and any other possibilities that occur to you. We won't need a back-and-forth discussion like this one—just send your reactions along, and we'll look at them when they get here."

Vintner closed. "Even with all that's happened, you're still scheduled to beat the Chinese to Saturn by over two months. Short of getting Reactor 2 back online"—the science adviser looked questioningly hopeful—"we don't think this affects your outbound mission plans. We thought it important that you know as soon as possible. We'll keep this channel live for the next two hours, in case you need to get back to us with any questions or observations. Over to you."

The view of the Oval Office was replaced by the presidential seal and the word "Suspended."

Fang-Castro turned in her chair and said, "Stay, Mr. Crow, while I get Dr. Johansson." Fang-Castro called the engineer and said, "Becca, I'd appreciate it if you could come to my office at your earliest possible convenience."

Becca and Sandy were having lunch in the Commons. The past month got to the Awkward-Couple-Having-Frank-Conversations phase. Becca saw an opening and went for it. "Sandy, why did you hit on me? No BS."

Sandy looked embarrassed. "Well, honestly? Because you're cute . . ."

"That can't be the only reason."

"And because I liked you and you seemed to like me, and because I was pretty sure you'd say yes. And . . . you talked to me like I was a real person and not a wad of money."

"That I'd say yes?" Becca rolled her eyes. "Boy, do you have any idea what comes out of your mouth? Really?"

"I knew you'd jump on that, which isn't fair—"

"What?" Her implant pinged her. The message from the captain on her subcutaneous earplug saved Sandy from hearing exactly what Becca's reply would have been. She swallowed her words, along with the last of a sandwich. "That's the captain. Gotta go."

"Think about being fair," Sandy said.

"Fair? Oh, later."

On her way to Fang-Castro's office, Becca thought about the pros and cons of their relationship.

Plus points: the sex was fabulous and shipboard duties were actually giving her time to address the urge. The boy was easy to talk to. He respected what she did, and didn't think he was more important than her job. And he was interested in repeat performances. Big, big plus.

Minus points: *he can be an amazing ass, when he tries. Even when he doesn't try.*

Which, she sighed, was pretty much what she'd been told in advance, so it wasn't like she could feign surprise to herself.

And back to the plus point: so many repeat performances!

Conclusion? What the hell, she didn't really have any more reason to kick him out of bed now than she'd had to not get in bed with him in the first place. So far, the sex and company were definitely worth the aggravation.

But what was that thing about being fair?

Was he suggesting that she was unfair?

He'd plainly said . . .

Fang-Castro's door pinged. "Come in."

Becca stepped through, where she found Fang-Castro and Crow sitting together.

"What's wrong?" She scowled. "The ship's fine."

Fang-Castro held up a placating hand. "Easy, Becca. Mr. Crow and I just received some unfortunate news from Jacob Vintner. It seems the Chinese ship did an unexpected midcourse burn that's advanced their arrival time at Saturn by more than three weeks. That still gives us a two-month lead over them, but it's making the President a little nervous. We're wondering how your investigations are going . . . about squeezing more performance out of the engines?"

"Huh." Fang-Castro caught a mutter, something about "armchair, backseat-driving politicians." Becca took a chair, and looked up at the ceiling for a moment, ran through the possibilities. "We've got more simulations to run. We've already decided that we don't want to kick up our acceleration burn. This late in the trip, it wouldn't buy us much time, anyway. But we're thinking we might be able to squeeze out more deceleration after turnaround. If we can stay at maximum velocity longer, that'll shave off some time. I'll tell the guys we're gonna do it and run the numbers tonight."

When Becca had gone, Crow said, "Were you aware that Johansson is involved in a sexual relationship with Darlington?"

"Yes. They seem to be conducting themselves with some discretion, so it's fine with me. I understand it's had a pretty powerful negative effect on the Hump Pool."

"So you're also aware of the Hump Pool."

"Part of the job description, Mr. Crow. I have not bet on it, of course. People believe that I have . . . mmm . . . monitoring sources which they might not have."

"They think I do, too. I've been informally approached to monitor the situation, vis-à-vis Fiorella. I refused."

"If that pool hits a half million . . ."

"It'll take off. I gotta say, if that goddamn Darlington's taken an interest in Fiorella, as well as Johansson . . . it'd be a shame if that blew up, if our movie star beat the shit out of our chief engineer."

"I think I might bet on the engineer, in that case," Fang-Castro said.

"You'd lose," Crow said. "Check Fiorella's in-depth dossier sometime. She was running a street gang in Bakersfield when she was twelve. But I'm not too worried. I don't think anybody's going to attack anybody, not over Darlington. As for the Hump Pool, there might be some trouble there, if it gets big enough. I'll keep an eye on it."

"Do that—and keep me informed."

32.

With the asteroid belt coming up, Joe Martinez began running a plaster-and-paint school. The trainees included both Sandy and Becca, since both were adept with the eggs—Sandy from his journalistic and documentary excursions, and Becca from her occasional trips out to the radiators, which she insisted on inspecting in person.

Plaster-and-paint involved repair of collision damage, an ongoing issue for the *Nixon*. Most of the repair work was done by his own maintenance crews, but he trained extras in case there should be a substantial, but non-fatal, hit, which would require large crews both inside and outside.

The *Nixon* was traveling a hundred times faster than a high-speed bullet. A millimeter grain of interplanetary sand packed the same wallop as a rifle slug when it hit the ship at a hundred and forty kilometers per second.

The ship was covered with microseismometer sensors. They dutifully picked up the small but sharp impulses of sand strikes and relayed the information to the maintenance computers, which pinpointed the spot on the ship where the hit had taken place. The *Nixon* averaged about one hit a week, which wasn't a lot, considering the distance they covered in that time. Each hit was shortly followed by a visit from a service egg. The divot got filled with structural composite putty and epoxy overcoat. The entire EVA took less than an hour.

"The thing about interplanetary space, as you all should know by now, is that it's astonishingly empty," Martinez told the crew. "The asteroid belt is only a little less astonishingly empty—I'm thinking we might get one hit a day out there, maybe two dozen total for the transit. None of them, I hope, will be larger than the ones we've already seen. The odds of a hit inconveniencing the power plant or heat radiating system are really, really small."

Becca jumped in: "The odds are small, but just in case, we need to go through the protocols for dealing with the strike in those areas. I've got a lot of stuff to tell you, but mostly it boils down to this: if we take a critical hit on the engine or the radiators, you call Engineering and you wait for specific instructions. You don't go off on your own or I honest-to-God will murder you. Is that clear to everybody?"

Everybody nodded.

"What happens, er, if the hit's bigger than a grain of sand?" asked one of the trainees who hadn't read the handout.

"That's why we're training you extras," Martinez said, "because if that happens, it's gonna be a major clusterfuck. How major, depends on where it hits. The real problem of the asteroid belt is not only are the sand-sized hits more common—we can handle those—but we've also got some bigger rocks out there. There are a hundred times fewer one-centimeter rocks out there than millimeter ones, so there's a better than even chance we'll never encounter one, on the whole trip. Even in the asteroid belt. That's a good thing, because an impact with a centimeter-sized rock would have the explosive force of several kilos of high explosive. Containing something like that would be a struggle—that's why we have the nose and tail cones."

"What about ten-centimeter rocks?" asked the same trainee.

"That could be a total disaster, again, depending on where it hit."

"We couldn't dodge it?"

"No. We cover more than a hundred thousand kilometers every fifteen minutes—a third of the distance from the earth to the moon. We simply can't track rocks that size, that far out. The good news is, the chances of hitting something that big are far less than one percent. Far less."

"Be like losing the lottery," Sandy said.

Martinez scratched his chin: "Interesting concept—losing a lottery. I've never heard of such a thing."

After they finished the inside class, they went outside in the eggs, to practice the plaster-and-paint on simulated hits. They were being monitored by Crow, who monitored all EVAs. The entire interior of the ship was covered by vid monitors, and the vid was cached for later viewing, if necessary. The exterior was of more immediate concern; Crow worried that if somebody were to sabotage the ship again, the attack well might come there and so real-time surveillance was in order.

He listened to the eggs going out, watched them by tapping into Martinez's vid feed, then tapped into the private comm channel between Darlington and Johansson, and listened for a while.

One of his surveillance computers automatically monitored all shipboard communications, and a relational app alerted him to problematical talk and provided a written transcript—but those were just the words. They didn't catch tone and the unvoiced emotions that directed it; there was no substitute for the occasional direct audio surveillance.

Crow was a bit surprised those two had fallen into bed. Not that he hadn't expected Darlington to make a move at some point; really, the only question was how soon. Johansson, on the other hand . . . he'd have guessed she was too wrapped up with her work—obsessed might be more accurate—to consider any distracting personal involvements. The boredom of interplanetary flight was a bigger factor than he'd realized.

He would have to remember that if he ever found himself in this kind of insane situation again. Not that he was planning to.

Their conversation was work-related discussion interspersed with personal chat. It had taken nearly three weeks for the honeymoon period to wear off, and since then they'd slipped into mismatched couple behavior.

He was sure they'd deny the couple part. The mismatch, no one could deny. They squabbled. It was none of that "opposites attract" nonsense; they were just different. Johansson's single-minded, utterly dedicated work focus didn't stay at work; it carried over to her approach to her entire life. She behaved as if everything in her existence was a chore, and she liked the chores.

Right now the squabble was essentially territorial, although Darlington didn't seem to realize that. Playing in Johansson's quarters meant they were playing by her rules. She'd defined the scope of the relationship from the very beginning. Keeping physical matters on her turf reinforced that authority. Served Darlington right. He so took it for granted that he called the shots in these sexual liaisons that he couldn't wrap his head around why this one was discomforting him so. He'd made the first pass, but then she'd grabbed the ball and called the plays after that.

But . . . something else came through the squabbling, something the computers and transcripts wouldn't flag. After listening for ten minutes, he thought, *Damnit. They're falling in love.*

That could be bad both ways.

He considered Darlington to be one of his troops. Troops were always better when unencumbered by attachments, especially attachments to critical personnel. There might even be more complicated sexual arrangements, he worried, that could turn into bitterness and strife. For example, what was going on between Darlington and Fiorella? Did Johansson know about it? Was there anything to know?

Darlington was his ace in the hole, but he wasn't a very stable ace. So far the relationship seemed to be working for Johansson and Darlington, but if, or more likely when, it went south . . .

He figured Johansson was far less likely to fall apart. She had fuckin' balls. Except . . . she counted for a lot more.

It was a classic risk vs. threat. More likely that Darlington would melt down, but all they'd lose would be a card he might never have to play and a cameraman. More likely Johansson would keep it together, but if she didn't, there went the ship's most important crew member.

"I got a fuckin' soap opera," he said aloud. "We got three hundred contingency plans, and not a single one for a fuckin' soap opera."

33.

The *Nixon* was ninety-three days out, eight hundred and ten million kilometers from Earth, six hundred and twenty million from Saturn, and on the far side of the asteroid belt. Becca rode a transport cart down the axle to the service egg bay, sucking on the morning's third bulb of coffee as she went. The day before, the *Nixon* had reached the point where it would stop accelerating outward from the sun, turn tail-forward, and begin the three-month process of decelerating into Saturn.

Becca had spent the day supervising the first controlled shutdown of the *Nixon*'s propulsion system since they'd left Earth's orbit. Shutting down was less dangerous than start-up, but not a whole lot less tricky. Strictly speaking, it was unnecessary. The thrust of the four VASIMRs was low enough that firing broadside for a few hours would hardly affect their trajectory. But the techies running the simulations were antsy about those sail ribbons running at full velocity. The sims said they'd be fine in a rotating reference frame, but better to err on the side of caution and slow that molten metal down as much as they could.

Engineering had to ramp down the output of the reactor, turbines, and generators while shutting down the VASIMR engines and slowly winding down the radiator system. Not too fast or the system would overheat; not too slowly or the heat exchangers would freeze up.

The shutdown wasn't complete. Becca didn't want to restart the radiator system from scratch; cold starts were always rough. Happily, there was no need to. The reactors could churn out power indefinitely, and she'd had them wound down to the point where they'd be supporting the radiators at minimum output. She could bypass the main turbines and generators entirely, run the auxiliary power system—more than enough to maintain ship's power and the heater and control systems for the heat exchangers and radiators—and toss in a bit extra to give the molten metal ribbons something to do as they cycled from nozzle to collection boom and back down into the heat exchangers.

The process wasn't all that difficult and they'd practiced it in Earth orbit. This wasn't for practice, though, and there were no rescue ships if something went wrong.

It all went smoothly, though, and the *Nixon* went into free fall.

At that point, the attitude thrusters went to work, a complex and delicate orchestration of impulses that slowly rotated the entire structure—booms, struts, axles, and modules—a hundred and eighty degrees, so the engines were pointing away from the sun, and what had been the forward part of the ship was now facing back the way they came.

The crew wasn't overly worried about impacts on the engines. Their cross-section was small, and they were now well clear of the asteroid belt; in fact they were approaching Jupiter's orbit. Jupiter, fortunately, was far away. Becca didn't have to be concerned with the Jovian gravity well or the massive radiation belts. Even Jupiter's leading and trailing Trojan asteroids were far off: their orbit simply made for a mental benchmark.

The next one would be the rendezvous with Saturn.

On this day, she and her crew would bring the engines back online, essentially, shutdown in reverse. Again, as they'd practiced so many times in Earth orbit, it would be a slow and coordinated ramping up of reactors, turbines, generators, engines, while bringing the radiator system up to full speed.

If everything went as planned, they'd be at Saturn in a little over three months. Things had been going smoothly since the shutdown of Reactor 2. Both the flyby of the sun and the transit of the asteroid belt had been as uneventful as statistics had predicted, given good engineering.

The shutdown of Reactor 2 still nagged at her. If she'd been able to keep both reactors up and running, they'd be looking at a Saturn arrival in a little over a month and a half, instead of three months away. They weren't in any danger of losing the race to the Chinese—they'd already made up for the nine-month launch lead the *Celestial Odyssey* had, which was now only a little farther from the sun than the *Nixon*. The Chinese ship was coasting along at less than twenty kilometers per second, even after its unexpected midcourse boost. The *Nixon* was speeding away from the sun at more than a hundred and seventy kilometers per second. They'd get to Saturn with months to spare.

But still . . . Reactor 2 nagged.

As the cart approached the service egg bay, her mind turned back to the day's itinerary. This was perhaps the most critical point in the ship's journey; now they had to start decelerating or they were all on a one-way trip to some not-very-nearby star. Ironically, the loss of Reactor 2 actually made her job easier. They only had half as much power to manage and they still had close to full capacity on the radiators, so nothing there was being pushed to its limits.

Doing it right required paying attention to detail, but it was the kind of power plant operations work that made her the most comfortable— the boring kind. Take it up five percent. Check all the settings. Double-check the settings. Take it up another five percent. Check the settings. Double-check the settings. Rinse and repeat until done.

She didn't even need to be in the engine room for this one, so she was going to be keeping an eye on the performance of the radiators from outside. Sometimes you picked up on stuff just watching the equipment run that you didn't get from the instrument readings. Sandy would accompany her so she could get a hard copy record of whatever she saw and take advantage of his multispectral cameras and extensive range of optics. Whatever she found worth recording he'd capture six ways to Sunday, and she'd review it at her leisure.

When she arrived at the service bay, Sandy had finished loading his camera gear into his egg and was chatting with Joe Martinez. Martinez had his slate plugged into Sandy's egg, checking out all the relevant preflight specs.

"Morning, Joe," she said, as the transport stopped and she pushed herself off, got her feet stuck to the floor.

"Becca . . . already checked you out, you're good." He touched his slate and said to Sandy, "And you're good, too."

"I already knew that, having done exactly what you just did," Sandy said.

Martinez shut down his slate and said, "Two heads are better than one, especially . . . I say, especially . . . when one of them is yours. That problem doesn't come up with Becca, of course."

Becca yawned: "I gotta pee before I go out."

Sandy: "You haven't already?"

"Yeah, but I had two more bulbs of coffee since then and I could really use another." She handed Sandy a sack: "Peanut butter sandwiches and a bag of cookies. We might be out for a while."

"Hmm. Junk food. My body is my temple. Do I want to stick sugar and fat into it?"

"You might, if we have a problem, and wind up being outside for five or six hours."

"Good point." He stuck the sack in a plastic box next to the egg's pilot seat.

Becca yawned again and said, "You guys are playing tonight, right?"

"Seven o'clock. We've got three new covers of Eye-Shine songs, so you'll probably want to be there."

"I can hardly wait." She wandered off to the restroom and was back three minutes later. "Let's get out there and get it done. Wendy's ready to push the button. Sandy, you got the macro on?"

"I do."

"Let's go, then."

"Have fun, you kids," Martinez said. "Don't stay out too late."

The next two hours were carefully choreographed, a virtual textbook exercise, and thoroughly documented. It wasn't as bad as the cold starts had been in Earth orbit. The radiator ribbons were still moving, the reactors were simmering along at ten percent output, and the heat exchangers and sodium boilers were primed and simmering, like a stove set on very low.

Becca was in frequent contact with Greenberg as they worked through it, and she and Sandy cruised the radiator mechanicals as they worked toward full speed. Becca pointed Sandy at a couple of items she'd wanted documented: the exact way the edge of the molten ribbon flowed from the outer end of the slot nozzle, some details of how the ribbons got collected and shunted down the masts.

It was dim out there: the sun was still the sun, but drastically shrunken: pea-sized.

There was no planetary light to fill in the shadows. Jupiter was nowhere close, and Saturn was still a long way out—although they'd been past the orbit of Mars and through the asteroid belt, and were approaching the orbit of Jupiter, the planets were nothing like evenly spaced: Saturn was twice as far from Earth as Jupiter.

Sandy finished another scan of the slot nozzle and asked, "Now what?"

"Let's just back off for a while—probably ought to go back in, but let's give it another hour."

"All right."

"How come Fiorella's not out here?"

"After the turnover operation, we had about as much as we needed for her show. She talked to Wendy about what she'd see today—Wendy said there wouldn't be much—so she's trying to scrape some kind of feature story out of the garden guys."

"That ought to be exciting. I hear they thought they had an aphid last week."

"Turned out not to be true. It was a flake of the dry fertilizer they use."

Becca laughed and said, "And you ran right over to cover the nonexistent aphid?"

"Hey, it coulda been a big story."

Becca made sure they were on a private channel. "Can I get serious for a moment?"

"Yeah?"

She could hear a little resignation in that drawn-out word. "I'm feeling like we need to talk about what's going on between the two of us. And I'm going to need you to talk back for a change. Please?"

"Oh, Jesus . . ."

"We've been keeping company, as my folks would put it, for two months now, and I'm still not sure how deep I'm in. For me, that's a long relationship."

"I guess it is for me, too," Sandy acknowledged.

"You think I don't know that? I knew that about you the day after we first met. The other women on the team made sure I knew about you. You think you don't have a reputation that precedes you?"

"Ummm, I don't think about it."

Becca sighed. *Guys!* "I'm sorry. That's not really what I wanted to talk about and I'm not trying to put you on the defensive. It's just . . ."

Becca took a deep breath. *I'm finally getting to the point,* she thought.

"It's not that I don't like it, it's just I don't exactly know what that is. I'm not sure there's a future."

"If this is about us breaking up . . ."

"What? No! No, no, no! I mean, I'm really enjoying this. Whatever it is."

Deep breaths, just breathe, she thought. *Damn, I hate Talks.*

Engineering pinged.

"Hold on," Becca said, "Wendy's calling. Back to you in a minute."

Becca opened the two-way comm to Engineering. "How's it going, guys? I'm seeing temperature fluctuations in Exchanger 1. Anything I need to worry about?"

Greenberg came back: "Becca, it doesn't look like much from here. We're getting a few hiccups in a couple of the heater coils. Minor current spikes. We'll stamp 'em out."

"Okay, Wendy, but sooner rather than later, okay? Turnaround's enough work without distractions. Let's kill this one, pronto."

"Sure thing, boss. I'll ramp up the damping algorithms another notch. That oughta do it."

"Good. Stay on top of it."

Becca switched two-way back to Sandy. "Hey, you listen in on that?"

"Yeah, what's up?"

"Not much, some rattles in the gears. Do me a favor, though, feed me an external shot of Slot Nozzle 1, the outboard half? IR, false color mapping, like you did back when we were doing the Earth-orbit tests? Can you do that?"

Sandy was a few hundred meters away: "No problem, I've had an IR camera running. Just let me switch to wide-angle"—there was a pause— "Okay, should be getting the IR feed on screen four"—another pause— "Okay, I just kicked in the color thermal map post-process on the vid. You seeing that?"

"Yeah, it's good. I'm copying Engineering in on this." Becca opened a conference channel back to Engineering. "Wendy, I'm feeding you Darlington's IR view of Nozzle 1. See that hot spot between Plates 87 and 91, about seventy percent out from the mast? I think that's where the fluctuations originate. Try dialing back the heaters around there."

"I agree. We've already been focusing on that section," Greenberg said. "We'll sweat the small stuff, doncha worry." Wendy clicked off.

Becca switched back to the private link with Sandy.

"What was I saying? Oh yeah. I'm liking this. A whole lot. I think you are, too. You're sticking around, anyway. It's just that . . . when we get back, I expect I'm gonna go home to Minnesota and you'll be going back to Pasadena. That whole shipboard romance thing, and that'll be it.

"I'm really not sure I want that to be it. I'm still working on it. But I'd really like to know how you feel about this . . . 'thing' . . . between the two of us. You ever thought about moving to Minnesota? Okay, not much to surfing there, but at least we're not topping fifty degrees in the summer." Becca took a deep breath. "Okay. That's your cue. I'm done. You've got the floor."

Sandy was silent.

"Sandy? What's on your mind?"

"Well, I hadn't thought that far ahead."

"Well, maybe it's time!" Becca blurted exasperatedly. Damn, this mattered. She was surprised by that.

Another ping: "Wait one, Wendy's pinging me again." Becca went back to the engineering channel.

"What's up?"

"We sent a power-back command, but Heater 1-89's still pumping out full heat. What do you rec—"

34.

And then the engineering operation stopped being routine, and turned into a nightmare, a train wreck. Everything happened in a fraction of a second, but Sandy's combat-trained brain played it out in slow motion, so he wouldn't miss any of the uglier details.

The radiator boom-wall ruptured right next to the hot spot his IR camera had highlighted. Molten radiator metal poured out of the breach, a surreal liquid explosion of silvery blobs moving at different speeds. One droplet of spray, traveling at over one hundred kilometers per second, pinged on the large front port. He instinctively recoiled—sniper! Then his explosion reflexes kicked in. Look for bricks coming down.

He leaned on the joystick, realizing in the first second that he would be hit. The bigger blobs moved more slowly, like oncoming cars, but there was no hole in the spray he could duck into. He couldn't move the egg fast enough to avoid all of the molten metal. A major hit on that big Leica-glass window would be very bad. He needed to rotate the pod to get the window out of the line of fire. The egg's least sensitive equipment was located in the bottom, where the heavy mechanicals were, and Martinez had given him the good training. He started spinning the egg so the bottom would take the impact.

He didn't quite make it, but it was good enough. The impact came a second later, on the corner of the utility cradle, below his seat. It felt like the rubbery impacts of a bumper car at a carnival, but a *lot* harder, but that was okay, because it came through his butt. If he'd taken it on the face, even if the window had held, which was doubtful, he'd be looking at a fractured vertebra.

Then the electronics started screeching at him, and the life-support indicators went to a screaming yellow. And though he was upside down to Becca, he saw a barrel-sized slug of molten metal slam into her egg at head-on-auto-collision speed.

No sound, other than his own electronic warnings: he was locked on Becca's channel but heard not a word or a scream, the vid was down, nothing but the sight of the egg getting hit, and the egg flying off, tumbling, at ten, twenty, thirty meters per second. He wasn't sure. His own egg was rotating, and she'd passed out of his field of view.

"Becca's hit, oh fuck oh fuck, Becca's hit, I'm going that way, I'm going that way . . ." He slammed over the joystick.

Nothing happened.

He slammed it again.

Nothing happened.

Martinez: "I'm coming, I'm coming . . ."

Sandy called Becca once, twice, three times, got nothing back.

One of the techs called from the egg base: "Sandy, your egg's screwed. Stay off the electronics . . . stay off the electronics . . ."

"Becca's hit, you gotta—"

His microphone shut down—Martinez could do that from his command egg—and Martinez said, "Shut up and listen. I'm in my egg, but it's gonna take a couple minutes to get out there. The data feeds say you've got a fire in the R-Box, you've got to pull the flush ring for R. Can you pull the ring?"

The emergency panel was overhead and Sandy swatted the cover away, saw the red flush ring for R, and pulled it.

"R ring pulled. Joe, you gotta move. She was hit hard. Jesus, she was hit, I can't see her, my maneuvering gear is all red—"

"Sandy, I'm losing your data feeds, I don't know if it's the fire, I think that's gone but it's possible the metal is still hot and is reigniting, but the feeds are going down one by one."

"What about Becca? You gotta get going . . . you gotta go—"

"Do you have a status on your air?"

"No, not anymore. I'm dead in the water, man, all the vids are going out, they went yellow and then red and now they're going out. The LEDs are still powered, but they're going to red, too, I'm not gonna be any help."

"Listen. Did you take that bag of cookies with you?"

"What? What? Cookies . . ."

"Listen to me, man. The cookies. Did you eat the cookies?"

"What the fuck are you talking about, Joe? Are you out—"

Martinez's voice was cool, but sharp: "Sandy, this is important. Did you eat those cookies?"

"No, no . . . I . . ."

"Look at the bag. Is the bag normal, or is it all puffed up? Is it fat?"

Sandy looked at the lunch box—the container where they kept the food, picked up the bag of cookies. It looked like somebody had been pumping air into it.

"It's fat. It's like a ball."

"Goddamnit. You're leaking air, your pressure is dropping. Hold real still, spit a little, just easy, small drops of spit . . . see which way the spit drops drift . . ."

"Tell me about Becca . . ."

"Becca's a separate problem and we're working on it," Martinez said. "We've also got to work on your problem. Spit."

Sandy spit, and the tiny drops of saliva hovered in front of his face for a second, then another, and then they began drifting down to his right. As he did that, he heard Martinez shouting over the open link, "Elroy! Elroy! Call Butler and see what the situation is with the other eggs," and "Sandy, what happened with the spit?"

"They're drifting down to my right, not outward . . . it's not centrifugal force . . . they're going down behind the seat, I can't see . . . Joe, I think if there's a crack, it's probably in the bottom of the interior shell. I can't reach it."

"Shit. You smell anything?"

"No, I—"

Sandy's microphone went dead, and so did the sound feed coming in; a new red LED light began blinking up and to his left. Now he really was dead in the water, and not only that, he was isolated from the others.

He couldn't see the ship itself, but he could see one section of the radiators, which seemed to be moving along in a smooth flow. It had been the other one where the problem occurred, he thought.

The interior lights flickered, and another LED popped up: the lights had gone to emergency battery power, and the emergency batteries were in the ceiling, away from the impact zone. He should have light.

Anything he could do to help himself? Nothing came to mind. He looked up at the emergency box, and a half-dozen additional flush rings. Couldn't hurt to pull them, he thought: they were basically fire extinguishers, mechanically operated, and the egg was dead, anyway. He pulled them all, one at a time.

His egg continued its slow tumble, the ship was now below his feet. Then he picked up Becca's egg. He almost missed it: it looked like a large dim star, and he wouldn't have noticed it at all except that it was moving. Maybe three or four kilometers away, he thought, though he didn't know for sure.

Nothing, nobody was going after it.

He screamed at it: "Becca! Becca!"

35.

Captain Fang-Castro sucked thoughtfully on her second bulb of pouchong of this watch. The delicate tea soothed her nerves and gave her something to do with her hands. Bridge watch was uneventful on the *Nixon*, and thank God for that. Still, it meant the officer of the watch mostly had little to do but sit in the big chair and look, well, watchful.

Fang-Castro liked to keep busy. Doing nothing, even watchfully, made her fidgety, and a fidgety commander was not good for morale. Consequently, tea was usually in hand.

The crew was excited about midcourse turnaround. It was the first tangible evidence of progress since they'd completed their slingshot pass of the sun, and it meant they were more than halfway to Saturn.

They were two and a half hours into restart and the engines were up to three-quarters thrust. Fang-Castro was finishing her tea when the faintest of shudders rippled through the bridge.

"Nav, what was that!" she snapped. "Comm, give me Engineering and patch Mr. Martinez in."

Navigation came back instantly: "Command: we experienced a lateral impulse, ship's aft. It turned us slightly off course. Attitude control is bringing us back on heading." A second later, "Our acceleration is dropping rapidly. It looks like the engines are shutting down."

"An impact?"

"Don't know, ma'am, we're inquiring."

Frank LaFarge, who was on engineering watch, spoke up. "I'm not seeing damage indicators commensurate with an impact big enough to shift our heading."

Comm spoke up: "Engineering's on."

"Dr. Johansson, what just happened?" Fang-Castro kept her voice calm and level, belying her twitching gut.

"Captain, Greenberg here. Becca's on EVA, observing the radiator ramp-up. We've lost contact with her. Radiator Boom 1 experienced a blowout. We don't know how serious it is, but we're hemorrhaging radiator melt. I've initiated rapid shutdown and containment procedures on the damage."

"Are we in any immediate danger, Dr. Greenberg?"

"I don't believe so, Captain."

Nav came back: "Command, we're accessing the fore cameras, we'll have them up in a few seconds."

Comm: "We have Mr. Martinez on—"

Fang-Castro: "Nav, hold the pictures. Comm, show me Joe: Joe, what happened?"

"I'm really busy right now, ma'am, so I gotta be short." Martinez was buckled into his egg. "We blew a radiator, looks like, some of the melt hit Becca's and Sandy's eggs. Sandy's damaged but I think recoverable if I can get out there, but my best bet now is that Becca's gone."

"Gone? You mean . . ."

"Dead. The monitoring vid showed her getting hit by a wad of metal the size of a chair. Hit hard, head-on. The shell's intact . . . maybe . . . but the cradle, power system, propulsion, they're trashed. Her egg's been hurled away from us. I gotta go, I gotta go, if I can get the goddamn garage door open, I gotta go . . ." Fang-Casto heard him shouting at somebody, "Get off the line: get off the fuckin' line, get off the fuckin' line and get me out there . . ."

Fang-Castro: "Keep me informed when you can, Joe."

"Yeah, I will, ma'am. Sandy's losing power, we're losing his data feeds, get me out there, you motherfuckers, I don't care about that, use the crank, use the fuckin' crank if you have to and get into suits. I'll bring Sandy back into Bay 12."

The captain went back to Comm: "Get me the command link to Dr. Johansson's service egg."

Two seconds passed. "Now, Comm."

"I'm trying, Captain, but I'm not getting a ping back."

"Pull up the last feed you have. Ten seconds' worth."

Two more seconds passed and the main screen lit up, showing the vid from the egg's internal safety monitor camera. For three seconds, it was just Dr. Johansson peering intently through the main port. Then sudden darkness on the port, interior lights coming up instantly and Dr. Johansson's head slamming into the inside of the port hard, very hard, and her head snapping back, as the vid feed dropped off-line.

Comm spoke, barely audibly. "After that we just have maybe three seconds of low-grade telemetry, but it's showing cascading failures, one subsystem after another. Environmental's out, atmosphere toxin levels skyrocketing, there's a breach somewhere, the egg is losing pressure fast. . . ." Her voice trailed off.

Shit. Double-shit, thought Fang-Castro. "Get me any of the other working channels. Try Mr. Darlington's egg."

"Trying all channels."

A moment later, she heard what sounded like breathing. "Mr. Darlington?"

"Yes. Yes. Jesus, who is this?"

"Fang-Castro. Are you injured?"

"No. Becca's been hit, hard. I can see her egg some of the time, I'm rotating, can't stop it, but she's way out there. You don't have much time. I think she's taken a lot of damage. I don't see anybody after her. You gotta get going—"

"We've got everything under way, Mr. Darlington. You hold on tight there. Joe, Mr. Martinez, is on the way out. . . . I don't see you on my screen."

"I don't see you, either. All the vid and all the audio channels seem to be out, except this one. I can't reach Becca. Joe oughta go after her, if he can. She's gonna need air, for sure, and probably power, her heater could be down."

"Mr. Martinez is coming up on you," Fang-Castro said. "Get ready for recovery. And I'll say again we're on top of the situation."

She clicked away and said, to Navigation, "Get the aft view on my screen."

The aft view came up.

"Spot Dr. Johansson's service egg."

That took a few seconds, but the camera finally locked on the egg and began zooming. There was nothing but empty space between the excellent lens and the egg, no heat ripples, no dust, no humidity, and when the camera got out to full zoom, and a further digital zoom was applied, they could see that the egg had been totally disabled. The metal slug that had hit it had taken out power, propulsion, comm. The shell looked intact, but it was splattered with now-frozen radiator metal. There was a crack in the view glass behind which Johansson had been sitting, visible between splashes of metal.

Somebody on the bridge said, "Oh, my God."

Fang-Castro said, "Comm. Get me Mr. Martinez if he'll take the call."

Martinez came up: "I'm closing on Sandy's egg."

"Yes. I can get him on the command channel, I've spoken to him. He knows you're about to do the recovery. Your assessment of the impact on Dr. Johansson's egg is correct. I'm afraid there's no prospect that Dr. Johansson has survived."

"Okay. Listen, Sandy can be a handful. If you'd get the people he talks to—Fiorella, Crow, and get Dr. Ang for sure—get them down to egg operations to meet him when he gets out of his egg. I don't know whether he's physically injured—"

"He says not."

"Okay, but his head's gonna be seriously messed up. I don't know if you're aware of his relationship with Dr. Johansson . . ."

"I am. And I will get you that help. Also, I'll have Comm patch my command channel into your egg so you can talk to him." She clicked off: "Comm: patch my command channel through to Mr. Martinez. Also, order Mr. Crow, Dr. Ang, and Ms. Fiorella to report to my quarters, immediately. If I'm not there when they arrive, I will be shortly."

She went to Engineering: "Dr. Greenberg? Where are we?"

"Off-line and shutting down. We're shutting down everything as fast as we safely can."

"Inform me if you start seeing more anomalies."

"Yes, ma'am. We need to talk to Becca as soon as she can get back online, this is a rather complicated situation."

"Do everything you can, Dr. Greenberg. Consider yourself in charge until I tell you otherwise."

"Oh, no . . . oh no."

Greenberg was no dummy.

With the situation stabilized, Fang-Castro turned the bridge over to the second officer, told him to get the off-watch executive officer up to the bridge as fast as he could be roused from his sleep time. "I will be in my quarters for a few minutes, but available at a second's notice. Comm, keep me active all the time. And get me Joe Martinez right now."

Martinez came in over her implants as she walked down to her quarters. "What's your status, Joe?"

"I'm grappling onto Sandy's egg. Man, the kid's got some reflexes: he flipped the egg over when the radiator blew and took most of the damage on the corner of the undercarriage. I'll have him back in half an hour. We're gonna have to take this slow, the whole hookup's pretty unstable. But I'm talking to him on the command channel and I think this is gonna work. He's leaking air, but he should have plenty to get him inside."

"Good. We'll see you there."

The second officer: "Ma'am, we're getting a flood of inquiries about the shudder that went through the ship."

Shit and double-shit. "Tell Comm to put me on the ship-wide."

"Comm: you're on, Captain."

Fang-Castro said, "Your attention, please. This is Captain Fang-Castro. We experienced a difficulty on engine restart. This was the shudder some of you may have felt. The ship is in no danger whatsoever. Please continue with your normal operations. Engineering is shutting down the engines while they analyze the difficulty, so the ship will be in free fall for a while longer. I'll inform you of our status further when we've fully evaluated the situation. Captain out."

Crow, Fiorella, and Ang were waiting at her cabin door. Crow asked for them all, "What just happened?"

"Come inside," Fang-Castro said.

She shut the door behind them. They all remained standing as she told them about the accident, and Fiorella buried her face in her hands and Ang said, "Oh my God."

Crow shook his head.

Fang-Castro: "I want you all to come with me down to the egg section, to meet Mr. Darlington. I suspect you're all aware of his relationship with Becca. We're not sure how he'll handle it. He's a young man . . ."

Crow put up a finger.

"Mr. Crow, you have something to tell us?"

"Sandy's not exactly what he appears to be, or rather, he is, but he's also quite a bit more. We've held it close, but he's actually one of my people. I expect all of you to hold this confidentially, but Sandy was an army officer in the Tri-Border fight, and not just an officer, but in a rather . . . extreme . . . or elite . . . outfit. He saw quite a few of his comrades killed. His friends. He suffers from post-traumatic stress syndrome, which accounts for his somewhat . . . lackadaisical . . . attitude. From which he has been recovering, as you may have noticed. He's been extremely effective in his job—in all his jobs. But: what this will do to him, I have no idea."

"I do," Ang said. "I will meet you down at the eggs. I need to run get my bag."

Fiorella was speechless. For almost the first time in her life.

Fang-Castro asked her, "Are you all right?"

"No. Yes. I mean . . ."

"I know what you mean. Let's get down there."

Martinez maneuvered Sandy's egg up to the garage, and two space-suited techs hooked up the egg and pulled it inside. The air lock was resealed, and the interior atmosphere checked for any toxic emissions from the egg. There were none; if there had been anything coming out, it had been harmlessly outgassed into space.

The lock was pressurized and the rear garage doors opened. Sandy

had no power in the egg and the techs didn't want to power it up, should
there be some problem, so they opened his access hatch with a hand
crank.

He was met by Fang-Castro and the others. Sandy eased out, looked
at their faces: "She's dead, isn't she?"

Fang-Castro said, "She was killed instantly."

"Are you going after her egg?"

"No," Fang-Castro said. "We need to concentrate our resources on
the crisis here. Going after her would present an unnecessary risk."

"Then don't do it," Sandy said. "Dead is dead. No point in throwing
good bodies after a dead one."

Ang muttered, "Oh, boy."

Sandy gave him a toothy grin: "Dr. Feelgood. I hope you know what
I need."

"I do. Where are you at?"

"About a five and going down. I was at a nine when the metal hit
the fan."

"Are you using any drugs?"

"Stims, from time to time. Not for several days."

"No street drugs?"

"No."

"Adrenal implants?"

"They've been pulled." Sandy looked at Crow. "You told them."

Crow nodded: "Had to."

Ang said, "Roll up your sleeve. I'm going to get you started."

Sandy nodded and smiled and pulled his sleeve up. Ang pushed the
pressure injector against his arm and said, "Here it comes."

Tears started running down Sandy's face and Fiorella put an arm
around his waist and said, "We'll walk you back," and Crow patted his
shoulder and said, "Captain Darlington. I just . . . I just . . ."

Sandy thought through the drugs, *So that's what Crow looks like
when he's sad . . .*

Later that evening, Sandy was lying on his bunk, watching an
incoming episode of *Celebrity Awards*, with Kilimanjaro Kossoff—

KayKay—in a stunning red half dress taking a golden trophy for her sponsorship of a massive troop of penguins being relocated in Antarctica, away from their particular melting ice shelf. "When I saw those birds . . . penguins are actually flightless birds, which a lot of people don't realize . . . when I saw those poor birds, I just knew in my heart . . ."

His door buzzed, and though he didn't feel like talking to anyone, he said, "Come in," and the door unlatched and Crow came through and tossed him a can of beer. He had another for himself, and dropped onto Sandy's chair.

"How you doing?"

"About as well as usual."

"I don't know quite what it's like—the drugs."

"It's like somebody removed a couple of cc's of your brain," Sandy said. "I don't feel much concern for anything, or anybody. I really don't. Ang will start pulling the drug levels down in a week or so, and if he does it right, I'll be all smoothed out by the time we reach Saturn. Crazier than a fuckin' bedbug, but smoothed out."

Crow stared at him for a minute, then said, "Really?"

Sandy popped the top off the beer: "Really. I'm surprised you haven't done this."

"I've lost a couple friends," Crow said. "But when we lost them, we didn't know it. We kept hoping. We only knew they were lost when they never came back. That takes the edge off. We're still kind of hoping, you know? Like maybe they bailed out and are living in Istanbul or something. The other time . . . You know I was married?"

Sandy smiled at him: "That seems uncharacteristically optimistic of you."

Crow hunched forward in his chair. "Yeah. She was the daughter of a Marine Corps general. A flier. In his spare time, he liked to go up in those little stunt jets, fuck around. He'd take her up with him—she liked it—and one day, something broke and he stuck the goddamn jet right into a goddamn mountain. The last thing he said before they hit was, 'I'm sorry.' He was talking to her."

"Ah, boy."

"Didn't do the drugs," Crow said. "I wanted to feel it. I think if anything like that ever happened again, I'd do the drugs."

"Which is why I'm sitting here watching this moronic vid with a smile on my face," Sandy said. "They got good drugs now, man. You're still all fucked up, but it doesn't hurt as much."

"Huh." Crow looked at the screen and asked, "You mind if I watch for a while?"

36.

Fang-Castro was entirely certain she was the unhappiest ship's captain in the universe, or maybe just the galaxy. The radiator blowout had been about as bad a disaster as one can have in space and still live to regret it.

The blowout had left the *Nixon* adrift, though it was still tearing along at over a hundred and seventy kilometers per second. They had no propulsion. The VASIMRs were cold and useless contraptions without the necessary gigawatts of power.

There was plenty of electricity from the auxiliary power plants to run all the onboard functions. Life support, computing, communications, none of those were in any danger. They could survive just fine, for a few years.

But they weren't decelerating and they should be. If that didn't change, they were on a one-way trip out of the solar system. A year would see them passing the orbit of Pluto. Two and they'd be through the Kuiper belt. A century would pass before the *Nixon* would reach the Oort cloud as a lifeless tomb carrying the corpses of ninety people who'd died long, long before. The stars were millennia beyond that.

But the aliens . . .

What kind of civilization had built something that could traverse those distances? She couldn't imagine. And why had they come, stopped at Saturn, and then left again? Even less fathomable. Her mission was supposed to bring back answers to those questions. Now she wasn't absolutely sure she'd be able to bring back her crew.

Fang-Castro looked around the table. Crow looked impassive, as usual. No, more like implacable. The man was not happy. She didn't blame him in the least. Bad enough having an accident that killed someone, bad enough for it to be their chief engineer. Bad enough that it left them adrift, at least temporarily, without propulsion.

Worse that it was Becca Johansson. Fang-Castro had come to genuinely like her. Totally different cultures, totally different upbringings, but they'd both grown up to take no nonsense from anybody, to follow the facts where they led, and to never, ever yield unless they had to.

Martinez—the chief of operations, or head handyman, take your pick—Francisco, the exec, and Darlington rounded out the group in the room. Darlington was not involved in the discussion, but was recording it: he'd insisted on carrying through with it, and Crow had asked Fang-Castro to allow him to do it.

They all turned as Wendy Greenberg walked into the room. She looked flustered. "I'm sorry I'm late, we wanted to pull the latest out of the engines and out of Nav."

She took the empty chair and Fang-Castro nodded and said, "All right, let's begin. It's oh-nine-hundred, October 28, 2067. It's one day after midcourse flip-over and the heat exchanger accident that shut down our propulsion system and killed Chief Engineer Dr. Rebecca Johansson. A full report on that death will be filed later. I've instructed Mr. Sanders Darlington to fully document this meeting."

She looked around at everybody, then continued, "Dr. Greenberg . . . Wendy . . . I do appreciate the situation you've found yourself in. I understand your people have been working nonstop to understand the situation and figure out what we're going to do about it, and you may not have reached any final conclusions, yet. Tell us what you know, because we are looking at a number of critical decisions that need to be made very soon."

"Let me start with a quick review," Greenberg said. She touched her slate and looked at it. "Yesterday, when we had Reactor 1 up to eighty percent output, we suffered a side blowout in Heat Exchanger 1 below the slot nozzle about three-quarters of the way outward on the nozzle boom. We're still investigating the cause of the blowout, but we registered a control anomaly in one of the heaters in the vicinity of the blowout before it occurred. We were in communication with Dr. Johansson over how to deal with the anomaly when the blowout occurred.

"At 1:17 P.M., ship's time, Dr. Johansson's service egg was struck directly by a large slug of radiator melt, several hundred kilograms, traveling at tens of meters per second. Essentially all onboard systems—power, propulsion, communication, life support—were instantly disabled or destroyed. The impact threw the egg away from the ship at substantial velocity. Mr. Darlington's egg was also struck by escaping melt, but the damage was less severe and Mr. Martinez brought him safely into the hangar bay."

She touched her slate again, scrolling. Greenberg had had a taste of the same drugs that were smoothing out Darlington.

Greenberg continued. "As soon as Engineering registered the blowout, we initiated an emergency full shutdown. We dropped partitioning baffles into HE1's melt reservoir, which were successful in slowing and eventually stopping the hemorrhaging of radiator melt into space. We were able to recover much of the melt using the procedures we developed after the first radiator test in Earth's orbit. We still lost a few tons of metal, but that's well within our reserve allowance for the heat exchanger system, especially in our new situation. Which brings me to the measures we are currently recommending."

Fang-Castro said, "Excuse me, but for the purposes of this record I would like to insert that all evidence shows that Dr. Johansson was killed instantly upon impact. Accordingly, we concentrated our efforts on containing the damage to the ship rather than recovering her damaged egg. A trajectory for that egg has been calculated and has been entered into our ship's records, as a contingency in the unlikely event that there should someday be the possibility of a recovery." To Greenberg, she said, "Go ahead, Wendy."

"Yes. At this time we don't think we can repair the breach in the heat exchanger wall. It's right below the slot nozzle, which is a very precisely designed and controlled assembly. We can't patch the hole without altering the behavior of the nozzle in that area and, as we've seen previously, the radiator ribbon system is challenging to control and even more difficult to model. We don't feel comfortable that we can repair this section without risking a major failure on start-up."

She looked around the table, and then spoke directly to Fang-Castro:

"Fortunately, this should not be necessary. With only one functional re-actor, we do not need the entire capacity of the heat exchanger-radiator system. We think we can wall off the heat exchanger and terminate the slot nozzle just inboard of the damaged section, which will still leave us with seventy percent capacity on that side. We plan to make the same modification to the undamaged HE2 system to keep performance sym-metric. That still leaves us with the capability to dissipate a hundred and forty percent of the entire output of Reactor 1. That's pretty much it for the moment."

"So we won't be going out to the Horsehead, or wherever," Fang-Castro said. "How long before we're up and running again?"

"I can't give you a good estimate, yet," Greenberg said. "I don't think a week. The heat exchangers need to cool down enough that we can work on them. While we're equipped to make these kind of modifica-tions, it's not something we ever had to do in the field."

Fang-Castro turned to the exec: "Mr. Francisco, what does Naviga-tion tell us?"

"Ma'am, the good news is that we're in no immediate danger. When we can get power back, we've got enough reserves in our water tanks that we can still make a rendezvous with Saturn. We could even return to Earth directly if we had to, although it would be slow and life support might be stretched very thin."

"And the bad news?"

"The bad news is that we're still outward bound at full velocity, so we're going to overshoot Saturn's orbit. Every day without propulsion adds fifteen million klicks to our overshoot. We won't be able to make a direct rendezvous with Saturn. We'll fly on past, bring the ship to a full halt, and then fly back to Saturn."

"And we have the reaction mass for that."

"Yes, but we don't have unlimited amounts. Flying that second leg from beyond Saturn back in, the maximum velocity we can achieve is around twenty-five kilometers per second and still stay within our mass budget. The way Nav figures it, every day of overshoot costs us nearly a week on the trip back in. What it comes down to is that we've already lost almost two weeks on our arrival time and every additional day that we're in free fall delays our arrival at Saturn by another week."

Fang-Castro nodded. "Our ETA was February 15. Another week's downtime, Dr. Greenberg, moves that out to, hmmm, April, days after the Chinese are projected to arrive. That's not really acceptable."

Martinez asked, "Wendy, why can't we shut down Exchanger 1 and run all the waste heat from Power System 1 through Exchanger 2? That would be a quicker fix."

Greenberg looked worried. "That's a really asymmetric situation. Especially since we'd be running Exchanger 2 at full load. We're talking about nearly five gigawatts of heat. It's not just a matter of opening a couple of valves. Plus, we've never fully simulated that scenario, let alone tested it in the field. You've seen how unstable the system can be. I can't say it won't work, but I think we're more likely to break something badly trying."

"All right, then let's table that idea," Fang-Castro said. "But we'll hold it in reserve. Dr. Greenberg, if I'm not convinced you can bring the system back online in less than a week, I'm likely to change my mind. Getting the engines back online is our first priority. Anything your people need, and any extra personnel you need, they're yours. All of the ship's resources are at your call. Coordinate with Mr. Francisco on this."

She looked around the table: "Anything else? No? Then let's do it. Mr. Darlington, you can shut down the recording. Mr. Crow, if you could linger a moment."

When they were all gone, other than Crow, she asked, "Sabotage?"

He shook his head. "This time, I don't think so. It was too uncontrolled, and if things had gone differently, could have killed the ship. I don't think there's a reasonable . . . mmm . . . process that a saboteur could have followed to create that result. I've been looking at it very carefully, talking to my people back on Earth, and we're agreed on that. Our best guess is a fabrication flaw: at the end of fabrication, back on Earth, we were simply moving too quickly. Another month, we might have caught the flaw."

"Good." She smiled briefly and said, "You're not nearly as paranoid as everybody thinks."

He ventured a smile himself: "Too paranoid is as bad as not paranoid enough. We stand on a rather narrow ledge: that keeps it interesting."

When he was gone, Fang-Castro, still in her chair, tapped her slate. A document had been winking at her all morning, and now she opened and scanned it, though she already knew most of it.

". . . the impact of the molten metal slug on Dr. Johansson's service egg quickly disabled it. The ship had high-bandwidth communication for 0.8 seconds before that channel went down. Consequently, we have full telemetry as well as the vid feed from the internal safety camera for that brief period. Dr. Johansson's egg was facing the nozzle assembly when it blew out. The slug of metal hitting the egg was comparable to a front-end automobile collision at highway speed. As the egg was flung back at high velocity, Dr. Johansson's body slammed into the forward console. Her forehead made full contact with the upper display. Her body rebounded backward, but there were no indications of voluntary motion in the fraction of a second before we lost vid.

"The impact possibly broke her neck, very probably gave her a fatal concussion, and at an absolute minimum knocked her out. There is no possibility she retained any consciousness.

"Low-grade status-sensor telemetry continued for another 3.1 seconds before cascading and catastrophic system failures disabled all communications from the egg. During that time, life-support monitors reported falling pressure in the cabin as well as rapidly increasing contamination of the air. We can't tell from the incomplete data if this was smoke from onboard fires or ruptures of chemical lines or scrubbers that allowed toxins to enter the air system. Within seconds, at most, the air inside the cabin became fatally unbreathable and/or vented into space. If the impact did not kill Dr. Johansson outright, she died very quickly from asphyxiation or toxin inhalation."

Ah well, Fang-Castro thought, as she filed the report.

Becca.

37.

Greenberg tilted back and closed her eyes, just for a second—though she didn't know exactly how long the "second" lasted. The night before, she'd had the granddaddy of all cliché anxiety dreams: all the reactor tests were going wrong, every Level 2 tech had called in sick, she had totally forgotten Fang-Castro was showing up to inspect their progress, she really needed to pee, and on top of all that she'd somehow neglected to get dressed so she was floating next to the primary coolant control panel, naked, when Fang-Castro and Francisco entered the compartment.

None of that resembled the actual case.

The whole crew was running on illegal amounts of stims, but things were getting done. Short of any unexpected problems, they'd be moving again five days after the accident; maybe less.

Desperation was the mother of, well . . . something . . . and she desperately wanted to avoid cross-coupling asymmetric heat flows or any of the other dubious suggestions she'd heard. Previous discussions between Fang-Castro and the late chief engineer notwithstanding, Greenberg was going to run the power plant by the book.

What she was actually doing, she thought, was *scheduling*, rather than engineering. She'd read somewhere that the most successful generals were not the combat heroes, but those who could best manage traffic, and get fuel and food and ammunition to those who needed it.

Greenberg worked out ways to cut corners, to schedule work in parallel, even to schedule jobs by temperature. As much as possible, work that could be done on a hot heat exchanger was scheduled for the very beginning and very end of the repair queues. She'd been able to get some repair teams on the job within hours of the status meeting the morning after the accident, instead of having to wait a full day for the radiator metal reservoirs to come down to safe temps.

Conversely, as soon as all the fixes that demanded low-temp conditions were completed, she'd ordered the heaters turned on to bring the melt reservoir back up to operating temperature. She had given that word the night before, and currently was waiting on the inspection of the last of the high-temp work.

Becca might have been a tiny bit better as an engineer, Greenberg thought, *but I'm a better manager.* She was currently avoiding doing the one thing that Becca wouldn't have avoided: she refused to get in the hair of people who already knew what they were doing and were doing it as fast as they could. Becca would have been on them with a whip, and that would have slowed things down.

She was still sitting with her eyes closed—only for a second—when her wrist-wrap tapped her, and she checked her slate: and she got the sign-off by the inspection team. Time to start making radiator ribbons.

She had a few new moves here, as well. Previously, they were in no hurry to fire up the engines—back then, a few hours one way or another hadn't mattered. Now they did. Her magneto-dynamicists had burned up the models and figured out that radiator ribbons separated by more than ten meters didn't really interact with each other. When it came to radiator sail stability, it didn't matter whether Engineering extruded the ribbons one at a time or started up one in every dozen ribbons simultaneously. It required more people to monitor status boards when fifteen new ribbons got extruded at once, but that was all. She had the people . . .

She touched her comm controls, straight through to Fang-Castro: "Captain, we're ready to start generating real power again. Should be about two hours from start until we have you at one hundred percent. Awaiting your command."

"Thank you, Dr. Greenberg. Great job. You're instructed to bring Reactor 1 up to full power."

Greenberg: *And now we'll find out if I'm as good a power engineer as Becca thought I was when she made me her second.*

Two hours later, she decided she was. Power-up came off without a hitch, and the *Nixon* began its long deceleration burn. They were still half a billion kilometers sunward of Saturn, but it would take until the end of January to kill all of the ship's prodigious velocity. By then they'd have overshot their mark by nearly a hundred million kilometers.

The race to Saturn was far closer than the most pessimistic of the mission planners expected.

There'd been no earlier formal memorial ceremony for Rebecca Johansson: too many people who knew her well—the engineers—would have been unable to attend.

The memorial was held the evening of the restart.

Many people cried.

Sandy simply sat there, feeling—and looking, he thought—fairly stupid. In addition to messing with your hormones, the drugs did take out a piece of your brain.

Maybe he should just stay on them forever, he thought.

Real feelings had never really worked that well for him.

38.

Fang-Castro ran into Sandy as they converged on the Commons. As the captain, she did not touch subordinates for good, legal reasons. Now she hooked Sandy's shirt with a couple of fingers and pulled him aside.

"How are you? Dr. Ang told me you're coming off the drugs."

"Just in time for New Year's," Sandy said. Becca had been killed two months earlier; they were approaching the orbit of Saturn, though they wouldn't be stopping there. And, "Thanks for asking, ma'am. I'm feeling fairly bad. Going through the brooding phase, as he calls it. The what-ifs. Dr. Ang tells me that's good. I'm getting my mind back."

"The post-traumatic stress . . . ?"

"I've dealt with it, you know, for a while. This is a bump in the road, but I'll be okay."

She touched his arm: "Very good. I pressed Mr. Crow on your previous service, so I'd know what I was dealing with. I have a good deal of admiration for you, Captain, and you are a most excellent cameraman, as well. I would be pleased to have you on any of my ships, even if you *were* in the army."

"Thanks . . . I'll remember that, ma'am."

They went on to the New Year's celebration.

New Year's Eve aboard the *Nixon* was one for the record books, Fang-Castro thought, as she and Sandy entered the Commons. People had celebrated the coming of the new year for millennia, but never before in a spaceship over a billion kilometers from Earth.

And despite the cheerful dressing, there was a touch of melancholy to it, as well—they were still feeling the loss of their chief engineer.

But as Sandy had said, on the day of the accident, probably in shock but also in truth, dead was dead. Rebecca Johansson was slipping irretrievably into the past, and here, in the present, Phillip McCord, a Nobel physicist, the only Nobel on board, was serving as a most excellent bartender, pouring a most excellent champagne.

The champagne was courtesy of Fang-Castro herself. She'd had a few cases laid in to herald their year-end's arrival at Saturn. It would have been impossibly wrong to let the combination of the holiday season and the successful completion of their voyage go uncelebrated. The occasion was, unfortunately, not quite the one she'd planned.

Her first officer was standing at the observation window, and she wandered over to him. "Evening, Salvatore."

"Evening, ma'am." An uncomfortable look flitted across his face: her use of his first name.

"This is a party. Relax."

"Trying to, ma'am. It's quite a view, isn't it?" He nodded toward the window.

Once every minute, the living modules' rotation brought Saturn into view. It was an awesomely beautiful sight, hanging so close by that you could almost reach out and touch it. Except that it wasn't. The nearness was an illusion; Saturn was twenty-one million kilometers away.

That was half the distance from Earth to Venus, a distance at which you'd expect to see planets as nothing more than pinpoints of light. Saturn, though, was huge, so that even at this distance, the flattened sphere looked to be two-thirds the size of Earth's moon.

The crew members could easily see its lovely bands of tawny clouds; the sharp-eyed might even convince themselves they could make a disk out of the orange, Mars-sized moon called Titan.

Most mesmerizing, of course, was the massive, pearly ring system, half again as wide as the full moon. People had no trouble seeing the fine dark band of the Cassini division splitting the A and B rings, and fine grooves within the rings themselves.

Because of the breakdown at turnover, the *Nixon* was still traveling at seventy kilometers per second out of the solar system. This was the nearest they would come to the magnificent planet for some time. It would be another month before the crippled propulsion system could bring them to a halt, ninety million kilometers beyond their goal. It would take almost two more months to fly back in and establish an orbit around Saturn . . . assuming that nothing else went wrong.

Francisco was thinking along the same lines, and said, as the planet rotated out of sight, "We're cutting it fine, aren't we?"

"We play the hand we've been dealt," Fang-Castro said. She looked up at the massive view screen at the end of the Commons. The picture showed a hundred thousand people jumping up and down in Times Square. Just for this single night, they'd gone to what Martinez was call-ing "Eastern Standard Fake Time." The scene they were watching on the screen had taken place more than an hour earlier, but it was just coming in now. "Four minutes until the ball drops. I'm going to go mingle. If you have a moment, go say something cheerful to Darlington, if you please. When we sing 'Auld Lang Syne' . . ."

"I will do that, ma'am."

The minutes counted down, and when the ball hit bottom, every-body but Fang-Castro got kissed at least once, and then Darlington, in his best singing voice, and with Martinez's arm wrapped around his shoulders, and Fiorella's around his waist, led the way:

"Should auld acquaintance be forgot . . ." And others began to join in, "and never brought to mind . . ."

There was melancholy, at least some: they were so far from every-thing, farther than any human had ever been from home. And then there was applause, and the party really began.

Five minutes after the ball fell—time for the singing and the kissing—the vid message came in from Santeros.

"I can't honestly say I can really appreciate how you all must feel, so far from home," the President said, from the huge view screen. "But yours is one of the most important missions ever undertaken by man-kind, and for the future of your country. I wish you—I wish all of us—the very, very best in the New Year. Please, please be safe: America treasures each one of your souls. I tried to come up with some substan-tial way to reward the members of your crew for your efforts. I could hardly find anything appropriate, but I can say, and this will be announced publicly tomorrow, that each and every one of you has been awarded the Presidential Medal of Freedom, the highest non-military award your nation has."

She paused, to allow for applause, and though she'd recorded the message eight hours earlier, she got it: the Commons erupted in cheering and applause, and the President smiled into it.

"In addition to that—Mr. Martinez, Mr. Darlington, would you approach Captain Fang-Castro now? Thank you."

Fang-Castro, puzzled, looked at the two smiling men as they came to stand on either side of her.

The President continued: "At my direction, and with the concurrence of the Congress and the secretary of the navy, Naomi Fang-Castro is hereby promoted to the permanent rank of rear admiral. Gentlemen, if you'll do the honors."

Fang-Castro actually felt a little sag in her knees. She looked at the grinning Martinez and Darlington, who stepped in front of her and showed her the golden shoulder boards with the single star of a rear admiral (lower half).

"You fabricated these down in the shop, didn't you?" she asked.

"Yes, ma'am," Martinez said. "Carbon fiber—probably the most resilient shoulder boards ever made. We put some excellent sticky tape on them, so they won't come off until you want them to."

He and Darlington pressed them over her regular boards, and they stuck there, just as Martinez promised.

Then the President said, "I'm sure you've already done this, but join me now:

"Should auld acquaintance be forgot . . .'"

39.

Launch plus a hundred and ninety-five days, eighty million kilometers from Saturn. It was February 7, 2068, back on Earth, but that didn't mean as much to the crew as it used to. The *Nixon* had become their world. It was on its way back in to Saturn, had been for a week. Their velocity was up to a piddling twenty kilometers per second and would only get a bit higher; reaction mass was in short supply. They still had eighty million kilometers and six weeks to go before they'd get to Saturn.

Crow sat with his feet on his desk and tapped at his slate, looking at the numbers even though he already knew them all, and they wouldn't change. Six weeks: and it wouldn't be long after that when the competition showed up. Fang-Castro wanted to have some idea where they stood with the Chinese before that happened.

Crow had been working all of his contacts, both those with access to human intelligence and the techies who pulled things down out of the sky and up out of the buried fiber-optic cables that connected Chinese military installations.

He was met with very little resistance—one middle-level CIA bureaucrat had objected to what he called the "over-allocation of resources to this single project," and a half hour later had taken a call from the director, in person, in which he learned that the director had taken a call from the President, in person, and the President had mentioned the bureaucrat's name, and not in a kindly fashion. Did the bureaucrat have Arctic-quality survival gear? If not, he might start looking into some.

Resistance melted like ice cream on a hot sidewalk.

Even with good cooperation, Crow didn't know much more now than he'd known when he started.

But he did know a few things.

One thing he knew for sure: there was one person on board who was as unhappy as he was: Admiral Naomi Fang-Castro. She had all his reasons and then some. He was responsible for ship security? Fang-Castro was responsible for the ship, period. He looked at the time, sighed, and walked down to her private office, tapped the comm button by her door. A moment later her voice said, "Come."

He nodded and said, "Admiral," and took his chair; Fang-Castro poured a cup of tea and pushed it toward him. It had become a ritual they both enjoyed, when enjoyment was on the table.

"Anything?"

Crow shook his head. "No. It's driving me crazier than it is you. I truly believe we have a spy on board, who has some method of communicating with the Chinese. Probably the Chinese."

"All those analysts at the NSA, there are supposedly tens of thousands of them, they can't find anything?" Fang-Castro asked.

"That's not the problem," Crow said. "There are no countermeasures that can keep me from collecting information, but there *are* countermeasures. Ninety-nine percent of the information we're taking in is actually noise, or active disinformation. The opposition knows they can't prevent us from tapping in, not entirely and not for very long, so they try to bury us. I can see the forest for the trees, but almost all of the trees are fakes. They are there to lead us down the wrong path. Admiral, everyone lies. All the time."

Fang-Castro: "You're saying there's no way to ferret the truth out of the noise?"

"I'm not quite saying that. We have tools. Contextual analyses, time-stamp discontinuities, tail-thread stubs, meta-patterns, and a lot more that the supercomputers can throw at the problem. Most of the time they'll tell me what's a bogus plant and point me toward the one true oak. But this time we're playing for the highest stakes in at least half a century, maybe ever, and everyone's pulling out their A Game. The disinformation is fierce and sophisticated.

"My best thread says the Chinese are behind the sabotage. That might be true. It might also be a plant by one of the other geopolitical unions, who wouldn't mind seeing the relationship between the two superpowers get chillier, especially if one of them, or both, is about to acquire starship tech. It could even be disinformation by a faction within the Chinese government. Santeros doesn't have a monopoly on hawks."

"What about sabotage on the Chinese ship?"

"Don't know. Anyone with a decent-sized infrared telescope could figure out that we had a problem when our heat signature and trajectory changed. Post-launch-boost phase, the *Celestial Odyssey* has mostly been in free fall. If they're having propulsion system problems, they wouldn't be anywhere as obvious. Maybe that midcourse burn of theirs was a glitch, not a plan. We just don't know."

"So that's it?"

Crow hesitated, and hesitated some more, and his eyes went down then cut toward her, and finally he said, "On New Year's, just for that night, you told me I could call you Naomi. I need to call you Naomi again. Just for a few minutes—this is way off base, but . . ."

"You're not going to make a pass at me?" She was amused.

So was he. "If your preferences were different . . . you're probably my type. But no. I'm not gonna make a pass."

"So call me Naomi. For a few minutes."

"Thank you, Naomi. I've been involved with discussions between the President and her advisers. They believe it's not necessary to bother you with them. So I'm putting my ass in your hands, so to speak."

The intelligence nets on Earth, along with the agencies' science people, Crow told Fang-Castro, had determined that the Chinese ship's midcourse burn had not only advanced their arrival time by weeks, it had seriously hampered their plans for establishing orbit around Saturn. They would go into the Saturnian system five kilometers per second hotter than they'd planned. The intelligence coming in suggested that the burn had been devised under direct pressure from the general secretary.

"The problem is, Naomi, that the *Celestial Odyssey* may not have the reaction mass to kill enough velocity to achieve a close orbit around Saturn. It's possible that they've been able to lighten their ship enough to make some kind of orbit, but that is not likely," Crow said.

"Why wouldn't our people tell me that?" Fang-Castro asked.

"Because it's equally unlikely that the Chinese decided to go ahead and commit suicide. They're up to something and the intelligence guys think that smells like trouble for us. The reason they're not talking to you is, *they* want to decide how we react. They don't want you getting out the law books and deciding on what to do about a distress call, *they* want to decide. They've worked up a bunch of different scenarios, including saying, 'Fuck it, let 'em die.' Depending on what we find at the alien site, of course."

"I wouldn't do that—let them die," Fang-Castro said.

"But what do you do if Santeros, backed by the secretary of the navy, calls Francisco and tells him that you've been relieved of command, and he's the new commander—and 'fuck it, let 'em die'?"

"Francisco wouldn't do it," she said. "That's why he's my Number Two."

"But what about your Number Three, Naomi? And so on."

They sat and stared at each other for a moment.

Then she asked, "What if the Chinese planned for the midcourse option in advance, and they've got a leaner, meaner ship that can make it to Saturn, establish orbit, and make it back?"

"That's the best case. That's what we're hoping for. But honestly? Nobody thinks it's likely. Burning through the extra reaction mass when they left Earth orbit would have bought them a lot more time than the midcourse burn. Everybody now agrees that was a Plan B. Another possibility is that they're going to orbit much farther out, well beyond Saturn's rings. That'll reduce the delta-vee requirements for establishing orbit, but it would leave them with a several-day trip time between their ship and the alien whatsit. That's more than inconvenient, it's unpredictably dangerous. They don't have any more ideas than we do what or who is there, or what the environment is like around the alien station."

"Somebody suggested to me that they might have some kind of small return ship attached to the *Celestial Odyssey*."

"We've discarded that idea: more intelligence," Crow said. "They've got a couple of buses, like ours, to get them back and forth from the alien site, but that's it. No way the buses could get the Chinese crew back to Earth. They're also talking about other possibilities—that they'll loop around Saturn, use what delta-vee they've got to get into a closed orbit around the sun, that might pull them close enough to Earth for a rescue mission."

"I was twiddling with my slate, with John Harbinson, and . . . mmm . . . that would take them years," Fang-Castro said. Harbinson was the onboard nav guru. "Would they have enough consumables to do that?"

"Unlikely. The thing is, we can't discard the possibility that they are really down to Plan C. In other words, acts of desperation. In that case, there's a fair possibility that whatever they've got planned won't work. Best-case scenario from Santeros's point of view is that their ship gets destroyed. Worst case is that it survives, with the crew alive, but it can't establish close Saturn orbit. In that case, they start screaming for help."

"And we could help them, once we take on water for reaction mass."

"Let me say this in Chairwoman White's voice: 'We know the crew on board the *Celestial Odyssey* is mostly military, and real military, guys who've been fighting Islamorads in the Western Provinces for years. We're gonna give those guys access to the most advanced ship the U.S. has ever built? Plus, whatever we find in Saturn's rings? Is that even under consideration?'"

Fang-Castro smiled at Crow's mimicry, and asked, "Crow, is Crow really your name?"

"No."

"You might as well tell me what it is—I can always look for your smiling face in the academy yearbooks."

"It's Crowell. David Crowell," Crow said. "Nobody's called me either name for years. Even my wife called me Crow."

"I guess it goes with the job," Fang-Castro said.

"Yeah. Anyway, White is furious at the very thought of allowing Chinese troops on the *Nixon*. That's what she calls them—Chinese troops."

"International law says I would have to help if the Chinese ask, and I can do it. If I don't, I could be charged with murder. Rightfully so, in my opinion."

"And that, Naomi, is why they're not talking to you. They want to decide."

"I'll tell you what, David. It appears to me that we're looking at the first real interplanetary bureaucratic clusterfuck."

"Yes. And I'll tell you what, Naomi: if push comes to shove, and I do mean shove—I'll back you up. All the way. I will."

40.

Fang-Castro's implants pinged. Her eyes popped open as she tried to remember why. Then, Ah!

She slipped out of bed, dressed in her plain tan NWUs as quietly as she could, stepped out of the bedroom, closed the door, left the cabin, and walked down to the Commons. There were a dozen other people there, mostly the night shift, picking up coffee, along with a few day-shift workers who appreciated historical markers, even if they couldn't particularly see, feel, hear, smell, or taste this one.

Most of those were looking out through the big port window. Fang-Castro got an orange juice and went that way, watching a countdown that popped up on a corner of the screen, something like the New Year's countdown.

Hours before, they'd begun to bend around Saturn. In three minutes, they'd close that first loop: the official seal on the fact that they'd shed enough of their excess velocity and achieved a closed orbit around the enormous planet, bound by Saturn's gravitational pull.

They were late. The original plan had placed them at Saturn for Christmas. Instead they'd arrived just in time to celebrate the start of spring. Like that mattered, 1.3 billion kilometers from home.

What mattered was that the Chinese were only two weeks behind them.

Two minutes, one minute, ten seconds, zero.

"There it is," somebody said, and there was a smattering of applause.

"It's a big deal, ladies and gentlemen," Fang-Castro said. "We're there." She watched the planet swinging by for another moment, then walked back to her cabin. Fiorella would be doing a brief rendezvous broadcast in the morning, and Fang-Castro wanted to look good.

Sandy said, "Anytime . . ."

His egg had been basically unrepairable after being hit by the molten radiator metal, but he, Martinez, Elroy Gorey, and a couple of other techs had pulled the undamaged Leica optical glass off the old egg and reinstalled it on another one. He wasn't using the Leica glass at the moment, because the standard egg glass softened Fiorella's image.

Fiorella was floating fifty meters away, and Sandy slowly closed from a wide-angle image of Saturn, and a slice of its rings, to a close-up of Fiorella's face.

Fiorella said, picking up from what Fang-Castro had said a couple of times in that morning's interview, "Rendezvous—it was a big deal. For those of us who witnessed the entire project, it's hard to believe that only two years ago, most of us would never have thought we'd leave the surface of the earth. For those of us who had, we'd gone no further than Earth orbit, a trip that takes not much longer than an ordinary jet flight from Los Angeles to London. But to think we'd be orbiting a planet over a billion kilometers from home! A bare year ago, the Chinese construction of a Mars transport had been state of the art: just a few months to Mars, if you caught the right launch window. This new technology, encapsulated in the *Richard M. Nixon*, could make that run in a third of the time and it could fly almost anytime it wanted. How proud President Nixon would be if he could see us now!"

She went on for a while, talking of the frustration of crawling back to Saturn after the ninety-million-kilometer overshoot—though a funny definition of "crawl." Twenty-five kilometers per second was roughly twenty-five times faster than the speed of a standard rifle bullet, but compared to the flight out, at a hundred and fifty kilometers per second, it felt like crawling.

"As beautiful as it is, it will take us a week to move in from this preliminary orbit to what we hope and believe will be an alien space station. Saturn is gorgeous, but its rings are nothing more than a beautiful buzz saw of orbiting debris, mostly water-ice, with some rocks included. Our destination is technically called the C Ring's Maxwell Gap, near the innermost part of the ring system. The gap itself is almost entirely free of debris—but to get there, we're going to have to avoid the saw blade. This will be the most delicate part of our whole flight: this crew is up to it, but you'll want to stay tuned. Aliens on tap!"

Three-two-one. "Okay . . . we're out," Sandy said.

"Look at my lipstick."

"It's fine. You gonna change blouses?"

"Yes, and I'll get rid of the necklace and mess up my hair. This has to look as informal as possible."

When they were ready, and she'd changed, Sandy said, again, "Anytime."

Fiorella flashed her Number 1 smile: "Hi, kids. As I suppose most of you know by now, the third-graders at La Canada Elementary School in La Canada-Flintridge, California, and the fifth-graders at Hillside Elementary in Cottage Grove, Minnesota, have made a special request that was forwarded to us by President of the United States Amanda Sentaros . . . Oh, Jesus, I fucked that up . . . Santeros, Santeros, Santeros . . ."

"Yeah, and now you do need to check the lipstick," Sandy said. "When you fix that, pick it up at, uh . . . special request . . ."

"Okay." She fixed the lipstick. "How's that?"

"Good. Do it anytime."

". . . Cottage Grove, Minnesota, made a special request that was forwarded to President of the United States Amanda *Santeros*. The kids asked for a tour of Saturn's rings, and that's what we're going to give you guys, right now."

Santeros spoke to Crow and Fang-Castro in one block of verbiage, because of the time elapse in the transmission back and forth:

"I'm fully aware of the dangers of trying to get into the alien object too quickly. That has been repeatedly pressed upon me by my scientific advisers, to the point of being tiresome. I leave to you the tactical details of doing that, but would remind you that we've lost a lot of time. A lot of time—and our Chinese friends and allies are coming in fast. We still don't know exactly what they are doing, but do not underestimate the dangers here. We are pressing the Chinese government for details of what they expect from us, if anything, but they are being remarkably reticent. Mr. Crow is aware of the many scenarios we have been discussing, and can provide the command with details of these discussions, but I say again: you must move as quickly as possible, now, and you must take great care in any approach from the Chinese. With the time lag we have in the broadcasts, we may not be able to provide timely advice, or provide . . . timely discussion with the Chinese . . . over any difficult situations you may encounter. We're counting on you to act in the best interests of the United States. . . ."

When she was done, Fang-Castro said, "Oh, boy."

"Yes," Crow said. "That was a very complicated way of saying, 'If you screw it up, you're on your own.'"

The trip from Earth to Saturn had been the fastest done by any human-built craft, ever—so fast that collision with even a brick-sized object would have been a disaster. But space was remarkably empty, even of sand-sized objects.

Saturn's ring system was another matter. The rings were only tens of meters thick, but that space was filled with icy objects of all different sizes. If the *Nixon* crossed the densest rings it would inevitably be struck multiple times by hail-sized and larger—much larger—ice balls moving at many kilometers per second relative to the ship.

Their goal, the alien mystery, orbited Saturn within the translucent C Ring's Maxwell Gap. The *Nixon* could safely orbit within that region, twenty-seven thousand kilometers above Saturn's cloud tops, if it could get there.

The Maxwell Gap was near the innermost edge of the huge ring system. Between the gap and deep space was a fifty-thousand-kilometer disk of icy projectiles. If the *Nixon* tried to come into Saturn on a straightforward equatorial path in the plane of the rings, it would be sliced in two by a twenty-meter-thick buzz saw of ring-particle impacts before it got one percent of the way in.

Instead, the ship approached on a vector that was tilted at thirty degrees to the ring plane, decelerating the whole way on an inward spiral, reminiscent of the one that had taken them out of Earth orbit.

It was a week's work for the VASIMRs to slow the ship enough to bring it into a circular orbit that threaded the Maxwell Gap; along that spiral trajectory the ship had to cross the ring plane many times. Each ring encounter lasted only a few milliseconds, but they were potentially lethal ones.

Fortunately, Saturn's rings weren't uniform. They were divided into thousands of ringlets and lesser gaps, like grooves on a giant celestial record. The inbound trajectory wasn't a simple smooth spiral. The deceleration was carefully modulated and timed so that each ring crossing would pass through one of those myriad smaller gaps that subdivided the ring system.

Ship's navigation had carried the burden of responsibility for this segment of the flight. This was not the usual preset deep space trajectory, determined well in advance of the flight. From far off, Saturn's rings appeared stable and fixed, but those ringlets performed a constant and chaotic dance with gravity. Gaps would shift kilometers inward or outward. Sometimes they disappeared entirely. Changes could happen in weeks, sometimes days; it was impossible to plan out a precise trajectory far in advance of the *Nixon*'s arrival at Saturn.

So the nav crew actually had to "fly" the ship in, working with a constant stream of communication between the astronomers, Navigation, and Engineering. Navigation would say where they hoped to take the ship, the astronomers would tell them what gaps were close to their desired path, Navigation would calculate a course correction, and Engineering would execute it or tell them it wasn't feasible and they'd better look for a different gap.

It was nerve-racking. Haggard didn't begin to describe the flight crew's appearance by week's end.

The majority of the ship's complement, who weren't involved in the life-and-death decisions, had an entirely different experience. They were entranced. Saturn, ten times the size of the earth, was a beautiful object to behold. When the *Nixon* made its first pass by Saturn, outside the F Ring, the flattened disk of Saturn, all by itself, spanned a fifty-degree field of view and the rings, the most gorgeous planetary system known to humanity, filled the sky.

People couldn't get enough of the spectacle. The Commons was always packed to capacity. Anyone whose duties didn't require them to be elsewhere crowded to see the amazing sight that swept past the window. They marveled at the huge pearly-white arcs of the rings and the perpetually fascinating colors of Saturn's cloud bands striped with tawny hues of oranges, ochers, tans, salmons, more different and delicate colors than most of the crew had names for.

The ring crossings were even more popular, if that were possible. Approaching from the sunlit side, the rings grew ever bigger in the window until they occupied the entire view. Unbelievably detailed and striated, rings became ringlets, ringlets parsed into sub-ringlets, ever-finer textures that grew and grew and then suddenly they were through the ring and looking at empty space. Half a rotation of the living modules, and the rings came back into view, sometimes glowing with ghostly pale backlighting from the sun. Where Saturn's shadows fell across the rings, they were visible only as dark sweeping silhouettes that blocked out the distant stars.

The flight crew's anxiety never managed to infect the spectators. Intellectually, the spectators knew that ring crossings were one of the riskiest parts of the mission. They just didn't feel it. They'd survived a close pass by the sun, a crippling accident at the orbit of Jupiter that had killed one of their own and nearly ruined the mission, months in space far beyond the reach of the rest of humanity, and here they were. Deep in their emotional cores, they knew nothing would go wrong.

They were right. Nothing did go wrong. The ship took some minor hits from some minor bits of ice in the gaps. Nothing the structured foam hulls and carbon composite skeletons couldn't handle, and nothing that service egg jockeys couldn't repair once they were settled in.

Each pass through the potentially hazardous ring gaps came more quickly on the heels of the last. The first ring crossings were separated by a day and a half. Just before the *Nixon* finally settled into the inclined circular orbit that threaded the Maxwell Gap, the crossings were three and a half hours apart.

Then they were close.

"What do we know?" Fang-Castro asked.

They were gathered in the Commons, which had been declared temporarily off-limits to anyone not invited—not because there were any secrets, but because there wasn't enough room for everybody who wanted to attend. The chairs were mostly occupied by the science crew, along with representatives from Navigation and Engineering. Sandy was recording the meeting, which was being transmitted directly back to Earth on an encrypted link.

"We're poking at it with everything we've got," said Barney Kapule, a ranging and surveillance expert, one of two on board. The two had been chosen for their expertise in operating the onboard telescopes and the associated cameras. Everything they saw in their scopes was on its way back to Earth within milliseconds.

What had appeared two years earlier to be idle speculation by Richard Emery, the vice chair of the Joint Chiefs of Staff, was close to spot-on.

"This is no moonlet," Kapule said. "Our primary object is the size of a minor moon, an oblate spheroid a good five kilometers in diameter." He tapped his slate and a vid of the object popped up on the oversized Commons vid screen. "It has minimal perturbing effect on the rings, so it has to be very low in density. In other words, we think it's hollow, so it's not a natural object. Whether it ever was a natural object, we don't know yet. The surface is irregular. At this distance, we can't tell if it's natural weathered material, you know, roughened up by occasional small impacts over the years, or an artificial shell with a lot of hardware stuck on the outside."

"Why can't we see it better?" John Clover asked.

"Because it's dark—not exactly stealth-black, but the surface is very, very dark, shading to a lighter gray at both of the poles," said Candace Frank, Kapule's associate. She touched her slate and brought up a different view of the object. "Whether or not this was intentional camouflage, it made the primary difficult to pick out in the Maxwell Gap as anything more than a minor moonlet. But it is more, a lot more. Not only do we have the primary, but it has a substantial retinue of dozens of additional moonlets, considerably less than a hundred meters in size. They appear to orbit in a fixed formation with the primary, and statistically there's no possibility that the formation is natural. They were placed where they're at. Whether they're physically connected or just station-keeping, we can't tell at this distance, but they're all associated with each other."

"In other words, we don't have one alien object, we got a whole bunch of them," Fang-Castro said.

"Even more than we've been talking about," Kapule said. A new view came up, one that seemed sprinkled with salt. A group of thin red rings popped up, surrounding each white grain. "We're seeing hundreds, and maybe thousands, of pixel-sized glitters of light that move between the primary and its moonlets and out into the rings and back again. Whatever they are, they're always moving, like a swarm of bees around a hive . . . not to suggest anything invidious here."

"What are the patterns?" Fang-Castro asked. "Is that a defense system?"

"Yes, we have an analysis," said Don Larson, the mathematician and former founder of the orgy club. "To go back to the bee metaphor, it's more like they're gathering honey and bringing it back to the nest, rather than performing any kind of defensive maneuvers. They're not particularly fast . . . fast enough, but not way fast . . . and their actions are deliberate, rather than random. Even if not designed for defense, they could certainly be used that way. To see them at this distance must mean that they are some meters in diameter. If they are metallic, and if enough of them hit the *Nixon* as quickly as they are moving now, they could tear us apart. It'd be like being hit by cars driving at highway speeds. In other words, they seem to be gathering honey, whatever that is, but like honeybees, they could bring out the stingers."

Fang-Castro shook her head. She wanted none of that. The *Nixon* was not an armored warship.

Over the next several days, the steady minuscule thrust of the *Nixon*'s engines gradually warped its orbit, changing its inclination until the *Nixon* was orbiting within the Maxwell Gap in the plane of the rings. Simultaneously, they crept up on the alien constellation. Navigation and the surveillance people fed a steady stream of vid to the computers, where image analysis software tracked the motion of each of the bees. Sophisticated statistical modeling looked for any changes in the pattern of their collective motions, any indication that they were responding in any fashion to the approaching spaceship.

From Earth, they got a steady stream of essentially useless speculation about the nature of the constellation: the scientists on the *Nixon* saw everything hours before the earthbound analysts, and by the time their speculations got back to the ship, it had all been thought of.

Fang-Castro said to Crow, quietly, "David, the politicians and the military seem strangely quiet."

"By design, I think," Crow said. "Almost anything they say, the Chinese would pick up, one way or another. Not the encrypted stuff, but just chatter in the hallways. Which tends to be fairly accurate, if you're in the right hallway."

None of the analysis picked up changes in the behavior of the alien artifacts. The bees appeared to be as oblivious to the presence of humanity in the solar system as the starship had been two years earlier. Still, the *Nixon* held back, stabilizing its position at three hundred kilometers from the constellation. This was plenty close for the *Nixon*'s best telescopes—they could see ten-centimeter details on the alien facilities and the bees.

And they launched two recon shells, basically small, slow rockets equipped with cameras and designed to be extremely visible to radar and even visual detection, the better to signal peaceful intentions. The recon shells did a complete loop around the station, broadcasting a three-hundred-sixty-degree view of it.

They watched for a day. The nature of most of the bees became apparent, although the ultimate purpose of their activities was still mysterious. Most were ice-catchers. They hunted for ring debris. Some of them looked for chunks of ice comparable to their own size, latched onto them with grapples, and hauled them back to one of several moonlets. Others had large scoops and swept up ice gravel and sand, the way a whale scooped up plankton. This was also ferried to the moonlets. Another much smaller group of bees shuttled containers of some kind between the moonlets.

None of the bees seemed to be equipped with armaments, not even so much as a cutting laser. The same seemed to be true of the moonlets and the five-kilometer primary. The surfaces were mostly natural rock, porous regolith dotted with various alien assemblages that were mostly unrecognizable. A few were clearly antennae of some kind or another; none looked anything like a beamed energy or projectile weapon. The constellation seemed to be entirely unarmed.

The primary rotated slowly with a period of four hours, further evidence of its artificial nature. A natural moon this close to Saturn would've been tidally locked, just as Earth's moon was to its parent planet.

At Fang-Castro's command, the *Nixon* moved closer, then paused again. During the primary's second rotation, after the move, the *Nixon*'s computers spat out an anomalous delta.

A previously jet-black spot on the surface of the primary had turned light gray. During the third rotation things began to get genuinely weird. The black spot was now bright white and surrounded by concentric rings in rainbow colors. When the polychrome target came over the horizon on the fourth cycle, it was glowing dimly.

As the primary's rotation brought it around toward the *Nixon*, the glow brightened and coruscated until it could be seen with the naked eye through the windows of the *Nixon*, sparkling in the distance like a glass crystal spinning on a string and catching the sun.

The glow began to fade again after the target passed the median line until it was almost extinguished by the time the target had rotated past the horizon.

The fifth rotation repeated the light show of the fourth. The message was clear: "We know you're here."

Who or whatever "we" meant.

Naomi Fang-Castro took slow, shallow breaths and sipped her tea as her most senior crew members took their seats for the morning briefing, chatting with each other, making last-minute slate checks. Her face was calm, peaceful in its thoughtfulness.

That was entirely for show.

Aliens were no longer a distant, hypothetical consideration, not with *Nixon* parked next door to the primary. When everybody was settled, she put down her cup, and the chatter ended; the crew had learned early on that this was the signal that the meeting was about to begin.

"We're skipping the usual status reports," Fang-Castro said. "Have them recorded before dinnertime. I assume everything is nominal. Our sole business this morning is to decide on our next move. John, what's your take on what we know?"

Clover put down his triple-strength espresso, put his fingertips together, and said, "They're inviting us over for coffee and Danish."

"This is being recorded, John, so . . ."

"I'm somewhat serious. Look at their behavior . . . and lack of it. They take no apparent notice of us until we settle into our position. They keep doing business as usual. There's no evidence of weaponry or hostility. The colored lights are not in any apparent way a warning. We don't know what those colors mean in their culture, obviously—white is for mourning in Korea, black is for mourning in the West—but it seems likely that given the colors they've chosen, which they probably know are attractive to us, they're inviting us in, rather than warning us away."

"Where does that conclusion come from?" asked Martinez. "That those colors are attractive?"

"Our astronomers have done an analysis of the colors, and they are quite pure, they are very specific wavelengths—there's nothing in the UV or IR ranges, as though they were spattering us with everything. That suggests that they know what wavelengths we see, and that . . . give me a little rope here . . . suggests that they may very well know which ones we like," Clover said. "So we show up, but we do nothing. Eventually, they take the initiative. They set up a pretty little light show, designed to catch our eye, and just in case we're really thick, it shines brightest when it's pointed directly at us. Then they sit back and wait. How could that not be taken as an invitation?"

Imani Stuyvesant, the exobiologist, waved a stylus. Fang-Castro nodded at her. "Are you sure? Maybe that is the wavelengths they see best. Or maybe they don't even see the patterns the same way we do. Honeybees and birds see flowers a lot differently than we do."

Clover smiled and tapped his fingertips together. "If you were talking about human equivalents, Imani, you could be right. But aliens, I'd say it's pretty much guaranteed that they won't see exactly the way we do. There are all kinds of animals on Earth that don't see exactly the way we do. What would be the odds that the alien sensory apparatus, their eyes, would respond anything like ours? The astronomers and physicists started taking measurements like mad when it began"—Clover nodded companionably toward Bob Hannegan—"and all they saw was visible light. No other kinds of radiation. It was tailor-made for our eyes. The light show was purely for our benefit.

"So I just gotta figure, if they know that much about our physiology, they have some idea of how we respond to stimulus. The word that came to mind when I saw that display? Pretty. It was a sparkly, colorful, enticing bit of eye candy. It was presented to us the way we'd hang a shiny bauble on a string and hold it up before a baby, just to get the kid to reach out for it. You really think that was coincidence? Or miscommunication?"

Clover continued: "Remember, they could have been looking at our TV shows for a century. Beings who could build these artifacts and travel between stars almost certainly have some sense of curiosity, or self-preservation. If they could see our TV signals, they surely would have at least looked at them. Any analysis of our TV signals would tell them a lot about us: not just the culture, but our level of tech and everything else. Everything we do winds up on TV."

Martinez raised a stylus: "What if it's a deliberate trap?"

Clover shrugged. "Could be, but why go to the trouble? They can build starships that use antimatter for fuel. If they wanted to smack us upside the head, it's not like there's much preventing them from doing so. Why play games? It's like the question of why they didn't accelerate an asteroid into the earth, to wipe us off the face of the planet. They could, but they haven't. That suggests they don't want to."

Fang-Castro pulled the argument back in. "If the aliens are intentionally deceiving us, I don't think there's anything we can do about it. That's the bottom line. So we can sit out here and dither, or we can go in. We keep watching and analyzing, of course, but we're not going to turn around and head home." She allowed herself to show a bit of a smile. "So, I agree with John that we've received an invitation to reach out. We are going to reach. I won't risk ship-critical personnel in the first team we send to the primary. Unless anyone has a relevant objection, I will assign Captain Barnes to command the first contact team. He has combat command experience and is also heavily trained in combat trauma medicine. His second will be Lieutenant Emwiller, for the same reasons. Bob Hannegan and Imani Stuyvesant will cover physics and exobiology, John Clover will see to the cultural issues, Sandy Darlington to make the record. Ms. Fiorella will probably try to assassinate me for not including her in the trip, but I'm afraid she'll have to wait. Sandy, your first duty will be documentary, but if you should have a moment to make some vid that Ms. Fiorella can use, I'm sure she will appreciate it."

"I will keep those priorities in mind," Sandy said.

"Good. Do that." Fang-Castro turned to Martinez and said, "Joe, I'm sorry, but you're not on this run." His face fell. "Next to Dr. Greenberg, you are the single most vital person to keeping this ship running. If things work out as we hope, you'll have plenty of future opportunities, but for this expedition I want you to pick one of your assistants, whoever has the most experience flying a bus."

"Elroy would be good for it. He's good in space and has a lot of on-the-spot creativity, and I know he's anxious to get out there."

"Done, then. Tell Mr. Gorey." She looked around the room, which included several members of the contact team. "I want you all to be ready to go in six hours. Do what you need to get ready. I would suggest naps. And, Mr. Crow?"

"Yes?"

"I believe you'll find Ms. Fiorella out in the hall. Disarm her, and send her in."

41.

Rested and equipped, but not fed—they were uncertain about the availability of alien restrooms and although some facilities were built into the EVA suits, nobody enjoyed using them—the exploratory team assembled in the air lock of the storage and shuttle bay. The bay could be pressurized for shuttle maintenance and other on-site activities, but normally it was left open to space.

The seven-person party, led by George Barnes, a marine captain, suited up. The short-range shuttles, designed to carry up to twelve people and convey a substantial amount of cargo, were boxy skeletal affairs, similar in size and shape to double-decker omnibuses, so, naturally, that's what they got called.

Barnes was soft-spoken and meticulous. Sandy had always been a bit suspicious of marines during the Tri-Border fight, as they seemed willing to trade casualties for easy movement. That is, they used lighter weapons than Sandy thought reasonable. Faced with a Guapo hardpoint, they'd tend to do recon with a live patrol, then attack with backpacked munitions. The army would check it with drones of various kinds, both fliers and crawlers, and once the extent of the hardpoint was determined, the army had no qualms about calling in the air force with thousand-kilo bunker-busters, or toasting the place with a fuel-air heater.

On the other hand, good marine officers were just plain good officers, and Barnes was affable enough. Along with Sandy, Barnes taught a couple of popular physical-fitness courses.

As Barnes hand-checked the readouts on all seven suits, he took a call from Fang-Castro. "Captain Barnes, your party will be enhanced by one extra member. She'll be there in a couple of minutes."

"Yes, ma'am. Who is it?"

"One guess."

Fiorella showed up two minutes later, still pissed. "I imagine you set Fang-Castro straight," Sandy joked on a private channel.

Fiorella bared her teeth.

Sandy said, "Seriously, did you pee before you left? You have a bladder the size of a thimble."

"Yes. I peed. Now shut the fuck up."

"Keep your teeth off your lip—you won't be able—"

"Shut up."

"I gotta tell you one more thing, before you tell me to shut up again."

"Tell me."

"I brought the mini-Red with a Post-it pad. You can stick it to the bus rail and focus it on your face as we go out, and talk to it on a side channel. When we get back, we can intercut your commentary with the documentary photos."

"Sandy . . . but wait. You knew I was coming?"

"No, but I've been exposed to your powers of persuasion," Sandy said. "I suspected I might be seeing you."

"Sometimes I think you're brighter than I give you credit for," Fiorella said. Pregnant pause. "But only sometimes."

The *Nixon*'s buses weren't pressurized. The upper deck was equipped with seats and harnesses and umbilical connectors for space suits that provided life support, power, and communications. The suits were comfortable; they'd been designed to be lived in for up to thirty-six hours. They'd support a human being for longer than that, but things would start to get ripe. Food, water, waste elimination, air recirculation, were provided for. A built-in sponge bath, not so much.

The suits even offered entertainment: the heads-up virtual screen could show movies, vids, reading material, even games, whatever the wearer had uploaded into the suit databanks, or had transmitted to it. None of the team had bothered uploading data for this trip; boredom seemed unlikely to come up inside Saturn's rings, with the vast delicately colored expanse of Saturn itself hanging to one side and aliens awaiting them.

Beneath the seats, the life-support system sat on top of an open framework equipped with grapples, maneuvering actuators, and tie-downs. The front of the bus was equipped with manipulator arms, like the claws on a lobster. At the rear end of the bus were the rockets. The bus "cruised" at a maximum ten kilometers a minute, a snail's pace by the standards of space travel, but entirely sufficient for the bus's normal operating range of a thousand kilometers.

The first trip to the alien constellation's primary would be an easy half-hour run, and over that distance, fancy orbital mechanics didn't come into play: Gorey could fly it by the seat of his pants.

The five-kilometer primary was impossible to miss if you knew where to look; it was dim and dark, but it was twice the size of the full moon. When they were loaded, strapped in, checked one last time by Barnes, Fang-Castro gave them the go-ahead.

Barnes said, "Mr. Gorey. You've got the wheel."

The bus unlatched from the ship, Gorey gave it a tiny boost to the left, pointed it slightly inboard of their alien objective, and opened the engines. The bus's quarter-gee acceleration brought them to their cruising velocity in barely over a minute; it felt oppressively heavy to people who'd been living in a tenth of a gee for half a year.

Hannegan, the physicist, said, "My God, when we get home, it's gonna hurt, the gravity is."

"That's why you've got to keep coming to the PE classes," Barnes said. "If you don't, going home won't just hurt, it'll kill you."

Sandy kept his high-resolution cameras running all the way in, with the recordings retransmitted to the *Nixon* as they were made. Gorey stopped the bus ten kilometers out. Fang-Castro asked, "Anything?"

"Not that I see," Barnes answered.

They'd agreed that purely passive reconnaissance was the safest course. No laser altimeters or radar-mapping, nothing beamed at the alien structure, nothing that could be interpreted as hostile or invasive. They thought they'd been invited . . . but what if they were wrong?

The bus trip had been timed so that they'd arrive shortly before the primary's rotation brought the rainbow target in line with the *Nixon*. The scientists had wanted the bus to loop around the primary, so that they'd have a minutely detailed record of its entire surface, but Fang-Castro had vetoed the idea. The bus would never be out of sight of the *Nixon*, not on the first trip.

Barnes: "Here comes the target."

As the alien sphere turned, the rainbow target slowly appeared, brightening and sparkling but now something new happened. A hundred meters off to one side of the rainbow, a new, smaller bull's-eye target began to glow, in repeating concentric rings of yellow, green, and blue that shrank toward the center and disappeared.

Barnes: "John, is that a landing port?"

Clover said, "Can't see what else it could be."

Barnes said, "Admiral, unless you object, I'm going to have Elroy take us in. Otherwise, we'll be waiting another four hours before you're line-of-sight with us."

"I concur," Fang-Castro said.

"Elroy . . ."

Gorey took them in. As they closed, a port began to open in the middle of the smaller rainbow target, and a massive shelf pushed out.

"One damn fine mousetrap," Clover laughed.

"Not helping, John," Barnes snapped.

Sandy glanced at Fiorella, who was smiling into the mini-Red she'd stuck to the rail of the bus, talking a kilometer a minute.

Barnes: "That shelf could take the bus. Do we land it? Or do we leave the bus hanging? If we land it, it'll rotate out of sight."

There was a long silence, then Fang-Castro said, "We now agree here that you should land the bus. Then, if you're asked to leave, or pushed out, you'll have something to leave with—you won't be hanging on the wrong side of the primary without a ride."

Barnes: "Take it in, Elroy."

The bus landed on the primary without incident and extruded the Post-its to hold it to the surface. As soon as the bus was secure, the crew began unplugging from the bus and to go on full internal suit support.

Barnes worked through the agreed-upon procedure: "Everyone stay together. Check your tethers. I don't want anyone flying free. Nobody touch anything without my approval. Nobody armed except Emwiller, and make sure your weapon is safed, Sally. No other external equipment except for Sandy's camera gear. Ready?"

They were ready.

"Then let's go."

They floated just above the regolith of the primary. As soon as they moved away from the bus, maneuvering with their suit thrusters, a line of glowing dots appeared on the regolith leading toward the rainbow target. The dots flowed toward the open port.

"Interesting," said Hannegan, the physicist. "The surface doesn't change, it's like the light is moving through it. I'm guessing some kind of cellular automata or nanobots, they're what's making the lights. Nice. The ultimate programmable signage. You getting this, Sandy?"

"I am now." Sandy was pointing his camera at the surface, cranked up to maximum magnification. In his viewfinder, he could see the surface was packed with speckles that brightened and darkened in a coordinated way. They reminded him of the chromatophores he'd seen on the skins of squids and octopi.

The crew floated through the open port into a white, cube-shaped chamber, large enough for a small orchestra. The door that was open to space was behind them, but there was a closed door in front of them. A green pad the size of a dinner plate was next to the closed door.

Barnes looked at Clover. "What do you think?"

"What does green mean, on traffic signals almost everywhere on Earth?"

Barnes shrugged, reached forward, and punched the button.

The door behind them closed and a light winked on Sandy's camera: "George, I just lost the link back to the *Nixon*."

Barnes tried calling the *Nixon*. There was no response. "The interior must be EM-blocked. Why am I not surprised? Okay, people, we are really on our own now. You follow my orders. You do what I tell you, when I tell you to do it. You do not take the initiative, not if you ever want to come back here again. We take everything slowly."

Gas began venting into the chamber. When it hit one atmosphere, according to their suit gauges, the inner door opened. They moved forward, and somebody muttered, "Standard air lock . . ."

When they'd all entered the second chamber, the door behind them closed. The room was larger than the first, but not much, possibly ten meters long and eight wide, also a featureless white with diffuse lighting. The only item in the room was a stand-alone console toward the back of the room. A meter and a half high, it would've been impossible to miss even if the room had been as cluttered as a secondhand junk store: it glowed with flickering bands of rainbow colors and looked disturbingly similar to an antique jukebox.

Words appeared in the air above the console that read: "You can remove your helmets. The air is sterile and breathable to Earth standards and is maintained at 21 degrees Celsius." In a few seconds, the words changed to Chinese ideograms, followed by Arabic and Russian, then a half-dozen other languages, before it cycled back to English. Barnes looked over at Emwiller and said, "Sal, I'm cracking my helmet. If I collapse, get everyone out of here, pronto. Shoot out the air lock if you have to."

"Wait, wait, wait . . ." said Stuyvesant. "What if there are biologics in here?"

"That'd be another unnecessary mousetrap," Clover said.

"They could be unintentional—"

"We haven't seen anything unintentional so far. . . . I believe the air will be safe."

"I'm going to unseal," Barnes said. "Sally, stand by."

They all watched as he unclipped the faceplate on his helmet and took a deep breath. And held it. And let it out and took another. He took a few more breaths and licked his lips, tasting the air, and finally nodded. He pushed the faceplate closed again, resealed it, and said, "The air seems to be okay, but I want everybody to stay sealed. When we get back, I'll go into isolation to check for biologics. Let's go to Post-its."

They all reached down and threw switches on the legs of their EVA suits. When upward pressure was placed on a boot, a pressure switch would cut the electrical charge and the boot would peel away from the floor with about the same resistance as Earth gravity.

As they all stuck to the floor, or deck, or whatever it was, new words appeared over the polychrome console. "Please say something to me."

"Speakers and mikes, now," Barnes said, and they all went to external speakers and microphones.

The phrase repeated in the same other dozen languages they'd seen in the first message.

Barnes said, "Hello. We're from Earth. Uh, the third planet in this system."

Colors shifted across the sides of the alien console making it look even more like a jukebox, and then it spoke: "American English. I can speak in American English. Now, what questions do you have?"

Barnes asked, "Who are you?"

The jukebox said, "I am not a 'who' but a 'what.' I am a low-grade artificial intelligence tasked with answering questions. I am programmed to understand thirteen human languages, five of them based on the probability of being the first-contact languages. In order, the probability for first contact was American English, Chinese, Russian, Arabic, and Portuguese. I am not a fully intelligent AI. I chain rhetorical logic via a statistical grammar. Though it may sound as though I'm being conversational, in fact I am always responding directly or indirectly to questions. My data storage has the answers to 71,236,340 explicit or implicit questions. I can synthesize new answers from those I am preprogrammed with, but at times you will ask questions for which I have no answer, to which I will reply, 'I don't know.'"

Barnes asked, "Can we set up camera equipment to record this conversation?"

"Yes. I will wait."

Barnes nodded at Sandy, who'd had the mini-Red under his arm, recording first contact as clandestinely as he could. Now he broke three more cameras out of his carrying case and began setting them up in the bare room.

Clover asked the jukebox, "Are there any other species here now?"

The AI said, "No, you are the only species here at this time."

Clover: "When are you expecting others to arrive?"

"I don't know. That is not an omission from my database. There is no predefined schedule for arrival. Previous intervals between arrivals have ranged from two years to three hundred and ninety-six years."

"Who made you?"

"I don't know."

"Where are your makers?"

"I don't know."

"Why don't you know?"

"When they left, they didn't tell me who they were or where they were going."

"When did they leave?"

"One thousand seven hundred and fifty-three Earth years ago."

Hannegan: "How old is this facility? The aliens . . . uh, the beings who recently left, they weren't your makers?"

"This depot is 21,682 Earth years old, and I don't know if the species that recently departed were my makers, because I don't know who my makers were."

Stuyvesant: "Can you tell us what the other species look like?"

"No. There may be some visual recording facilities on this depot, but I do not have access to them."

Stuyvesant: "Do you provide this service to species other than humans? Do you speak languages not derived from Earth?"

"Yes."

Barnes: "How can you run this depot with so little critical information?"

"I do not run this depot. It is separately automated. I am here to answer questions."

Hannegan muttered, "Not very helpfully, so far."

Clover wagged a finger at him: "Are you programmed to deny us information about your technology?"

"No. Ninety percent of my information is about technology. I contain complete descriptions, operation details, status reports, maintenance records, documentation, and instructional and design manuals for this station, and for its satellites."

Barnes: "Tell us all about the depot."

"That would not be a good idea."

"Why?"

"I would not know what you would want to know. I would start with the first facts in my memory and proceed through the databases in an orderly manner. Done orally, it would take seventeen Earth years. Do you have sufficient time?"

Clover: "Don't you have more efficient ways to transmit information than talking?"

"Of course, but I do not know which ones of them, if any, are usable by you. Technology changes very rapidly. In comparison, language changes extremely slowly. I doubt you are equipped with I/O protocols from even a century ago. But English, as spoken several centuries ago, would still be comprehensible to you today. If you have communications specialists I can talk to, we can probably find a mutually agreeable protocol."

Clover: "And you are willing to transfer that data to us?"

"Yes."

Barnes held up a hand to slow him down, then looked at the jukebox:

"You say you can't tell us about your makers or other species. Is that because you are prohibited from sharing that information, or because it's not in your databases?"

"Your question is not entirely correct. I do have some limited information about my makers and other species, but you have not asked the correct questions to elicit that response. As to your other point, I am not prohibited from answering any questions for which I have information. Everything I know or can synthesize is accessible to anyone who asks me questions."

Clover jumped in: "What would be the correct questions that would elicit your programmed response about your makers and the other species?"

"The correct questions would be: First: 'Are your makers afraid of us?' The correct answer would be, 'Not at this time.' Second: 'Should we be afraid of them?' The correct answer would be, 'Not at this time.' Third: 'Should we consider them hostile to our species?' The correct answer would be, 'No.'"

Emwiller looked at Barnes: "Sir, should we be trusting these answers?"

Barnes shrugged: "I don't know."

Clover asked the jukebox, "Is there some way we can determine if you're telling the truth or not?"

"Not that I am aware of, but I have not been programmed to lie. I am not an advanced AI. I cannot construct elaborate fabrications. If I were to mix false information with the true, it is likely the questioner would eventually find a discrepancy or contradiction in my answers. Lying would also interfere with my function, which is to provide instructional information on how to best make use of this depot and to ensure that visitors do not harm the depot or themselves unintentionally."

Clover turned to Barnes: "What we have here is the 'all Cretans are liars' problem. Its responses make sense, but this could be a very elaborate fabrication. I'd say that either this machine is pretty much as it seems, or it's much more sophisticated than we can imagine, a very high-level AI, well beyond our systems, masquerading as a low one. I think we have to assume the former until proven otherwise, because there's not much we can do if it isn't true."

Hannegan said, "But if it feeds us incorrect information on physics, we'll find that out pretty quickly. I personally don't care if it's lying about what the various species are like, if it could deliver, say, a thirtieth-century *Physics Handbook*."

Stuyvesant: "That's a little parochial, Bob."

Hannegan: "Yeah, well, what if he could deliver a thirtieth-century *Biochemistry Handbook*?"

"That would be helpful," Stuyvesant admitted.

Barnes said, "Our jukebox raised another concern. New question: Why do we have to worry about harming ourselves or the depot?"

The jukebox said, "This depot has technologies and artifacts from many different species. No visitor could be familiar with them all. Some of these devices are dangerous if misused, the same way a milling laser is dangerous if misused."

Clover nodded: strange technology, strange tools.

The jukebox: "Also, there are containment modules that should not be accessed without proper instruction, as they currently hold a total of eight hundred and forty-nine tonnes of antimatter."

"Holy shit," Hannegan said. "Uh, where did all this antimatter come from?"

"It's manufactured here."

Before anyone could say anything, Barnes barked, "All right, everybody, speakers off, intersuit comm channel 7, full encryption, wait for my lead."

When everybody had gone to encryption, he said, "This is exactly why our mission was top priority for the U.S. We need to secure this, or make sure that nobody else gets their hands on it. That is a buttload lot of antimatter. Bob, thoughts?"

The physicist had been looking off in a distracted way and tapping the fingers of one hand together. "Yeah, I'm doing a little mental arithmetic here. If the Wurlitzer is telling the truth, that's on the order of a teratonne explosive equivalent. Call it a million of those H-bombs the superpowers used to stockpile. Which immediately has me wondering, first, where is it? And second, how are they making it? Related to that, where are they getting the power to make it?"

Barnes said, "Numbers one and two are what most concern me. Plus, there's a number four: Will the answer-bot tell us how to make it?"

"Let's go back to the jukebox." They turned back to the answer-bot. "Excuse us, we need to discuss the information you imparted."

"My programming informs me that is very common with first arrivals and I am not programmed to take offense in any way. Do you have any other questions at this time?"

Hannegan cleared his throat: "Uh, you said this depot stored over eight hundred tonnes of antimatter. Where? And how?"

The jukebox said, "The constellation of small moonlets you see associated with this depot are the containment modules for the antimatter. The material is in the form of iron-58, which is electromagnetically isolated from the walls of the modules."

Hannegan raised his eyebrows: "Anti-iron? We can barely manage anti-helium. How do you make this and where do you get the power? For us, manufacturing that quantity of antimatter would require roughly a year's worth of solar output."

There was a perceptible pause as the answer-bot considered its answer. Then:

"I can't give you an accurate answer to your first question unless your engineers can establish a high-bandwidth I/O path. Very inaccurately and roughly, the transformation reaction makes use of a supersymmetric resonance to convert protons to antiprotons. An analogous lepton pathway produces positrons. Assembling those into neutrons and higher-order nuclei is a straightforward exploitation of a subset of localized D brane excitations to chain up isotopic ladders of least resistance—"

Hannegan said, "Okay, stop. I get it. We'll wait for the interface."

"As for your second question, this depot taps the rotational energy of Saturn for power. The reaction pathway is approximately twenty percent efficient. Consequently this depot can produce something in excess of one billion tonnes of antimatter before Saturn's rotational period will be significantly altered."

Hannegan glanced at Barnes, then asked, "Can you provide engineering designs and instructional manuals for the antimatter production and containment facilities?"

This time there was no hesitation in the response. "That information is exportable to all species."

Barnes said, "I think that's enough for this session. We should return to our ship now. Are we allowed to return at any time?"

"Yes, at any time."

"We will bring engineers to discuss a high-bandwidth I/O pathway. May they come at any time?"

"Yes, at any time."

Sandy cut in. "Speaking of which, can you establish a link so that I'll be able to transmit directly to our ship from here?"

"EM-blocking is an initial precaution. The security system will establish a communications link for you before your next visit."

Fiorella, who'd kept her mouth shut, jumped in: "George, please: give me one minute. Or two minutes. No more than two minutes. Three at the outside."

Barnes grinned and said, "Two minutes, Cassie."

Fiorella moved up to the jukebox with Sandy switching between cameras to provide a range of views. She asked the machine, "Do you have a name?"

"I have understood that you call me jukebox."

"That's because you look like an antique music machine from Earth, called a Wurlitzer. Could we name you Wurly?"

"Yes."

Barnes groaned, Clover laughed, and Fiorella asked, "Wurly, do you have any historical records? Of events in other systems?"

"Yes. My records contain a generalized history of this galactic arm."

"If you have no information about other species, how can you have a history?"

"Because the history has no specific information about other species. The species are designated by number and date of emergence and tradable items. Specific information on the species is not available through my memory banks."

"That information must exist somewhere."

"Yes, that is logical."

"Do you have tradable items stored here?"

"Yes."

"Do we have access to them?"

"Under the terms of tradable items, yes. However, you must have items to trade."

Now Clover got back in: "How can we provide items to trade if our technology is so much lower than star-traveling species?"

"Most tradable items are not technological. One questioner referred to an antique music machine. Music machines are often tradable. There is a trade AI that will determine if your music machines are tradable, and if so, what level of trade you may access. In general, these are not valued highly, as it is very likely that other civilizations already have music machines resembling yours, and manufacturing specifications can be simply transmitted, which is vastly less costly than carrying physical goods between stellar systems. But the actual alien machines may be valued by collectors in some cultures, as visual artworks are in yours. Some musical compositions might also be tradable, for similar reasons."

Sandy: "We gotta have a hundred and fifty instruments on board—I've got eight guitars down in the fab shop area, and we've gotta have a million songs on file, from Bach to Kid Little."

Barnes said, "Yeah, yeah, we'll discuss that later."

Clover raised a finger. "Uh . . . Wurly . . . are there any classes of trade goods that we 'primitives' might have that would garner us more trade credit?"

"You are not considered 'primitives,' merely less technologically advanced."

Clover muttered into a private comm channel, "It doesn't get sarcasm. Probably not a high-level AI, as it says . . . or it's a great faker."

The answer-bot continued. "Physical art artifacts are valued by species with similar sensory systems and possessed of an inclination toward acquisitiveness. These are worth something. Comestibles can also be rated highly, especially those that cannot be duplicated based on the transmission of data."

Stuyvesant jumped on that—her specialty, biology. "Oh, come on. You're telling me different species from entirely different ecosystems can eat each other's food?"

"Very rarely. On the infrequent occasions when the biologicals are compatible, though, those can be highly prized trade goods."

Clover said, "Makes sense to me. How much were rich folks in Europe willing to pay for spices a few hundred years ago? Stuff we take for granted, like peppercorns. A king's ransom. And that's not an exaggeration."

Stuyvesant pondered for a moment. "Hmmm, there's the commander's tea—you can't transmit 'specs' for that. And I've heard rumors there's some pretty good booze squirreled away somewhere."

Clover winced. "I'll work on a list."

Barnes got back to the jukebox: "Is there any limit on the number of trades?"

"Not exactly. Trade items are evaluated by a trade computer and assigned a total numerical value between 1 and 8. You may leave the items and choose trade items with a similar total value."

"Was that top number chosen because your makers use a mathematical system with a base eight?" Stuyvesant asked.

"I have no information about my makers."

"Is your native mathematical system in base 8?"

"Yes, except for our mathematical computer languages. However, when speaking with you, I convert all numbers to base 10."

Stuyvesant: "When you have new arrivals, does the station provide them with a relevant environment, as you did with us?"

"Yes, if it is within the station's means. Not all species can be accommodated. Those that cannot be accommodated always have means to maneuver in space, so they do that."

"Do all species require gaseous environments?"

"No. Some require hybrid gas-liquid environments."

Clover: "Does the size of your entry air lock and entry hall suggest that other species may be quite large?"

"Yes."

"This was supposed to be my two minutes, goddamnit," Fiorella said. To the jukebox: "Wurly, do you have a message for the people of Earth?"

"Yes."

"What is it?"

Wurly said, "Hello, people of Earth."

Fiorella: "Anything more?"

"No."

Barnes muttered, "Well, shit, that was inspiring. I'm calling an end to this . . . again. Everybody ready? Let's go."

Leaving was as simple as the arrival. From the bus, Sandy fired the contents of his camera's memory back to the *Nixon*. It was gone in a few seconds; they were gone in another minute.

42.

Back at the *Nixon*, the contact team stepped through the air lock and found themselves face-to-face with a room full of people, easily half the ship's complement, clapping, cheering. Fang-Castro was leading the cheer and even Crow was smiling.

The commander stepped forward. "Congratulations to you all. You just made history." She turned to Sandy. "Mr. Darlington, job well done. The recordings and data you beamed back are already on their way to Earth."

To the rest of them, she said, "I'll give you a half hour to decompress, and use the facilities, but then I need you all in the Commons to discuss what you learned. Captain Barnes, you're headed for isolation, but we've got vid and sound ready for you. We are indebted to you for your courage in making yourself a guinea pig: I will recommend to the commandant of the Marine Corps that you be awarded the Bronze Star. I believe you deserve better than that, but nobody has yet defined our aliens as an enemy force. In any case, I'm sure we are all inspired by your selfless act."

Another round of applause, and seven of them began peeling off EVA suits while Barnes clumped away to the isolation suite.

The Commons was jammed: the entire first contact team was there, with all the department heads, and all the individual scientists, no matter the discipline. Sandy set up his cameras, set to record and transmit, and Barnes, relaxing in the isolation suite, gave a brief summary, and then said, "I think you've all seen Sandy's movie by now, so you really know as much as we do. The question isn't what we got, the question is, what does it mean? That's more in your territory than mine."

Crow jumped in immediately, addressing himself to Fang-Castro: "Ma'am, one thing is already crystal-clear from the vid. If the jukebox, uh, Wurly, is not lying to us, then everything we hoped for and feared is about to happen. The aliens are about to deliver technology that could unbalance the world's power structure. In my opinion, that's the number one thing that our strategists on Earth have to think about. The other stuff is interesting, or, I should say, fascinating, but the tech . . . that's beyond important."

Barnes got back in: "I'm a little skeptical. Total strangers, 'benevolent' aliens give us incredibly valuable and very dangerous tech? They're handing the family jewels to someone who could potentially be their enemy. What's the catch?"

Fang-Castro nodded, looked at Clover: "John?"

Clover took the cue. "Y'know what I think? I think they're pump-priming. I think they're giving us technology that they expect will make us more valuable to *them*. I don't think this is charity or altruism. I think this is self-interest. Remember, they already have met us, in a very real sense. They know our languages. We don't know how they know—maybe their supercomputers just analyzed radio broadcasts. But however they got their hands on the information, they know a lot more about us than we know about them. Besides, it's not like this costs them anything."

Crow cleared his throat. "I'm in agreement with John on this one. There's nothing the aliens could give us that would make us a credible threat to them. We don't know who they are, or where they're from. One thing we do know is that they could be an existential danger to us, if we tried to mess with them. So there's no downside for them in giving us this stuff, and there might be a considerable upside."

Sandy interjected, "You don't think antimatter technology makes us a lot more dangerous?"

"To ourselves, maybe, but not to them," Crow said. "Try this thought on for size. Suppose the U.S. were to give Jamaica, with whom we're none too friendly these days, all our military designs and knowledge. What could they do with it? Attack us? Sure, they might get in one slap. Then we'd wipe their island off the face of the planet. At the first White House briefing on the starship's arrival, the military science guys told

President Santeros that one of the reasons we had to come out here was because a starship was inherently very dangerous. Slam one into the earth at running speed and there's a good chance you make humanity extinct, or at least push it back to the Stone Age."

Martinez joined in. "That's just the technology we know about. All we've seen is a starship that is a century or so ahead of our engineering. From what we've seen here and been told by the answer-bot, we know it's not their first or only one. A ship like the one we detected may take a century or more to make a trip between star systems. The 'bot said it was installed seventeen centuries ago. How many millennia ago did the makers build their first starship? Three? Four? Ten? And what about the other species, the ones who aren't the makers? And who built that damn primary thing twenty millennia back?"

Crow nodded. "Exactly. They're not just a century ahead of us, they're thousands of years ahead. We don't really know how many. So why not give us tech that might make us more valuable to them? Or, maybe, just to make us like them a bit better? Trinkets for the natives."

Clover looked thoughtful. "Yeaahh," he drew out. "Maybe they've been doing this long enough that they're a real good judge of who'll make a good future trade partner. Or maybe it's just a shotgun approach: they try this on every potential partner. If it works out, great for both parties. If the indigenes screw themselves over, no skin off the aliens' butts. Assuming they have butts. If we get too big for our britches and turn hostile, they'd wipe us out and go on to the next species. There's lots of fish swimmin' in the Milky Way. Hell, maybe it's never worked, but they figure it doesn't hurt to try again."

"So that's the big picture? We get this stuff because they think it will make us more valuable, but if we don't play like good little boys and girls, we're history?" Fang-Castro asked.

Clover said, "It's probably not that simple. We might even be completely misjudging the situation. But it might be prudent to assume the worst in this case and behave accordingly. . . . I'm particularly concerned that we can't get any information on the aliens, of whom there seem to be several varieties. I'd like you all to think on questions that might circumvent that prohibition and ones that would illuminate why it exists in the first place."

Crow nodded in agreement. "Security always has a reason. We need to understand theirs."

Fang-Castro said, "Another conversation with Wurly—God, I can't believe you did that, Cassie, but I think we're stuck with it now—anyway, another conversation with Wurly is our top priority, along with that high-bandwidth link the answer-bot offered us. First priority on next contact is engineering and communication. We'll have a new team leader in Lieutenant Emwiller, in keeping with the idea of some basic military-style discipline while on the primary."

Sandy held up a hand, and Fang-Castro nodded at him. "If I'm not out of place, I think it might not be a bad idea to take a guitar and an amp with us. And maybe, if they want to go, Joe Martinez and Crow. We could talk to this trade-bot they've got, give them a musical demo, see if they want to trade, and for what. My concern is, we're doing fine right now—but what if they cut us off for some reason? What if we . . . or the Chinese . . . do something to piss them off? I think packing away as much stuff as possible, as quickly as possible, might be a good idea."

Fang-Castro said, "Yes. That's good. Get the equipment ready. Whether or not Mr. Crow would be a valuable musical addition to your team, I would like to have a security expert take a look at the inside of that place. If Mr. Crow agrees . . . ?"

"Absolutely," Crow said.

Martinez said, "You know I'm hot to go, under any conditions."

"We should start getting responses to first contact from the earth-based people in four hours or so. Let's plan to launch again in twelve hours, to meet here in eight to discuss Earth-expert concerns and suggestions. Between now and then, I want seven hours of sleep for all team members, with meds as necessary," Fang-Castro said. She thought for a moment. "Okay. That's it. Everybody: brainstorm ahead of time and see if you can figure out some questions that might get us more information on the prohibited topics."

Second contact.

On the first trip out, Sandy had kept all of his cameras fixed on the primary at different focal lengths. On the second trip, he put one camera in tourist mode, recording sweeping views of Saturn along with the rings seen nearly edge-on, a thin white line bisecting the sky, most with the alien artifact somewhere in the picture. And he spent time recording in detail both the bees and the antimatter storage units.

On the second trip in, with Martinez at the wheel, they moved more quickly, and stayed longer. They were all more relaxed than they'd been yesterday, but this time, they all kept their helmets on.

Emwiller to Wurly: "We've brought along a communications technician to determine what data interface would be mutually compatible. How should we proceed?"

The jukebox glowed a pure yellow, then flickered through the spectrum. To its right, a section of what they had thought was a seamless wall slid aside. "Down that corridor, I have another avatar by the entrance to the storerooms. Your technician may converse with me there."

The tech, Hal Emery, walked over and looked down the hall.

Crow muttered: "He's going alone?"

Emwiller called, "Hey, Hal, you want company?"

He waved her off. "S'okay. Hall's only five meters long and it's mostly empty."

Clover said to Wurly, "If we understand correctly, once our technician has set up the data link, you'll be transmitting to us all the information on your antimatter technology?"

"That is not correct."

Clover: "You said yesterday that you needed the high-speed data link to convey the information."

"That is accurate, but the link itself will not be sufficient. My analysis suggests that your equipment does not have sufficient transmission bandwidth to accept all the relevant data in what would be a reasonable time here, given your life-support systems. I will provide all the requested data in a quantum storage unit. I will also provide a reader for the quantum storage unit, also called in English a QSU. The first portions of the I/O transfer will include specifications for construction of the reader, should you need backup readers. The quantum storage unit reader is capable of feeding seven hundred and forty of your high-bandwidth channels simultaneously, if equipped with appropriate outputs. The data reader, however, is itself a very sophisticated device. Its interfaces are not currently compatible with your computer technology. You will have to adapt."

"Will the information be in English?"

"Partly in English, but largely in mathematics. Some new words will be introduced and defined."

Emwiller: "Can you give us backup QSUs and readers, in case we run into technical problems?"

"Yes, I can provide eight quantum storage units and eight readers."

Emwiller wasn't ready to let go. "Our I/O links are pretty fast. Can you transmit the basics of the theory and technology to us on how to build the reader?"

"Yes, I can do that. With the bandwidth I expect you to provide, it will take approximately three weeks to provide all the information on the reader, itself. It is not a simple device, and a wide variety of other technologies must be explained in detail before you can build it. Many of the design specifications are on the atomic level. Some even require customized nucleon lattices. There are components whose functional configuration demands the precise placement of considerable quantities of individual atoms. It is a large amount of data."

Hannegan said, "We shouldn't have expected it to be easy, but precisely placing umpteen trillion atoms? Yeah, that'll take us a while to figure out."

He thought for a minute. "Let me ask you this: Do you have compilations of physics, chemistry, and biological processes that could be transmitted separately and more quickly over our limited bandwidth?"

"Yes. If you wish to prioritize those among the goods you trade for.

Other species have done so. When shorn of false trails, error, discussion,
and philosophy, much of this galactic arm's research into those areas can
be delivered in approximately six days, four hours, three minutes, and
7.4 seconds, if your technician's description of your I/O processes and
bandwidth is correct. If you choose this trade, the trade system can establish a parallel I/O link."

Hannegan said to Stuyvesant, "The admiral'll have to sign off on
using our trade points for that, but I think that's the way to go—get as
much of basic science as we can, while we can, in the I/O stream. We can
pass the science along to Earth as quickly as we get it. If the ship gets
blown up on the way back, we're gonna lose both the readers and the
QSUs, anyway. . . . Better to have the science, than a little bit of random
tech about the QSU readers."

Stuyvesant nodded: "I agree. Let's get that started."

The jukebox spoke up, unprompted: "Your communications technician wishes to speak to you about placing a communications link on the
surface of the station. He cannot reach you with your radio/video link."

"Why not?" Hannegan asked.

"Unregistered electromagnetic radiation is suppressed between
rooms in the station. Not all the trade items stored here are neutrally
receptive to electromagnetic radiation."

"I'll get it," Emwiller said. She walked toward the hallway where the
tech had gone.

Crow said, "I'll come with you."

Sandy handed him the mini-Red that Fiorella had been using: "Take
this. It's running."

When they were gone, Clover glanced at the other crew members,
then asked, "Is there a God?"

Wurly: "Concepts of God are extremely varied but the consensus of
the varied species put the probability of the existence of God at forty-
two percent."

"Really?"

"No, not really. I was programmed to answer in this way. Concepts
of God are so varied that no computation is possible."

Stuyvesant: "John, did you catch that? His maker had a sense of humor."

Clover nodded: "Yes. Wonderful."

Clover asked, "Your lack of information strikes us as a form of secrecy. Why so much secrecy?"

The answer-bot rippled mauve and puce for a second.

"This question is frequently asked, in various forms, by new arrivals. The purpose of depots like this one is to allow contact between alien species without direct contact. Early on, direct contacts were tried many times, by many different species, in many different ways. It almost always went badly. With few exceptions, alien species are too different from each other to allow constructive interaction. At best the efforts were extremely discomforting to one or both of the contactees. At worst, one or both found the other genuinely repugnant in some way.

"Contact invariably began with good intentions and no thoughts of hostility. Almost invariably those intentions failed. None of the failures were productive, and some of them were catastrophic. Eventually the surviving species still capable of interstellar travel devised this system of depots to safely provide some degree of cooperation and interaction.

"The depots provide two services. They are fuel production and storage facilities for antimatter-powered starships, and they are 'trading posts' of a sort. Arriving ships have automatic access to the antimatter storage vessels. In addition, they may offer trade goods, which are scored by a trade computer. They may take away items from the storeroom with similar scores, up to eight."

Clover was intrigued: "There is no medium of exchange? Just a scored swap?"

"That is correct. It is very difficult to measure the relative value of alien goods to other alien species. Our trade computer is highly sophisticated, but even so, there are continuing efforts to upgrade it."

Clover said to Stuyvesant, "Well, I'll be sheep-dipped. The advanced interstellar culture operates on a barter system. Never saw that one coming."

He turned back to Wurly: "You said with few exceptions there were problems. But there were exceptions? There were species that did get along well?"

"Yes. There are several pairings of cooperative species and even a sequence of similar species based on what Earth science would call convergent evolution. I have no information on those species."

Clover said, "About this trade system . . . the trade items seem fairly trivial in value compared to the cost of actually retrieving them. The ship that just departed was several cubic kilometers in size. Why are these ships wandering around the galaxy? Trade can't be the primary motive, can it?"

Wurly said, "No. Most ships that stop here are colony ships, on their way to colonize new planets. A certain percentage of technological societies severely damage their own planets before they become mature enough to understand the damage they are doing. In the past, a number of species have gone extinct before they achieved interstellar flight because of that damage, usually through runaway biological warfare or atomic warfare, with its consequent radiation poisoning. Those that do manage to survive despite badly damaged planetary ecosystems often look for a place to begin again to assure species survival. Planetary systems are quite common, although those that fit specific biological niches and that are not yet inhabited by advanced sentient creatures are not. Therefore, colony ships. Precise statistics are not available because of potential sampling error but it appears that between fifteen and twenty percent of advanced star-faring civilizations will sponsor at least one colony ship."

Stuyvesant asked, "Why would they stop here? It can't be to pick up antimatter: they would have done that at their home system and they'd already be traveling as fast as it's possible to travel with any given technology. . . ."

Wurly said, "No, the primary purpose for stopping is to restock supplies of consumables. Even with advanced recycling systems, some material is eventually lost and so stops are necessary. Water, for example—it would be possible to take along enough water to replace that lost on a multi-century flight, but that would add hugely to the mass that needs to be moved. The antimatter here is used simply to get them back up to traveling speed. The actual stop is made to restock consumable supplies harvested from the planetary rings."

Clover said to Stuyvesant, "Saturn's not just a recharge station. It's a convenience store."

Emwiller, Crow, and the comm tech came back, and Emwiller said, "We're gonna have to fab an interface to one of several possibilities suggested by the station, and the station will provide a constant-broadcast link back to the *Nixon*. We can't do it here. The most important thing we can get out of here will come over the I/O connection, so we need to head back."

Sandy asked the jukebox, "Wurly, could you direct us to the trade computer?"

"Yes, it is down the hallway number 2, opening to your right."

Sandy said to Emwiller, "We've got two guitars, a bass, and an amp with us. I think we should take the time to get them evaluated."

Clover said: "Stuyvesant and I have lots more questions, and Hannegan, too. . . . Every minute brings up amazing stuff. Give them time to talk to the trade computer."

Crow said, "I'd like to look around some more, anyway."

Emwiller nodded: "Okay, but if it's gonna take a while, if it's like a DMV or something, you gotta be willing to cut it off so we can head back."

The evaluation didn't take long. The trade computer was parked in a short dead-end hallway, and when they approached, it asked, in Wurly's voice, "Trade items for evaluation?"

"Yes."

"Please provide a simple description."

"Three musical instruments operated by vibrating strings which cause sound waves in gaseous atmospheres, and an electronic amplifier, powered by a battery."

"These are somewhat common instruments, but have some value, as well," the computer said. "Can you demonstrate their function?"

"Yes. It'll take a minute to plug in . . ."

They plugged in, and Martinez said, "We oughta go with our best number."

Crow: "'Yellow Dog Blues'?"

"That's what we got."

Sandy, "Okay, 'Yellow Dog Blues,' let's do it right: Everybody ready? Uh-one, anda-two, anda . . ."

"Yellow Dog Blues" lasted two minutes and nine seconds and when they finished, the computer said, "How many units of the instruments and the amplifiers can you deliver?"

"How many do you want?"

"Seventeen. For seventeen units, each unit consisting of three instruments and one amplifier, we will award you two-point-five points. Eight points is the maximum we may allow."

"Two-point-five? Shit, you're a tough audience. Okay, you got a deal," Sandy said.

Crow: "Seventeen units—is that in base 8, or base 10?"

The computer said, "Base 10. When communicating with you, all numbers are in base 10."

At the jukebox, Emwiller asked, "I think we understand the rules by which this depot operates, but what happens if someone breaks them? For example, what if a ship tries to take more than its share of goods or insists on approaching a depot when another ship is docked here?"

Wurly said, "The depots have some defenses. While you would find them overwhelmingly effective, most species that can build starships could overcome them. The network relies on disincentives. If a ship knowingly violates the rules of conduct, that information is propagated over the network to the security systems on all the depots. For some period of time, access to those depots is denied to other ships belonging to that species. The length of time depends upon the seriousness of the violation."

Emwiller persisted, "But what if some species ignored those denials and took what they wanted by force? What would prevent them from doing so?"

The answer-bot flashed silver, red, and lavender. "I do not know of any such occurrence. There's nothing in my historical records to indicate that that has ever happened, although those only go back 21,682 years. Also, I cannot find any information that would constitute a useful reason for this to happen. Essentially, it would require disabling a depot to overcome its defenses, rendering it useless for any future visits."

Emwiller started to ask another question, but Clover interrupted. "I think I get it. Destroying a depot to get what you want, when it gives stuff away freely, would be killing a goose that laid the golden eggs. You could, if you're shortsighted." He stopped, thought for a moment. "I wonder, can a species that embarks on multi-century voyages be short-sighted? Good question . . ." He looked off, lost in thought.

"John!" Emwiller snapped.

"Ah, yes. I was saying . . . you could do that, but then the sanctions would kick in, and your only options would be to cooperate or to continue to kill the geese. Mass goosicide eventually takes down the network, and then where are you for interstellar travel? Besides which, at sub–light speeds, this would take millennia, maybe hundreds of millennia. How many species have policies that are stable—and homicidal— for that long?"

"The only reason that could make sense for doing this would be to force policy, to blackmail the trading system into doing what you want or risk further destruction. But there's no one making policy! The depot network just does what it does, following a set of preestablished rules. You can't threaten it, because it lacks volition. It'd be like trying to threaten, oh, Sandy's camera—'Give me what I want or I'll destroy all your fellow cameras, mwahahaha.' Yeah, that'd work." He laughed. It echoed deafeningly in the chamber.

Stuyvesant said, "So, basically, you're saying that the system is stable and robust because it's too simple and dumb to be broken?"

Clover nodded: "Yup. I think so. A primitive barter system, a really simple set of rules, and no system of flexible governance. I think you can 'game' it about as well as you can game a toaster."

Sandy, Crow, and Martinez emerged from the side hallway without instruments: "We got two and a half points," Sandy said. "It's something. Let's see what some of the commander's tea and Clover's booze"—Clover winced again—"will get us."

43.

Fang-Castro poured two cups of tea and pushed one toward Crow. "Any change?"

Crow took a chair, shook his head. "No. The Chinese will be entering orbit tomorrow. Not only are they not talking to us, the Chinese government isn't saying anything useful to ours. We haven't seen any rendezvous craft splitting off, and it still looks like their ship'll be coming in close, inside the D Ring. It'll pass less than five thousand klicks above Saturn's atmosphere. It's coming in on a conventional high-inclination trajectory like we did, presumably to avoid ring particle impacts."

Fang-Castro took a sip of tea and said, "That's all by the book. It's how I would do it if I were commanding their ship. Come in steep and make your burn as close to Saturn as possible to get the most benefit from the delta-vee. Does that fit with your briefings?"

"Yes. Except my guys don't think they have enough reaction mass to achieve orbit. At least, not any kind of an orbit that would leave them in a position to resupply their tanks, let alone rendezvous with the aliens' depot. They'll be stuck, powerless, in orbit around Saturn. That's one case. The other is that they don't achieve Saturn orbit at all, in which case they've got a very long trip back to the inner solar system, and they're still powerless."

"Okay. What do we do about it?" She cradled her cup and looked at him patiently.

Crow sipped tea, said, "You gotta give me a list of your teas when we get back."

"It's a short list, but a good one. Of course, if Darlington has his way, it'll all be traded away. Enjoy it while you can."

"I will. Santeros and her group haven't made decisions yet, about the Chinese. Or, at least, not any she has communicated to me. I think it will depend upon the circumstances and whether the Chinese request our assistance. Then she'll weigh the options and tell us what actions to take. If any."

"It's coming down to what we talked about, David," she said. "If the Chinese government privately requests assistance as one government to another, that's for Santeros to work out. If the *Celestial Odyssey* directly issues a distress call or a request for aid and assistance, it's my decision, and it isn't even a hard one. We assist. To whatever extent is necessary to assure the safety of their crew, if not their ship."

"The President might order otherwise."

"The President doesn't get to decide. The Law of Space is clear on this point. When not in time of war, if a space vessel or establishment issues a distress call, any other vessels or establishments that can render assistance must do so, as long as it does not put them in danger. It's like maritime law but it's got much bigger teeth. If an oceangoing vessel is in bad trouble, people are likely to die. In space, it's a certainty. Failure to render assistance is classed as contributory homicide under international law," Fang-Castro said. "If I render assistance against the President's orders, she will have me court-martialed when we return to Earth. If I fail to render assistance in accordance with her orders, the International Court of Justice will try me for homicide and they will convict me, with a sentence of life in prison."

Crow said, "It is this president's policy not to allow U.S. military officers to be subject to trial by the International Court."

"That does not reassure me, David. My predecessor on the space station had to deal with the mess created the last time the U.S. flouted international space law, back in the early fifties. Look it up. 'U.S. Interops Space Litter Fine' will get you there. That president stood tough, until he discovered how powerful passive-aggressive disapproval can be in space. The U.S. cannot afford to be a pariah among the spacefaring players. Santeros will turn me over, when it sinks in just how much protecting me will cost the U.S."

"You're sort of skipping over an important point, Naomi," Crow said. "We're required to render assistance if it doesn't put us in danger. But

what if it does? Who decides what constitutes danger? What happens if
Santeros and her intel people decide that taking Chinese troops into an
unarmed vessel is automatically dangerous, and they communicate that
to you?"

Fang-Castro looked up at the ceiling, thought about it, then looked
back at Crow and smiled. "You know what? If they did that, and I ordered a rescue anyway, then it would all come down to what the Chinese
did. If we rescued them, and that was it—we simply hauled them back to
Earth on friendly terms—then Santeros wouldn't do anything. I might
not get another star, but that would be the end of it. On the other hand,
if the Chinese did try to take our ship, and I survived, then I'd probably
be court-martialed and convicted."

"Yes." Crow put his fingertips together. "It ain't pretty. So what are
we going to do?"

"Well, I think you should get word of this conversation back to
Santeros, so we don't wind up putting ourselves in a mutually untenable
situation. Convince her to leave the decision to me, and I'll take full responsibility for whatever happens. She can find reasons to do that—for
example, our comm lag is now so bad that she would be unable to provide me with minute-by-minute orders, and blah-blah-blah. Her PR
people can handle it."

"I don't know if they'll go for that, but I can try," Crow said. "They
may try to download about a thousand different scenarios on us, everything they can think of, with specific orders for each one."

"Tell them not to do that. If I tried to follow their scenarios, something inevitably would get screwed up, and they'd get blamed," Fang-
Castro said. "No. You tell them if something goes wrong, I'll take the
blame."

"I'm not sure they're so worried about who to blame—it'd be you, no
matter what happens—as they are genuinely worried about what would
happen if the Chinese got all this tech, and we didn't. If they grabbed
our ship, and, you know, took it and kept it."

"I worry about that, too. Which brings me to something else I need from you. I need you to analyze the security situation should we be required to take an indeterminate number of crew members from the *Celestial Odyssey* on board."

"We're working on that."

"David, I've never asked you this, but it's time to put a few more cards on the table. How many trained military personnel do we have on board the *Nixon*?" She held up a hand to stop him before he began to answer. "In total. Not just the official complement, but including the ones you had placed undercover among the regular crew members. Like Sandy Darlington. No, you don't have to give me names. Not yet. I just want the head count."

Crow didn't hesitate. "We have fifteen. Including the official eight, you, and First Officer Francisco."

"Mmm," Fang-Castro said. "I'd hoped for a few more. What's the latest guess on how large the Chinese crew is?"

Crow shook his head. "No change there. It can't be fewer than twenty-five. We can't imagine any way, technically, to run that ship with fewer people. Fifty might be a plausible guess. But it could be larger than our complement, maybe over a hundred."

"David, that really doesn't help at all," Fang-Castro said. "You better start grinding out your own scenarios. And we better hope that the Chinese have their situation under control, and this doesn't come up."

Crow said, "We'll get those memory things from Wurly, those quantum devices, the next time over. Supposedly, that's everything they've got—science, tech, everything. We could simply say that we didn't want to get in an untenable position here, given the lack of cooperation from the Chinese government . . . and then leave."

"What would Santeros say to that?"

"Listen, what Santeros wants is every bit of information we can squeeze out of the alien station, and she doesn't want the Chinese to get any of it," Crow said. "She knows that's probably not possible, but that's the baseline of what she wants."

"I don't see any way that could happen."

"There's one way. We get everything, and decide to leave. The Chi-

nese know that if we leave without them, they're all dead. So they have to
come with us, and we agree to take them, but we don't give them time to
download everything themselves. Then we've got it, and they don't."

"That's a dangerous game," Fang-Castro said. "If we've got it, but
they don't, then our ship is in real danger. The Chinese could decide that
it's better to destroy us than let us get back to Earth with the alien tech.
Or they could decide that they've got to take our ship, and take the tech."

"Yes."

"Or they could launch a very small conventional warhead that we'd
never see—if they haven't already done it—and simply steer it into us,
while we're on the way back. The *Nixon* goes up in smoke, and who
knows what caused it?"

"Yes."

After a moment, she asked, "What do you think, realistically, is the
best possible outcome, other than we get it all, and they don't get any?"

"Ohhh . . . you know, the *Odyssey* started out as a colony ship, set up
for a very long mission. What they could do, simply, is wait us out. When
we leave, they go into the station and do just what we did. Get it all. Then
the competition moves back to Earth. And that's fine. The Chinese have
some great scientists, but so do we. The competition would be pretty
even. Could even become cooperative."

"Would Santeros go for that? Or do we come back to the idea that she
wants all of it, and she doesn't want the Chinese to get any of it?"

"I don't know. I think she'd go for it if she had no choice. I really
think she's waiting to see what's going to happen with the Chinese ship.
If it makes a good orbit tomorrow, and doesn't need help, maybe that's
where she'll leave it. But that woman is always looking for an advantage.
This game is nowhere near over."

44.

The *Celestial Odyssey*'s trajectory was very tight and its speed was way too fast. The Chinese ship would hit closest approach at over fifty kilometers per second. The Chinese would have to kill more than half of that velocity to get into a circular orbit. Plus, their trajectory was still inclined fifteen degrees to the ring plane, and even if they achieved orbit, they'd need yet more delta-vee to turn their orbit into one that brought them into reasonable proximity with the alien depot.

The *Nixon*'s nav crew said the *Celestial Odyssey*'s approach would bring them through the ring system out of view of the *Nixon* on the first pivotal pass. At the Chinese ship's velocity, the most critical part of the encounter was going to be over in less than an hour. The *Nixon* wouldn't be able to see the ship again until well after it passed periapsis.

Joe Martinez had a fix for that. He and Sandy modified two recon shells, fabbing lens extenders for the standard camera lenses. Martinez launched his do-it-yourself reconnaissance satellites into polar orbits, a half an orbit out of phase. That way, at any moment, one satellite had a view above the ring plane and the other below. The solution wasn't perfect: the two cameras gave them only ninety-five percent coverage, but it would have to do.

By that "night"—ship's time—the Chinese ship was still in free fall, closing in on Saturn faster and faster when it should have been decelerating. The nuclear thermal engines, monstrous as they were, still only provided a fraction of a gee. With dozens of kilometers per second to shed, the Chinese ship's burn should have started hours before.

"They don't have the reaction mass," Fang-Castro told Crow.

"I don't think so. They're not going to make orbit."

The *Celestial Odyssey* finally began its retro burn. They were as far from Saturn as the moon from Earth, but at their velocity, that was nothing.

Navigation: "Admiral? They're not correcting their trajectory. Periapsis is dropping. They're barely going to clear Saturn's atmosphere."

"Mr. Crow," asked Fang-Castro, "do you have any reports of trouble aboard the *Celestial Odyssey*?"

"No." Crow amended himself. "At least, not as of two hours ago."

"Comm, keep monitoring for a distress call," Fang-Castro said.

Nav was losing her voice: "They're still not correcting their periapsis! They're going to hit the upper atmosphere!"

Martinez: "Oh hell. I've got it." He looked bemused. "They're crazy. They're going to try aerobraking."

Crow: "What?"

"They're going to try to skim through the atmosphere deep enough that they can shed some velocity through friction. It's been considered standard operating procedure on any Mars mission. But they're nuts. Mars is one thing. Saturn's another. Different atmosphere, different gravity profile, and, uh, three or four times the velocity? It's nuts."

Twenty minutes before close encounter, the *Celestial Odyssey* cut its main engines. Everyone looked at Martinez.

"Oh, yeah, that's right. They've got to get the orientation and angle of attack absolutely perfect. Can't come in tail-first, they'll burn off their engines. Even if they get their attitude right, they can't come in too shallow or they'll skip along the top of the atmosphere like a stone on a lake. There wouldn't be enough friction, and they won't kill enough velocity. On the other hand, if they come in too steep, they'll just be another meteor."

The Chinese ship's image on recon shell's camera's IR channel, a bare handful of pixels, had dimmed sharply when the engines cut out and dimmed even more as the engines cooled. Now it began to brighten again.

"Hope they tied down everything good. Aerobraking's a bumpy ride," Martinez said. "These boys have got some major balls, I can tell you that."

Nav: "They are definitely slowing down. They're shedding significant velocity."

Fang-Castro: "Enough to put them in a closed orbit?"

"Nowhere near, but probably more than enough, before they're done, to shed the excess velocity they piled on with that midcourse burn."

Fang-Castro looked over at Crow, an unvoiced message going between them: *Maybe we dodged a bullet.*

"Uh-oh, that's bad," Martinez said. Fang-Castro and Crow looked back at the display. Trailing the IR blip of the *Celestial Odyssey*, there were sparkles. Bright pixels that quickly winked out.

"Something's burned off. Nothing should be burning off," Martinez said. "They wouldn't have an expendable heat shield. They figured something wrong. They broke something."

"Comm, any messages?"

"Nothing, ma'am."

"Hope they didn't burn off their comm antennas," Martinez said.

A minute or so later, the IR image of the *Celestial Odyssey* started to dim, as it left Saturn's atmosphere. "Navigation, what's their trajectory?"

"Still open, ma'am. They don't have orbit, yet."

Fifteen minutes passed, then twenty. No call. Nothing. Fang-Castro waited for the Mayday call. Nothing.

The image of the *Celestial Odyssey* suddenly brightened; simultaneously, Martinez called out, "They've started retro burn, again!"

Cheers broke across the bridge.

"Let's keep the discipline, people," Fang-Castro said, though she felt like cheering herself. It was space: it made a family of everybody. *The President doesn't get that*, she thought. *She probably never would.*

45.

Zhang Ming-Hoa glanced at the date readout in the corner of his view screen: Tuesday, April 3, 2068. They were a billion, three hundred million kilometers from Earth and orbiting Saturn. That was the good news.

"Mr. Cui, cut those alarms off. They're not telling me anything I don't know and they're making it hard to concentrate," he said.

The captain of the *Celestial Odyssey* was a large, stocky man, with a reputation for being imperturbable, bordering on the impassive. He also had a reputation for being something of an irresistible force in the elite Chinese Yuhangyuan Corps. It went with his bulk.

The culture of the Corps favored *yuhangyuan*—astronauts—who were slight of build. In the early days of Chinese space travel, when each additional kilogram put into orbit greatly increased the cost and difficulty of a mission, this tradition had meant something. Small spacefarers made for smaller, lighter weight spacecraft. The Chinese space program could not have advanced as rapidly as it did with average or larger-than-average *yuhangyuan*.

That was decades in the past, but tradition changed slowly. The only group that put more of a premium on small size and weight were racing jockeys. Zhang's imperturbability, merged with single-mindedness, had carried him through the training academy without any disciplinary incidents, despite the hazing of his classmates. The nicest nickname he'd ever had there was "big ox."

His instructors, despite their skepticism over his physical suitability, knew officer material when they saw it. Faced with difficulty and even outright hostility, Zhang remained calm, quiet, and thoughtful. Very little fazed him.

For that reason, the bridge crew began to worry when he repeatedly muttered the obscenity *ta ma de* to himself. That was more what they expected of First Officer Cui. Cui Zhuo better fit the image of the stereotypical *yuhanguan*: she was small and wiry, even by Corps standards, and entirely perturbable. Where Captain Zhang carefully pondered a course of action, First Officer Cui responded instantly and instinctively.

Her quick reactions were also what stood between her and a captaincy. Within hours of entering the academy, an upperclassman, noting her unusually slight build and reddish brown hair, dubbed her "Mouse." Within a day that had changed to "Ferret," and freshman Cui had the classes' first disciplinary mark.

Her instructors noted her ability to command respect, but felt she needed thorough tempering before she'd be ready for command of her own. She wasn't there, yet.

The alarms died, and Zhang said to Cui, "Well, we're alive, anyway. For now. Is there any other good news?" He looked to Navigation. "Mr. Sun, what do you have for me?"

Sun checked her console. "We are in orbit about Saturn, sir. The aerobraking maneuver and retro burn were . . . successful."

"You don't look very happy, Lieutenant. I take that to mean it's not a very good orbit."

"I'm afraid not, sir. It's very eccentric—we're barely captured. Apoapsis will be, umm, about half a million kilometers. It'll be about two days before we make a close pass by Saturn again and can do another retro burn to circularize our orbit."

"Cui, you and Peng look even less happy than our navigator. Enlighten me."

The first officer and helmsman had been worriedly conferring over his console. Cui looked up.

"Sir, the external tanks took a lot of damage during aerobraking. One or more of them may be repairable, but we've lost what reaction mass they still had. That's about six hundred tonnes of liquid hydrogen gone. The internal tanks won't provide enough delta-vee to get us into a proper orbit and rendezvous with the alien operation. We're going to need to aerobrake again on the return pass, to shed enough velocity."

Zhang's mood turned grimmer than it already had been. "Those *ben dan* and their damned simulations. The plasma sheath was nowhere near wide enough to protect the upside tanks. We're fortunate the whole ship didn't burn up."

He looked around the half-empty bridge: another brainstorm of the groundpounders in Beijing. The decision-makers had decreed that stripping the ship of all nonessentials, both people and equipment, was the path to beating the Americans to Saturn. By the time the designers had gotten done repurposing the *Martian Odyssey*, they'd turned it into one of the most automated ships that had ever flown. The *Celestial Odyssey* could get by with half the operational crew of a typical ship of its size.

It was a damned stupid idea, in Zhang's judgment. That judgment, he'd kept to himself. Another tradition of the Yuhanguan Corps: you not only followed the orders that were handed down, you made believe you were enthusiastic about them. Once you were in space, you could pretty much do what needed to be done, but until you got there . . .

Zhang knew it was the same for the Americans who went to space, and the Indians and the Brazilians, when it came down to it. It wasn't culture, it was politics.

Those same politics had him here at Saturn. He'd seriously considered turning the assignment down. He'd been told the choice was entirely his. What they hadn't had to say was that if he did turn it down, his career would come to an end. He'd shrugged, maintained his placid exterior, and thanked them for the glorious opportunity.

Well, it was a glorious opportunity, and it had gotten him to a part of the solar system he never in his wildest dreams imagined that he would see. However, it would be nice to live long enough to enjoy the memories, and he was starting to have some concerns about that.

Zhang said, "Well, nothing to be done for it. Mr. Cui, see how much repair work the crew can manage in the next two days and send me a report. You have the bridge. I'll be in my office."

He pushed himself free of his chair, his weightless bulk moving easily across the bridge and down to his private office. Once settled at his desk, there were plenty of other reports to be studied.

The external tank situation was, indeed, bad. Beijing had been crazy to order that desperate midcourse boost. He'd been even crazier to pretend to believe their reassurances that the aerobraking maneuver would come off without a hitch. But their best experts had been so confident, *ben dan* every one of them, and he wasn't going to disobey a direct order on nothing more than a sinking feeling in his stomach.

They'd cut free the downside reaction-mass tanks. Those would've burned away during aerobraking anyway and probably taken the whole ship with them. That lightened the ship, but cost them a third of their storage capacity. They still had the three upside external tanks, plus the internal tanks. That would provide them enough delta-vee capability to get home in a little over two years. It was well within the safety margin of life support and supplies. Control thought it an entirely workable plan that would get them to Saturn nearly a month sooner. They might even still beat the *Nixon* if the Americans suffered more bad luck. Zhang suspected the *Nixon*'s troubles involved more than luck.

Except, Beijing's plan hadn't worked well enough. The Americans had beaten them to Saturn by over a week. The preliminary damage report stated that the aerobraking maneuver had irreparably breached one of the external tanks; maybe the other two could be repaired. The downside bay doors looked to be inoperable; half their complement of runabouts and service eggs were useless unless they could get those doors open. That was going to substantially slow down refilling the reaction-mass tanks. He hoped the repair team could do something about the doors, and do it quickly.

Worst of all, they hadn't arrived at their destination, not really. They'd still need to make another pass through Saturn's atmosphere before they'd be able to match orbits with the alien operation.

Zhang jotted off an order to have the ship's stores re-inventoried and a rationing schedule drawn up, in case things got worse. He was fairly certain they weren't going to get better.

He and the management team ran on stims, and by the next morning, had a better idea of the range of their problems.

"The external survey crew says at least one of the external tanks can be repaired," Cui said. "That'll take at least a week. The second tank we're not sure about yet, but I think we can do it."

"We have to do it," Zhang said, "so let's enter that as repairable."

The third tank was a complete loss.

"We can't do anything with the tanks before our next pass through the atmosphere. Since the bay doors don't appear to be damaged, most likely heat warping has jammed the releases. Let's get Maintenance to focus on that."

More stims, and a few hours' sleep, and another day.

The morning brought an extended contact with Beijing. He'd started it with as complete a report as he could provide, including specific data that showed they'd hit Saturn's atmosphere precisely as the ground-pounders had recommended: and they'd still been badly damaged.

Mid-morning had brought a long message from the chairman and his scientific counsel. That had been an exercise in tap-dancing, everybody agreeing that nobody was to blame for anything, that everything had been done according to the best protocols.

That ended with the chairman turning to the screen and saying, "Zhang, you know how much I wish I could be there with you. I have nothing but admiration and respect for the way you and your crew have conducted yourselves. . . ."

When he'd finished, Zhang thought that he'd actually sounded sincere, and that he may actually have been.

Midday brought the inventory reports.

Zhang looked them over glumly. On the plus side, they weren't going to run out of food or water. Hydroponics could provide them with a nutritionally adequate diet for an indefinite time. Oxygen and water could be regenerated. The problem was that spaceships didn't have perfectly closed recycling systems; some chemicals were consumables they couldn't produce on board.

Zhang supposed the mission planners had done well. They'd taken a ship designed for multi-month trips and fitted it to support a crew for years. Since they had no idea what would be found at Saturn or how long it would take to explore, they'd been able to squeeze in almost five years' worth of life support. There was a good fifty percent safety margin over the optimum mission duration built into that.

The mission, though, was no longer running at anything like the optimum profile. If they couldn't get back to Earth in three years, max, they'd be in trouble. They really needed the two salvageable external reaction-mass tanks to hold through the next aerobraking.

Zhang drifted from his office down the passageway to the bridge. Seventeen months in zero-gee had been a hard regimen to live with. He'd been skipping days in the gym while confronting their difficult situation, and the ship's physician was going to beat him up if he didn't get back on schedule.

He'd told the doc, "If the aerobraking doesn't work, I'm going to die. So are you. Why spend our last moments worrying about whether our hearts would be healthy back on Earth? Once we know we're going to survive, I swear, it'll be an hour a day, every day."

"I don't believe you . . . sir," the doctor said.

"Remind me to have you pushed out the air lock for insubordination," Zhang said.

Now he floated into the bridge, strapped himself into the captain's chair, and brought up the status screen. Everyone at their stations? Yes. All sections reporting everything that could be locked down, was locked down? Yes, except for the maintenance team in the downside bay. They'd been working on the door mechanisms and reporting good progress.

"Cui, tell Maintenance to have the team in the bay finish what they're doing and strap down. This is going to get bumpy."

Again.

He'd pressed the geniuses on Earth to provide a better set of navigation parameters for the next pass through Saturn's atmosphere. They'd been both sympathetic and largely unhelpful. Their computer models still suggested much the same trajectory and angle of attack that had caused them grief on the first pass.

Chedan!

From their viewing ports, Saturn looked less like a planet than a landscape. The horizon line was nearly flat at this close distance, the cloud tops below them streaked with tawny shades of yellows, oranges, and dusty greens. Far ahead, the broad bands of the ring system filled

the rest of the sky, their knife-like precision contrasting sharply with the
fuzzy fringes of Saturn's atmosphere. The whole image looked unreal,
an airbrush fantasy.

Cui said quietly, "Here we go."

The ship began to vibrate; just a bit for the first few seconds, then
more strongly. The view through the port was obscured by a faint reddish haze that quickly yellowed and brightened, and negative gee forces
pulled the crew forward in their seats.

The incandescent plasma sheath made the ports almost too bright to
look at. Atmospheric friction did its job, converting the kinetic energy of
the *Celestial Odyssey* into heat and sound. The scream of the wind pen-
etrated the hull as a rattling roar. For minutes that seemed much too
long, the cacophony continued, then the ship bucked violently, and simultaneously a new alarm fired.

Through chattering teeth, Zhang called, "Helm, status."

"We're losing more pieces of the external tanks! I don't think they're
going to hold."

"Navigation, how much more of this?"

"We're most of the way through, sir. Another two minutes and we'll
have shed enough velocity to handle the rest of the re-orbiting on our
own."

"If we make it that long," Zhang whispered to himself. If they didn't
burn up. Even if they didn't burn up, they might not have external tanks.
If that was so, he thought, *We are screwed.*

Time dragged on, until it seemed impossible that the ship wouldn't
fly apart: but it didn't. Gradually the buffeting diminished, the incandescent glow outside the windows dimmed, and the roaring wind
quieted.

The *Celestial Odyssey* was free of Saturn's atmosphere for a second
time.

Zhang: "Navigation, you have a burn that will normalize our orbit?"

"Relaying it to the helm now, sir."

"When you can, Helm, if you will."

Peng: "Acknowledged, sir."

A moment later he initiated the command sequence. Thrusters fired, rotating the ship one hundred eighty degrees. The main engines cut in, ten huge columns of blue-white-hot hydrogen plasma jetting from the rocket nozzles into space ahead of the ship. The *Celestial Odyssey*, much lighter than it had been when it left Earth, decelerated at a steady half gee. Fifteen minutes of this would have the ship in a much tighter orbit, from which they could work their way into the Maxwell Gap.

"Mr. Cui, what's our status? Just the high points, if you will."

The first officer scanned the ever-lengthening list of status summaries scrolling onto her screen. Maintenance had nothing new to say about the external tanks, but it was assumed that they were pretty much useless. Worse than useless, dead weight—they'd have to be cut away from the ship to reduce its mass before they returned home.

"Sir, I . . ." Then she stopped and turned pale. It took her just a fraction of a second to collect her thoughts, but the rest of the crew caught her hesitation. The bridge went silent.

"Captain . . . Engineering reports that we lost . . . we lost containment on the downside hangar bay. The seals on the doors failed. Thermal stress plus physical shock . . ." She shook her head violently and resumed in a stronger voice. "The bay depressurized. Maintenance has been unable to raise the work crew."

Zhang: "Comm, get me a feed, now!"

A virtual screen flicked into visibility, mid-bridge. Everything looked intact in the bay. No equipment had shaken loose from its tie-downs. The doors appeared solid. It was a deceptive appearance. Toward the forward end of the bay, four figures floated in harnesses tethered to the wall. Unmoving figures.

"Get a medical team to the bay! Now! Now!"

"On their way, sir, but I don't think it's going to make any difference," Cui said. "The data stream says the bay depressurized ten minutes ago."

O jiangui, thought Zhang, *o jiangui, o jiangui . . .*

46.

The transfer of the memory modules and the readers was routine. The eight modules looked like 2.5-centimeter carbon-fiber dowel rods, each twenty centimeters long, with a needle-thin, gold-colored metallic strip on one side. The strip was gold-colored because it turned out to be gold. The rods looked like carbon fiber, because analysis showed that each module had a carbon fiber shell.

The readers looked vaguely like office paper-printers, black cubes that measured fifty centimeters in each of the three dimensions, with rubber-like legs at each corner of the bottom. The top had a slot that would take a memory module.

The readers ran on direct current electricity but had an alien I/O port. Converter ports would have to be fabricated. Wurly interrupted the regular I/O flow to the *Nixon* to insert an operating manual for the readers, along with instructions for converting the I/O port.

Each reader and each QSU module came in its own container, again, of carbon fiber. They were ferried back to the *Nixon* in a heated case built by Martinez and Sandy in the fab shop, one set at a time: Fang-Castro wouldn't risk losing all of them at once, or even two of them at once, in a freak accident.

Sandy called Crow from the primary: "We got the last five and a half trade points. They gave us one point for the oboe and the bassoon, apparently there're no double-reeds in their trading stock. Forking over most of the commander's tea and Clover's liquor got us three more points. Oh, yeah, and we got half a point for the music collection, although the trade computer discarded ninety-nine percent of it. John says we could learn more about our alien friends from what they kept and what they rejected."

"We kept a record of what they took and what they let go?"

"Absolutely."

"They keep Beethoven and Mozart?"

"No. They kept Bach, Vivaldi, some guys I never heard of from the late nineteenth century—Erik Satie?—then a twentieth-century group called Motörhead and some American Indian drumming songs, and most recently, a Russian group called Rape the Whirlwind. They didn't take Kid Little, which tells you something about their taste."

"Yes, it does, but I don't care. What'd we get the other points for? Don't tell me they went for those fake disks and the disk player."

"Absolutely. The computer suggested that we could bring more of them, and get more points, but we have to wait sixty-four years."

"Unbelievable." When Martinez had learned that the trade computer was interested in archaic music machines, he'd fabricated a mid-twentieth-century disk player that played thirty-centimeter plastic disks through a crystalline pickup that vibrated according to an arrangement of grooves on the disk. He got the specs from a vintage recording club, and he and Sandy printed out everything but the pickup in a marathon five-hour fab session. The pickup was fashioned from a diamond-stud earring they extorted from the surveillance tech—"But they were given to me by my former fiancé"—and cut with a laser.

"Unbelievable, yup. I got the feeling we just got patted on the head for handing over some nice woven baskets. Do you care?" Sandy asked.

"No."

Crow rubbed his eyes: he'd had nothing but catnaps for two days, relying on stim tabs to get him through. They were starting to take their toll.

The powers-that-be back home were making life difficult, demanded constant updates on the status of the Chinese mission. By virtue of its proximity, the *Nixon* had a better idea what was going on with the *Celestial Odyssey* than Earth did, but that didn't mean they had a very good idea.

That problem was complicated by the light-speed time lag. The round-trip time for communication was over two hours, and that was unavoidable. Santeros didn't much care. Whatever was going on back home wasn't waiting on the speed of light. As soon as one of her queries

came in, he had to jump on it and formulate a response, regardless of the
time, day or night, or what else he might be doing.

Further, the Chinese were still uncommunicative. There clearly had
been considerable damage to their ship. Their external tanks were either
destroyed or badly damaged. They could see Chinese work crews cutting away what remained of the tankage. The main superstructure ship
appeared to be intact.

His implants beeped at him, and he nodded, sighed, and headed
down to Fang-Castro's office.

She looked at tired as he felt. "Talking to the President again?"

"Yes. Same old thing. Anything change? No. How about now? Anything change? No." A thin smile flitted across his face. "It's like dealing
with a kid: 'When are we gonna get there?'"

"All right," Fang-Castro said. "They're telling us that we need to ensure that the Chinese don't get access to the AI in the depot, at least until
we're gone. I'll be ordering the deployment of armed personnel at the
depot landing pad and the access port, round the clock. Do you agree?"

Crow pursed his lips. "This is theater, correct? Drawing a line in the
sand that they know they can't cross without risking war?"

"Entirely. We can't fire on their personnel for the same reason. We
look tough, but if the Chinese push the issue, we give way. I'm betting
the Chinese won't risk it. If it did come down to a fight, we'd lose. We are
most likely seriously outmanned and outgunned."

She continued: "Our ship is also more fragile than theirs. If they
were to bring the fight to the *Nixon*, they very likely have armaments
that could entirely cripple us. Whereas we, in turn, have little if anything that could touch their ship. Unless you have an ace up your sleeve
you haven't told me about?"

Crow shook his head. "No. When the planning devolves down to
'Who can wave the bigger gun?' it's moved beyond my scope of authority."

"All right, then. I'm assigning four-person teams, two at the landing
pad and two at the port. Three teams, eight-hour shifts. I will hold back
Sandy Darlington. He will continue to document this encounter—I
mean, both with the alien primary and with the Chinese."

Crow nodded. "I wish I could provide you with better options, but I'm as blind as you are. I'll keep hammering intelligence back on Earth to try to get more information about the Chinese's intentions, but I'm not hopeful."

His slate pinged. Sandy Darlington, urgent. Any urgent call from the alien primary was a priority.

He said to Fang-Castro: "It's Darlington, urgent, from the primary. I better take it."

"Yes."

Crow tapped the link and Darlington's face came up from his in-suit camera. He said, "Hey, big guy. How they hangin'?" and flashed his toothy smile.

"Sandy, I'm talking to the admiral."

"Oops. Sorry, ma'am. Anyway, I was, uh . . . hanging out here . . . uh, just bullshittin' with Wurly—"

Crow said, "Sandy . . ."

"Ah, sorry again, ma'am. For the language. Anyway, I thought of a couple of questions that nobody else has asked, and I asked them, and I thought I better get the answers back to you."

Fang-Castro said, "Do you want to share the answers with us, Mr. Darlington, or do you plan to continue bullshittin'?"

"No, ma'am." The toothy smile again. "I asked, 'Wurly, when you said we get eight memory modules and eight readers, did you mean, we, from the ship here now? Or did you mean we, as a species?' Wurly said, 'You, as a species. We have eight memory modules to dispense and eight readers.' I asked, 'Can't you make more?' and he said, 'We do not have the facilities here to fabricate more, although we have the information to do so. Therefore, the number of physical readers allotted to one species is limited.' Then I asked, 'When you said we get up to eight points, is that for our species, or for this visit?' He said that it's for our species. If we want more, we have to go to a different depot, or wait sixty-four years, when we'll become eligible again."

Fang-Castro and Crow looked at each other, then Fang-Castro asked,

"You mean . . . if the Chinese show up and ask for the memory modules and readers, they won't get any? Nor will they be able to trade?"

"That's what Wurly's saying, ma'am. Then I thought, 'You know, old Crow's gonna want to run off with both the memory modules and the readers, and all the trade stuff, leaving the Chinese holding an empty bag. More than that, he's probably gonna want to slap a chunk of C-10 on Wurly and blow the shit out of him—sorry again, ma'am—so the Chinese couldn't even find out what we'd done.' So I asked Wurly if there were more Wurlys, and there are. It will take them ten hours to bring out a replacement, plus all the other computers can act as Wurlys if necessary. So we probably can't go around blowing them all up, even if we knew they wouldn't retaliate. Bottom line is, we've got all the hardware.

"They could get instructions for the reader, and maybe even the information that's on the memory modules, through Wurly, but it would take them forever. I asked how long it would take to download all the QSU information through our I/O, and Wurly said it would take two hundred and twelve years. The Chinese can get the basic science over the I/O link. Hell, a lot more than basic science. But the complete manu-facturing and engineering specs? Those're on the QSUs.

"But here's the key thing: Wurly answers all questions that he knows the answer to. If we run off with everything—the Chinese are going to find out. All they have to do is ask."

Fang-Castro said, "Mr. Darlington, stay where you are. I'm going to run this by the brain trust, and see if there are more related questions for your old pal Wurly. Oh, and we'll get Santeros and her people off their asses."

Sandy said, "Ma'am, as you know, I served in a military intelligence unit . . ."

"Yes, I have been briefed on that."

"Mr. Crow believes there is a spy on board. Or at least, believes it's possible. I would suggest that you, mmm, hold this information very tightly. You need to know it, and Mr. Crow needs to know it, but if there's a spy, and you talk to your brain trust, the spy is going to hear about it. I don't think that would be good—though, of course, it's your call, ma'am."

"Thank you, Mr. Darlington." She went silent for a moment, looked at Crow, who raised an eyebrow.

Then: "I think perhaps you're right, Mr. Darlington. We will hold this to the three of us."

47.

Zhang contemplated the surveillance vid playing on the bridge's main screen. The American survey team had departed the artificial planetoid that appeared to be the primary alien base. They'd been making daily visits for as long as the *Celestial Odyssey* was close enough to observe them. Presumably the Americans had started sending over teams as soon as their ship had settled into position.

Zhang had positioned the *Odyssey* on the far side of that body from the *Nixon* but much closer in, just fifty kilometers from the alien base. Zhang could appreciate the Americans' caution; they were the first ones to approach this enigma. He recalled an Americanism—the first pioneers were the ones with the arrows in their backs.

That was a benefit of being second on the scene: now Zhang knew that the aliens wouldn't instantly initiate hostilities. In fact, given the repeated visits of the survey team, it appeared that they wouldn't engage in hostilities at all. Further, it appeared, the Americans had found something worth making repeated trips for.

At this close distance, surveillance probes weren't even required; not on this side of the planetoid, anyway. The ship's telescopes could resolve centimeter-sized objects on its surface. First Officer Cui had joked, "From here, if they wave at us, we can tell if it's a friendly greeting or if they're giving us the finger."

Nobody had waved. Until now, it had looked like the Americans were entirely ignoring the Chinese, continuing their predictable routine of visits. The new vids, though, showed a second shuttle vehicle arriving at the planetoid just as the survey team was about to depart. It landed and deployed four people, who took up stations in pairs at the landing pad and the access port to the planetoid.

Thanks to that centimeter-scale resolution, the vid clearly showed that all four were armed. It appeared that the Chinese presence was being acknowledged.

Cui pushed for a confrontation. "Sir, the Americans can't lay unilateral claim to the planetoid. It violates the Law of Space Treaty. Not even considering that in all likelihood there are intelligent beings in that planetoid, with their own sovereignty. We need to press the issue."

"Mr. Cui, before relying on space law to back your outrage, you might wish to recall that our original mission was to establish a sovereign colony on Mars. Also, this planetoid falls below the ten-kilometer limit for sovereign territory. While its resources must be shared, to some degree, any party can lay claim to it for such things as exploitation of mineral rights. I don't believe we have a lot of legal push.

"Now, the local sovereignty issue, there may be something to that." He thought a moment. "We don't even know what the aliens' desires are in this matter. They might be entirely happy having more than one group of humans visit them. They might have means to enforce those wishes, regardless of those of the Americans. We will send a party over. A diplomatic party. Let us see if we are welcomed."

"Sir! May I volunteer to lead the party?"

Zhang shook his head. The last thing a possible first contact with aliens—and a definite contact with probably-antagonistic Americans—needed were the diplomatic talents of someone as temperamental as his first officer. He kept those thoughts to himself. Instead, he said, "Mr. Cui, I really need you here, capable of making on-the-spot decisions for the ship. Furthermore, we know nothing about the aliens, but it's possible they might take umbrage if approached by less than the highest-ranking entity. This task falls on me."

More importantly, he thought, *I'm less likely to get us into a dustup with the Americans.* Beijing had been clear to him on that point: keep the aliens' knowledge out of the hands of the Americans at all costs . . . short of starting the next superpower war.

Two hours later, a short-haul tug departed from the *Celestial Odyssey* with five space-suited crew. A fifty-kilometer run didn't require anything like the shuttle, and Zhang didn't want to risk it on so uncertain a mission. Really, prudence dictated that he shouldn't be there at all.

Unfortunately, there was no one on the ship who was better qualified to deal with this unpredictable and delicate situation. If worse came to worst, his first officer was entirely capable of commanding the vessel for a return trip to Earth. She'd not likely make any friends along the way . . .

And they had yet to settle the question of whether the ship was capable of bringing the crew home alive and whole.

Zhang had done what he could to minimize the potential for loss. He had a bare minimum complement accompanying him. The contact crew included Lieutenant Peng Cong, who was without question the best pilot on board and Zhang's personal favorite. A short-haul tug did not usually require fancy piloting, but this was not a usual run, and evasive action might prove necessary.

Dr. Mo Mu was a research biologist and medical officer and one of the oldest and most experienced crew members. He might have some insight into the nature of the aliens and if there were an accident . . . or incident . . . his skills might save someone's life. He was also, frankly, expendable; there were several other people on board the ship with advanced medical training. Dr. Gao Xing Xing was an astrophysicist, best in her class at Beijing University, smart as a whip, and very, very fast on the uptake. She was along to study alien technology and science. If first contact failed catastrophically, there'd be little for someone of her skills to study, and she served no function in the operation of the ship. So . . . also expendable.

Zhang hated planning this in terms of who he could afford to sacrifice. He'd just lost four crew members in the bay depressurization, including two engineers. That had been an unavoidable accident. It still ate at him. Consciously choosing who was dispensable, to put them on this mission, it didn't sit well. It was especially difficult when he knew that the people he'd chosen for this trip thought that he'd honored them by doing so.

He was too soft. He needed to be more dispassionate.

Then, there was the fifth team member, one the captain wouldn't mind seeing expended. Second Lieutenant Duan Me wore two hats on the under-crewed *Celestial Odyssey*. She was a plant biologist, in charge of the ship's hydroponics, and as such she kept the crew well fed.

She was also the ship's political officer, the voice, eyes, and ears of the Party. On first meeting, you'd be impressed by her charm and humor, Zhang thought: she was a compact, solidly built woman who liked a good laugh. She also liked digging in the dirt, of which, she complained, there was far too little of in hydroponics.

She was the kind of person you'd want to confide in . . . unless the conversation turned to politics. With her, it inevitably did. Then she gave old Mao a run for cultural purity.

She had made it entirely clear that while she might be a mere second lieutenant and he was captain, she would be going on this little jaunt. Strictly as an observer, of course, to ensure that Beijing got an accurate report of the behavior of the Americans. No interference, she wouldn't think of it.

If Zhang could have thought of a way to release her tether and make it look like an accident, he would have been tempted.

Fifteen minutes in flight had them at the planetoid. Zhang had timed the launch so that the landing pad and apparent access port were facing the *Celestial Odyssey*. He preferred this encounter take place within sight of his ship, not to mention out of sight of the *Nixon*.

The four Americans took no action until the tug got within about a kilometer of the surface, when two of them unshouldered their weapons. Zhang signaled Peng to bring the tug to a halt. He toggled a common comm frequency, stood up, and held his arms far out from his sides.

"Gentlemen, I am Captain Zhang Ming-Hoa, commander of the *Celestial Odyssey*. May we have permission to land?"

One of the Americans, Zhang couldn't tell which one, responded, "I am sorry, sir, but we must regretfully decline your request. We are under strict orders that no one is to land here without the explicit authorization of Admiral Fang-Castro. We have received no such authorization."

"My apologies for my forwardness, but under the law of space, unless you have filed a claim on this body, we are entitled to land on it just as you have," Zhang said. He discreetly signaled Peng to start moving the tug in. Slowly. Very slowly.

"Sir, I am not trained in space law. But we are under orders from our commander." One of the Americans noticed the tug was approaching. He stiffened and nudged his companion. Very quickly, the other two Americans unshouldered their arms.

"Please, sir, stop your approach. Our orders are to take all measures necessary to prevent unauthorized landings." The American who had first unshouldered his weapon began to raise it to the ready position. Slowly, the other three followed suit. "Sir, we are authorized to use force. Once again, halt. You will not be warned a third time."

Ta ma de. They were going to push the issue. They must be bluffing. They were almost certainly bluffing. But he wasn't a hundred percent sure. Zhang signaled Peng and the tug came to a halt.

The American said, "Sir, we have a remote relay point flying in station with the primary. We ask that you contact our commander, Admiral Naomi Fang-Castro, for permission to land. If she agrees, we will stand down here. We our transmitting the link, which is a standard inter-ship channel."

The link came in and Zhang turned to Duan. "Your advice?"

Duan said, "They're bluffing."

"Probably. Almost certainly. But if they aren't, they'll kill us."

Duan's face was impassive, but she was sweating, Zhang thought. She didn't want to make the call, because whatever call was made, there'd be criticism in Beijing. On the other hand, if she didn't make the call, she would be showing an unseemly deference to the captain.

She said, "We should consult with the minister."

Ah. Nice move, Zhang thought. Consulting with the minister would take hours, which they really didn't have. "If we consult with the minister, we'd have to go back to the ship, which would appear to be a retreat, which would be undesirable," Zhang said. "So. I will consult with Fang-Castro."

"You must insist that we be allowed to land," Duan said.

"Of course," Zhang said. He nodded at Peng, who also served as comm officer. Peng picked up the link through the American satellite and called the American ship. The call was answered by the American comm officer, and a moment later, Fang-Castro appeared on the screen.

She spoke in Mandarin: not the best Mandarin, but good for an American: "Captain Zhang. I hope you managed the aerobraking without damage or injury. There was cheering on our bridge when you came through intact."

Zhang smiled. "I appreciate that, Admiral. Alas, we did not. We have suffered a number of casualties, and substantial damage, which we are still assessing, as I'm sure you know. At the moment, however, we wish to approach the alien planetoid, but we have been met by armed members of your crew, who are refusing us access. As you know, this is a violation of basic space law, and we must insist on access."

"And you shall have it, Captain Zhang," Fang-Castro said. "But not immediately. I will be frank with you. Inside the primary, or planetoid, we have found an AI computer which is willing to divulge a substantial amount of information on alien science. We have broadcast a vid of this AI—"

"I have seen this," Zhang said.

Fang-Castro said, "Captain, your English is far better than my Mandarin. Might we switch to English?"

"If you prefer, of course," Zhang said. Duan nodded: she'd matriculated at UCLA.

"Thank you," Fang-Castro said. She looked down—at a slate, Zhang thought—then continued. "The AI has established an I/O link on which to transfer this data. We have been accepting data for six days. The AI tells us the transfer of certain kinds of scientific information will be complete in two days. When it is complete, we will leave this station, and you will be free to access it. The reason we refuse access now, quite frankly, is that you frighten us. Our intelligence agencies tell us that you have a military crew—even your scientists have military status. We have very little military aboard, which creates a problem for us, as I'm sure you recognize.

"We are not refusing you access because we want to keep you away from the AI computer, but because we want to keep you away from our crew and the equipment we have on board the primary, and because we want to finish downloading the scientific information. If we allow you on board, we would essentially be at your mercy, since you can stay here longer than we can. So, that is our position. In two days, we will depart this station, and will leave it to you."

She continued: "As an indication of our goodwill, we will further tell you that this station is a refueling depot for the alien ships, and also a trading station. We have asked the computer if we are allowed to trade, and have been told that we are. Trade values are assessed by an alien onboard computer. Each species is allowed to leave items valued at eight points by the aliens, and once we leave eight points in value, we will be allowed to take away alien items valued at eight points. We were granted a full eight points. This ship will take four points in value and we have indicated to the trade computer that you should be allocated the other four points and the computer has agreed that this would be appropriate. So, as a gift, we give you those points, in the hope that you will accept our difficult position with goodwill. We ask you to wait two days. Then, the station will be yours."

Zhang said, "This will require some consultation. I am sorry that we frighten you, for I assure you, that is not our purpose here. We have questions, however, which our experts in Beijing will want answers to. Have you met the aliens?"

"No. There are no aliens here. The primary is a remotely controlled station that creates antimatter as fuel, and stores the antimatter in the fleet of smaller moonlets that accompany the station. Trade goods are exchanged purely through a computer-mediated barter system. Alien visits are extremely rare. We have found the onboard AI to be extremely forthcoming on all these matters, and our experts tell us this is so simply because the aliens have no reason not to be, and some reasons why this . . . position . . . may benefit them."

"So the planetoid contains nothing but this cooperative AI and the trade goods?"

"That is correct. It's essentially a warehouse. The I/O interface is complicated, but we have managed to establish one. If it had been simple, we would have already finished downloading the alien information, and would have gotten out of your way already. Since ours—American and Chinese I/Os—are compatible, and we will have no further use for our gear when we leave, we will leave our connection intact for your use, if you wish to use it."

"Understood," Zhang said. "I will return to my ship now for consultation, which will take some time. I will contact you when we finish."

Fang-Castro said, "Captain Zhang, I would point out to you that if your consultations are anything like ours, this will take quite a long time, because of the light-speed lag. By the time they are done, there should be very little time left before the *Nixon* departs. Perhaps we could both suggest to our governments that slightly prolonged consultations on Earth . . . would obviate our problem. If they last long enough, the *Nixon* will be gone."

Zhang said, "I will point this out."

Fang-Castro: "Assuming that everybody sees the wisdom of that, I would tell you that the *Nixon* has excellent fabrication and repair facilities. If there is anything we can fabricate for you, or any repairs that we could assist you in, we would be happy to do so."

"Thank you. We need to finish our assessment of the damage we have taken. I will call you personally if we have need of your aid."

Back aboard the *Celestial Odyssey*, Zhang ordered the contact crew into a conference room, and called First Officer Cui to join them. The video of the encounter with the Americans was already on its way back to Earth, and now he said, "Feel free to speak your minds."

Cui and Duan glanced at each other—the video of this conference would be on its way to Beijing as they spoke. Zhang said, "I'm serious about that. We need to plan our next move, and I want more than just the thoughts in my own head. We also need the thoughts of our experts back home, and quickly."

Cui spoke first. "Sir, I think it was a mistake not to push the issue and attempt a landing. I do not think there is any doubt that the Americans were bluffing. They can't afford to initiate an attack."

Zhang shook his head. "Officer Cui, I am nowhere so free from doubt as you are. I believe your assessment is correct, but I also believe we both might be wrong. The consequences of an error in judgment are so severe that I want us to pursue all other options before we force a confrontation with the Americans. Be assured, I will force that as our last resort. Not as our first. We explore other options before we risk even the smallest, most unlikely possibility of . . . an international difficulty."

"Sir?" Dr. Mo, the biologist, spoke up. "There is a great deal more to this complex than the planetoid that the Americans have sequestered. There are myriad smaller moonlets that are clearly alien constructions, and uncountable numbers of small autonomous spacecraft traveling between them and the rings and the planetoid. The Americans can't be everywhere at once."

"True," interjected Cui, "and the Americans have no force of authority beyond a physical presence. They could order us away, but they would have no means of backing up their order. They would never risk initiating an attack by their ship on ours. Their vessel is obviously fragile, it's a flying bundle of twigs. Even our light armament could permanently disable it in a matter of minutes. Their poorest tactician would understand this."

"That, I entirely agree with," replied Zhang. "Still, they may devise some kind of a response. We may not get more than one chance at this. Do we just pick a target at random? I'd rather spend that chance on better than the flip of a coin."

"I have a suggestion." Dr. Gao, the astrophysicist, looked at her data slate. "Our instruments picked up low levels of radiation from many of the moonlets. I mean *really* low, nothing that would be hazardous to people, not even with prolonged exposure. But the interesting thing is that some of the spectra show a slight energy spike at 511 KV. That means positrons. Antimatter. Not much, just a handful of particles, but something has to be generating those positrons. That technology has to be associated with this antimatter storage that Fang-Castro spoke of. If we should go examine one: it would establish our right to work among the alien artifacts, and there'd be nothing the Americans could do to prevent it."

Zhang punched through to Comm: "Put a chart of the planetoid and its accompanying fleet on the conference room screen."

The map popped up a moment later, a complicated skein of artifacts encircling the planetoid, the moonlets flying in a steady formation, other, smaller ones moving between the moonlets and the rings.

"There's the one we want," Gao said, tapping one of the smaller vehicles, which was moving toward the nearest of the moonlets.

Zhang turned to the political officer. "Mr. Duan, do you see any aspects of this plan which conflict with our orders from Beijing?"

Duan considered the matter for a double handful of seconds before replying. "Sir, I don't see anything in this plan that contravenes the Party's instructions. But I feel I must register an objection to your actions at the planetoid. We had clear instructions not to engage with the *Nixon*."

"Which, Mr. Duan, I followed to the letter. I did not engage the American ship directly in any fashion. I tested the waters . . . and their resolve. The verbal exchanges were meaningless theatrics. We learned what we needed to know without engaging." He turned to Cui. "Mr. Cui, I want you to work up a list of personnel for the shuttle mission to the moonlet. I want everyone on that trip who could possibly be of any use in investigating the alien technology. If we're fortunate, this won't be the only opportunity to study their technology, but we can't count on that. Assume the worst about the Americans: that is our one and only chance."

He then turned and spoke directly with the camera that was recording and transmitting the conference. "To you experts in Beijing, I would suggest that the American commander was probably telling the truth, and that her assessment of the balance of power between our two ships was accurate. Therefore, I believe that the *Nixon* will be leaving in two days. I don't believe that she was being entirely candid with us: there may be other issues here, but we can't know what they are, unless there is some special intelligence of which I'm not aware. I believe that there would be some profit in investigating the moonlets, and perhaps some legal precedent would be set by doing such an investigation. However, I will suspend any further action from this ship until we have time to confer with you in Beijing. We have much work to do in repairing this ship, and we will do that, starting immediately. We await your counsel."

48.

President Santeros: "The goddamn Chinese ought to learn how to speak proper English. I've got this Mandarin translator telling me what the chairman is saying, and I have no way of knowing if he's getting the implications right, and the goddamn Chinese don't speak in anything but implications."

Out of sight, behind her, the chairwoman of the Joint Chiefs stuck the knuckles of her fist into her mouth, to keep from laughing. Santeros, who apparently had a monitoring screen in front of her, snapped, "I saw that, White . . ."

Crow, sitting in the conference room next to Fang-Castro, muttered, "Just tell us what they fuckin' implied."

Fang-Castro: "Shhh," although nothing was outgoing at the moment. It was wall-to-wall Santeros, with a few advisers, from the Oval Office.

"Anyway," Santeros said, "the Chinese are screaming at us and say that they will gather a coalition of other geopolitical entities to penalize us for this blatant violation of space law. They insist that their crew be given access to the alien primary, and say that they will begin immediate investigations into other alien vessels in the fleet around the primary. However, there's a goddamn implication that they won't act until they can get agreement from the other geopolitical entities, and that will take about, mmm, two days . . ."

Crow said, "All right. We won."

". . . But you better be prepared to get the hell out of the neighborhood. All that stuff about leaving trade points was fine, and helping with repairs, that's good, but sooner or later, they're going to find out about the memory modules, and the fact that we're sneaking away like a thief in the night. Then, the shit's gonna hit the fan. We gotta hope you can get out of range before that happens."

Fang-Castro called Zhang. The Chinese comm said, "Our commander has been promoted. You may call him Admiral Zhang now. We will put you through."

Crow, standing to one side, whispered, "They didn't want him negotiating with a superior officer. They jumped him two ranks. If he's a Chinese admiral, he technically outranks you now. He'll have two stars."

"I'm sure I can handle it," Fang-Castro said. She smiled when Zhang came up on the screen. "Sir. First, congratulations on your promotion. Our intelligence people have kept me briefed on your personal background, and I have to say, I'm honored to be dealing with you."

Zhang's face crinkled with something that might have been embarrassment. "Thank you. It appears that my superiors will order me to make a landing under . . . any circumstances . . . when they have finished Earth-side negotiations with other nations that are as outraged by American actions as we are."

"We understand," Fang-Castro said, to a minute nod from Zhang.

And there it was: the deal was done. "We will be vacating the primary as soon as possible. In the meantime, is there anything we can do to help with your repairs?"

"Possibly. We understand from some of our astronauts that when the *Nixon* was a space station, you had on board three Mitsubishi Force 5 printers. If you still have these on board, we would wish to borrow one."

"Stand by, Admiral, let me talk to our head of maintenance." She lifted her slate, tapped it, got Martinez on-screen: "Joe, do we still use Mitsubishi Force 5 printers?"

"Yes, ma'am, we've got three of them."

"Would it be possible to move one to the *Celestial Odyssey* in a timely way?"

"Uh, we'd have to figure out a way to isolate it, package it. We can't just shove it out in space, you'd have some differential contraction among parts that wouldn't be good. Probably put it on a bus . . . I'd have to make some measurements. Yeah, I could do it, given twenty-four hours. Be a lot quicker if you'd let them come over with their tug if it's got a pressurized cargo hold. We could just push it in. We could do all that in a couple hours."

"Stand by on that—I'll let you know."

"Do they need carbon fiber? We've got a ton of it we'll never use. Actually several tons, we never took it out. They might be able to use it to repair their tanks, and not have to hitchhike back with us."

"Good thought. I'll ask." Fang-Castro went back to the link to Zhang. "Admiral, uh, I don't want to embarrass anyone, but how many people fit in one of your tugs?"

"Up to fifteen . . . why?"

"We're still a little nervous about your military capability. My maintenance chief says that we do have that printer, as well as several tons of carbon fiber, and we could allot you some of that if you need it. The fastest and easiest way to get that to you would be for you to send a tug over. Our shuttles aren't pressurized and the maintenance man is worried about differential contraction under temperature extremes. But if you sent a tug over with fifteen crew aboard . . . we would be inclined not to open the air lock."

Zhang smiled. "You Americans are too paranoid. We will send the tug with the pilot and a copilot. Tell us when to come. And thank you. I will ask about the carbon fiber."

When they finished talking, after more pleasantries, Crow said, "We need to get that video off to Earth right now. If this is a ploy . . ."

Fang-Castro said, "You must be one of those Americans who's too paranoid."

Crow: "The I/O's got what, twenty-eight hours?"

"That's what Wurly tells us . . . if nothing breaks. I just wish we had more bandwidth to Earth. We're archiving most of it."

Greenberg came up: "Ma'am, we're ready to go. Everything looks nominal with the engines."

The printer delivery went without incident, and the Chinese pilot seemed genuinely grateful, joking with Martinez's men as they moved the massive piece of machinery into the Chinese tug, along with two tons of raw carbon-fiber stock.

Twenty-eight hours later, John Clover was interrogating the jukebox as the I/O stream was coming to its scheduled end. Direct vocal interrogation of the jukebox had slowed since the I/O link went up, simply because so much more critical information could be passed over the link.

The vocal material had, as a result, gone to what nine-tenths of the *Nixon*'s crew dismissed as "anthropological." Clover persisted, right to the end.

"Wurly, you said you can provide us with operational logs for the station, correct?"

"Yes, for most of them. No, for a few. I cannot provide detailed security logs, only summary reports."

"Why is that? Can I talk to the security system?"

"Security data can include the detailed activities of visitors to the depot. In the case of sanctions, where that information needs to be promulgated to the rest of the depot network, it must include species-specific information that exceeds the normal privacy protocols. Consequently, access to the detailed logs is not allowed. That information is not accessible to external systems."

"Then the security system contains explicit details about the species visiting the depot?"

"No, even the internal-to-security database contains the bare minimum of identifying information, only enough to recognize a species if it shows up again and to allow other depots to impose mandated sanctions against that species. Still, it is against depot rules to access that data, and attempts to do so will be met with penalties."

"What is in the summary reports, and are we allowed to see them?"

"The summary reports contain security-related status information about the station. For example, the approach of your ship. The details are completely scrubbed from the summary. No one could identify your species or its origin from the summary information. You are allowed access to any information I have. None of my data is restricted."

Sandy had stuck a camera to a wall to record Clover's interrogation attempt, and had then stretched out on the floor in an attempt to nap: he couldn't do that in an upright position, nor had he trained himself to do it simply by floating in a zero-gee state. Clover spoke to him: "Well, the jukebox spins an airtight yarn. There's no point in trying to get around its own security, because it doesn't know anything it won't tell us voluntarily. Plus, I'll bet you anything that trying to circumvent its protocols breaks the rules."

Sandy asked, "Wurly, does trying to circumvent your protocols break the rules?"

The answer-bot spoke up. "That is correct. As long as no harm is done to my systems, though, the sanctions are small because the effort cannot gain anything. There is just enough of penalty to discourage species from trying."

Clover asked, "Have there been any sanctions applied during this depot's operation?"

"Yes, thirteen times, all for minor breaches of protocol. Would you like the summary reports?"

"Yes. Also, are there summary reports that list arrivals and departures that don't result in sanctions? If so, I would like those also, and time-stamped."

Sandy keyed a private channel to Clover. "What are you up to? Are you going to get us in trouble?"

Clover shook his head. "Nope, I've got an idea, and I was just making sure it's completely legal." He turned his attention back to the answer-bot. "Wurly, I'd like to get the environmental logs for this room and any other habitable portions of the depot. Not the minute-by-minute logs, just anytime there's a significant adjustment to the environmental conditions—lighting, temperature, atmosphere—and I'd like that time-stamped. Is there a problem with that?"

"That is a legitimate request." The console's colors mirrored a warm sunset. "I've extracted the data you requested and directed it to the uplink your technician set up. It will increase the time of the I/O flow by .013 seconds."

Clover keyed his comm back to Sandy: "You see that?" He chortled. "We may not know exactly who visited or where they came from, but we know when, and if they behaved, and the environmental data will tell us a hell of a lot about their biology. I just scored major demographic data on the populations of alien species in our neck of the galaxy."

"Good job," Sandy said. He yawned. The I/O link went down and Wurly said, "Data transfer through the I/O link is now complete."

"Thank you," Clover said. "Wurly, I have—"

Fang-Castro crashed the party. "For all members of the contact crew, the I/O record is now complete, or so we have been told. Return to the *Nixon* immediately, or make arrangements to hitchhike back home with the Chinese."

"That's us," Sandy said on the private link. On the public link, he said, "Yes, ma'am. It'll take a minute to pack up my cameras."

Clover asked, "Wurly, do you have any final message for the people of Earth?'

"Yes."

"What is it?"

"Hello, people of Earth."

Sandy: "I think that's a glitch. It's the first glitch we've had from him." He patted the jukebox on its carapace. "Thanks, pal."

A tech came out of the room where the I/O harness was attached.

He said, "Let's haul butt."

Thirty-seven hours after Fang-Castro first spoke to Zhang, she called back: "We are starting our main engines. We thank you for your courtesy in waiting for our departure."

Zhang nodded. "May you have the best of luck in your return. We hope to see you there someday."

"Someday," Fang-Castro said.

Zhang winked out.

The *Nixon* left Saturn on Sunday, April 8, 2068, but it wasn't a day of rest. As soon as Fang-Castro issued the burn order, the VASIMR engines set about pushing the *Nixon* out of the Saturnian system.

The exit trajectory was similar to the one that had taken them away from Earth more than eight months before—a long, slow spiral outward while the VASIMRs piled on enough thrust to finally break the ship free of Saturn's grip. Unlike that launch, this was no tentative departure, no slow and careful ramping up of the reactors and the engines. In less than two hours, Engineering had the engines sucking down every bit of power Reactor 1 was capable of generating.

The engine ignition that signaled their departure from Earth had been a novel experience and symbolically profound for everyone on board, unimpressive as it was to the senses. Eight months later, it was another story. Firings were now routine; in truth, most of the crew had had their fill of engine starts and stops. Of space travel, really. They just wanted to get home.

As the *Nixon* gradually put distance between itself and the alien depot in the Maxwell Gap, it pushed out of the ring plane as it expanded and inclined its orbit. An hour of thrust had it a thousand kilometers from the depot and the Chinese. Halfway through its first orbit, as the *Nixon* threaded its way back through a gap in the ring plane, they were far enough from the alien constellation that it was invisible to the naked eye.

By the following morning, the *Nixon* had completed three outward spirals on its winding path to free flight. It was a comforting fifteen thousand kilometers farther out, in an orbit that was inclined four degrees to the ring plane. Another day's worth of thrust doubled that. Saturn was still an overwhelmingly impressive presence in their sky, but it was dwindling. It remained paramount for the engineering and navigation teams that had to calculate and recalculate the trajectories that would let them safely thread the gaps in Saturn's rings on each half orbit's ring plane crossing, but even their vital job was becoming routine. By the end of Day Three, they'd be safely beyond the outer limits of the A Ring, where the ring plane was mostly empty space.

Just as when it had left Earth, the *Nixon*'s velocity dwindled as their orbit expanded. That peculiar logic of orbital mechanics by now felt normal to the *Nixon*'s crew. That trade-off would continue as they spiraled away from the ringed giant, but nine days of this would see them entirely free of Saturn's pull.

49.

With the Americans leaving, there was no particular reason to rush to the alien planetoid. A number of critical repairs were being completed on the *Celestial Odyssey*, and Zhang wanted them done before they were distracted by the larger mission. Too many people had already died because of problems with the ship.

The American printer and the extra supply of carbon fiber could be crucial to the effort: the maintenance crew, what was left of them, told Zhang that they could probably repair one of the badly damaged reaction-mass tanks.

They already had plans, the result of a flash-design program in Wenchang. They were also looking into the possibility of fabricating tankless tanks out of water-ice taken from the rings, that could be attached to the exterior of the ship, cut up with lasers, and fed into the internal tanks as those emptied on the way back. That was iffy.

Still, things were looking up.

Finally.

So they took it slow.

Wenchang ground control was understanding; the politicians, less so. The Americans carried on board a very effective and attractive female propagandist who had given the alien information-bot a cute name, which had inspired a number of retail efforts and three copyright and patent lawsuits. She had also subtly and with humor created the impression that the Americans were the generous, idealistic ones, even providing the Chinese with repair equipment. The Chinese had no answer to that: their own trained propagandist had been off-loaded at Earth, part of the weight-reduction program when the ship was being stripped for speed.

Beijing pressed for action. Since the Americans had investigated only the primary, the Beijing brain trust suggested that Zhang's crew investigate the rest of the constellation of alien artifacts, as well as the planetoid.

The thinking went like this: Zhang's crew should gain access to one of the moonlets, taking care not to interfere with its operation, while collecting as much data as possible. If the Americans were to be believed, there would be no aliens there—but then, the Americans hadn't looked.

If there were aliens aboard the moonlets, let the anthropologists and the diplomats do their job. The military was absolutely not to engage unless they were attacked first and retreat was impossible. First Contact was worth a few human lives.

Absent an alien presence, they should pursue a secondary, and more aggressive, goal. The alien facilities deployed uncountable numbers of small autonomous spacecraft. Some of them scavenged Saturn's rings, apparently for water ice, and brought it back to some of the moonlets. Others shuttled between moonlets. They appeared to lack armament, or even much in the way of tools.

Ground-based analysis suggested that they were simple collection and transport devices—but however simple they were, they deployed alien tech. The large number of such craft, their small size, and their swarm-like behavior, strongly argued that they were not individually important.

They were the station's equivalent of ants foraging in the grass. The analysts also guessed one ant would not be particularly missed, as long as the rest of the hill was not disturbed. Capture an ant, preferably alive rather than dead, but either way, get one aboard a tug and get the tug and its treasure back to the *Celestial Odyssey*.

Because the Americans would be periodically watching the Chinese activity around the alien planetoid, it would be best if they never got a hint that one of the ants had been captured. The ant, after all, would probably become the major piece of alien tech actually back on Earth.

After two days of repair work, Zhang signaled to Beijing his willingness to move toward contact. It seemed little enough to get the politicians off his back, especially since the repairs were going well. He directed Cui to draw up plans for two contact parties, one to investigate the planetoid, the other to look at the rest of the constellation.

Cui: "Sir, I would request that I be allowed to lead the first contact to the planetoid."

Zhang said, "I was thinking of doing that myself. However, you may be right: we need decisive short-term thinking there, rather than a more leisurely process. Put yourself down to lead the planetoid team. What about the other team?"

Cui leaned almost imperceptibly toward Zhang and lowered her voice just a notch. "Sir, thank you for allowing me this opportunity. For the other team leader, I would suggest Duan Me, as a way of forestalling, mmm, personnel difficulties."

Zhang nodded: "Do that. Your recommendation suggests to me that you may actually have a future in the navy."

"Thank you, sir."

"How long will it take you to draw up your crew list and give me a prospectus on your investigations?"

Cui held up her slate. "Sir, I need to put my name at the head of the planetoid list. Otherwise, you could have it in ten seconds. As is, it will take me perhaps a minute to transmit it to you."

"Excellent, Cui. You do that. I'm going down to the maintenance bay."

Because the crew didn't do just one thing at a time, Cui had managed to signal to the prospective members of her crew, and Duan's, to make themselves ready for their separate missions.

There wasn't much to do, other than to check the EVA suits and vehicles. Cui would take the tug to the planetoid: they had measured the extruded landing shelf and determined that the tug would fit.

Duan would take a separate group in the shuttle to investigate the antimatter storage units and the service modules known as ants.

They waited until the *Nixon* disappeared behind the bulk of Saturn, on one of its outward spirals, and launched the shuttle and the tug within minutes of each other. All communications would be deeply encrypted.

Cui took the tug directly into the landing shelf and put it down. Having watched the news broadcasts from the *Nixon*, they knew the process, and Cui led the crew members through the air lock, and into the main room.

Ahead of them, they saw a machine that resembled an old-time jukebox, such as those they'd seen in museums in Shanghai. Letters formed in the air above the jukebox, and without waiting for the Chinese script to form, Cui said, "We bring you greetings from the People's Republic of China."

The jukebox said, "Mandarin. I speak Mandarin. What do you wish to know?"

"Do you have anything to say to the people of China?"

"Yes."

"What would that be?" Cui asked politely.

"Hello, people of China."

Zhang watched the shuttle go with some apprehension. Duan was not impetuous, but she was terribly ambitious. An ant would be coming back with them, whether or not it wanted to. He was not sure that an ant was worth the risk. Duan had been told emphatically that she was not to insist, but Duan was ambitious.

Zhang went back to the bridge to watch.

The scopes and radar watched as Duan and the shuttle attempted to match speeds with one of the ants. If they could do that, they could simply pull the alien craft aboard, and bring it back. The ants, however, eluded the shuttle, apparently with an effective proximity control that steered them away whenever the shuttle got too close; and the ants were much more maneuverable than the Chinese craft.

After a few fruitless attempts, the shuttle moved on to investigate one of the moonlets. A few minutes later, there was a burst of traffic from Duan. "Arrived, no incidents. Unpacked. All fine."

Excellent, thought Zhang. *Right on schedule.*

Cui went directly to the technology.

"We are told that the humans who just left established an I/O connection between your computers and ours. Can we use that?"

"Yes."

"What kind of information was transmitted to those humans?"

"They used four trade points to obtain scientific findings in physics, chemistry, and biology. They also received technological information regarding the engineering of interstellar capabilities appropriate to this facility. That information is available to all visitors."

"Including construction of antimatter manufacturing and storage facilities?"

"Yes."

"Where is the I/O port?"

"There is a hallway opening to your right. I/O equipment, including that left by the first humans, is there."

Cui turned to Wong, the senior tech, and said, "Let's go look."

The Chinese scientists sent to investigate the moonlets began with surface readings, which showed faint gamma emissions from inside the moonlet. They'd quickly congregated as close to the source as they could get. Although the surface of the moonlet was covered with what appeared to be natural regolith, like any normal moonlet, the soil was studded with plates, protuberances, and sockets, none of whose function was at all obvious to the scientists. In addition, faint light splayed across the regolith, as though the surface of the moon were one giant computer display.

When the scientists brought microscopes to bear on the surface, they discovered it was covered with small organelles, most likely extraordinarily sophisticated nanobots. They seemed to operate like a loose mesh network, neighbor communicating information to neighbor.

Samples of the regolith, including myriad bots, were scooped into isolation canisters. The scientists were delighted to see that the soil kept twinkling, at first with faint random flashes. The flashes started to settle into larger patterns, expanding circles, stripes, checkerboards.

Without a signal to drive them, there was no meaning or content to display, but it proved that the bots' communication network was still functioning.

Duan asked Chang, one of the engineers, what the tech might mean.

Chang grunted and said, "One thing it means is that somebody is going to make another trillion yuan from these things. Just not us. What you're looking at is microscopic machines. We've been talking about them for years but nobody's got there yet. If we can reverse-engineer these things, we can get fifty years of tech in one leap."

Duan was pleased by that; still, it wasn't the big prize. It wasn't aliens, it wasn't starships, it wasn't antimatter technology. Aliens, especially, seemed in short supply. She wondered what Cui was finding on the planetoid.

Cui asked, "We would like a summary explanation of the trade items. We were told by the last human group that you would allow us to trade up to eight points, and that they used four of those points, leaving us another four. Is that correct?"

"That is correct. There is a trade computer down the hall to your left. It can send a list of tradable items, and their cost, that is, their score, to the I/O port you are using. You may select from the list."

"Are these technological items?"

"Most are not. Most are artistic items involving visual and aural arts, items used in food preparation and sensory stimulation."

Wong said, "I think he just offered us vibrators."

Cui: "Shut up."

At the moonlet: while the biotechnologists were gathering nanobots from the surface, the seismologists were trying to find out what lay under the surface. What their sensitive microphones heard was disappointing: all of it was mechanical or electronic in nature. Not that any of them knew what aliens were supposed to sound like, but steady, repetitive, monotonous sonic signatures were not the hallmarks of active, intelligent life. Furthermore, no definite entry ports had been found. The few possible ports would accommodate nothing larger than a hamster.

Chang said, "Maybe the aliens are hamsters. I always thought hamsters acted suspiciously."

"Shut up," Duan said.

Possibly the moonlet was inhabited, by very quiet, intelligent, alien rodents. But probably not. The consensus was that this was not going to be the day for First Contact with another species.

The seismologist determined that the shell of the moonlet was quite thin. The geologists were equipped with drills and even small mining charges.

"Do we crack the shell?" Chang asked.

Duan shook her head: "No. The instructions are quite clear. Nothing that could be interpreted as an attack. We should see to the ants."

At the planetoid, Cui had gone out through the air lock to call Zhang and the bridge crew.

"The I/O connection is fine. We can hook right in and start the I/O feed back to the *Odyssey*. The question is, should we do that, or should we fabricate our own equipment? Ours is better—not faster, but more robust. And I worry that the Americans may have done something to the cables. Is it possible to insert something into the cables that would turn the I/O output to garbage, or noise, or add error somehow?"

"Yes, that would be possible," said one of the *Odyssey*-based techs. "But we would see that almost instantly. I would suggest you get the specs for fabricating our own I/O, but also, begin transmitting through the American connection. We could transmit to a sequestered computer to make sure that the input is not contaminated."

On the moonlet, Duan took a call from one of the team members designated as an explorer. One of the ants was sitting on the surface of the moonlet, attached to one of the hamster-sized ports. The machine was less than a kilometer away.

After signaling to the *Celestial Odyssey* what they were about to do, they moved the shuttle to the site discovered by the explorer. Duan took a message from Zhang: "The Americans are coming over the horizon. You won't be visible to them for another hour, because of the rings, but then they will be able to see you, if they look at the right place. So, either hurry, or hide."

Duan signaled, "We will hurry first and hide later."

At the planetoid, Cui asked, "How long will it take to transmit data at the current output rate of both science and technological information?"

The jukebox—now renamed the Narcissus, for the flower held in Chinese folklore to represent the intellect—said, "At the previous I/O rate, approximately two hundred and twelve Earth years, one hundred and six Earth days, seven Earth hours, sixteen Earth minutes, and 24.5 Earth seconds."

Cui and Wong looked at each other. "Narcy . . . uh, how much did you give to the other humans?"

"All of it."

"All of it? Why would it take us two hundred years to get it, if they got all of it in a week?"

"The first group of humans also received memory modules containing the most detailed technological and manufacturing information, which is the bulk of the information. The fundamental science information only was transmitted on the I/O link."

"Then we also want memory modules."

"Only eight physical memory modules and eight physical module readers are allotted per species. More cannot be fabricated on this facility, which is designed for storage, rather than the manufacture of consumer goods. The first group of humans took all eight."

"*What?*"

On the moonlet: the ant—the alien artifact, whatever it was—more closely resembled a crab than a worker ant, with a flattened, domed fuselage and multiple mechanical appendages that extended from its midsection. None of the appendages could be interpreted as a weapon. They were all tipped with grapples, manipulators, or sockets, presumably for interchangeable attachments like tools. Nothing that would fire a projectile or a bolt or beam of energy, nothing that even looked capable of delivering a shock.

Duan signaled back to Zhang: "It's some kind of drone, we think. No visible defensive or offensive capability."

"How big?"

"A meter and a half long. Appears to be inactive. We've probed it with every nondestructive tool we've got—millimeter waves, soft X-ray, active sonar and passive sound detecting equipment. There's a little hum, but not much."

"Could you, uh, pick it up?"

"We'll try."

They tried, but the artifact was immovable. A docking collar locked the fuselage to the port that went into the moonlet. The tips of several appendages were firmly embedded in complementary fixtures arrayed about the port.

"That isn't going to work," Duan called. "We need to talk here."

"Americans are almost around."

At Duan's direction, the crew tried to pry the appendages loose and rotate the docking collar, but got no movement with the degree of force the mechanics were willing to risk. The only response of the automaton was that faint internal hum increased when stress was put on the appendages.

They considered the option of cutting it free. Their cutting torches ought to be up to the task. But was it a good idea?

As an option, it was the last resort. They had no way of knowing how much damage they would do to the automaton by cutting away pieces of it, especially powered components, as the hum suggested they were. They might end up with a dead and dismembered spacecraft, pieces of alien space junk. How much could they learn about the technology from an entirely nonfunctional device?

Before going the meat-cleaver route, they opted for precision surgery. The docking mechanisms were active devices. If they could shut down the ant, they might be able to decouple it from the moonlet. The scientists and technicians now had 3-D models of the innards of the spacecraft, the fruits of the multispectral scans. A lot of what was in there was unidentifiable or incomprehensible. Just what was that thing near the bottom front that looked like a kidney?

A lot, though, was recognizable. Conduits and cables look much the same no matter who built them. They could see lumps that they could tell must function as motors or actuators, odd as they looked, just from where they were and what they were attached to.

There were a handful of larger modules. Those had to include fuel and storage tanks, computing and data-handling functions, and a power source. Assuming, of course, that alien engineering design followed anything remotely like human engineering principles. It was a large assumption, but they'd been able to recognize conduits and cables and motors, so it couldn't be all that different.

There had to be signals to the motors telling them what to do and power so that they could do it. The electrical engineers started tracing conduits back from the motors. One by one they eliminated modules from consideration, as the scientists peered anxiously over the engineers' shoulders and kept checking the time. They worked it down to two candidates. One was likely the computing unit, the other the main power supply. The one with the larger cables? Probably power.

They might be wrong, but disconnecting either ought to shut down the spacecraft. They had twenty-five minutes to do one or the other before the Americans would be looking over their shoulders. Rebooting the artifact might be tricky, or impossible, but at least they'd have an intact machine.

"Cut the power supply," Duan said. There wasn't time to consult with Zhang on the decision.

The engineers worked rapidly, calling out for tools and instruments that were delivered to them instantly by the surrounding team. Like field surgeons, they contemplated their alien patient. They were down to eighteen minutes to complete the operation. They decided where to make the first incision.

Zhang was talking with Cui, with increasing exasperation about the information feeds, and about the fact that the Americans may have tried to sneak away with the most important information dispensed by the information-bot.

He was doing that when the screens carrying the feed from the ship's telescopes flared white, at the same moment that blinding light poured through the ports on the bridge.

Cui, several kilometers away, was looking toward the ship as she spoke to Zhang, and saw the ship flicker, as though it had been lit by lightning. An instant later, though, the ship remained as it had been.

On board the *Celestial Odyssey*, the radiation alarm sounded for a fraction of a second and went silent. As it went silent, all the ship's screens, all the interior lighting, went dark. Zhang heard a panicked scream, he didn't know from whom; it was almost immediately stifled by the embarrassed crew member.

The windows' glare had been dazzling; anyone looking out a port had been temporarily blinded, although the flash had been several kilometers away.

After a long five seconds, lights began to come back, as well as the various vid screens.

"*Shenme zai diyu?*" That was the helmsman, Lieutenant Peng. His voice was high, panicked. Zhang knew who had screamed.

Zhang took a calming breath before he spoke. "Mr. Peng, that was a nuclear explosion. The ship's systems and power went down because the electromagnetic pulse tripped the safeties."

"But, sir, the shuttle!"

Zhang managed to keep his voice from shaking. "Cong, there is no shuttle. Not any longer," he said very softly.

"Admiral?" The navigator on watch, Lieutenant Sun, spoke up. "I'm confirming that. There's nothing on the scope."

"No shuttle?" asked Peng.

"Peng," replied the navigator, "there's nothing. No moonlet, no shuttle. Everything that was there . . . everyone . . . gone. Vaporized."

The helmsman began to sob. It was not professional. Zhang found it entirely understandable.

"Mr. Lei, ship's status now, if you please."

The watch officer was already hard at work. "No physical damage likely, not at twenty kilometers. The EMP might have fried some hardware. We're pretty well shielded against that—original ship's design in case it got caught by a really bad solar storm or a coronal ejection mass. But that's a whole different level from a close-by nuclear pulse. The major systems will be okay or have backups. We could lose some lesser equipment. I'll have a survey done now."

"What about the radiation flash? What effect would that have on the crew?"

"I don't know. The hull would protect us from normal background radiation, but a short, intense dose like this? I don't know. I will talk to Medical. We may want to start everyone on radiation sickness preempts, just in case."

"Do that. Mr. Sun, what is it?" The navigator was signaling urgently.

"Captain, we may have another problem. Those small autonomous spacecraft, like the one we were trying to catch? A lot of them, hundreds it looks like, are changing trajectory. They're moving in our direction."

Ta ma de, thought Zhang, *we kicked the anthill.*

50.

Francisco, the executive officer, had the watch when the bridge klaxon sounded the three-note tone that signaled a radiation emergency. Startled, he lost his grip on the slate he'd been reading; the slate slowly fell to the end of its tether.

He ignored it. "Comm, kill that noise. Engineering, Science, talk to me. Frank, you first."

Lieutenant LaFarge scanned his console. "It's a real alert, sir, not a computer fault or test run. Outside sensors reported a radiation spike. Safety systems kicked in like they're supposed to and set off the alarms."

Comm spoke up. "Confirming that, sir. It's a radiation storm alert." All over the *Nixon*, except in the shielded engineering module, warning lights and bells were going off, while the computer system's voice instructed personnel in the unshielded sections to immediately go to their nearest hidey-hole.

"We're ten AU from the sun. It has to be one hell of a big solar event for us to notice it way out here. Why hasn't space weather sent us an alert?" The Earth-orbit monitoring stations had near-instantaneous response times. They couldn't beat the initial X-ray burst to the *Nixon*, but their warning should have arrived by now.

"Sir?" Albers Janssen was at the science station.

"Go ahead, Albers."

"I don't think it was the sun. The directional data says the burst came from the general direction of the alien depot. That's well off the sun line. Also, the burst was too short for a solar flare or coronal mass ejection." Janssen peered closely at the time plots. "Make that two short bursts, close together. A small one and then a much bigger one." He switched his attention to the spectral plot. "Aw fuck. The main spikes are gamma, not X-ray—511 keV. That was an antimatter detonation."

Fang-Castro hurried onto the bridge: "What happened?"

"We think the Chinese may have triggered off an antimatter explosion," Francisco said.

"Oh, no. Can we see them?"

Navigation: "No. We'd have line of sight, but the edge of the ring is in the way. We should have visual in . . . eight minutes."

Cui turned as the air-lock door behind her closed: she didn't know why it had done that.

Suddenly feeling alone in the universe, she called the *Celestial Odyssey*: "Sir: What happened? Something is happening here."

Zhang came back: "Cui, evacuate your crew immediately. Duan's crew apparently set off an antimatter explosion and the ants are beginning to cluster between us and the planetoid. We need you back here, until we can reassess our status."

"Yes, sir. The crew is out of touch at the moment—immediately after the flash, the air-lock doors closed, separating me from the crew. There is no . . . Wait one . . ."

In front of her, the air-lock doors were opening again: inside the lock, she saw her entire crew.

"What happened?" she asked Wong. She kept the relay open to Zhang.

"We've been ordered out of the planetoid. Narcissus told us we have to leave. I have vid, sending now."

The vid popped up on a display screen.

Narcissus said, "There has been damage to the depot. Containment Module 7251 was disrupted. Members of your species intercepted one of the antimatter transport units while it was docking with the containment module. It appears that they tried to disable the unit, leading to a failure of its isolation vessel. The vessel contained 2.5 grams of antimatter. That explosion, in such close proximity to the containment module, caused it to fail as well, resulting in a larger explosion. Sanctions apply. Access to this depot and my database are denied, effective immediately."

Wong tried to shift blame, to keep the planetoid open: "We didn't do this. It was an action by another ship, not authorized by us."

Narcissus said, "Sanctions automatically apply to all vessels of a species. You have five Earth minutes to collect your equipment, secure your suits, and vacate this room. In five minutes the security system will discontinue life support, evacuating the atmosphere and ceasing illumination and thermal regulation. In six minutes, further countermeasures will be taken."

Wong asked, "What countermeasures?"

"I do not have that information. That information is available only to the security AI."

Wong had heard enough. To the crew, he called, "You heard it, everybody. Get it together and let's get out. Narcissus, for how long are the sanctions in effect?"

"Physical damage to a depot is a very serious security breach. Fortunately, Containment Facility 7251 was almost empty. The damage was limited to its destruction, so suspension of all depot privileges will only be in effect for one hundred and forty-four Earth years. Life-support services will end in four minutes. Further countermeasures begin in five."

Wong said, "People, into the air lock. Don't start cycling yet." And, "Narcissus, why didn't your security system prevent this kind of tampering?" The AI had indicated the depot's defensive capabilities were superior to human technology. There should have been a specific warning, he thought.

"If an unauthorized ship or one of unknown origin had attempted to access the containment facilities, the security system would have instituted protective measures. This was not a ship of unknown origin. It was one of your species' ships. Once I informed the security system that you had been given the safety protocols and basic operating instructions for using this depot, your status was changed to authorized. There was no a priori reason to believe that you would not follow the safety protocols, considering the hazards to you and the depot and the penalties that could incur. By the time the data stream indicated that a safety was being breached, there was too little time for security units to arrive before containment failed. Life-support services will end in four minutes."

Wong tried one more time. "Narcissus, the first ship did not convey the safety information to us. We did not know about the safety protocols."

"I would not know that, nor would the security system. It is in the interest of every species to make sure that none of its ships interfere with the depot's functioning, to avoid sanctions. Life-support services will end in two minutes. Further countermeasure begin in three."

There was no point arguing with the answer-bot. The team finished stowing their gear, secured their suits, and Wong entered the air lock and the interior air-lock door closed. The space-side door opened, and they found Cui hanging in space, just outside.

Cui saw herself on the vid, and killed it. "We don't know what range Narcy was talking about when he said, 'further countermeasures.' We need to get back to the ship. Everybody into the shuttle."

Another minute and they were gone.

"Admiral Fang-Castro, Mr. Crow wishes to speak to you. Shall I put him through?"

She said, "No, not at the moment. Wait—tell him to join me in the conference room in ten minutes. And Hannegan, Clover, Martinez, Barnes, and Darlington. I want them there, too. Tell Darlington we're going to have a conference, we'll want a direct link to Earth."

Fang-Castro spent ten minutes assessing the situation from the bridge. The *Celestial Odyssey* was right where it had been and a tug was headed back toward it from the planetoid. There was no sign of the larger shuttle.

Francisco said, "They were messing with one of those storage units and it blew. That's why we got two pulses. I bet they tried to grab one of the bees, and something happened—could have been a self-destruct mechanism to keep that from happening—and that took out a second storage unit."

"What's our radiation status?"

"We're fine. They may not be, depending on how close they were to the explosion."

"Any other damage?"

"No."

"Comm, call Zhang."

A moment later Comm said, "Admiral, they acknowledged the call and declined it."

"Might be too busy to talk to us," Francisco said.

"Or too angry," Fang-Castro said. "Comm, reach out to them every half hour or so. If they answer, put it through to me. I'll be in the conference room. I want everything that happened since the blast, including the blast, encrypted and forwarded to Earth. I want that done immediately, with a top-priority tag on it."

"Yes, ma'am."

When Fang-Castro got to the conference room, the others were all waiting, Barnes by vid from the isolation suite. She nodded at Darlington and said, "Link this to Comm, highest encrypt, top priority, tagged for the President."

Sandy nodded and when the link was set, Fang-Castro told the group what had happened.

When she finished, Crow held up his stylus: "We must have told them that the trailing moonlets were antimatter storage?"

"Of course," Fang-Castro said. "We also told them that the bees were apparently gathering something, but we didn't know what, or why."

"Didn't we ask Wurly?" Clover asked.

"We asked Wurly for all information concerning the moonlets, the bees, and the primary, including technical drawings, manufacturing specs, and everything else we could think of," said Martinez. "He agreed to give it to us as part of the tech package. But we were so busy gathering information, and checking the validity of what we could see, and making valid copies of it, we haven't had a chance to look at much of it. We never looked at the details of what the remotes were doing, because we figured we could do that anytime."

Crow said, "I'm sure the survivors on the *Odyssey* are talking to Beijing. What I need to get clear here, now, is that nothing we did caused the accident—that we are not to blame."

"That is correct," Fang-Castro said. "Mr. Francisco has suggested that the Chinese may have tried to capture one of the bees. That would have been tempting—they're small and they're genuine alien tech. If they could have gotten a bee back to Earth, it would have been worthwhile. We didn't try it because we didn't have to, and we didn't actually have time, with the Chinese pushing on us as they were."

"So we're not to blame," Crow said. "Whatever happened, is the Chinese's own doing."

"Yes, that's correct, in my opinion." She turned to Hannegan. "I'd also like some reassurance that the aliens haven't been . . . fooling us. Did they actually deliver what they said they would?"

Hannegan cleared his throat. "We've been looking at the science data ever since the I/O went up. There's an awful lot of it. All the theory behind the production of antimatter, all the underlying supersymmetry stuff. That's a far cry from working technology, but it'll still give us a twenty-year jump on the underlying hard science. A lot of theoretical-physicist food fights are gonna get settled when we get back. To me, it looks like Wurly really has given us exactly what it promised at the first meetings."

Martinez held up a finger. "But understand, we got the science over the I/O link, but not the tech specs for actually building much. That's on the quantum storage units."

"Where are you on testing the actual readers?" Crow asked.

Martinez shook his head. "We're sorting out the electrical connections now. They're not hard, but we don't want to screw anything up, either. With everything else we've had to do . . . What I'm trying to say is, we could probably start testing them tomorrow, or even tonight, if you're in a rush. We haven't done it yet."

A call popped up on the corner of the conference room screen: Francisco calling. Fang-Castro tapped her slate, and Francisco's face appeared: "Admiral, we're getting a broadcast from Wurly. Or the primary.

It's very short, it's in all the languages, it says we're barred from contact
with the primary and all the other alien tech for one hundred and forty-
four years. It's a loop, playing over and over."

"Anything else?"

"That's it, ma'am."

Fang-Castro said, "Thank you," tapped her slate, and Francisco disappeared. She asked, "Anybody?"

Clover said, "Hey, it told us the rules right at the beginning. It's never
done anything to deviate from those rules. It even told us why those
rules were in place, and we pretty much played out the part it said we
would. Less than two weeks into our First Contact, and we've managed
to piss off the other party. Well, it would be pissed off, if it had any feelings to be pissed with."

Crow said, "Stop saying 'we.' It wasn't us, it was the Chinese."

Clover shrugged. "An irrelevant distinction, I suspect. As far as the
AI is concerned, all us humans look alike. I imagine that millennia, or
megayears ago, when the face-to-face contactees got into their planet-
killing disagreements, they didn't much concern themselves with exactly which members of the other species had committed the unforgivable
offense. I think we came out of this pretty well—a little foul, a little
harm. It only banned us for a hundred and forty-four years. We got off
easy! That's almost nothing when you consider the timescales of interstellar travel."

"All right, John," Fang-Castro said. She turned to Crow. "Mr. Crow,
do you have an opinion on our current situation's security? Does the AI
or anything else in the depot pose a threat to us, in your opinion?"

Crow tapped his fingers together thoughtfully. "I'm more concerned
with the Chinese. If they attempt further tampering with the depot, its
security systems might be inclined to take countermeasures. I don't
think it would distinguish between them and us. As John pointed out,
its policies operate species-wide.

"And I'd point out, they banned us—they didn't tell us to give anything back. And as far as we know, we have it all. And as far as we know,
the Chinese don't have much. They didn't have time link to the I/O and

we got all the available QSUs. That strikes me as a pretty unstable situation."

Clover said, "About an alien threat: if there is one, we have no idea what form it would take."

Barnes added, "We never saw any visible weapons, but there's so many things a facility like this might be able to do. Some kind of super cybervirus trashing our computers? A swarm of bees chasing us down— we have no idea what their capabilities are. Nanobots, like the ones on the surface of the depot's primary, gobbling up the ship from under us?"

Clover said, "You guys work too hard at your nightmares. Blowguns would be a lot easier."

Crow: "Blowguns?"

"Yeah, these guys are making anti-iron by the ton, remember? So a little magnetic peashooter firing BBs at us, that's what I'm thinking. Except each BB is like getting hit with . . ." He looked at Hannegan. "Well, I don't know. You tell me."

Hannegan punched a few numbers into his slate and volunteered, "Something like a kiloton of TNT?"

Clover laughed: "That's the ticket! Beats poison blow darts all to hell. And it's not like they'd have any shortage of BBs. Oh yeah, the AI could've slammed us good if it wanted to. But it hasn't, so it probably won't."

Crow said, "You've been leaning on that theory pretty hard, the 'they haven't, so they won't' theory."

Clover shrugged: "It's what I got."

51.

Zhang Ming-Hoa was having a terrible day and it wasn't going to get better anytime soon. Communications with Beijing had been running nonstop since the accident, on an excruciatingly slow cycle. Beijing would ask a question or make a suggestion. He'd get it more than an hour after they transmitted it. He'd reply. They'd come back with a response two and a half hours later, unless they decided to think it over, in which case later still. And on and on and on.

The explosion had occurred while the alien constellation was on the far side of Saturn from Earth, so the first Beijing had known of the disaster was a short message Zhang had sent back after the ship had come off of emergency status. Their reply was terse: Is the *Celestial Odyssey* operational? No recriminations, no expressions of concern, no queries about the crew. Just, are you operational?

He didn't know if he should take that as a good sign or a bad one. It didn't much matter. The mission was in shambles. It had fallen apart, failed to achieve every one of its objectives.

No, that was wrong. This wasn't some anonymous "mistakes were made" scenario, not even some third-party "the captain is responsible for a ship" rhetoric.

He had done this. He had caused this. The failures, the losses, they were due to his mistakes. His plans, his strategies, his errors in judgment had cost them. Half the crew vaporized in an antimatter-driven fireball. The shuttle, vaporized. All but nine of their space suits, vaporized.

Were they operational?

Technically, yes. Was this survivable? That was a whole different question, and the one foremost in his mind. His primary obligation was to get the remainder of his crew home alive. He wasn't sure that was possible; they might already be dead men walking.

He felt most guilty over the death of Duan Me. He'd disliked the political officer, not as a human being, but for what she did. He'd idly wished her ill.

Now a completely illogical part of his mind felt culpable in her death. He knew it was ridiculous; the universe did not bend to his will to determine who lived and died. She would have been no less dead if he had loved her like his mother. He knew that. He still couldn't throw off that extra load of unreasonable guilt piled on top of the immense load of entirely justifiable guilt he carried.

Somehow he had to push all that aside and manage the welfare of the rest of his crew. The explosion hadn't killed them, not directly, anyway. The ship's surge protectors and electromagnetic pulse firewalls were there to protect it from a major solar event. No one had tested it as a defense against a nearby nuclear detonation, but it had worked well enough. All the major circuits and power subsystems were intact. Some lesser stuff had been fried. The ship was functional—what was left of it after the aerobraking maneuvers, the only catastrophe that wasn't entirely his fault.

But they'd been counting on what was left of the ship to operate at a hundred percent of capability. That was no longer possible. Some of the damaged subsystems were certainly not repairable. How many, they didn't know yet. They might not have an exact count of how many they'd lost until after the repair attempts failed, but there was no doubt that the number was considerably larger than zero.

Those repairs would be slowed for weeks or months, by the deaths of so many people. The loss of all the scientists, tragic as it was in human terms, did not directly affect the running of the ship. The loss of pilots, maintenance technicians, and engineers did.

Zhang had been prudent enough not to send over anyone absolutely vital to ship's operations, but even so they were now operating with barely better than a skeleton crew. They'd hoped that they might repair one of the badly damaged external tanks with the carbon fiber and printer donated by the Americans. Now they no longer had the personnel to do that. The ship's status would not be clear for some time, but it was somewhere between "bad" and "disastrous."

That wasn't even considering what the aliens might do. Hundreds of the autonomous spacecraft, the worker ants, had positioned themselves between the *Celestial Odyssey* and the alien constellation. The ship's instruments had picked up very faint positron signatures. Regardless of whatever the aliens used them for, each of those ants was a flying nuclear weapon.

Zhang ordered the *Celestial Odyssey* to back off, very slowly, very cautiously. The maneuvering engines drove the slightest of orbital changes, increasing the gap between them and the aliens by less than a meter a second. It was nothing that should alarm them or trigger an attack, but it had been enough to substantially increase the distance between the ship and the ants since the explosion.

The flying bombs hadn't moved forward. They'd stayed where they were, letting the *Celestial Odyssey* pull away. That was good news . . . unless the aliens were waiting for the ship to be safely far from the facilities before they vaporized it with a score of antimatter detonations. Who knew?

Meanwhile, the military and political gamers in Beijing were trying to work through the various scenarios confronting the ship.

With the total loss of the external tanks, the *Celestial Odyssey*'s delta-vee capabilities were much reduced. With some effort, they could whip up enough to get them a Hohmann transfer to Earth, with a small safety margin for the unexpected. Of which, so far, there'd been no shortage. Just one problem. It would take six years to get back. That wasn't survivable.

Beijing thought differently, perhaps? Zhang didn't know for sure.

With more than half the crew gone, the survivors might be able to stretch supplies out considerably longer than otherwise. The Beijing experts politely requested Zhang confirm the situation. Sighing, he set his quartermaster about taking inventory, following orders but knowing that Beijing was thinking about it the wrong way.

The limits weren't food, air, and water. It was about turning what was to have been a three-year mission into a much longer one. The ship's designers had considered an extended mission of five or more years, but they hadn't considered a ship so badly damaged and incapacitated.

Engineering and Environmental thought they could keep them all alive for two and a half more years. Sufficient repairs to the life-support and engineering systems might let the engineers nurse them along for three.

Zhang wasn't taking any bets on that. So far, the gods he didn't believe in had not looked favorably upon this mission. So, a four-year mission? Probably. Five? Probably not. Six? Forget it. The vessel that passed by Earth six years from now, seven and a half years after it departed, would be crewed by corpses.

They considered throwing additional velocity at the problem. If the *Celestial Odyssey* used up all its reaction-mass reserves, they could trim a year off the transit time. Meaning that they'd die two years out from Earth instead of three. Zhang asked Navigation and Beijing to consider more desperate scenarios.

There was one. It almost worked. If they topped off the remaining tanks and burned all their reaction mass leaving Saturn, they could pile on enough extra velocity to drop the transit time to Earth orbit to under two and a half years. That was survivable. The catch was that once they got there they'd have no delta-vee left for matching Earth's orbit and another ship would have to rescue the crew.

There were a couple of problems with that. First, they'd pass Earth's orbit moving twelve km/s faster than the earth. Second, the timing was imperfect. Earth would be tens of millions of kilometers away. The only ships that existed that were capable of those kind of delta-vees and long-distance travel were the *Celestial Odyssey* and the *Nixon*.

Could the engineers build a rescue ship fast enough to do that? Perhaps: desperation was an excellent motivator.

Zhang had the unpleasant feeling that Beijing wouldn't mind at all if the *Celestial Odyssey* and its remaining crew simply disappeared. They'd achieved nothing of value, which made them a political and scientific embarrassment. He did not, of course, voice that opinion to his superiors. He was considerably more candid with his first officer.

"Mr. Cui, what's your take on Beijing's plan for getting us home?"

"Well, sir, I think it could work." Cui Zhuo didn't say more. She looked acutely uncomfortable under the placid gaze of her commander.

"Acknowledged. Do you think it will work?"

"Sir, may I speak freely? And will this go no further than between the two of us?"

Zhang nodded.

"I don't believe them. Uh . . . I'm not saying they're lying," she nervously backtracked, "it's just that it would take some effort to get a rescue ship out to us, and, well, I don't think we're Beijing's most favorite people right now. You in particular. I mean no offense, sir, but many of the crew consider this to be your failure, and they're people who have worked with you and like you and respect you. I can't imagine our superiors in Beijing have a higher opinion of you. I think this could start off with the best intentions and if the wrong people decided not to push the project, well, schedules slip. And then where are we?"

Cui looked about the room nervously. It was apparent she was worried that perhaps she had spoken a bit too freely.

"Relax, Zhuo, I share your concerns. I don't think we can count on Beijing to get us out of this predicament. Amend that: I'm almost certain of it. I think we must turn to the Americans for assistance."

"Sir? Is that a good idea? Beijing—"

"Zhuo, my time has evidently passed. Your time may or may not arrive, depending on what happens next. Let me suggest something to you. Again, to you only. One of the last things you elicited from Narcy was that the Americans had taken away some memory capsules, with technical specifications for entire alien industries, and, through the I/O port, they'd taken away scientific information that would give a boost of decades in hard science, and who knows how much in soft. Have I expressed this accurately?"

"Yes, sir."

"So if this ship dies, then Beijing will be left with two options: let the Americans have those industries, or shoot down the *Nixon*. If they shoot down the *Nixon*, and I think they might do that, then there might very well be a war. I don't know what would happen in a war—"

"Sir, I'm sure there are options other than a nuclear war."

"Of course. Like a trade war. If the Americans put an embargo on Chinese goods, and threatened anyone who traded with us with further sanctions, well, they'd fall into a Depression. But we would fall into something much worse. With a billion people sloshing around the country without food or work . . . who knows what might happen? I'm sure Beijing has worked through these scenarios. What I'm suggesting is, we request a rescue: actually, we leave them no choice in rescuing us. And we suggest to Beijing that once we are aboard the *Nixon*, we may have some . . . mmm . . . influence on the distribution of the alien information."

"Sir . . . you would try to seize their ship? The Americans must have countermeasures."

"Let's not look that far ahead, Zhuo. Let's just say our presence might have some effect on how things work out." Zhang looked at the time panel on his slate. "Beijing will be waking up. I'm going to go talk to them. About this possibility."

"Sir, do you want me with you?"

"No. I have other things for you to do. How's our reaction mass?"

"We're only about ten percent, on the remaining tanks, sir."

"Hmm, we'll need more like fifty percent and we'll need it soon. Assign everyone we can possibly spare to ice collection and hydrogen refining. Round-the-clock shifts. Also, I need some orbital calculations done that Beijing won't find out about, depending on how they receive my suggestion. Our navigator, Lieutenant Sun, how does she feel about me?"

"Oh, she almost idolizes you. She'd follow you to the end of the universe. She's very young." Cui touched her lips. "Sorry, sir, I didn't mean that the way it sounded."

"That's all right, I get your point. In this situation, it will perhaps be a plus. Her service record shows that she's ambitious. Few *yuhanguan* rack up so much flight experience so quickly. Landing on the crew of this mission at the age of twenty-eight shows that she's bright and good at what she does."

"Sir . . ."

"A bright, young *yuhanguan* with ambitions will take risks an older one would not, and what I'm planning will be risky. Send her up, would you? I'll talk to her as soon as I finish my argument to Beijing."

"Sir . . ."

"Zhuo, you need to get busy. One way or another, we're going after the *Nixon*. With Beijing on board, or without them."

Zhang's proposal made the hour-plus-long trip to Earth. Beijing considered it for four hours. The reply made its hour-plus-long trip back to the *Celestial Odyssey*.

When the reply came in, Zhang was alone in his private quarters; had Duan been alive, she would have been with him, but Duan was now an ever-expanding cloud of atoms. The message came in a highly encrypted block of vid from the defense minister himself, who smiled tightly as he said hello; the smile disappeared as he continued.

"Admiral Zhang, your suggestion had already been considered here in some detail. Your analysis is correct: we really cannot afford to let the Americans get all of this technology to themselves. They are pushing us into a corner and they must be aware of that and the dangers that creates. I'm quite sure they don't want us cornered. They had hoped to get away with this banditry, of course, but we cannot let them. We understand that much of the damage to your ship was done by what, in retrospect, was the inadvisable midcourse burn and then the necessity of the aerobraking maneuver.

"We accept responsibility for those errors: they were ours, not yours. We believe that two things could be done to rescue you: you could return via the two-year transit plan, and we could build a ship to pluck you from that orbit, or you could simply wait there, in a safe orbit, and we could send a rescue ship. We could, in fact, build that ship and get it there in time to rescue you. But that would not solve the problem of the Americans getting the alien science and technology. Therefore, we are going to announce, with great loss of what the West thinks of as our face, that our ship is so damaged that no feasible rescue is possible, unless done in cooperation with the Americans. We will announce that you will attempt a rendezvous. What happens then . . . we shall see. Now, you have on board, as a survivor, your first officer Cui. I have seen photographs of her and she is quite attractive. She also speaks English. We will have her interviewed by a reputable Xinhua reporter, in which she expresses the desperation of your condition. That script is being written now. We have created an attractive husband for her here, and two children, and they will add to the plea. Our . . . experts . . . tell us it will go viral, worldwide."

When they were done, Zhang had to laugh. Not a happy laugh: the cynicism of international politics had always astonished him, and he'd not been disappointed in this latest example.

He floated out to the bridge, where Cui was waiting nervously. She said, "Yes?"

"Congratulations, Cui."

"Sir?"

"On your marriage. And the babies. You have such pretty babies."

"Sir?" She thought he'd lost his mind.

"Did I mention that you're about to become a movie star?"

52.

A week and a half after the *Nixon* departed the Maxwell Gap and the alien depot, the *Celestial Odyssey* followed. It was a very different kind of departure. The *Nixon*'s exit had been excruciatingly slow, tiptoeing away from the debacle of humanity's first contact with an alien intelligence. It had only managed to fully escape Saturn's pull a day earlier.

In contrast, the Chinese left with a massive push. Ten blue-white plasma jets poured from the reactors at full thrust. In a few hours, they generated as much boost as the *Nixon* managed in three days. The Chinese gamble was a race between the tortoise and the hare, turned on its head. In the long run the *Nixon* could outpace the *Celestial Odyssey* tenfold. The short run was a different matter.

Lieutenant Sun's models had confirmed Zhang's instincts. The *Nixon* was a million kilometers from Saturn, far from the *Celestial Odyssey*, but it was only moving away at nine kilometers per second. That velocity would steadily increase, day by day, but the *Nixon* would be gaining only a few kilometers per second each day.

The *Celestial Odyssey* was traveling twice as fast and it would pick up even more velocity with its course correction burn. It'd lose speed relative to the *Nixon* as it coasted in free fall, but the Chinese ship would put as much distance between itself and Saturn in a day as the *Nixon* had in eleven. By then the *Nixon* would've moved on, ever-accelerating, but the *Celestial Odyssey* still had the sprint advantage.

With some midcourse corrections, as soon as they got an exact fix on the Americans' intended flight path, the Chinese ship could catch up with them in a little over a day and a half. They'd both be about two million kilometers from Saturn and their velocities would match. A rendezvous was achievable, a rescue possible.

The scopes on the *Nixon* easily picked up the Chinese exit burn. The ten plasma exhausts were impressively bright even from a million kilo-meters.

Fang-Castro had been eating breakfast in her quarters with Marti-nez, talking about the condition of the ship and the testing of the alien readers, when Francisco called from the bridge. She tried not to jog to the command station, the better to maintain her dignity.

"Not another antimatter depot?" she blurted.

"No, the flare's continuing and we're not seeing any gamma rays. The Chinese are leaving. It's the only thing it can be."

She watched for a while, then said, "Department head meeting in half an hour. Comm, let everybody know."

"Yes, ma'am."

Fang-Castro went back to her fake scrambled eggs and real oatmeal.

The duration of the burn was a surprise. "Admiral, they're not head-ing back to Earth as fast as I would've expected," said Harbinson, from Navigation, at the meeting. "Unless they're planning a big burn later, which wouldn't be a very efficient use of their reaction mass, it'll take them two and a half years to get home."

"They took a lot of external tank damage during the aerobraking," Martinez said. "Maybe this is all they've got. They escaped retrograde, like we did, the fastest way to drop down to Earth's orbit. Or maybe the depot's security AI ordered them to go, and they're simply hightailing before something bad happens."

"All speculation. We'll have a better idea after they do their course correction burn," said Fang-Castro. "Nonetheless, I'm happy to see the last of them. We're fortunate we beat them to the depot and that our bluff worked. The shoe could've been on the other foot." She turned to the President's liaison. "Mr. Crow, do you have anything to add?"

Crow nodded. "I hope you're right . . . about seeing the last of them. We have some intelligence that has suggested that Beijing is looking into various rescue plans. We've also heard that Beijing has told Xinhua to reserve a block of vid time for a special presentation"—he looked at the time code in the corner of the room's vid screen—"about forty-five minutes ago. We'll see it in another thirty, if it's relevant. We have to consider the possibility that they're not headed for Earth—that they're coming after us."

Fang-Castro looked at him for a moment, then said, "Oh . . . no."

Oh, yes.

As soon as the Chinese burn began, the information ministry released the pretaped interviews with Zhang, in Chinese only, and Cui, in Chinese and English. Her children were seen on swing sets at a Chinese elementary school, with their handsome father, waiting for Mom to get home . . . if only the Americans would help.

The *Nixon*'s leadership was still sitting in the conference room, waiting, more than anything, when the first reaction arrived, Santeros herself, from the Oval Office:

"The goddamned Chinese are asking for a rescue. They say the *Celestial Odyssey* has calculated a trajectory that will pair up with you in a day or so. . . ." She called off-screen, "Is that right? A day or so? A day and a half?"

She turned back to face Fang-Castro and the others. "A day and a half. They issued the goddamnedest propaganda vid you ever saw, the *Odyssey*'s first officer, cute as a button, hoping we'll help, pictures of her kids at their school, waiting for Mom. She speaks English . . . the vid's gone viral, it's on a half-billion phones in India alone, probably a hundred million here. . . . We're gonna cut it in at the end of this briefing so you can see it yourself. We got all the big brains working on a reaction, but I'm telling you, there's no way we can say no. Not with those kids on the swing set. I suspect they're about to produce a vid of her breast-feeding the little fuckin' crotchfruit.

"So, you need to start thinking about how to contain the Chinese, because they're coming for you. What's gonna happen then, we don't know, but we're working on scenarios. You better start working on some of your own, you know the ship better than we do." She looked to the side again, this time asked, "What? What? Oh, yeah." She turned back to the camera. "Some of our guys think that they're, well, they're gonna try to take the *Nixon*. Take the alien tech. Can't let that happen. That's the first priority: they cannot have the tech. Let us know what you're thinking. . . . Here comes the vid."

The rest of the day was taken in video-conferencing, with the tiresome round-trip time in the discussions.

Toward the end of the day shift, Ferris Langers pinged Fang-Castro; a ping with an urgent tag. She was in the bathroom. Fang-Castro had a number of informal rules, which, though informal, were quite clear to her staff. One was that if a ping was labeled urgent, it goddamned well better be urgent. The goddamned was not articulated but was well understood.

She touched her slate, audio only. "What is it, Lieutenant?"

"Ma'am, I've been running the numbers of the Chinese ship. The solutions don't make any sense for a return to Earth. I guess I'm confirming what everybody's saying. They're coming after us."

"Would you care to elaborate on that?" A pro forma request. She'd known what the Chinese were doing since the moment Crow suggested it, even before the call from Santeros.

"The *Odyssey* just completed their inclination and course correction burns. When I figured up their new trajectory, it was still directed at the inner solar system, but it came close to ours. I ran the timeline forward, and it wasn't just close. In a little more than a day, they're going to be at about the same place in space that we will, with a similar velocity vector."

She commed Crow. "Mr. Crow, the Chinese have corrected course, and there's no longer a question. I need you in the conference room, fifteen minutes. Bring all your ideas."

"Yes, ma'am."

She closed the link. After issuing several other peremptory comehithers, she poured a cup of tea, cradled it in her hands, and thought very hard about just how much trouble they might be in.

When Fang-Castro arrived at the conference room twenty-two minutes later, she was gratified to see that everyone she had summoned was already seated. Crow, looking pensive; Martinez, almost sleepy, which meant he was thinking hard; Major Barnes, freshly out of medical isolation, intent; Fiorella, engaged; Lieutenant Langers; and Greenberg, the chief engineer. All swiveled in their chairs and looked at her as she entered the room. Darlington didn't; he was busy checking the settings on the recording equipment. Langers kept glancing down at his slate, where orbital models were running.

"Mr. Darlington, you're ready?" Fang-Castro asked.

"Yes, ma'am. We're on the air, straight back to the Oval Office."

"Then let's proceed. Lieutenant Langers has confirmed that the Chinese are coming after us." She nodded toward the slightly nervous navigator. "Mr. Langers? You have the floor."

The soft-spoken officer kept it short and concise. His summary, accompanied by a few plots brought up on the conference room vids, barely took longer than his original phone call to Fang-Castro.

Greenberg was incredulous. "We're not helpless! We have power and plenty of delta-vee to spare. If we thrust at ninety degrees to our current trajectory, it would add, oh, a week, maybe, to the trip back. Then our course'd be well clear of the Chinese."

Fang-Castro looked at the navigator, who was tapping away at his slate. He shook his head. "That won't do the trick. We'd be a hundred thousand kilometers off to one side when the *Celestial Odyssey* passed us, on their current trajectory. The thing is, they'll pick up on a course shift pretty quickly, and once they do, they can adjust their trajectory accordingly. They've got over a million kilometers to cover before they reach us. If they can manage a lateral burn of a kilometer or so per second, they can track us. Seems likely."

Fang-Castro thought about that. "And, without the additional forward thrust from our engines, they'd catch us even sooner."

Langers nodded. "By an hour or two."

"There's also the question of how the Chinese would react to an attempt to elude them and how Earth would react," Crow said. "If we successfully stay away from them, they die."

"So we're going to have visitors," Fang-Castro said. "We need to prepare the ship for them. I don't mean baking cupcakes. We can't allow them to capture the ship, take it away from us. I need ideas on how to secure the ship and the alien tech from possibly aggressive moves."

Fiorella asked, "What if they're on a suicide run? What if their plan is simply to take us out? If they do that, nobody gets the tech, and everything goes back to the status quo. From their point of view, that might not be an undesirable outcome."

Martinez, now looking so sleepy that his eyes were almost closed, said, "Then we're fucked. Excuse the language. I've thought about that, about what we could do about that, and my answer is, 'Not much.' Depending on what they've still got aboard, there's lots of ways they could kill us. So I go back to a variation of John Clover's fundamental position on the aliens. . . . Since there's nothing we can do about it, if they intend to blow us up, we might as well plan on the basis that they won't."

Fang-Castro nodded, but said, "Mr. Crow, Major Barnes, Captain Darlington—I want you on military status, now, Sandy—and Mr. Martinez, I want you to brainstorm that whole proposition: Is it really true that we couldn't do anything? If they don't blow us up, what can we do to secure the ship from a takeover? We need procedures for taking the Chinese on board, without jeopardizing our own position. I want complete recommendations in four hours: that will allow the ship warfare experts on Earth to view this vid, confer, generate their own recommendations, and get them back to us. Four hours, people."

Barnes held up a hand, and Fang-Castro nodded to him: "Major Barnes."

"Ma'am, we need to do more than plan for ship security. We also need to plan for what we'd do if security fails and the Chinese manage to take over the ship. That might be a small possibility, but we have to consider it."

Crow interjected: "You're right." And to Fang-Castro: "He's right."

"I'm sure he is," Fang-Castro said. Back to Barnes: "Do you have any practical suggestions for, um, a post-takeover scenario?"

"Yes. I'd suggest that we set up some kind of kill switch that would allow us to destroy the alien tech if we needed to. Joe tells me we're shipping everything that came over the I/O link back to Earth as quickly as we can, but it's not fast enough. I suggest we take down all other high-speed commo links with Earth, and use them to speed up the I/O, to capture as much of that as we can before the Chinese arrive. And maybe even refuse to allow the Chinese aboard for as long as possible so we can keep sending it."

LaFarge, the comm officer, said, "That would double our I/O rate, but we still wouldn't manage to get a significant fraction of it back. We might get ten percent of it, instead of eight."

"Yeah, but who knows what might be in the additional two percent?" Martinez said. "Be worth doing, in my estimation."

"Then we'll do it," Fang-Castro said. "Major Barnes—expand on the kill switch. I don't quite grasp where you're going with that."

Barnes nodded. "If the Chinese managed to take the ship, they could probably figure out a way to get a package or several packages, containing a reader and a memory module, back to Earth, no matter what happened to our ships. Put them on a simple rocket, launch it in the proper orbit. Maybe it doesn't arrive for ten years, but so what? They'd still get it a hundred and thirty years before we did."

"Maybe we ought to consider that," Crow said. "We've got eight copies—"

Martinez said, "We don't have time. We'd have to fab a rocket, work out the orbits . . . they're going to be here in less than a day. If I had a couple of weeks, maybe. But this wouldn't be a simple project."

Barnes said, "To finish my thought . . . if we can't launch our own rocket—and even if we did, I suspect the Chinese would see it, and could probably intercept it, either here or at the earth, and either capture or destroy it—then we should protect the memory capsules and the readers from a takeover. We should fab a box, a safe, out of materials on hand, load it with magnesium from our Mayday flares, and build in a coded trigger. Then, we give triggers to Admiral Fang-Castro and a couple other people. If the Chinese take the ship, we tell them what we've done, and tell them if they interfere with the box, we'll blow it. We'll already have a tech edge on them, from the I/O material. If we do this, it'll at least give the top people on Earth a chance to work out a compromise."

Fang-Castro scratched her nose, then said, "Mr. Crow."

Crow smiled. "Major Barnes has nailed it. This would give us an ultimate fallback."

Barnes: "Keep in mind, we wouldn't even have to use the box if we decide ten hours from now that we don't need it. But if we decide a day from now that we desperately need one, but didn't have it, it might be too late to fab one. We could fab it now and decide later if we need it."

Fang-Castro looked at Martinez and said, "Build it."

"Yes, ma'am. Though . . ."

"What?"

"Ah, I just hate the thought of blowing all that tech. We've got that science stuff on the I/O, but building the tech from first principles is gonna be a nightmare. It's like this: suppose I went back to the 1700s and cornered Ben Franklin and handed him the plans for a laser, and asked him how quickly he could whip one up for me. Even if he fully understood the concepts, he simply wouldn't have the tools. He wouldn't even have the tools to make the tools. Hell, he'd probably electrocute himself trying—he just got lucky with that kite and lightning stunt. That's where we're at. We blow that tech . . . well, we might get some of it in less than a hundred and fifty years, but we won't get all of it. I bet we wouldn't even get most of it."

Crow said, "Joe, it's not really about what mankind would lose: it's about the competition between us and the Chinese."

Martinez nodded. "I know that. But I don't want mankind to lose it. I don't want to lose it. I won't be alive in a hundred and fifty years. I want to see what's in the alien package. Like, now. Before I die."

Fiorella and Sandy put together a quick vid of Fang-Castro graciously agreeing that the Americans would do everything possible to rescue the Chinese. Fiorella's carefully crafted commentary left no doubt that American science, technology, and humanitarianism—the Americans were risking their lives—were key to rescuing the cruder Chinese mission, to allow Cui to get back with her handsome husband and pretty

children. She didn't say that, but everybody watching the vid understood it.

"I think you just made Ultra," Sandy told her, when the vid had
been dispatched to Earth. "Santeros will owe you big-time, and as big
a bitch as she can be, nobody ever claimed that she didn't take care of
her own."

"I'm not one of her own," Fiorella protested.

"Not exactly, but she'll feel the debt. Not a bad place to be," Sandy
said.

Fiorella thought about that, then changed the subject. "You're done
with your meds now, right?"

"Yup."

"How are you feeling?"

"Still hurts, but I'm functional. What happens is . . . Do you want to
hear this?"

"Yes."

"What happens is, your brain gets stuck in a feedback loop. Why
did this happen? Is there something wrong with me that it keeps
happening—first in the Tri-Border, and now here? What could I have
done? What could I have said to her that I didn't? You get these flashbacks and every time you flash back, the loop intensifies. The meds
break the loop and smooth out the thought processes, and eventually
time starts to erode the power of the flashbacks. Somewhat, anyway.
Still get them, but less frequently, and with less force. So. That's where
I'm at."

"I asked because . . . Fang-Castro says you're back on military status.
Which means, if there were a conflict with the Chinese . . ."

"You're worried that I'm fragile."

"I worry about *you*."

"I'm good. And sad. Both at once. But: functional. My brain's working again."

"We're sure that's a good thing?"

Sandy gave her his toothy smile: "You gotta work with what you got,
sweetheart. I just try to keep up. . . ."

53.

The alien tech was kept in one of the rooms that earlier had been used as a temporary jail. Because it had been specifically designed for that purpose, it had been lined with thin sheet steel on all six sides, which effectively made it a Faraday cage, shielding the room from most electromagnetic radiation.

With a heavy, nearly unbreakable lock, it would also resist physical interference, for at least some period of time. All by itself, it might serve.

"The only problem," Martinez said, as he, Sandy, and Crow stood in the room, looking at the carefully packaged alien tech where it sat on newly fabbed plastic shelves, "is that it's too big. Any amount of explosive big enough to guarantee that the tech would be destroyed might also knock a hole in the ship."

"Not good," Crow said.

"We need a small, tough isolation box, inside the hard room, connected to a little tiny receiver buried in the wall outside the steel, where the Chinese can't see it. If we keep the fire in the box, and put the box on a heat-resistant stand of some kind, that'll restrict the fire until we can get inside the room and kill it. And we probably ought to have a camera inside the room, in case they figure another way in."

"Box won't be that small," Crow said. They all looked at the readers, which were the size of a standard office printer.

"Why not just fab a box for the memory modules?" Sandy asked. "Kill those, and the readers are useless, anyway. I mean, maybe we could take four readers, and give four to the Chinese, and we could all race to see how they worked. We could even call it a sign of goodwill."

Crow said, "You've been thinking about this."

"My history in the Tri-Border: trust no one, everything breaks, nothing works as advertised, and if anything can go wrong, it will."

"And you're so young."

"But getting older by the minute," Sandy said. "I can fab the steel box, if Joe can work out the kill trigger switches, which is going to be the hard part. I'll need to measure the modules. Actually, I can scale them with one of my Reds."

"How long will that take?" Crow asked.

"I can fab the box in a couple of hours," Sandy said. "Compared to building a guitar, it's nothing. If we get Elroy to work with Joe on the kill trigger switches . . . I don't know, we should be done before midnight?"

Martinez nodded: "But we'll have to hustle."

The dinner briefing was quiet. Not much had changed. Santeros had confirmed the ship's preparations for the Chinese, "although I'll be pretty goddamned unhappy if you blow that tech."

Sandy had finished the box and gave a brief description of the work: "Made out of steel, with a steel lock. It'll have a bed of raw magnesium taken from Mayday flares. I didn't want the magnesium to actually touch the memory modules, in case there might be some chemical reaction, so I fabbed a tray that sits inside the box, near the top, with individual grooves for each module. The tray's made of non-reactive plastic, so the modules should be fine. That's ready to go. Joe can tell you about his switches."

Martinez said, "We created two electronic ignition circuits inside the magnesium bed—this is a very thin layer of the stuff, because it burns really hot, and we want it to burn out in a hurry. The circuit is battery-powered—two batteries sit inside the box, and either one can provide juice to the firing circuits. It's got a radio link to a coded transceiver embedded in the wall of the room that would be almost impossible to find—it's about the size of your little fingernail. Only two people know where it is, and the Chinese, even if they knew, would virtually have to tear the middle of the ship apart to get at it. Anyway, it's a deadman circuit. If it doesn't get a picosecond ping from at least one of the kill triggers each second, it'll go off. Just in case the Chinese do manage to find the transceiver or otherwise isolate the box from a possible kill signal. We built three triggers for Admiral Fang-Castro to distribute as she wishes. We assume the actual holders of the triggers will be secret, trusted people known only to the admiral."

"This all makes me very nervous," Fang-Castro said. "Though it's exactly what I asked for. How do we fire the switches, if we need to?"

He reached down into a briefcase and pulled out three gold slate styluses. "These actually work, of course. If you drop them, throw them, whatever, nothing happens. But if you look carefully at the middle of them, you'll see a very faint line. That's a cut point. You turn the two halves against each other, rotating them, it doesn't matter which way, then just snap it in your hand. Like you were breaking a wooden pencil. It takes some effort, more than breaking a pencil, but nothing that would be a problem for any active person. No way that could be done accidentally, both the turn and the snap. Do it, and BOOM. The box blows."

"Are they armed?" Barnes asked.

"Yeah, they're functional, but the box isn't. Not yet. I'll arm that just before the Chinese come aboard. Once that's done, it's done." He pushed the styluses across the table to Fang-Castro, who pulled them in, looked at them, and said, "God help us."

Barnes asked, "What about the stuff in memory? The stuff we got through the I/O?"

"That's a little easier," Martinez said. "We suggest that the I/O material be sequestered in the main memory banks, at a location known only to Admiral Fang-Castro and her most-trusted people, and accessible only with a code. We should make it accessible through any terminal. If we hit a crisis point . . . somebody accesses the memory and hits delete."

"I don't see why that's necessary," Greenberg said. "The Chinese can't make use of our data. We've been scrupulous about following the security protocols. Every bit of alien data that came in over the I/O is quantum-encrypted and the intermediate stores are scrubbed as soon as the backup's been verified. We can't even read our own records. The only copy of the decryption key is in Santeros's hands. We've never seen it, it's never been out of secure storage. Without it, the encryption's unbreakable. The Chinese can't get in. If there's even the least chance of keeping or regaining control of the data, we can't consider throwing away knowledge we won't get for another hundred and fifty years."

Crow shook his head. "That's just it. As far as we know, the encryp-

tion's NP-complete, secure even under quantum attack for aeons. But we
might be wrong. The encryption could've been compromised from the
beginning. Look what happened with the American atomic secrets during World War Two. The country built an entire top secret town out in
New Mexico, and guarded it with the most paranoid military men you
could imagine, and every bit of tech was stolen and delivered to the Russians. There are back doors into a lot of supposedly secure systems. The
sabotage of the *Nixon*'s power systems demonstrates that we can't blindly
rely on a belief that we're impregnable."

He looked around the room, then continued. "Even if we are . . .
today . . . well, if I were the Chinese and I got my hands on that datastore,
I would fund the mother of all Manhattan Project hacks. It might take
me a century to figure a way in, but if there was any way in, I'd find it.
That's a long-term view. The Chinese are good at thinking long-term."

Barnes said, "I kind of don't like the whole 'accessible from any terminal' business. If I were the Chinese, and I took over the ship, I'd make
sure that no terminals were accessible that they weren't watching. Even
if I had to shoot them out. I'd be a lot happier if we had the same kind
of kill switch we're using with the QSUs. Something that would send a
signal directly to a receiver hidden someplace, that would invoke the
memory-wipe. Primary memory *and* system backups. We should be able
to do that, shouldn't we?"

Fang-Castro nodded at Martinez, who sighed and said, "Yeah, we
can do that. But this stuff really does scare me. The thought of losing all
that information . . . I can't sleep thinking about it."

And more to worry about.

Fang-Castro nodded at Barnes. "Major Barnes: your assessment of
our overall physical security."

Barnes picked up a coffee cup and said, "It's pretty simple, ma'am. If
they attack us, we're screwed. We have no major weaponry. The *Nixon*
has very little maneuvering capability and it is very slow to respond."

He turned the cup in his hands, as though warming them. "Even if
the *Celestial Odyssey* has no traditional weaponry whatsoever, which I
would hardly assume, they can cripple us. All they have to do is maneu-

ver alongside us, turn tail on and rake their exhaust across one of our radiator masts or booms. The nine-thousand-degree plasma'll take it out in an instant. That's it for us. We've got no propulsion without the radiators. The auxiliary power plant system can provide us with ship-support power forever, but without the big generators online we've got insignificant thrust."

Fang-Castro: "So with hardly any effort on their part, they can leave us adrift in space with no damage to the rest of the *Nixon*, no immediate loss of life, zip. A perfect surgical strike. There is absolutely nothing we can do to prevent it. If we try to outmaneuver them or counter with our own engines, they are ten times more nimble than we are at our best. If they want to disable us, they will."

Barnes nodded: "Yes. Then, if we assume they don't do that, and we take them on board, and they managed to hide some weaponry . . . well, we have a dozen sidearms and four Taser rifles. The Tasers will disable any EVA suits I've ever heard of, and at lower power stages will take down a human. But frankly, that's not much equipment, if we're facing a take-over by trained military personnel with more sophisticated equipment."

"We can't allow any weaponry on board," Crow said to Barnes. "I assume your marines will take any baggage apart, molecule by molecule."

Barnes said, "Yes. Frankly the biggest danger is that they'd take a weapon away from one of us, get a group of us together as hostages, and threaten to start executing people. So we need really good weapon control. Weapons only to people who really know how to control them."

Crow nodded.

And finally, Fang-Castro asked, "The *Odyssey* hasn't even asked for help, yet. Not ship-to-ship. I don't want to call Zhang, I'd rather have him do it. But suppose we manage to take the Chinese on board and all they really want is help. Where are we at on consumables? Do we need to transfer some from the *Odyssey*? How would we do that?"

The meeting went on for two hours.

Then Comm pinged them: "Admiral, the *Celestial Odyssey* is call-ing us."

54.

A day and a half after departing the Maxwell Gap and the deadly alien constellation, the *Celestial Odyssey* was closing in on the *Nixon*. The two ships were separated by a few thousand kilometers, and the gap was narrowing at a kilometer per second.

Zhang was considering the good news: the *Nixon* had stayed its course and made no efforts to evade the impending encounter. They had sufficient reaction mass to follow the *Nixon*, however it maneuvered, but the ship was badly battered, and he didn't want to put any more stress on it than he absolutely had to.

Cui pushed for contact with the *Nixon*: "Sir, we're only hours away from the *Nixon*. Shouldn't we contact the Americans and ask for rescue?"

He smiled what he hoped was an enigmatic smile: "I feel that ambiguity serves us better, for the moment." Seeing that Cui was not satisfied, he said, "Speak plainly, Cui."

"I don't see how that helps us. In fact, I don't entirely understand why you didn't reach out to her much earlier."

"This isn't about the *Nixon*. It's about the people on Earth, playing their games. We have not been entirely candid with those *ben dan* on Earth about the condition of our ship. I don't want anyone to know how damaged we are, how weak we are. People talk. If American intelligence learned what we know, the terms of the rescue might change. I want them frightened of us, I want to be treated as equals. Unfortunate victims of shipwreck, but equals."

Cui shook her head, still skeptical. "But how can we not look like a threat to them, sneaking up on them in silence? It's dangerous. They must be going crazy over there. It would make me crazy if I were their captain, this kind of suspicious behavior."

"No doubt it would, Mr. Cui, and it would make me crazy also. But tell me this: If the situation were reversed, what would you do? Would you initiate hostilities, fire upon the other ship? When it has not, in fact, overtly demonstrated a hostile intent? You, yourself, commented on how flimsy their ship is, how easily we could cripple it. Would you really fire upon us?"

She paused. "Uh, no. Not without an explicit authorization. Maybe not then."

Zhang nodded approvingly. "Very good, Cui, you're thinking like a space captain. You may get your own ship yet. If we live through this. The ability to put yourself in somebody else's shoes, that's a valuable survival skill in space. We have a lot more in common up here—and a lot more risks we share—than the groundpounders understand."

"All right, sir, but what if you're wrong about this? What if she has secret orders to finish us off? They've had time to fab a bomb . . ."

"Then we are at the mercy of Fang-Castro's conscience. She has as much space experience as I do, and I have as much faith in her as I would have in me. I know what I would do, without a moment's hesitation."

But it was all academic, anyway, Zhang thought. The fate of the crew of the *Celestial Odyssey* had been taken out of their hands a day ago, when they'd made the burn that put them on an intercept course with the *Nixon*. Either she'd rescue them or she wouldn't. Zhang had done the best he could.

Soon he'd know if his measure of the American admiral was correct. He and Cui headed for the bridge. It was time to play out the next scene in this drama he'd constructed.

"Comm, open a distress frequency channel." The murmurs between the bridge crew got momentarily louder; then everyone became very, very quiet, as Zhang's gaze swung around the room. He spoke calmly and clearly, with the utmost respect and deference, yet with no hint of subservience.

"This is the Chinese deep space research vessel *Celestial Odyssey*. We

are issuing a Mayday call. We are in distress and are in need of immediate assistance. Please respond."

He waved a finger at the communication station to close the channel.
"Comm, put that on a ten-second loop. Repeat it until we get a response.
When we do, patch it through immediately."

He smiled at Cui: "Now? We wait."

55.

Fang-Castro watched the rearward screen as the *Celestial Odyssey* closed on them. If she cut the engines, they'd arrive in ten minutes. She had no intention of doing that, because there was little doubt that the Chinese ship could fire up its engines to keep up with the slowly accelerating *Nixon*. The Chinese were two kilometers to starboard, well out of the path of the VASIMR engines' exhaust and safely distant from a collision course.

"Let's hear the hail," she said.

Summerhill, the comm officer, said, "It's recorded, on a loop."

He touched a button and Zhang came up, in the middle of a sentence: ". . . are in need of immediate assistance. Please respond." After a couple of seconds of silence, the recorded message started from the beginning. On the second repeat, Fang-Castro ordered it muted.

"Put me through to the *Odyssey*," Fang-Castro said. Summerhill touched another button and then pointed at her: "You're up, ma'am."

"*Celestial Odyssey*, this is the United States Spaceship *Richard M. Nixon*. We've received your distress call. Please stand by." She signaled the communications officer to close the channel. After a quarter minute, the muted distress message loop cut off.

"Good. They're listening full-time," she said. "Mr. Crow? Mr. Francisco? Anything you want to say before I proceed? This is for the official record."

Crow shook his head: "We've talked it through. Speaking officially and for the record, as the President's representative, I'm satisfied that we have prepared as well as we can for . . . whatever eventuality. I agree that under the accepted laws of space, we are required to perform a rescue of a ship in distress, if we are able to do so."

"Thank you," Fang-Castro said. "Mr. Francisco?"

"I agree with Mr. Crow, ma'am."

Fang-Castro signaled Summerhill to reopen the channel to the Chinese. "Ship in distress, *Celestial Odyssey*, this is Admiral Naomi Fang-Castro. What is the precise nature of your emergency and what assistance do you require? Over."

"Admiral, this is Admiral Zhang Ming-Hoa. I am very happy to hear from you. I will keep this brief: my ship was badly damaged during our aerobraking maneuvers at Saturn. Most of our hydrogen tankage is gone. Our remaining tanks cannot carry enough reaction mass to get us back to Earth before our life-support or engineering systems fail. We have expended almost all our reaction mass just to match velocities with you. In your vernacular, we 'need a lift.' Otherwise, we are all dead. Over."

Crow said, to no one in particular, "There it is."

Fang-Castro: "Admiral Zhang, do you need immediate retrieval? How much time do we have? Over."

Zhang: "We are not at imminent risk, but we cannot match your acceleration indefinitely. We will exhaust our reaction-mass reserves in less than half a day. Over."

"Admiral Zhang, we will consider your request and get back to you. Over and out." She turned to Crow and Francisco. "Let's adjourn to the conference room, where we can sit down and talk this out."

A moment later, settled into the conference room chairs, she said, "Thoughts?"

Francisco: "I suggest we drop the whole thing back into Zhang's lap. He's the one with the real problem. Supposedly. What should he do to convince us? He couldn't imagine we would take him at his word. He must have thought out what his next move would have to be. Let's see what that is."

Fang-Castro nodded: "Good point."

Fang-Castro asked Comm for a channel to the *Celestial Odyssey*. When Zhang came up, she said, "Admiral Zhang, we have considered your request. If your situation is as you state, we will take your crew on board. But—there is no delicate way to put this—you must understand that we are skeptical. We need to be persuaded that you are really in need of aid. Over."

"Thank you, Admiral. I understand your doubts. In your position I would share them. I have a proposal. We exchange delegations. Two of us will come over from the *Celestial Odyssey*. You may send as many of your crew as you would like to our ship to inspect it. You may ask any questions you wish of the crew; half of them speak English."

He continued, after a pause: "To ensure that this does not appear to be a useless exchange of hostages, I propose that I and my first officer come to your ship. We are willing to arrive at your ship before you send your representatives. The people you send to our vessel can be of as low rank and . . . frankly . . . expendable as you wish. Over."

Before Fang-Castro could reply, Crow silently raised a finger and slid it across his throat. Fang-Castro said, "Excuse me one moment, Captain Zhang. I will be right back."

When she'd closed the comm channel, Crow said, "This is extremely abnormal behavior for the Chinese. If Zhang is being honest with us, I can understand his coming over, if for no other reason than to be able to talk with you face-to-face and privately. The stakes are extremely high for him. But, he would be accompanied by their political officer, the highest-ranking party official on their ship. He'd leave the first officer in charge."

Fang-Castro understood that, in her blood. She nodded and re-opened the channel: "Admiral, I am puzzled by something. I would expect you to be accompanied by your political officer rather than your first officer. Can you explain? Over."

Zhang: "Ah, you have some familiarity with our protocols. The explanation, unfortunately, is extremely simple. Our political officer is dead. She died with half my crew in the antimatter explosion at the alien facility. We have barely enough personnel to operate this ship. We are running with a below-minimum complement. I'm offering to send over our two most senior command to help convince you of the gravity of our situation. Over."

"Thank you for that information and my sincere condolences on your losses. I'll get back to you as quickly as possible. Over and out."

Crow shook his head: "I don't see how we can refuse."

"A suicide mission?" Francisco suggested.

"I don't believe it," Fang-Castro said. "But we could insist on a scan before they board us."

Crow said, "That would also define the relationship. We're not just being friendly."

Fang-Castro: "Unless somebody has a better suggestion, I would assign Sandy Darlington to go over, with his cameras, so we can see in real time what he's seeing. He can take direction from Martinez and Greenberg, and if they kill him, we still get back, because he's not critical to our operations. And you, Mr. Crow. Since you speak Mandarin, you might overhear something—"

"And if they kill me, you still get back," Crow said, with a grin. "That works for me."

Francisco nodded in agreement.

Fang-Castro reopened a channel to the Chinese captain.

The extensive and unrestricted videography was acceptable to Zhang. He was eager to proceed; he reminded Fang-Castro that unless she decided to order the *Nixon*'s engines shut down, their two ships would start to separate in less than half a day and rescue operations would become increasingly difficult, maybe even infeasible.

"I will order the engine thrust reduced, which will allow the radiators to continue operating," she said. "They're a little touchy, and we don't want a cold restart. My first officer will speak to yours, about the details of the rendezvous."

56.

Just past midnight, *Nixon* time, transports left the Chinese and American ships. Fang-Castro had decided that requiring Zhang to come on board first was perhaps insulting. And she didn't see much risk in a simultaneous exchange.

Sandy said to Crow, who was driving the bus, "I hope she's right. I got this funny feeling between my shoulder blades."

"Could be shingles," Crow said.

"Or possibly a sniper."

"You take your stims?" Crow asked.

"Does a chicken have lips?"

Crow considered, then said, "I don't know what that means. It could go either way."

"Yeah, I took the stims. But fear alone would keep me awake."

As the *Nixon*'s bus passed the Chinese runabout, Sandy waved at the space-suited figures strapped to the framework of their craft. It was similar in concept to the *Nixon*'s eggs, but meant to carry more than one person outside the *Celestial Odyssey*. Rather than working from inside, as with an egg, the Chinese craft would ferry several space-suited workers to any point on the ship, and then release them to work as individuals. One of the space-suited figures waved back. The larger one, he thought.

Crow nudged him. "When we get there, don't say anything unless spoken to, and keep your replies as short as possible. I want you to be the silent guy with the camera. Don't volunteer anything. Don't ask any questions. That's my job."

"Got it. Sir. General. Field Marshal."

The *Nixon*, with its near-kilometer-long radiators and three-hundred-meter main axle, was larger than the *Odyssey*, but it was like a box kite made of balsa wood and string, long thin columns and beams tied together with graphene guy wire. The Chinese ship was only two-thirds the size of the *Nixon*, but it looked like a tank.

As they approached the massive deep space transport, Sandy panned his cameras over the surface of the Chinese ship, and Crow muttered, "Holy cow. Look at that. Get that."

"I'm getting it."

They were stunned by the damage. There were fused and torn moorings where, presumably, there had been external hydrogen tanks. There were none of those now. The hull was scarred and gouged where pieces of the disintegrating tanks must have slammed into the ship. It was obvious that the Chinese crew had patched things together rapidly and, so far, functionally, but there was no attempt to clean it up. Rough welds, overlapping plates, mismatched joints.

Crow said, "You can have it fast or you can have it right." The Chinese had been under time pressures that precluded "right."

"Can't believe they didn't breach," Sandy muttered.

Crow: "The Chinese know how to build a hull. If that had happened to us . . ."

They'd all be dead.

Sandy went to an open channel back to the *Nixon*: "Comm, are you seeing all this? Just checking."

"We see it. Astonishing. Keep it coming, Sandy."

They lingered for a few moments outside the Chinese ship, doing a complete vid scan of the exterior. When Sandy finished, Crow maneuvered the bus into the one operational shuttle bay on the *Celestial Odyssey*. It was a huge space, clearly designed to accommodate a surface-to-orbit vehicle. Now it contained nothing but a couple of runabouts and service pods. A second shuttle, they'd been told, was currently useless, trapped behind nonfunctioning doors on the other shuttle bay. The external vids might confirm that, once Martinez went over them. Sandy couldn't tell, from one look: there was simply too much patchwork on the exterior of the ship.

As Crow maneuvered into the shuttle bay, Sandy stuck the small hand camera on a side-support, with the camera aimed toward the air lock. If a bunch of Chinese troopers came boiling out to seize the bus while he and Crow were inside, the *Nixon* would see it.

While they waited for the bay to pressurize, Crow and Sandy disconnected themselves from the bus and pushed off toward the floor. The shuttle bay was zero-gee environment, as was the entire ship.

"They gotta have some kind of serious exercise regimen, or they're gonna drop dead when they get back to Earth," Sandy said.

"They do," Crow said, as though he actually knew. "And they got lots of meds."

"That shit can kill you all by itself," Sandy said.

The environmental all-clear had come through on their internal readers. As they stripped off their suits, the inner bay door opened and two people came in, led, Sandy noticed, by a young woman, about his age. A really, really cute young woman, small, slim, buff, who looked like she was made to ride a surfboard.

The two Chinese stopped a few meters from the two Americans. "Welcome to the *Celestial Odyssey*. I am Second Officer and Acting Commander Sun Yu Jie, and this"—she gestured to her left—"is our medical officer, Dr. Mo Mu."

Her English was excellent, with only the faintest hint of an accent. "Please do not be offended, but Dr. Mo is going to perform a body scan on both of you, to ensure that you are not bringing any weapons or explosives on board. I am entirely comfortable with the arrangements Captain Zhang has made, but some of my crew is nervous." She looked regretful. "They feel that we are at the disadvantage in this situation. This will relieve some of their anxiety and distrust, unjustified as it is."

Sandy gave her his toothy grin. "No problem! I'm Sanders Darlington. Everyone calls me Sandy—"

Crow's voice crackled in his earbud. "Zip it, Sandy."

Sandy said to the woman, ". . . and this is Mr. Crow, my assistant."

The woman smiled back and extended a hand to Crow: "Yes, Mr. David Crowell, the political officer. Ours, unfortunately, as you heard, was killed. She was loved by everyone. As, I'm sure, is Mr. Crow."

"Absolutely," Sandy said. "And by no one more than myself."

Crow said, "Mr. Darlington is our videographer and will be sending a vid stream of what we observe back to the *Nixon* for the experts there to evaluate. We understand that time is short, and I put myself and Mr. Darlington at your disposal. I'm sure you best know what we need to see to appreciate your situation and confirm Captain Zhang's statements. Not, I assure you, that we've been given any reason to doubt them."

Sun reached out to Sandy, and as they shook hands, she said, "Captain Darlington. I've been watching your vids since you left Earth. You are very talented. Welcome aboard."

Crow conjured up a look of regret, and said, apparently embarrassed, "The President is insisting on confirmation in a matter which has such profound international repercussions. If it were left up to me, we could dispense with all of this."

"The scan, then?" Sun asked. "You accept the scan?"

"Yes, of course."

"Do you wish to continue in English?" Sun asked. "Or go to Mandarin? I understand yours is excellent."

Crow didn't flinch. "English is fine."

With the formalities completed, and the body scans done, the four of them left the hangar bay for their tour of the ship. Mo also spoke English, and Crow engaged him in polite chitchat, inquiring of his family, wondering what it was like to practice space medicine on a trip like this, and admiring the spaciousness of the ship they were wandering through.

Sandy marveled at it: Crow was completely in character as a political functionary, a meet-and-greeter whose primary skill was to be disarmingly pleasant and a good listener.

Though it didn't demand any dissimulation to marvel at the scale of the Chinese ship. The *Nixon* was large in dimension, but very little of that was interior space. The *Celestial Odyssey* was all about carrying cargo, people, and equipment. Three-quarters of the interior was taken up with the propulsion system, mostly the huge internal liquid hydrogen tanks that provided reaction mass for the thermal nuclear engines, but the remaining quarter was still a lot of volume, especially in a zero-gee vessel that was carrying a fraction of the number of people it'd been designed for.

Crow consulted his slate and said, "We'd like to see the propulsion system and talk to a few of your engineers, if we could."

Sandy did vid of the conversation: most of the engineers spoke passable English, and Crow relayed questions from Martinez and Greenberg. At the end, he asked that their engine operation and refueling logs, from the time they arrived at Saturn, be transmitted to the *Nixon*. The engineers looked at Sun, who nodded.

Sandy didn't know what Crow was seeing, but nothing he saw suggested that Zhang had told anything but the truth. Sandy didn't understand, and wasn't interested in, most of the details of ship operations. But after documenting the activities of the *Nixon*'s crew for nine months, he had developed a feel for what were normal working situations in space.

This surely wasn't. There were many fewer workstations than the *Nixon* had, and two-thirds of them were unstaffed. Some of that might be differences in the way the Americans and the Chinese did things, but overall, the ship looked bare bones to him. The unused stations were powered down and there was a very, very thin layer of dust on the screens, about what you'd expect to see from a few days of non-use on Earth. But in a spaceship, in zero-gee? They must be having scrubber problems. Sandy made a note for his report.

The remainder of their tour didn't turn up anything to contradict the impression that the *Celestial Odyssey* was operating with a skeleton crew. Sun asked if there was anything else they needed to see.

Crow carefully consulted his slate one last time and, apparently chagrined, asked if it would be possible to see some of the crew quarters. He told Sun that he felt this was an invasion of privacy and that if she declined he wouldn't hold it against her or their evaluation. It would make his job easier, though, if she could accommodate this awkward, and in his view inappropriate, request.

She agreed to the request—the whole thing had been gamed by both sides, Sandy realized, and there were no unexpected moves—and took them to what amounted to a space-side barracks. Most of the Chinese quarters were laid out for three or four occupants, and a large fraction of them seemed to be entirely unoccupied. Unless the Chinese had very carefully staged all the living quarters, Crow's random sampling ought to yield a fair statistical estimate of the number of Chinese remaining in the crew.

Sandy dutifully vidded everything and then they headed back to the shuttle bay for the return trip to the *Nixon*. Crow amiably chatted the whole way, asking about opportunities for touring, even living in China. He thought there might be some prospect for posting to the diplomatic corps if he did well on this assignment.

Once they had jetted well away from the *Celestial Odyssey*, Sandy aimed his remote at the hand-camera, which unstuck itself, and as he stowed it, he said, "Jesus, what an enormous load of bullshit. The diplomatic stuff. You think they bought it? They know you're the political officer."

"What part did you think was bullshit?"

"The 'hail fellow well met' routine. Free-and-easy social banter isn't really your style."

"You really don't know my style, Sandy."

Sandy hesitated, then asked, "Do you?"

Crow shrugged, and they slid back to the *Nixon*. A minute before they arrived, he said, "I'll tell you what, Sandy. When John Clover interrogated the alien AI, he was more interested in finding out *why* the aliens were doing things than *what* they were doing. That's what I wanted to know. I didn't so much care what the Chinese told me. What I cared about was how they told it to me. What I learned is that they are scared. You, they paid no attention to, because they understood your function. But they were frightened of me, because they were afraid I might say no, and they understand me as the political officer. They are deeply suspicious of us, but they badly wanted my approval.

"That, more than anything I saw or you vidded, makes me think they're telling the truth. His crew has been traumatized and is operating under terrific stress. They're keeping a lid on it as best they can, but they're terrified. Unless their typical engineer is better at this game than I am, this isn't some crafty ruse to get on board the *Nixon*. They need us. If we don't help, they're dead."

After a minute, Sandy said, "All right." After another minute, "I'm sorta impressed, man."

Zhang and Cui inhaled the delicate vapors drifting up from the cups of tea that Fang-Castro had offered them. "Superb," Zhang said. "Better than anything I can get. When we are back on the ground, you will have to give me the name of your provider. I'm stunned that you, outside of China, can obtain better leaf than I can."

Fang-Castro smiled. "It's a side effect of our international trade. When you find out what I paid for this, you'll be amazed. The tea growers in China can make much more money selling their goods on the international market, than they can selling it locally. There's not a lot of opportunity on a space station to spend my pay. So most of it goes into retirement funds for me and my ex-wife, and our children's education. Tea is one of my few indulgences."

Zhang sighed. "I hope we will get to enjoy retirements. On that point . . . I am feeling pressed for time. May we discuss transfer arrangements, assuming your investigations confirm my claims and encourage you to a favorable decision?"

"I read the summary of your situation. You only have nine space suits and your pressurized shuttle was destroyed in the antimatter explosion? Other than a handful of service eggs, similar to your pods, we don't have any pressurized transfer vehicles, and our space suits are customized to the user. How did you plan to make the transfer?"

"Our suits are not so customized. We could either shuttle the suits back and forth or go to body bags. I'd prefer not to go to body bags."

"I understand."

"We would also wish to bring aboard personal items. We understand that they would be thoroughly inspected by your security people."

"Are you talking about weapons?"

"No, of course not. Just small sentimental items, and clothing and so on."

"We can take a limited amount of that. But it will all be closely inspected."

"Of course."

Fang-Castro's slate pinged. "Admiral? Summerhill, here. The bus with Darlington and Crow is back."

"Send them to the conference room, along with Mr. Martinez," she said. She turned to Zhang. "All right, sir, let's see what my people have learned."

57.

The transfer of the *Celestial Odyssey*'s crew took six hours in two shifts. Crew members collected personal belongings, packed them into standard Chinese military duffels, and carried them to the shuttle bay, where the bus from the *Nixon* was moored. Those chosen to go first got into space suits and shuffled onto the bus, for the short ride across. Cui would go with the first group, to command the Chinese on the *Nixon*. Zhang would go last.

On arrival at the *Nixon*, each Chinese crewman was put through a security scanner, and their duffel bags were both scanned and examined by hand. All personal items that might be considered volatile—a few bottles of perfume, soaps, and so on—were sequestered for chemical analysis, with the crewman's name written on the outside of a clear plastic bag containing the questionable items.

At the end, only Zhang, Second Officer Sun, and four other Chinese crew members were left aboard the *Odyssey*. As they suited up and prepared to board the waiting bus, Zhang looked around the shuttle bay for the last time. They were abandoning ship. He'd never had to do that before. He'd never lost a vessel . . . or the majority of his crew.

The level of failure that he felt, the deep melancholy, that was something he could barely endure. Every morning he woke from fitful sleep into a worse nightmare. He'd done his best to be a good commander, to make the right decisions, but all he could say of himself was that his very best had only been enough to keep a near-total disaster from being total.

He barely felt the bus accelerate away from his ship. He shook himself. He wasn't sure how much time had passed since he climbed onto the bus, probably less than a minute. All he had to do was wait. The fittings on their space suits weren't compatible with the ports on the bus, but for such a short operation it didn't matter. They could rely on their suits for life support during the transfer procedures.

Ahead of them was the *Nixon*; behind was his past. He watched as the shuttle bay grew smaller with distance. The lights were on, but there was no one left there to operate the doors.

The *Celestial Odyssey* would continue its voyage, the lights on but nobody home, as the Americans might say. For how long? Who knew? At their lowest power generation settings the reactors might run for many decades. Probably before then something would break and the lights would go out, leaving the ship a dark and powerless hulk.

For a while, though, the *Odyssey* would continue to function. Maybe, Zhang thought, long enough for Beijing to send out a recovery mission. More likely, given its condition, Beijing would abandon it. Perhaps centuries from this moment, space explorers would discover a mysterious, dimly lit ship, abandoned by its crew for reasons long forgotten, a *Flying Dutchman* of the Early Space Era.

A silly and romantic notion. Zhang's mind was wandering. So much fatigue. With his responsibilities over, for all practical purposes, he could barely keep his eyes open.

The receding shuttle bay looked dimmer, blurrier. He wished he could rub his eyes to clear them. That was something he'd always hated about space suits; if you got an itch, you couldn't scratch. Maybe he should just close his eyes for a minute, to see if that would clear his vision. He was just a package on the Americans' transporter.

They didn't need him.

Half an hour after leaving the crippled Chinese ship, the bus arrived at the *Nixon*. A white American egg hovered outside the bus bay, and Sun could see the young cameraman—Captain Darlington?—inside the egg, recording the transfer.

The bus edged into the *Nixon*'s air lock, settled onto the deck, where clamps engaged its legs. The bay doors closed and the hangar began to pressurize. Sun looked to Zhang. "Sir, we've arrived. Your orders?" She got no reply. She leaned over and poked at his arm. He didn't move. She tried again. No response. Tried again . . .

She hit her open channel button. "*Nixon*, we have a problem. Admiral Zhang is unresponsive. We need medical attention!"

The *Nixon*'s chief medical officer, Derek Manfred, rushed forward, along with marines there to process the new arrivals. Manfred and Barnes unclipped the inert captain's suit from the bus harness. There wasn't time to wait for the hangar to finish pressurizing. They ran with him to the air lock. Barnes radioed over his shoulder. "You can come if you wish, Lieutenant Sun, but we're not holding the air lock for you. Your call."

Sun followed her commander.

Fang-Castro, Cui, Crow, and a few others were waiting on the other side of the air lock. Barnes held Zhang's unmoving body while Cui pulled off his helmet and started in on the rest of the suit. Dr. Manfred moved in and shoved her to one side, gently but firmly.

He said, "Not breathing. No pulse. Shocking, now. . . . Nothing. Okay, last resort." The doctor injected Zhang with something and shocked him again. "Nothing."

Another shock, and another. Finally, to Cui: "I'm sorry, I can't bring him back."

Cui was stunned: "How could this happen?"

Manfred was doctor-cool: "I'd have to perform an autopsy to be absolutely certain, but the blood chem telltales are consistent with asphyxiation. Way too little oxygen, way too much CO_2. Something went badly wrong with the air mix in his suit."

Fang-Castro reached out and touched Cui's arm. "I am so very, very sorry, Lieutenant Cui. Admiral Zhang was unquestionably an intelligent and perceptive man and an officer of integrity. I was greatly looking forward to spending time with him in the coming months."

She straightened up. "Lieutenant Cui, I believe that you are the ranking officer and now in command of your crew. I welcome you aboard the USSS *Richard M. Nixon*. With your permission, we can transport Admiral Zhang's body to Medical. I'll have our very best technician, Joe Martinez, go over his space suit. Dr. Manfred can perform an autopsy, if you wish. We should attend to the task of moving the rest of your crew into the *Nixon*."

Sun said, "The suits were tested before we left. Tested. He should have been fine." She hesitated, looked to Cui. "Sir, your orders?"

Cui was still trying to get her bearings. "Uh, yes." She turned to Fang-Castro: "Thank you, Admiral, please go ahead with the personnel transfer. I want to be sure the rest of our . . . my . . . people are all right."

Cui Zhuo stared for a moment at Zhang's body, then turned to the shuttle bay air lock. The door opened—the bay was now fully pressurized—and the American marines were helping the final crew members peel off their suits. As the Chinese crewmen clambered out, the Americans helped them get their footing.

When they were all out, Cui barked an order, gave them a moment to focus on her, and took that moment to do a quick evaluation of the ranks. They all looked alert and in good health. Excellent. Manfred could check them over later.

"Your attention," she said. "We have some very sad news. . . ."

Lieutenant Peng looked like he might burst into tears. Dr. Gao's eyes were huge; eventually she would think to close her mouth. Sun appeared thoughtful. She wasn't surprised by any of that; she knew her crew. Cui would make a good commander, even if she lacked the seasoning of Zhang.

"Sun is your new first officer. Retrieve your duffels from the bus and carry them to the American marines for inspection. You will get individual receipts for your property."

Fang-Castro asked Crow, "What do you think, Mr. Crow? Anything catch your attention?"

"What happened to Zhang—that's not right. I don't understand that, and I need to," Crow said, flicking through the pages on his slate. "As for physical security . . . Most of their duffels were purely personal effects, plus some electronics, mostly standard brand-name slates, although we're checking them closely, of course. We found nothing hidden, nothing resembling contraband or an effort to circumvent our security. There were an unusually large number of drugs, along with the usual vitamins, headache remedies, and such. Their Dr. Mo said that they were primarily to offset the effects of long-term zero-gee travel and to counter any possible damage from radiation exposure at Saturn. It's plausible. Manfred and his medical people are doing analysis of all the various drugs as well as all the volatile chemicals carried aboard . . . mostly soaps, perfumes, deodorant, that sort of thing."

"Are we in danger?"

"No way to know. Zhang . . . Is there some kind of coup under way? There doesn't appear to be. As for them taking over the *Nixon* . . . If I were them, I'd be thinking about it. But a ship this size? With only eighteen unarmed people? Not if they don't hold Command and Control, for certain. Obviously we do not allow any of them into C & C. Not for any reason.

"We're going to lock down their quarters on a rotating schedule, give them limited access to the Commons and other areas, such as the gym, a limited number at a time. Restrict them to the living modules and elevators—no access aft to Engineering or to the storage and shuttle bay. I'd like to keep them out of the elevators, keep them confined to one section of one living module, but the shared facilities of the ship—galley, gym, medical bay, and so on, are distributed across the habitat sections, so we obviously can't completely restrict them."

Fang-Castro noticed a wrinkle in Crow's forehead. Probably the closest he ever came to a furrowed brow. "Unfortunately for us right now, the designers didn't plan this as a prison ship," Crow continued. "I would recommend that you set up a monitoring screen on the bridge, with continuous coverage of all internal cameras, and detail some of our marines to watch the cameras at all times. . . . This situation makes me more uncomfortable than I expected it to be. Especially the loss of Zhang. We knew quite a bit about him. About Cui . . . we know almost nothing."

"I'll take your recommendations for surveillance," Fang-Castro said. "We have them quartered in different areas of the ship, we've split up their sleep/wake schedule and require them to be in their beds during the sleep cycle, we split up exercise cycles and require them to attend," Fang-Castro said. "We've arranged it so that it would be hard for even half of them to congregate at once. We've taken their communication gear . . . I don't know what more we can do."

"I'll think of something," Crow said.

"Do we have some kind of anti-paranoia pill?" Fang-Castro asked. "If we do, maybe you should take one, David."

Crow was paging through his slate at a pace little short of frenetic. Fang-Castro said, "David. Relax. Have a cup of tea."

Lieutenant Sun followed Cui out of the shuttle bay toward a cart that was waiting to take them to the living module elevator. When they were alone, she opened a file of printed paper—hard copies of personnel lists with medical histories to be given to the *Nixon*'s doctors—and pulled two sheets of paper, checked the page numbers, and then pressed them together, face-to-face.

Cui: "What are you doing?"

Sun: "Creating a chemical reaction. There is a plastic coating on page fourteen that will be dissolved by the chemical treatment on page nineteen."

"What?"

Sun peeled the two sheets of paper apart and said, "Lick the corner of this page."

"What?"

"If you don't lick the page, in about"—Sun checked her implants— "three hours, you're going to spend several hours on a very pleasant trip."

"Yu Jie, what are you talking about?"

"You can thank me later, Zhuo, but we're about to take control of the USSS *Richard M. Nixon*. You will have your own ship, Captain Cui."

58.

"What?" Cui said it again, feeling stupid.

Sun said, "Short version, there's a drug in the *Nixon*'s air supply. It'll become active in less than three hours. The antagonist on this paper will block it. I can give you the long version, but first, lick the paper."

Cui refused to give ground. "You're my second. You may speak frankly, but you do not give me orders. I am your superior."

Sun shook her head. "You are not my superior officer. I operate under a mandate from the Party and the Ministry of State Security. Duan Me, the *Celestial Odyssey*'s political officer, reported to me. I report directly to the MSS. I am not obligated to follow your orders. Strictly speaking, you are obligated to follow mine. Lick. The. Goddamn. Paper . . . ma'am."

She offered the paper again. The expression on her face was fierce and imploring, both. Cui licked the paper, her eyes never leaving Sun's.

"Now. Tell me. All of it."

Sun told her.

Sun was *yuhanguan*. Yes, she had done everything and been on every assignment that was in her official dossier. Primarily, though, she functioned as a covert operative for the Ministry of State Security. She was thirty-six years old, not twenty-eight. Since Sun had turned twenty, she had been officially aging, on paper, one year for every two real years.

"I've had a longer career than most. That's just good fortune," Sun said. "Agents age out of the program when it becomes too difficult to reconcile their physical age with their paper one. I was lucky with good genes: I look unusually youthful, and I haven't started to shift into a middle-age appearance, yet."

Her apparent youth was used to place her in the lower levels of any command group, where she'd be less conspicuous, she said.

Her personal medication and toiletries were completely innocent. Her papers were not, and had been primed with several chemical agents. One of the agents was designed to incapacitate a large number of people in a large enclosed space in a short period of time, useful, on Earth, in terrorist hostage situations. Hardly ever likely to be needed in space, but how handy it was, if it were needed.

As soon as she had realized what dire straits the *Celestial Odyssey* was in, Sun had begun re-analyzing her options. After Zhang confided his plans to his officers, she reached out to several carefully selected crew members, the ones she was sure would be most patriotic.

Each was provided with an innocent-looking packet of paper—permanent hard records. All they needed to do once they were safely aboard the *Nixon* was to shuffle the papers while they were sorting their personal effects for the marines' inspection. After that, it wouldn't matter if the marines confiscated them.

The volatile contents from the papers started evaporating as soon as they were exposed to air. There was no odor. Within an hour, they'd have entirely evaporated and the ship's air circulation system would distribute the microencapsulated, aerosolized LSD derivative throughout the forward sections of the ship. The only air that wouldn't be contaminated was in the separately ventilated engineering and power plant modules.

On release, the encapsulation on the particles began to degrade. Three hours after release, the psychoactive component would be exposed, plenty of time for everyone on board the *Nixon* to have inhaled a dose. Shortly thereafter, anyone who had not taken the antagonist would undergo the very best psychedelic experience of their lives. None of that street shit; the chemists in Beijing knew how to make the really good stuff.

After that, the most time-consuming task for the Chinese would be shepherding happily incapacitated and distracted Americans back to their quarters. The best opportunity for clandestine release was during the Chinese's earliest time on the *Nixon*, when things were most chaotic and their activities least well supervised and restricted.

It was purely an accident of timing that it was late night, ship's time, when the unprotected crew would start tripping; Sun couldn't have planned that well, but she was fully prepared to take advantage of it.

Cui was amazed at the lieutenant's sureness. "You seem to have thought this through very thoroughly."

"I didn't come up with this entirely on my own," Sun said. "We started analyzing takeover scenarios for the *Nixon* and collecting intelligence in that direction the moment we realized what the Americans were up to. Truth, we didn't expect to exploit any of those scenarios, not without a direct attack on the *Nixon* that would lead to war. But, y'know, you do the analyses anyway, just in case, and for the intellectual exercise."

A surprisingly small number of Chinese, just seven or eight, could control the *Nixon*. With two shifts, the Chinese could maintain control for a considerable length of time. They couldn't run the ship; more Americans than that were required in Engineering alone. What those half dozen could do was dominate and command the Americans, as long as they were armed and the Americans were not. The part the MSS hadn't been able to figure out was how to gain control in the first place, other than by force.

"Admiral Zhang handed us that opportunity," Sun said, with a hint of gloating.

Cui was aghast. "Admiral Zhang was in on this? It's hard for me to believe he would've approved."

"No, he wouldn't have. That is why he is not part of the situation," Sun said.

The import of that sank in. "You killed him!"

Sun said, "The Party and the MSS came to the opinion that Zhang's myriad failings were putting the entire mission in jeopardy. He was becoming increasingly independent of the thought in Beijing, by our best planners. His reputation was useful: the Americans knew all about him. But he would have used his command weight to interfere with a takeover, even if he knew it was possible. He had a romantic conception of his job, as though he were an old-fashioned sailing captain. The fate of the *Celestial Odyssey*, and its crew, is as nothing, compared to the long-term interests of China. If we don't get the alien technology, we could be left behind for centuries, just as we were in the eighteenth through twentieth centuries, when we were forced inward. Zhang had become an obstacle to our interests."

Cui was still trying to grasp just what was happening. "Still, initiating an operation like this, without the approval of the admiral? What makes you think the crew will accept this?"

"Half of the crew are overtly with me. Nobody in the crew is anything less than wholeheartedly supportive of the State's mandates. The MSS wouldn't have let anyone on this mission who wasn't. Everyone has the same goals. The only differences are over what measures need to be taken to achieve them. Once a course of action has been settled upon, they will all fall in behind it."

Sun was right, and Cui knew it. The captain had hoped the matter could be resolved without confrontation. It was a laudable ideal. Not one, though, the real world would support. Without a show of strength by the Chinese, they had no chance of extracting any concessions from the Americans.

Salvatore Francisco had the graveyard watch on the bridge. Goddamn, what a long day it had been! He sucked at his bulb of coffee. He could've used a mug, but years of duty in zero-gee had made the bulb a comfortable and familiar item in his routine. The transfer of the Chinese had come off without a hitch, but there was so much planning involved, so many different issues and concerns, that it was exhausting monitoring it all. That wasn't even considering the political complications they were facing. Thank God he didn't have to worry about that.

Fang-Castro was getting some well-deserved sleep, and Francisco was scanning routine maintenance reports. Everything was nominal. The Chinese were settled into their quarters.

The new Chinese commander, Cui, had been given the schedule of who would be bunking with whom, and the dining and exercise schedules for the coming days. Each of the Chinese refugees had been assigned two American "supervisors," in most cases one of them military, to watch over them until they were properly settled in their quarters, made familiar with the operation of all the facilities, and locked down for the night.

The Chinese were being very cooperative. He was back to reviewing the engineering reports, post-start-up, when he noticed a scattered sparkling of lights in his vision, like the cosmic ray hits on the retina that happened every so often. Except there were a lot more of them, and they were increasing in intensity as well as frequency. A major solar storm? Radiation monitors were silent.

He blinked, shook his head, trying to clear his vision. Colors were starting to shift, the pale gray background of the text on his slate was taking on tints of green, purple, pink; they started to move and swirl across the screen. Something was wrong. He tapped the comm to Dr. Manfred's quarters. "Doc? Something's wrong with me. I need to see youuuu . . . riiiiight . . . aaaaawwwwaaaaaaaaayyyyyyyyy . . ."

He was having trouble speaking, or, at least, he felt like he was having trouble speaking. Maybe he was speaking just fine, maybe his words were stretching out like taffy taffy taffytoffeecoffeecarefree . . . What was he going to say? He couldn't remember. Words. They were just sooo interesting . . . taffytoffeecoffeecarefreetaffy . . .

He giggled. Low-gee was fun! He tossed his slate and gave it a little spin, watching it arc slowly toward the middle of the bridge, its shiny edges picking up the beautiful liquid light that was pouring from the control lamps and the glowing, wonderfully expanding data displays, flinging that light back at him, split into lightning shards of glorious, constantly changing colors and lovely sounds. *So this is what a rainbow sounds like.* The thought drifted through his head. *I never noticed before. The notes, and the colors, they're so solid. I could climb them. I wonder where they lead?*

It was very quiet throughout the *Nixon*. Most of the Americans were asleep; a few of them mumbled into their pillows. All of them were having the most wonderful dreams, the kind you hoped you'd never wake up from. They would wake up from them, in about ten hours. They'd be surprised at how much the waking world had changed.

The people who were still awake, the Chinese, their "supervisors," and the rest of the crew on duty, didn't make much noise, either. The Chinese who'd been offered the antagonist, the most trusted ones, were quietly going about their tasks. The rest of the Chinese, like the Americans, were too engrossed in the extraordinarily entertaining synesthesia surrounding them to say or do much.

Engineering was quiet, too, but it was operating normally. It was on its own air system. Nobody there, including Dr. Greenberg, who'd taken the late shift to supervise the next day's engine restart, noticed anything out of the ordinary. They went about their business, uploaded the routine status reports to the bridge, and supervised the smoothly running power plant.

In the living modules, those Chinese who weren't tripping gently removed the weapons and any ammunition they could find from their military escorts. They pulled the escorts into empty quarters and left them sitting or lying on the beds, enjoying their fantastic new world.

Two went off to the bus deck, opened the outer lock, and took the bus back to the *Odyssey*, where a nineteenth crewman, a volunteer who'd offered to risk his life to stay with the ship for a few more hours, had been hidden.

He was waiting, with the *Odyssey*'s armory, mostly handguns fitted with high-storage capacitor slugs, which would disable any living creature they hit, and perhaps kill a few.

And there were a few guns that were simply that: large-caliber weapons loaded with slugs that would kill without fragmentation ricochet or the power to do much secondary damage to things like a hull. . . .

The round-trip took barely an hour.

The nine functional Chinese crew members rendezvoused with Cui and Sun in the ship's conference room. From there, they moved to the bridge, where they removed the personnel on duty, save for the crew members staffing the communications, safety, and security workstations. Three stayed to watch over the controls and the tripping crew members. They'd need them later. The Chinese could control the rudimentary functions of the *Nixon*; those were sufficiently self-explanatory. The intricacies of real day-to-day operation? For that they'd need the Americans.

Three more positioned themselves respectively in life support, the galley, and at the dual air lock that led into Engineering.

The remaining two roamed the corridors of the *Nixon*, looking for any more incapacitated military personnel whose weapons they could confiscate and anyone who might still be wandering free. There were very few; at this late hour the only crew members who were up were the ones who were supposed to be on duty.

By the time everyone was in position, most of the night had passed. The eleven sober *yuhanguan* settled themselves down and waited for their compatriots and the Americans to sober up.

59.

Wendy Greenberg was the first crew member on the *Nixon* to notice something wrong. She was wrapping up her night in Engineering. She liked to be on-site for engine restarts. The confidence she expressed to the admiral about the state of the power plant wasn't false—but they'd had enough trouble with the power plants over the course of this mission that even when everything was running smoothly, and she had every expectation it would continue to, she wanted to be there during the run-up to ignition. Just in case.

Now she checked the time: 6:05 A.M. Her shift replacement was late.

That was not okay. Yesterday had been a little bit crazy, but her people had had plenty of time to learn that she was a little bit anal about punctuality. She would have words with somebody.

No point sitting around twiddling her thumbs, she thought. She went back to the endless task of filing operations reports. Definitely not the best part of the job.

When she looked up again, it was 6:20 A.M. That was more than not okay. Mildly steamed, she turned to one of the techs. "Julie, did Javier say anything to you about a shift change for today?"

"No, why?"

"Because he's twenty minutes late and I'm beat. I'm pinging his comm." *Should have done that at 6:01,* she groused to herself.

Julie Park: "He's not usually late for anything. He's as anal as you are, Chief."

"Or you."

"Let's face it, if you're in Engineering . . ."

Greenberg tapped the comm button. Nothing. Huh. "Hey, Julie, I'm not getting an answer, not even in pingback from his comm. Can you ping Javier from your slate?"

"Yup." A few seconds later, "Uh, problem, boss. I can't get a connection, either. Something's screwed up with communications."

By then, Greenberg was opening a line to the bridge. Except, it wouldn't open. She tried the communications station, then security, and finally the admiral's personal comm. They were locked out of the system.

"This ain't good. I'm going to find out what's wrong. Julie, you're in charge of the room until the next shift shows up or I get back. Whichever's first."

She launched herself out of the control room and down the corridor to the air locks. Park switched to the command workstation and had just started reviewing the status plots, when Greenberg returned. Barely a minute had passed. She was flushed and wide-eyed, out of breath.

"Wendy, what . . . ?"

"We're locked in. I cycled through the first air lock, no problem. When I got to the second, the door wouldn't open. The far-side door was wedged open, so the lock couldn't cycle. There was a woman on the far side, so I banged on the door. She turned around. I didn't recognize her. She was one of the Chinese we picked up, I think. She had a gun. She gestured with it for me to go back."

Park said, "Then we're in really bad trouble."

For the next three hours, everyone in Engineering who didn't absolutely, positively have to be monitoring the power plant and the engines tried to find a way to communicate with the rest of the ship. Nothing. They couldn't raise any of the stations in Command and Control. Not just security or communications, but the helm and Navigation were out of touch, as well. They couldn't even get through to the galley to order coffee, or send themselves a message to their own quarters. The whole intraship network was down. At least, it wasn't accessible to them.

Okay, hard decision time, Greenberg thought. *No helm, no navigation. We're flying blind. We should be on course, but we can't actually tell if our heading's drifted or what. Not good.*

She made the call. "Guys, let's shut everything down. We won't fire the VASIMRs up until the admiral says so. We're going back to standby status until we know what's going on."

Commander Fang-Castro rolled over and stretched. She'd slept excep-
tionally well. Remarkable dreams, surreal even for a dreamscape—more
intense, more vivid than any she could recall having before, but excep-
tionally enjoyable. Her wake-up alarm should be going off any moment;
she had an unusually reliable internal body clock. She clicked her implants.

After nine o'clock?

She'd badly overslept, and either the alarm hadn't gone off or had
failed to wake her. Someone should have called down from the bridge
when she hadn't relieved Francisco over an hour ago. She grabbed her
comm and hit the fast-connect for his. Nothing. No response.

His quarters, the same. Bridge and Engineering, the same. No one
was picking up her comm; she couldn't even tell if they were getting
through. She jumped out of bed, threw on her uniform, and headed for
the door.

It wouldn't open for her.

She was locked in her room, with no way of communicating with the
rest of the crew. She didn't have to be a genius to figure out what had
happened, even if she didn't know the details.

All right, then.

She put on her NWUs and clipped the kill trigger stylus to the side of
her slate. Then she retrieved her personal sidearm from a locker, pulled
her chair around to face the door from the far side of the room, and
cradled the firearm in her lap. It was turned on, unlocked and loaded.
Eventually, someone would be coming for her. She could wait.

Crow woke up a few minutes after Fang-Castro. No wake-up call, no
comm, and no exit. The good news was that nobody had come for him,
yet. They would, sooner rather than later.

Okay, priority one: making sure that he wasn't transferred to the
lockup. He had useful tools in his quarters, ones the Chinese wouldn't

know about. They wouldn't find out from the rest of the crew, because they didn't know about them, either. He needed an excuse for staying where he was.

He pulled out the data-hardened slate he used for communicating with the White House. It was set up so he could establish a secure connection to Santeros from anywhere in the ship. Useful previously, but now that worked against him. He drilled down into the slate's network protocols, as deep as he could go quickly. If he was lucky, the Chinese wouldn't have anyone who could dig that far down into an unfamiliar operating system. He hard-linked the slate to his quarters' intranet.

Next, work the same trick the other way around. He hacked into his room's net and changed its low-level protocols so that it would not establish secure outbound connections with anything except his presidential slate.

The slate? That was designed to work only for him, at least in the most-secure mode that was needed to connect to the White House. The log-in was biometrically linked to him. Nothing suspicious or unusual about that; every high-level diplomat's slate worked the same way.

If he was lucky, the Chinese would buy it. It shouldn't take a lot of luck; it was entirely reasonable that the man who had the direct ear of the President of the United States would be provided well-controlled and restricted ways of grabbing that ear.

He had to hope that whoever had masterminded this little coup was security-minded enough to appreciate how sensible this all was. Then all he'd have to do would be to continue to play relatively dumb, and they'd likely leave him where he was. Probably even let him link to the White House as much as he wanted, because they'd be wanting the ear of the President and they'd be wanting her to know just how bad, for the Americans, the situation was.

There was a lot more he could do from his quarters. Without checking, because his checks might be detected, he was pretty confident they'd be controlling the *Nixon* at the most superficial level. Unless the Chinese happened to have a serious cyber-expert among their survivors, it would be easy to circumvent blocks on the network and door lockdowns.

Easy, at least, when you had the equipment he had to work with, plus some carefully placed back doors.

But there was nothing more he was going to do. Not at this time. He wasn't a superspy from a badly written vid. He couldn't single-handedly wrest control of the ship from eighteen Chinese hijackers, at least not without them noticing and eventually figuring out who was doing it and where he was, and then he'd either be dead or find himself working from the naked-in-the-bare-cell scenario.

His tech prep done, it was time to clean up, to look the part he was playing. He shaved, trimmed a few errant hairs from his head, and took his best suit from the closet. Appropriately matching socks and a quick buff to the shoes. He contemplated ties, found one that complemented the suit and his eyes and gave himself a critical once-over in the mirror. He would do: he looked the part of a president's representative about to meet with the very highest level dignitaries of a foreign government. He hoped the Chinese would appreciate the gesture.

Just one last item. The kill switch. He'd picked up the stylus and slipped it into his breast pocket. It went nicely with the suit and tie. Didn't write too badly, either.

He sat down at his desk, pulled up some innocuous presidential briefings on his slate, and let his brain run overtime on the situation, while he waited for his captors to show up.

All over the *Nixon*, crew members were waking up, or coming down. On the bridge, Cui took stock: there were three unarmed Americans against three armed Chinese; five, including herself and Lieutenant Sun. The three Americans were coming to their senses. She could tell from their expressions that they'd rather be in dreamland. *Sorry,* she thought, *but this is reality and this is the new order.*

And, for the time being, the *Nixon* was her ship.

She didn't expect that status to hold indefinitely. Once an accommodation was reached over the disposition of the alien information, she'd be happy to share the command with Fang-Castro. She would even consider handing it back to her entirely, as long as the Chinese retained control of the weapons.

It could work. It would be like one of those countries back on Earth whose civilian government was supported by a strong and independent military. As long as principles and goals were agreed upon, everything was fine, and if there was a disagreement, well . . . The real power did not lie with the government.

She turned to the American at the communications station who was by now sufficiently un-addled to be both alert and fearful. "Lieutenant, what is your name?"

She consciously copied Zhang's command voice—low and soothing, but authoritative. "Don't worry. Despite appearances, you are in no danger as long as you cooperate, and I will not ask you to do anything that puts your compatriots or your ship at risk."

"Summerhill, ma'am, Albi Summerhill."

Ma'am, that was good. He appreciated the situation he was in. "Thank you. Mr. Summerhill, I'm going to need you to operate the communications console according to my instructions. My people understand your systems well enough to engage simple operations, such as temporarily shutting down internal communications, but not how to operate it fully. You understand what I'm asking of you?"

He nodded.

"Very good. Open a ship-wide channel, so that I can make an announcement to your entire crew. Signal me when you've done that."

Summerhill looked over the status board, pressed a few keys, and nodded to Cui. She nodded back in acknowledgment, and took a deep breath. The deepest one of her career; it felt like standing on the edge of a precipice, more exhilarating than terrifying, but some of both. Well, no turning back.

She leaped.

"Your attention, please. And good morning. I am Commander Cui Zhuo, of the People's Republic of China, and former first officer of the Deep Space Vessel *Celestial Odyssey*. I and my fellow *yuhanguan* . . . astronauts . . . are in command of the *Richard M. Nixon*. We expect to return command to you as soon as some concerns are resolved. At present we have locked your quarters and blocked internal communications for security reasons.

"We expect to restore normal functioning shortly. Please be patient, and I personally apologize for any inconveniences we are causing you."

She made a slicing motion with her hand, and then Summerhill killed the microphone. She nodded at him: "Thank you, Lieutenant."

Sun turned to the American sitting near the security station. "And you, what is your name? I'd like you to bring up some security information for me."

"Uh, Langers, ma'am, Ferris Langers. I'm usually at Navigation. I'm a navigation officer. I don't know a lot about this station."

"Can you perform simple operations, like locating a particular crew member or locking or unlocking a particular door?"

He looked at the panel. "Yes, I can do that."

"Please be sure, Mr. Langers. I would be very unhappy if you were to accidentally unlock all the doors or the communications system. The consequences could be tragic."

Langers looked at her face and then at her sidearm. "I will be careful."

"Are Commander Fang-Castro and Mr. Crow in their quarters? Can you open communications channels just to them and unlock only their quarters' doors when Commander Cui requests it? And do you have vid surveillance of their quarters?"

Langers tapped the panel and pulled up a few data lines. "They are both in quarters—or somebody is. I can unlock the doors, but I can't give you the vid. That's locked for reasons of privacy and only the admiral can override the locks. I can give you audio to both quarters, although they both have the option to kill the audio, if they wish."

Cui asked, "Lieutenant Sun, how is our complement?"

"Up to full strength, Commander."

"Lieutenant Langers, please open links to Admiral Fang-Castro and Mr. Crow."

Langers tapped the screen he was looking at, and then pointed a finger at Cui.

"Admiral Fang-Castro, Mr. Crow? This is Cui Zhuo. I would like to meet with both of you in the conference room. I'll be sending escorts to accompany you. They will be armed. Please don't attempt anything foolish."

She didn't wait for an answer, but gestured and Langers closed the channel. "Now, Mr. Summerhill, bring up the ship's logs for the past three weeks. My lieutenant and I have some reading to do."

Summerhill was sweating. "Some of the logs are encrypted, ma'am. I don't have the passwords or keys for those. Honestly, ma'am."

"Bring up what you can, Lieutenant."

 The first round of discussions between the Chinese and Americans went as expected: not well.

Sun had confirmed from the ship's logs what the AI told Cui at the alien station, that the *Nixon* had received eight data storage units of some kind from the alien station, and eight readers for the QSUs. The details were in the encrypted files they couldn't access.

She also divined, from the considerable amount of high-bandwidth data that had been beamed to the *Nixon* from the station, that a substantial store of information on the aliens or their technology must exist in the *Nixon*'s own databanks. The details were also not evident in the unsecured files in the datastore.

Cui and Sun were waiting in the conference room when Fang-Castro and Crow arrived, escorted by two crew members who were also members of the Chinese special forces, the Zhōngguó tèzhǒng bùduì.

Cui gestured at the chairs, but Fang-Castro shook her head. "Naomi Fang-Castro, rear admiral, U.S. Navy, 756-487-8765."

Cui shook her head: "Please. We need to talk this out. You are not a prisoner of war."

"Naomi Fang-Castro, rear admiral, U.S. Navy, 756-487-8765."

Crow said, "Admiral Fang-Castro would disagree about her status. She's a prisoner of war, because your acts are certainly acts of war. That's why she provides her name, rank, and serial number . . . in this case, her Social Security number. If you were not declaring war with your acts—"

"We were not," Sun blurted.

"—then you're pirates, for which the punishment in a critical situation like this, would certainly be death, for all the pirates." He paused, to look at the two Chinese officers, then continued. "Admiral Fang-Castro's reticence does not apply to me, of course, since I'm a civilian. I am willing to talk, and willing to report what you say to the President, although

I warn you, it would be advisable for you to give this up right now. The admiral is a humane person and I doubt that she would order any executions. Once I speak to the President, then this is all on the record. You will have declared war on the United States. I don't know if the chairman granted you the power to do that, but that's where we are."

Cui glanced involuntarily at Sun, then said, "Lieutenant Sun is our . . . new political officer. She would know more about the legalities than I do."

Sun said, "We anticipate returning the ship to your control amicably and quickly. Before we can do that, however, we need to work out a way to share the alien data that you took from the planetoid, and which the aliens intended for all mankind, not for the exclusive use of the U.S.A. I am quite sure that all the regional blocs would agree with us."

Crow smiled at her, shrugged.

"What?"

"We will give you what the President says we can. But I'm not going to do that on my own. If we're in a state of war, then giving you that information would be treason, and I could be shot. I would not enjoy being shot by my own people. And you won't get it from the admiral."

Sun: "We will get it from somebody."

"Good luck with that."

"I would point out that we could simply take the memory modules, and ship them separately back to Earth."

Crow shook his head. "No. You can't."

He told them about the burn box, and the secret switches.

The discussion went downhill from there. Cui made another appeal to Fang-Castro, who was still standing.

Fang-Castro: "Naomi Fang-Castro, rear admiral, U.S. Navy, 756-487-8765."

Sun turned to Crow: "It's time to talk to your president. You can establish a connection with that slate?"

"Yes, but not from here. There is a separately secured network in my quarters. It's tempest-hardened. That's the only way I can set up a line to our communications."

"Let me guess, you're the only one who can operate that slate."

Again, a smile: "It's standard issue for high-level diplomacy. Biometrically linked to me. Nobody else can start it up, and it'll shut down after three minutes if it doesn't sense my thumb. Oh, and it requires a live thumb. It can tell."

Cui looked at Fang-Castro, then at Crow, and sighed. She told the two special forces officers to escort the Americans back to their quarters. "Mr. Crow, Lieutenant Sun and I will confer, and then we will visit you, and perhaps speak to your president."

"I would hurry," Crow said. "You've cut the data stream to Earth and that will be noticed. We will have questions on the way back, by now. If they don't get answers, we might get a war even if you give the ship back to us—because one way or another, our president and military people will understand what has happened."

Cui nodded.

When they were alone, Cui asked Sun: "So, are we at war, or not?"

"Right now, we are Schrödinger's cat," she said. "We need to work on our talking points."

Fifteen minutes later, with Fang-Castro still confined to her quarters, Cui and Sun visited Crow in his. Cui instructed the bridge to reactivate the network in Crow's room and the adjacent corridor.

Crow could've done both, by himself, but wasn't about to reveal that.

Cui instructed Crow to initiate a link to the White House. Once he'd started the process running, she took the slate from him and walked out of the room. She got barely a meter away from the door when an orange alert came up on the screen: "Authorized network no longer available—suspending link initialization."

She stepped back into the room. The alert message was replaced by one stating that initialization had resumed. She stepped just outside the doorway and closed the door. The orange alert reappeared. The network was shielded and the slate locked to it, just as Crow had said. She stepped back into the room and returned the slate to him before the biometric authorization timed out.

Crow tipped his head: "You see?"

"I see."

In another minute, the slate finished initializing the downlink. Had they been close to Earth, Crow would have waited for a response from the White House server confirming the link. With more than an hour of light-speed delay, that was infeasible.

Crow looked at Cui, who nodded, and Crow looked at the vid screen, with a still image of Santeros smiling from the Oval Office.

"President Santeros. I am calling to inform you of some extraordinary events this morning. The *Nixon* has been seized by military members of the Chinese ship *Celestial Odyssey*. Admiral Fang-Castro has refused any cooperation with the Chinese and has indicated by her actions that she considers herself a prisoner of war. Her legal status, of course, would be up to you and to Congress, since she can't unilaterally declare war. At the moment, however, she is refusing the Chinese any cooperation."

He told Santeros that the burn box had been activated. He told her that the Chinese wanted to examine the alien datastore in the *Nixon*'s computer memory, and that he'd informed them that he didn't know the location, and that in any case, the files were fully encrypted and the only key to the encryption was on Earth, as the President knew.

When he finished, he nodded at Cui, who said, "Madam President, this is neither an act of war, nor of piracy. However, what the *Nixon* has done poses an existential threat to the Chinese people, more serious than any atomic bomb. You have, essentially, declared war on us by seizing all the memory modules from the alien planetoid, when they were clearly intended for all humans. There are eight QSUs. We want two of them. You may have two of them. The other four would go to the other major geopolitical blocs. If this is agreed, we will promptly turn control of the ship back to Admiral Fang-Castro."

She nodded at Crow and said, "You may close the link."

Crow said, "It'll be at least a couple of hours before we hear back—

probably more than that, especially if they have to fight a war first. What
would you like me to do in the meantime?"

Cui looked at him soberly. "You might wish to think about ways to persuade her."

Sun: "When I was going to graduate school at UCLA . . ."

Crow: "I would have guessed Berkeley . . ."

Sun: ". . . there was a saying. 'Better to ask forgiveness than permission.' If you deliver the QSU units to us—only two of the eight, along with two readers—you will present her with a fait accompli, and she will have to make the best of it. We return control of the ship to you, with certain safeguards, and there will be no war, no controversy, no piracy, no problem."

"Only the admiral has the power to do that, and she won't," Crow said. "Perhaps I should give you a few more details on the switches."

"Please . . ."

"You can't disable the burn box. Try to force your way into it, you'll trigger the devices. Remove the box from the strong room, they go off. Try to power them down without the release code, they'll go off. I don't know who has the switches: only Admiral Fang-Castro knows how they were distributed. If Fang-Castro is sequestered and you attempt to torture her for the information, the first trigger-holder to find out will burn the box. Really, over some long period of time, and with more of that gas you used on us—another, separate act of war, by the way—you might get some of the switches, but I doubt that you'll get all of them."

Sun looked at him, then said, "Shit."

Two hours later, one of the Chinese special forces officers escorted Fang-Castro to Crow's quarters.

"How's it going?" Crow asked. Cui and Sun were not yet there.

"I'm frantically bored," she said. "They've turned off everything inside my quarters. I can't even watch *Feeling Up Frankie.*"

"So maybe there is an upside to this mess," Crow said.

"How did they get away with that gas, or whatever it was?" Fang-Castro asked.

"I don't want to think about that, because I might have to find a pistol and stick it in my ear," Crow said. "My fault: I should have thought of it. It was some form of encapsulated LSD, I'm sure. It's powerful stuff."

"Do we have any?"

"I wish."

There was a ping at the door, and then Cui and Sun stepped in. Fang-Castro stood up, turned her back on them.

Cui shook her head and asked Crow, "Anything?"

"No, but it won't be long."

Fang-Castro broke her silence after fifteen minutes. Addressing Cui, she asked, "Do I have permission to return to my quarters?"

Cui shook her head: "No. You must hear what the President has to say."

Fang-Castro turned away again.

Santeros showed up five minutes later. She was seated at her desk, the pale greens of Washingtonian spring visible through the windows of the Oval Office. It had been a long time since any of them had seen trees.

With her hands clasped calmly in front of her on the desk, she said, "Good morning, Mr. Crow. I presume your Chinese visitors"—she paused very briefly at that word—"are listening in to this. If not, please let them know that I am glad we could offer them rescue and I have forwarded their proposal to my advisers for discussion. Convey my sincerest hope for a speedy resolution to this situation. Also, I've spoken to the chief of staff, who knows Admiral Fang-Castro quite well, and says that she can be quite the hard-ass. Inform the admiral that we do not consider her a prisoner of war at this point and that she can negotiate with the Chinese on behalf of the crew. She is not to negotiate the release of the QSUs or any other alien information. That is ours, and ours alone, pending discussions with the Chinese government. That's all for now, and TTTFO." Her hand reached over to click the off switch and the screen went blank.

Crow coughed, said, "Sorry, I'm a little nervous. You heard what we heard. Where does that leave us?"

Sun said, "Political doublespeak. I am familiar with it. They will discuss and stall for as long as they can. Eventually they will have to give in.

We hold the ship. One thing I did not understand—this 'TTTFO.' Code of some sort, Mr. Crow?"

He smiled blandly. "Of a sort, Commander Cui. It's diplomatic shorthand for the usual boilerplate formalities. Extend the other party the usual courtesies, try not to start a war, et cetera, et cetera."

Fang-Castro joined the conversation. "So we have nothing of substance back. I didn't expect we would. You are asking a lot of Washington, regardless of how much control you have over this vessel. Excuse my bluntness, but they are going to take some time over this."

Sun said, "Double shit."

"Yes. Now, as legal commander of this vessel, I need to talk in private with Mr. Crow. Regardless of what you may have effected, in the eyes of the U.S. government, I remain the only legitimate authority on this ship. I need to speak to Crow frankly about this situation, and through him, to the President. We can't have those discussions in your presence. It would be like me expecting to sit in on the private policy discussions of your top party officials in Beijing. If we can't have opportunities to talk in private, we can't discuss anything of substance. It simply will not happen—Washington would never permit it."

Crow did his best to look both sincere and harmless, and added, "I understand you'd consider this a risk. The admiral and I can meet here, and you can search my quarters again. You won't find any weapons or equipment a diplomat in my position wouldn't be expected to have. We have no arms, no means to communicate with the rest of the crew, and we will be locked in."

Sun hated the idea. Who knew what mischief they might dream up? Realistically, though, they were right. If this impasse were to end, they'd have to do more than glare at each other. Reluctantly, she nodded to Cui. "This is getting us nowhere, and we have matters of our own to discuss."

With curt nods, the Chinese left the room and the door snicked shut.

Fang-Castro turned to Crow. "David, I didn't think you had it in you. You had me totally convinced."

Crow raised an eyebrow. "Of what? That I could be diplomatic? It's necessary at times."

She chuckled. "No, it's more that you can come off as so middle management."

"Much of the time, I need to be not-noticed."

She understood. "One question, though—that TTTFO? That seemed to catch you up for a second."

"She surprised me with that," he said. "It's White House shorthand, usually applied to members of Congress. Means 'Tell them to fuck off.'"

61.

The Chinese returned to Crow's quarters about an hour and a half after they left. They knocked before entering, to Fang-Castro's surprise.

Cui smiled. "We understand your need for private communication and we want a proper resolution to the problem. In line with that, we've drawn up a schedule for the release of your people from their quarters. Not all at the same time, of course, but on a rotating schedule. I believe my people have also distinguished between crew members who are necessary to the continued operation of the *Nixon* and those who are merely passengers, like our scientists were.

"I think we have drawn up an acceptable duty roster, but please review it. We would also like to do a complete Engineering shift change. They have already been on duty for twice the normal time. We don't wish there to be any misunderstanding with the on-duty or off-duty teams, so we are providing you with a comm channel to both. Please inform them that you are authorizing this shift change and that we will be shepherding the new engineering team down and the old one back to their quarters."

Fang-Castro was rankled by having the terms of operation of her ship dictated to her. She swallowed her annoyance; the Chinese were doing the right things, but . . . they shouldn't have been there at all.

She issued the orders. "You don't think you can keep control of the ship indefinitely, do you? There just aren't enough of you to monitor everyone, everywhere, all the time."

Lieutenant Sun shook her head. "We don't expect to hold control indefinitely. Just until we get what we want: an equal share in the alien discoveries."

"We've already explained that full access to our computer system and data files is impossible without a presidential directive to release the crypto key, and hell is likely to freeze over before that happens," she said. "You might as well shoot us now, if that's what you're waiting for."

Crow said, "You're both military, so I'm sure you can understand this: getting superuser status on that system would be a breach of U.S. security on an unprecedented level. You'd have access to the designs and engineering information for the *Nixon*, all communications we've had with Earth, the security and crypto protocols that supported those communications, and every bit of political or military information that happens to be in the system. That would compromise U.S. operations for years. At the very least we'd have to treat every channel of communication as unsecured until it could be completely replaced and the code rewritten from scratch. If you can start mining our datastore, you don't just learn what data we're securing, you learn how we do it. It's not even open to consideration. If you think it is, imagine what your own superiors would say to the idea that you give us the key to the *Celestial Odyssey*'s datastore."

Cui looked at her feet: almost a concession of defeat. Then her eyes came up: "But the QSUs aren't encrypted. You give us two QSUs, and two readers, you jeopardize nothing—"

Sun: "Except your plan to dominate Earth's technology for a few hundred years . . . which is exactly what we can't allow. Give us the QSUs."

Fang-Castro said, "With our ship and people being held hostage, I can pretty much guarantee that Santeros won't negotiate over the QSUs. Even if she wasn't mightily pissed off. Her policy has been to never, ever give in to ransom demands."

Sun opened her mouth to answer, but Crow jumped in: "We need to relax. All of us. Leave it to the governments. Right now, the main thing we all need is patience."

The Chinese left again.

Fang-Castro said to Crow, "If we hint that we're willing to give a centimeter, Cui and Sun'll conclude we're vulnerable to pressure, and they will ratchet up that pressure in the expectation we will ultimately capitulate on all demands. We won't, but they will assume we will. They will make things as unpleasant as they possibly can to reach that objective."

"I'm worried they could decide that you're bluffing about using the kill switches, and they start shooting people until we turn over the QSUs. You've got to think about what you'd do, Naomi. If they say they're going to shoot one person every so many hours until we give in. If they don't think you'll give in, they'll start with you until, eventually, they work their way down to someone who will. Once that kind of bloodshed starts, it's hard to stop. Even triggering the kill switches might not put an end to it. A very few of our people still have access to weapons, and they might decide on their own to take the ship back. They might even succeed, if they got lucky. A truckload of people would die in the process, though."

"I have been thinking about that. But you know what? I don't think they'll do it. I don't think they have as much freedom to act as I do. If they start shooting people, it'll be because the chairman ordered them to. And that could lead to a war of some sort. Will the chairman go to war?"

"Don't know."

The Chinese and Fang-Castro put together duty rosters that let most of the *Nixon*'s crew move about the ship; the Chinese had to do that, simply to keep the ship operating. They maintained armed guards at key points, including the entrance to Engineering, and the bridge, where they monitored and controlled the communications, ship security, and safety workstations. Another person had to supervise life support and one more covered the cafeteria/commons. They agreed to let Fang-Castro and Crow consult in private. When they weren't talking, Fang-Castro was confined to quarters, except for mandatory exercise. She was allowed inbound entertainment vids.

Crow was not confined, but was allowed access to the ship for two shifts a day, sixteen hours. He spent most of his time talking either to Fang-Castro or to the personnel who still had access to weapons: there were seven of them, but only four were out at the same time.

On the second day, the Chinese government offered a compromise: Martinez and two Chinese engineers would fab a rocket-powered capsule that would contain two of the QSUs, and put them in an orbit back to Earth, where the Chinese would pick it up on arrival.

The American government refused to negotiate any settlement as long as the *Nixon* was forcibly held by the Chinese.

"Something's gotta happen," Crow told Sandy, as they sat in the cafeteria. "The Chinese don't have enough people to keep this up."

"I know. There are nineteen of them—turns out they had one hidden on the *Odyssey*, which I didn't find out until last night. That boy had some guts. Two of them, Dr. Mo and that Dr. Gao, they're not military and nobody's gonna make a guard out of them. So there are seventeen of them, including Cui and Sun, and that's not enough for everything they have to watch."

"How many do you think we could take down before things evened out?"

"Should we be talking here about this?" Sandy looked about, a bit nervously.

"Safest place," replied Crow. "They don't have enough people to monitor in real time, especially in the Commons, with the mikes picking up overlapping conversations. They don't all speak great English." He shrugged. "There's risk, but this whole business is well into risky territory. You think of a better place to talk, fine. You won't."

"If you say so. Okay, my best guess?" Sandy gave him the big goofy grin, just a couple of good ol' boys bullshittin' here, eating fake bacon and waffles. "If all your guys with guns could get out at the same time, and they probably could, if we worked it right . . . we could probably get eight of them before they could react. The problem is, they've got communications, and we don't. They'll know instantly that the shooting's started, and they've got better weapons. After we took out eight of them, they'd start getting some of us . . . and there aren't that many of us. And what do we do if they hole up and start taking hostages and killing them?"

Crow chuckled. "Want another cup of coffee?"

"Sure."

Crow got two more, sat down again, scratched his neck, and said, "Then there's the question of what happens if we're about to win. Would Sun do something to blow the ship? She wouldn't have to do much. A few shots into the cafeteria view window and the decompression would take out most of the crew . . . and kill her, of course, but maybe she'd do it."

"There's something else I've been meaning to talk to you about," Sandy said. "Way back when, I asked you if I could be a major, and you said, 'No, but you could be a captain.' Did I ever get that promotion? I mean, really? On paper?"

"To tell you the truth, I forgot all about it," Crow said.

"But when Becca was killed, and you had to tell the doc about my post-traumatic stress problem so he could rig the grief drugs . . . you called me 'captain,'" Sandy said.

"Just giving you a little more status in the eyes of the crew, you know. Letting them know you weren't just some jerk-off Hollywood videographer. . . . But if you're really worried about it, I can talk to the guys on Earth and get the routine started."

Sandy got his grin going again and slumped in his chair and said, "That's not where I'm going, Crow. When we went over to the *Celestial Odyssey*, Sun referred to me as 'Captain Darlington.' Showing off, like she did with you."

Crow rubbed a spot between his eyes and said, "Okay. I missed it, goddamnit. Where'd she get the 'captain'?"

"Curious minds . . ."

Crow glanced around the cafeteria. A dozen people, eating and chatting, two sleepy-looking Chinese . . . with guns. "They've not only got a spy on board, he could talk to them. Maybe talk to them directly, ship to ship."

"Yeah. So if you decide to cook up a little revolution . . . who do you trust?"

"Ah, Jesus."

As it happened, trust wasn't critical.

62.

No one was entirely sure what Lieutenant Albi Summerhill had in mind when he came on shift at the security station, midday on Sunday, April 29, 2068. He hadn't discussed plans ahead of time with anyone, hadn't even hinted at any. Maybe he hadn't had one. Maybe he just thought he saw an opportunity and seized it.

Whatever his reason and forethought, or lack of it, shortly after one o'clock in the ship's afternoon, when the Chinese soldier who was monitoring Summerhill's activities was eating his lunch, Summerhill attempted to surreptitiously unlock all the American crew quarters from the security panel.

Lieutenant Lei was not as distracted as Summerhill had thought. He pushed toward the console, his sidearm drawn, and ordered the lieutenant to relock the doors. When Summerhill tried to stall him, Lei attempted to push past and take control of the security station himself. Summerhill grabbed him, they wrestled, and Lei's firearm went off.

They recoiled from each other, the Chinese as startled as the American, the American bleeding from the back of the head and the neck. The blood dripped with surreal slowness as the American's body toppled slowly toward the deck.

As Summerhill and Lei began struggling, Lieutenant Peng Cong launched himself at them from the opposite side of the deck, leaving Ferris Langers unsupervised at the ship's safety and communication station. As Summerhill dropped toward the deck, Peng waved his pistol at Langers: "Call for help! Call for a medic," he screeched.

Langers hit the open channel tab, his call went out ship-wide.

"Shots fired on the bridge. We have a man down. We need medical personnel here, immediately."

Seconds later he got nearly simultaneous acknowledgments back from Doctors Manfred and Mo—"On my way," "Coming."

Peng swung himself back toward the bleeding American. Lei was attempting to staunch the flow of blood, but it was like trying to stop a river with his fingers. Summerhill began to shake uncontrollably.

Peng screamed at Langers, "Tell them to hurry, hurry, hurry . . . he is dying!"

Langers called again.

Too late.

Mo arrived first, Manfred a second later. Mo crouched next to Summerhill, his feet in the growing puddle of blood that seeped across the floor of the bridge. Mo touched Summerhill with an extension from his slate; Manfred crowded next to him, looking at the slate, then they looked at each other and simultaneously shook their heads. No heartbeat, no brain function.

Lei's bullet had ripped through Summerhill's carotid artery on its way into his head, through a piece of his brain, and out the far side of his skull.

Manfred stood up: "He's gone," he said.

Peng stood staring for a moment. Lei's gun lay on the floor, in the blood puddle. Peng turned toward Langers and extended his own pistol, and Langers put out his hands to fend off the bullet. Peng said, "No, no . . . take it."

He turned the gun in his hands and extended it to Langers butt-first.

Cui was in her quarters, Sun doing a check on her sentries when the call went out. "Shots fired on the bridge . . ." A moment later, "Dr. Manfred, hurry, hurry . . ." and in the background, the sound of heavily accented English, "Get back, get back . . ."

Sun bolted for the bridge, nearly ran into Cui running out of her cabin. "We're done," Cui said.

"We're not done," Sun snarled.

The bridge was locked: Sun called for Peng to open the door, but the door didn't open. Peng didn't answer.

"Something's going on in there. . . . Maybe Peng was shot," Sun said. She looked wildly around, then said, "The Commons."

"What?"

"The Commons, the Commons, that's where the most people will be."

"What . . ."

But Sun was already running, shaking loose her handgun as she went. There were fourteen Americans in the Commons, including the kitchen crew. Sun skidded to a stop as she entered: the two Chinese guards had drawn their sidearms and were facing the Americans across a narrow open space. Sun shouted, "Americans. Sit down. Sit down behind the tables."

"What are we doing?"

Sun commed Peng, then Lei, got no answer. She grabbed one of the Chinese guards and said, "Go to the bridge. Pound on the door. Tell them to hook me to Fang-Castro."

Crow was in his quarters when the call from the bridge went out.

If someone had been shot . . .

The walls of his quarters were made of hardened foam. There was one spot, indistinguishable from the rest of the wall, near the head of his bed, where it was just a bit softer. He forced his fingers into it, pushed side to side, thrust his hand deeper, and grabbed the butt of his Colt. He pulled it out of the wall, turned it on, did a power check.

Good to go.

Next he checked the door: to his surprise, it was unlocked. He turned back and checked his communication channels. The normal communication channels were open, and he pinged Fang-Castro.

"Yes, David."

"Shots fired, somebody's hurt, the comm's working and the doors are open."

"Then I'm going to the bridge."

"Get your sidearm, but stick it in your waistband. Don't carry it in your hand."

"Where are you going?"

"Don't know yet, I'm looking at my personnel screen . . . hang there just one second, I can give you a reading . . ."

He pulled up the personnel screen, went to mapping. There were no Chinese heading to either his or Fang-Castro's quarters. He could see two Chinese running away from the bridge. Barnes had armed himself and was setting up in the main hub intersection. Smart man. Francisco was still in his quarters, working his communications panel.

He tapped back to Fang-Castro. "You're clear all the way to the bridge. I'd say we've got about half the ship back, but I don't know the bridge status. Let me call Langers . . ."

Langers came up one second later: "Sir, we have the bridge. Summerhill's . . . dead. The Chinese here have given up."

"Hang on there, the admiral is on her way."

To Fang-Castro: "Go. Go. We got the bridge."

"Where are you going?" she asked.

"There's a crowd of Chinese setting up opposite Barnes. I'm going that way."

Before he went he called Greenberg and told her what had happened. "Jam the air lock. Don't let anybody through."

"Doing that now."

He took one last look at the personnel screen. Where was Darlington? He tapped a couple of keys and Darlington popped up. The Commons: with four Chinese and a bunch of Americans. He didn't bother to count them, just slipped out the door and ran toward the hub.

Everything froze. Armed Chinese and Americans faced each other, but nobody fired any weapons.

As Fang-Castro approached the bridge, she found a Chinese soldier standing outside. He started to draw his pistol, thought again, put it away. "I cannot get in."

Fang-Castro's slate was working again. She pinged the bridge and said, "I'm outside, with an armed Chinese soldier. His weapon is holstered."

Langers replied: "We have control here. The Chinese have surrendered their weapons. Uh, ask him for his."

Fang-Castro looked at the Chinese soldier, who'd overhead the call. The man scratched his face, and nose once, then said, "My commander is in the Commons. She wishes to speak to you. I have delivered the message, now I go back."

He left, and a moment later Fang-Castro walked onto the bridge.

Sun kept her weapon fixed on the line of Americans; three or four minutes after she'd entered the Commons, she was pinged by Fang-Castro, whose image appeared on the large view screen. She said, "Lieutenant Cui, Lieutenant Sun, you have lost control of the ship. Please surrender your weapons to the nearest Americans and we will settle this amicably, as we should have from the start. This is not a situation we can really resolve at our ranks—"

Sun cut in. "You may call me Colonel Sun. You still have not understood the situation, Admiral. We cannot allow you exclusive control of this technology. We demand that you and the rest of the non-critical Americans return to your quarters, where you will be locked down until we reestablish control here."

"We absolutely will not do that—"

"You had better," Sun said. "I tell you this. We cannot allow you the tech. I will begin executing the people we have here, one every five minutes, until you are locked down again. If anyone attacks us, I will do what I can to destroy the ship. I know I can blow at least two holes in it. I doubt that you'll survive. The five minutes starts . . . now."

Everybody in the room looked at the clock at the corner of the Commons screen. Eight minutes after twelve, straight up.

Two minutes into the count, with no reaction yet from Fang-Castro—she'd asked to consult with her command staff—Bob Hannegan, the physicist, held up a hand. "Colonel Sun, I need to speak to you for ten seconds."

Sun scowled at him. "Speak."

Hannegan held up a gold stylus. "This is one of the kill trigger switches." He gripped it and turned one side against the other. "And this is how it works."

Sun said, "Wait!"

Hannegan snapped the stylus in half, and said, "Ouch, I cut myself." And to Sun, "Now there's no reason to shoot anyone. The QSUs are gone."

As he said the last word, an alarm sounded, and he added: "There goes the fire alarm. There's a three-thousand-degree fire in the burn box."

Cui pinged the Chinese guard outside the strong room. "What is your status?"

"There are two Americans here, with guns, but they have not drawn them. My gun remains holstered."

"We have been told that a kill trigger switch has been fired. Do you have any indication—"

"Yes. I heard a . . . boom . . . one minute ago, and I believe it came from the strong room. One moment, another American is running here."

They waited and a few seconds later, the guard called again: "He has a fire extinguisher, which he says he needs to shoot on the outside of the burn box before the fire burns through. He says it will cool the box. Shall I allow him to open the door?"

Sun said, "Yes. Tell me what you see."

The guard called again a moment later: "It is very hot in here. There is a steel box sitting on what looks like ceramic bricks. The box is glowing red at the top and white at the bottom. The American is spraying it with a freezing foam which does not stay on, but the box is cooling somewhat."

Sun said, "I can't believe it."

She turned to Bob Hannegan and shot him in the head. Hannegan's body simply dropped straight down; he might have had a surprised look on his face.

Sun looked up at the view screen, where Fang-Castro had reappeared.

She shouted, "Admiral Fang-Castro. We demand that you return to your quarters. We have executed the first of your crew members, and will continue each five minutes until we are given access to the alien information."

"The alien information has been destroyed," Fang-Castro said. "Your own people can confirm this."

"I do not believe this," Sun shouted at her. "Even if so, you still have the I/O input. We demand that you return to your quarters, and return the ship to our control, so that we may access the datastore, or I will execute another crew member in"—she winked at her implants—"three minutes."

Fang-Castro said, "Killing people won't bring back the QSUs—"

"We can't take the chance!" Sun shouted. "If you don't believe me . . ."

She raised her gun, pointing it at Francisco.

Sandy shouted, "Wait, wait, wait . . . Colonel. I can fix this. . . . I promise you, I can fix this."

Sun was wild-eyed: "And how would you fix this, Captain Darlington?"

"Let me . . ." He picked up his slate and unclipped his stylus. "A datastore switch."

From the screen above him, Fang-Castro said, "Captain Darlington! Captain Darlington! Don't do that. Don't do that! That's an order."

Sandy looked up at the screen. "She's crazy, ma'am. She's going to kill Commander Francisco."

Sun said, "Give me that switch."

Sandy said, "No. Here. I'm going to fix everything." He snapped the stylus in his hands, and said, "The datastore is gone."

Sun shouted, "You are lying. You lie!" Spittle was flying from her lips as she looked around the room at the wide-eyed Americans. She pointed the gun at Sandy's head and shouted, "Admiral, you have ten seconds to surrender the bridge—"

Cui shot her in the back.

Sun went down and rolled over, her eyes open, catching Cui just before she died. Cui felt nothing for her at all. She looked up at the screen and said, "Admiral Fang-Castro, if you will put me on ship-wide comm, I will order my crew to lay down their arms."

Propulsion and Engineering's systems ran entirely independently of the rest of the *Nixon*. The shift on duty had no appreciation of how much the balance of power had shifted in a few handfuls of minutes.

"Hey, Wendy, the comm channels are all open again," one of her techs called out. Dr. Greenberg shook her head. Why did it seem like the interesting stuff always happened on her shift? So far, on this mission, "interesting" meant "bad."

Okay, maybe not bad this time, she thought. She opened a channel to the bridge, thought about asking, "Hey what's going on up there?" but decided on a more prudent formality, just in case she was speaking for history.

"Wendy Greenberg, here, chief engineer on duty. Can we have a status update? Over."

"Wendy? You guys okay? Langers. The Chinese have surrendered. Summerhill, Hannegan, and Sun are dead. Over."

There was a mutter all through Engineering: Summerhill was dead? But they had the ship back? Greenberg asked a tech, "Do I laugh or cry?"

When Fang-Castro and Crow got to the Commons, they found Sandy sitting in a chair next to a couple of Chinese soldiers. Sandy looked at Fang-Castro and said, "It's all over?"

"It's all over." She shook her head: "We lost both the QSUs and the datastore. Mr. Francisco?"

"Yes, ma'am?"

"Take Captain Darlington to the remaining lockup and secure him there. I'm placing him under arrest for ignoring a direct order under combat conditions."

Crow was dumbfounded. "Really?"

"I believe we could have negotiated—"

Clover jumped in. "You're wrong. You're flat wrong. Sun was nuts. She was going to kill all of us."

Fang-Castro snapped: "I didn't ask your opinion, Mr. Clover. This will all be subject to an inquiry. In the meantime, Mr. Darlington goes to jail. We've lost access to centuries' worth of knowledge that would have revolutionized the world as we know it. Mr. Francisco, remove him."

Sandy gave Crow the toothy grin: "Some days you ride the board, and some days the board rides you. That's just life, big guy."

63.

Santeros was all too aware of the light-speed delay. It was not improving her temperament. It would be difficult for anything to put her in a worse mood than the past week. Starting with god-damn Fang-Castro's taking the Chinese survivors on board the *Nixon*, and hadn't that worked out well?

Then came the takeover and the runaround she'd gotten from Beijing. This was an act of piracy, clear and simple. Or maybe an act of war. Nobody disputed that. How had Beijing responded? With the diplomatic equivalent of a shrugged shoulder and a mock-sympathetic "Life is hard, isn't it?"

And in the meantime, the Chinese had started a worldwide scare campaign: they were just trying to keep the Americans from keeping the tech that belonged to all humans. The scare campaign was gaining ground.

And that goddamn general secretary, Hong, was doing his best to piss her off even more. On the phone, just now: he didn't say it in so many words, but the condensed version was that she—the fuckin' President of the whole United fuckin' States—was being blown off!

She said her polite good-byes, wished the general secretary's family well, added under her breath that she hoped they'd all get tertiary syphilis, and slammed the handset down so hard that it cracked.

The bang made Paula White and Richard Emery, the chairwoman and vice chairman of the Joint Chiefs of Staff, wince. They glanced at each other. Santeros had a famous temper, but this was off the scale.

Carefully and quietly, White asked, "No improvement, Madam President?"

"Oh no, it's just great. Can't you tell from the expression on my face?" She caught herself and took a deep breath, swallowed. "I'm sorry, Paula, I'm taking it out on you and I should be taking it out on that asshole, Hong. He's got that grandpa face, and he's a bigger hard-liner than me.

Publicly, he's all wringing of hands and bemoaning the 'rogue activities' of the Chinese pirates. In private he's throwing a party. Hell, it's not even that private."

"Madam President," said Emery, "we need to up the ante. Put pressure on Beijing as well as prepare for the worst. Paula and I"—he glanced over at his boss, who nodded—"we think you need to start mobilizing. Take our forces up to Tier Three. And if this doesn't resolve soon, Tier Two."

Her chief of staff stuck his head in: "Ma'am, you've got a highest priority incoming from the *Nixon*. You're gonna want to look at it."

"How bad?"

The chief of staff scratched his head. "Honestly . . . I don't know. It's . . . I'm just going to spool it over to you."

"Give it to me in one word. Are we going to war?"

"Uh . . . no, but I'm not sure how much happier you're gonna be. Let me spool it over."

64.

Hong's call came just past midnight in Washington, early afternoon in a sunny, flower-scented Beijing. In Washington, Gladys's soft, synthesized voice spoke in the Oval Office. "Madam President, General Secretary Hong is on the line. May I put him through?" Santeros waved assent.

She said, "Mr. Secretary, we're going to need something that'll make both our populaces . . . and our governmental oppositions . . . happy. I'm getting a lot of push here just to have the Chinese rescuees shot outright, as pirates. No international tribunals, no repatriation. Just a bullet for each one."

Hong: "And I'm dealing with folks who think they're the Heroes of the Revolution. You shoot them and my administration won't stand. The MSS will have me replaced with someone even more intractable within hours."

Santeros chuckled. "Things don't move quite so fast here, but if your 'heroes' get their way and my opponents can pin that on me, the next sound you hear will be the House drawing up articles of impeachment."

Representative Cline shook her head vigorously no.

"Oh, face facts, Francie," Santeros said. "If it looks like I caved in to the Chinese pirates, and you don't support a motion to impeach, you'll find yourself ex-Speaker before you could blink twice."

Hong continued, "So, here's our proposed joint statement: our two crews had some communications difficulties to begin with. Language barriers, misunderstood orders, which created some confusion and concern, but it was all over nothing. I can toss in something about radical dissidents trying to foment trouble, not in concert with our policies. I'm sure you can come up with something about minor difficulties in the power plant delaying the restart of the engines. The important thing being that everyone is working together now in the spirit of international cooperation to see that both our peoples come home safely."

"That could fly, if your guys will go along. We'll have to shut everybody up when they get back, but I can do that on my end."

"And I can assure you that I can do it on mine. But I have to give the MSS a bone. They don't believe that all the memory is gone. They point out that you have three major computers, not one."

"You should know, you sabotaged one of them."

"I'm trying to be . . . cooperative here, and find a way to save both our asses."

"But primarily your own."

"Of course, and I'm sure that you have the same relative priority."

"Yes. I do."

"So. Since you say the memory store and the QSUs are all gone . . . here is our proposal."

Santeros had to struggle with the various interest groups involved—and talk to the top scientific experts—but in the end, acceded to the Chinese proposal.

One last task: put the screws to Fiorella. Santeros needed just the right news to be broadcast. . . .

Greenberg was sucking down a bulb of coffee when she took the call from the bridge. The *Nixon* floated in space, fourteen million kilometers from Saturn and 1.3 billion kilometers from Earth.

"Dr. Greenberg, this is Commander Fang-Castro. You have permission to bring the engines back online, full power at your convenience. Helm has sent the navigation coordinates to your station. Let's go home."

65.

Saturday, November 24, 2068—a hundred and fifty thousand kilometers from Earth. The *Nixon* was home.

That's how it felt to the crew, anyway. They were in Earth orbit. It was a large, elliptical orbit, never coming closer than fifty thousand kilometers to the earth and extending out beyond the moon. But it was an orbit; they were captured in Earth's gravitational field.

The *Nixon* would spiral in, reversing the course they had taken when they departed nearly a year and a half ago. Thanksgiving, two days earlier, had been a sober affair. Although Earth was tantalizingly close, less than a million kilometers away and rushing toward them, they still had too much velocity for orbital capture.

But nothing went wrong.

The least thankful person had been Fang-Castro. She had not taken the decisions of the two governments very well.

"I cannot believe you're asking this of me," she said. "You seriously expect me to scuttle my own ship?" She'd received outrageous demands in her time, but this was beyond all imagining.

Santeros was the model of calm. "Admiral, I am not asking anything of you. I'm *telling* you. This is what is going to happen. The *Nixon* will be abandoned, disposed of. The new Chinese Martian transport will retrieve you and your crew. They will bring you back to low Earth orbit. This has been decided. Debate is not being reopened."

"Then I'd ask you to relieve me of command. You can have somebody else take over for the rest of the mission."

The faintest of smiles played across Santeros's lips. "That wouldn't discomfit me in the least, but that's not how this is going to play out. There are issues of international politics that are far more important than you, and as far as that goes, all of your crew members put together. I want neither the distraction nor the questions that might be raised by a last-minute change of command. I need a good face on this. You're going to serve."

"Why should I?"

Santeros shrugged. "Because you're an officer in the navy. You guys always do what you're told first and resign later. If you want to resign later, be my guest."

Fang-Castro's shoulders slumped. Her hands gripped the arms of her chair. The knuckles were pale. She spoke softly. "You give me no choice. I've noticed that tendency in your administration. Anything else?" She didn't say, "ma'am."

"Thank you, Admiral. Look at it this way, Naomi: you have a certain . . . mmm . . . grip on my balls. That's a good thing, from your side. From my side, I'm used to it. There are more hands in my pants than you can believe. But, you know, play your part, and good things will happen for you. Play your part, and Crow will take care of the details."

The Chinese were unwilling to risk even the slightest chance that the *Nixon* could somehow unload the information on the alien technology. Since they didn't know how much memory the alien downloads would use, they were unwilling to let even the smallest objects leave the *Nixon*: a memory file could be made to look like almost anything, so they would not allow *anything* to leave the *Nixon*.

How to do that? The *Nixon* was diseased.

That was the report, a day after they achieved high orbit, when they'd already had visitors. Now the visitors were stuck, too.

Major Barnes came down with something that looked like a virus . . . but not quite like a virus. He'd been cleared through the quarantine months earlier, after breathing the atmosphere in the alien primary, and even now, didn't seem especially ill. Sore throat, pink blotchy spots over his back, legs, and arms.

Then Cui came down with it.

Fang-Castro made the announcement.

"The CDC has a man on the way up. The blood samples taken by Doctors Manfred and Mo suggest a virus, but it doesn't look like anything they've seen before. We're afraid it could have come from the alien environment, so the CDC's guy will be visiting us in a full environmental suit. Dr. Mo suggests that we really don't have much to be worried about, the bug seems easy enough to kill in vitro."

Ship-wide groans.

Sandy had been confined for a week after his performance on the bridge, but the confinement was obviously pointless—where was he going to run to?—and he hadn't yet been convicted of anything, though he surely would be. And he wasn't dangerous . . . and nine-tenths of the people on the ship thought he'd probably saved their lives.

So they let him out.

Fang-Castro told him, "Too many people in Washington know about this to let it go. You're going to spend time in jail."

"Not too much," he said, with his grin.

"If I were you, I'd brace myself," Fang-Castro said. "Among other things, Santeros is looking for a scapegoat."

Now, in Earth orbit, Sandy set up for an interview with Fiorella, announcing the onset of the plague.

"I probably wouldn't refer to it as the plague," Fiorella said.

"They want you to," Sandy said.

"Maybe. But I'm a journalist, not a lapdog," she said. "Really." She sounded slightly guilty. She'd had an extremely pragmatic talk with Santeros.

"I just take the pictures," Sandy said. "Really."

Clover cruised by. "One-point-two million in the Hump Pool. Not a single person has bet on tonight. Or last night or tomorrow night. So, I was thinking we ought to pull the trigger, but . . . you know, even though the whole concept of the Hump Pool is despicable, taking the money smacks of fraud. I'm getting mildly cold feet."

Sandy said, "If we pull the trigger, you could fund your own archaeological expedition. To anywhere."

Clover said, "My feet got warmer. Keep talking."

"I don't really need the money, but I *want* it," Fiorella said. "It's me that the Hump Pool is about. The assumption that I could never resist Mr. Money and Big White Teeth. I will not mind sticking it to them and turning a profit on twisting the knife."

Sandy brought out the teeth: "Dinner and a movie? Tonight at my place?"

"I'll be there at seven o'clock," Fiorella said. She threw her head back, released a well-simulated sexual groan, then straightened and said, "And I'm just warming up."

Clover rubbed his hands together. "I was hoping you'd talk me out of my spasm of righteousness. The Hump Pool was wrong. I'm defending the reputation of women everywhere by taking the cash."

"Absolutely," Fiorella said.

An hour later, she was live from the bridge:

"While the crew, including myself, and the former crewmen of the *Celestial Odyssey*, will have to spend some time in a Level Four biocontainment facility, now being fabbed in the new Chinese *Divine Wanderer*, there's not much doubt the viral visitor can be eradicated from our bodies. There remains the question of what will happen to the *Nixon*. Eradicating every last organic particle from this ship would be a vast task, not made easier by the fact that we'd have to do it in space. Preliminary tests have shown that this particle may not be killed by exposure to a vacuum. . . ."

She went on for a while, but the thrust was clear: a solution would have to be found for eliminating the contamination of the *Nixon*. The world could not risk the introduction of a new alien organism . . . or any other organisms that hadn't yet been found.

Later that evening, after another performance, she said hoarsely, "Damn, my voice is shot."

"Yeah, well, I'm pretty sore from bouncing that cot up and down. I'm thinking the real thing is a lot less work."

"Probably, and neither of us will likely get an Oscar for our performance . . ."

"Your moans were pretty convincing . . ."

". . . but you can't fault the pay scale."

"Amen, sister."

Clover was taking high fives in the Commons. He had a spaghetti pot under his arm, stuffed with currency.

Fang-Castro glanced around her bare quarters.

Saturday, December 1, 2068. She'd remember this date, the day she gave up the command of the *Nixon*.

The Chinese had been prompt and efficient. They could, in fact, have launched and arrived a day earlier than projected. It was the personnel on the *Nixon* who'd held to the original schedule, transmitting every last bit of their work to Earth . . . in native English and math . . . through a Chinese relay.

Not a lot of trust there. Not a lot of trust, anywhere.

Three Americans and two Chinese had died in her ship, though Admiral Zhang was probably dead by the time he arrived. There were four bodies in cold storage, and one was still sailing, in a broken egg, toward the outer planets. The thought of Becca Johansson, on her lonely voyage, still made Fang-Castro tight in the throat.

They'd also lost one cat on the trip: Mr. Snuffles had died of a heart attack three weeks out. John Clover had been devastated, but had said, "He never would have made it back on Earth, anyway. The gravity would kill him the first day. Better this way."

The living Americans—and the former crew members of the *Celestial Odyssey*, as well—would be going through meticulous body scans before they'd even be allowed in the Chinese facility, and then they'd be confined to the Level 4 biocontainment area until the docs were absolutely, one hundred percent sure that they'd eliminated the last of the . . .

Measles.

A mild, attenuated, fast-developing form of measles genetically designed to produce the raw material for a measles vaccine, should that ever be needed; and though it was attenuated, it nevertheless produced the blotching pink rash of regular measles. The only place where the regular disease occasionally popped up was the wilds of Marin County, California. If a few hundred parents hadn't resisted, it would have been eradicated there decades earlier. This outbreak had been brought up by the first visitor to the *Nixon*, a cheerful, politically reliable doc from the CDC.

With both the Chinese and American propaganda machines denying that there was any real danger from the "alien" virus, at the same time they used various ignorance-bathed celebrities to spread fear and misinformation through the Internet, most of the world had become convinced that the *Nixon* was a death machine.

A long-forgotten film from a century earlier, *The Andromeda Strain*, resurfaced on the Internet. Medical personnel—so they claimed to be—called and texted late-night talk shows, citing research that had shown how microorganisms could survive under the most extraordinary conditions. They reminded listeners how diseases on Earth had jumped between species, given the right set of chance mutations. Organisms that might normally infect an alien host might, and they emphasized the word "might," be able to make the jump to human beings.

Probably not. But maybe.

Santeros said it most plainly, in a talk on public television:

"Humans have encountered aliens. No one knows, for certain, what the *Nixon* might have brought back with it in the way of pathogens—germs. We are confident that we can eliminate any pathogens in the human body itself, but with the *Nixon*, that's a much different situation.

"We have consulted with the Chinese, European, Brazilian, African Union, and Indian governments. As much as it breaks my heart, the decision has been taken to destroy the *Nixon* in a way that will remove any doubt that rogue pathogens have been destroyed with it. . . .

"The only things to be brought back from the ship are eight alien machines, which will also be thoroughly decontaminated, and from which we hope and expect to derive much information about their computer technologies. As an act of goodwill between the U.S. and its many foreign allies, the machines will be distributed among the major states represented on the UN's Security Council. We hope, however, to develop a mutual research program."

But what to do with the *Nixon*?

De-orbiting the ship was unthinkable. It was far too large to entirely burn up; something might survive and contaminate the world. Crash it into the moon? It'd have to be monitored as a hazardous waste site indefinitely.

The only smart place to send the ship was to the ultimate incinerator. The sun. The *Divine Wanderer*, the *Celestial Odyssey*'s successor, could do the job; a ship that was designed to carry over a thousand tonnes of cargo wouldn't have any problem pushing around the four-hundred-and-fifty-tonne *Nixon*. A little extra water reaction mass from some strap-on tanks, some newly fabricated attachment mounts, and the Martian transport became the world's biggest and fastest tugboat.

The operation took a week.

On its second, and final, trip to the *Nixon*, the *Divine Wanderer* brought along service eggs, graphene cable, and sensor-laden tie-downs, and a full complement of riggers and jockeys. They'd only be pushing the poor *Nixon* at a few percent of a gee, but that was still several times more acceleration than the ship had been subject to before. A little extra rigging, just to make sure nothing broke loose. It was cheap insurance.

At six o'clock in the morning, Beijing time, President Santeros and General Secretary Hong jointly issued the orders to proceed.

The *Divine Wanderer*, grappled to the *Nixon*'s cold, dead VASIMR engines, began to push. Its nuclear thermal rockets thrummed at a comfortable one-third power for the next day, as the *Divine Wanderer* pushed the *Nixon* away from the earth and against its orbital motion about the sun. When it was done, twenty-seven kilometers per second of fresh delta-vee canceled out all but a few kilometers per second of residual orbital velocity about the sun.

The *Nixon*'s new course was confirmed. The *Divine Wanderer* released its grapples, turned tail, and headed back to Earth. The *Nixon* continued on, in a tight elliptical track with a perihelion of less than half a million kilometers. It would never complete a full orbit; the sun's radius was seven hundred thousand kilometers.

In just over two months, the *Nixon* would hit the sun at over six hundred kilometers per second, at least those few refractory bits that hadn't vaporized millions of kilometers out.

After six weeks of decontamination, the crew of the *Nixon*, and their Chinese guests, were released from biocontainment. The Americans were picked up, a few at a time, by Virgin-SpaceX shuttles, and returned to Earth.

John Clover was among the first to hit dirt: and feel the oppressive pull of Earth's gravity. He'd lost weight in his time in space and had worked out religiously. Still, gravity was a trial. On the other hand, he'd get used to it in a couple of months, and he'd have better than a half-million dollars, his share of the Hump Pool. Made him laugh to think about it.

In New Orleans, he stepped from the government autolimo and checked out his house. It was different. The steps were freshly painted. For that matter, so was the whole fuckin' house.

Crow had told him that the government would maintain it, but this . . .

"Aw, crap." He palmed the front-door lock and the door opened. The hinges didn't squeak. *Crap-crap,* he thought, *if they've messed with my stuff . . .*

Someone had straightened up the living room. Straightened up? They'd done a thorough cleaning, practically a remake. All his carefully tabbed and dog-eared papers and magazines, half-read books, the stacks of old journals by his chairs, all the stuff that had taken up eighty percent of the floor, it was all gone.

Assholes. It'll take years to undo what some brain-dead "organizer" had done to his filing system, he thought. Hell, it'd probably take him years just to find where they'd put all his stuff, assuming they hadn't thrown it out in some misguided fit of do-goodedness.

He needed a joint, he decided, hoping they hadn't thrown out his stash. He stepped on the loose floorboard to the left of the entryway to the living room. The floorboard flipped up and he reached for the rusty tackle box below it. He grunted as he pulled it up. Heavy. Inside there were fresh, wrapped kilo bricks. He peered at the label. They were from the government research farm in Kentucky.

An envelope was taped to one of the bricks, with a letter and a card inside. The letter said he was an authorized owner of the dope under federal law; the card identified him as a federal research subject, exempting him from Louisiana's antiquated prohibitions.

Both were signed by the surgeon general.

The card said:

See what the nanny state can do for you? Welcome home, John.
I'll call you. I need some jambalaya.—C.

Well, I will be blown, Clover thought, as he rolled a joint. He stepped outside to light it up: a calico cat sat on the neighbor's fence, a thin, feral feline. The cat narrowed his eyes and meowed, just once. Food?

"Back in a minute," Clover said to the cat. He'd always had a weakness for calicoes. He meowed once, and went back inside to look for the cat crunchies.

Good dope, even the possibility of a new cat.
Wonder if everybody gets this kind of welcome?

No. They didn't.

Fiorella said good-bye to Sandy at the back of the shuttle. "This whole criminal thing is bullshit," she said. "I'll do everything I can. I think I can probably do a lot. Santeros owes me. We've already got a petition going, almost everybody in the crew signed it."

"Thank you. For everything," Sandy said. "You gonna give me a kiss good-bye?"

"If I do, are you gonna try to squeeze my ass?"

"Maybe. Okay, maybe not."

She gave him a peck on the cheek and said, "Everything will work out."

"I know it will. I'll be seeing you around."

The FBI was waiting at the bottom of the stairs.

Whatever else had been said and done, Santeros still needed a scapegoat.

Sandy was arrested, placed in solitary confinement in Los Angeles, and the next day was flown to Washington, where he'd stand trial in federal court. Santeros had nixed a court-martial for the simple reason that nobody had actually taken the time to reactivate Sandy's commission in the army.

He had excellent attorneys. His father visited him every day and made it very clear that Santeros was going to get a half billion (or so) of adverse political advertising shoved down her throat at the next election cycle.

The trial itself was quite short, since the charges were designed to be undeniable. Sandy didn't bother to deny them, and pled *nolo contendere*. Most of the trial involved the pre-sentencing hearing, in which two dozen *Nixon* crew members defended Sandy's actions as necessary, sane, and probably the salvation of the ship; and former military colleagues represented him as an unsung hero.

Fiorella wasn't allowed to cover the case, because of the obvious conflict of interest, but she'd been interviewed on the top-rated CBSNN show *Sweet Emotion* and, in her Ultra-Star way, had dampened half the hankies in America.

The prosecutor, a civil servant but determined opponent of everything Santeros stood for, asked that Sandy be given forty years, as a way to embarrass her. The judge, a Santeros appointee, had been listening to the witnesses, too, and had a friendly conversation with an old college buddy currently working at the Justice Department; he cut the sentence as short as he possibly could.

Sandy got five years, in Leavenworth.

On the first day of winter, he was taken out of the Washington federal courthouse in handcuffs and leg chains. Onlookers and former cell mates thought he looked unreasonably cheerful for a man facing hard time at Leavenworth.

He was to be transported to National Airport, and from there, flown to Kansas City, for further transfer on to Leavenworth.

The first vehicle was an eight-person van, divided into four cells, cages within a cage. Seating was minimal, but not brutal: a city-bus-style plastic seat, with minor alterations to allow the leg chain to be passed through a steel loop welded into the floor. There was enough room that he could stand and stretch.

He was allowed a slate with one book on it for entertainment, no Internet connection. On this day, he was the only passenger. The trip to National would take a half hour, since the federal marshals driving the van were not allowed to exceed the speed limit.

They were moving at precisely eight o'clock in the morning, the time chosen to avoid reporters. The first stop took place four minutes later, outside the old Smithsonian building. The van pulled to the side of the street, and one of the marshals in the front got out, came around to the back, and popped the door. Crow was standing on the curb, and climbed into the cell next to Sandy's.

"I was wondering when you'd show up. I thought it'd be at National," Sandy said. Gave him the toothy grin.

"Man, with that smirk, you gotta be even dumber than you look," Crow said. "You're on your way to Leavenworth. You know what that means? You're gonna miss the best part of your life."

"I'm thinking not," Sandy said.

"Daddy can't buy you outa this one, pal. Not gonna happen. And all your shipmates who think you saved their lives? Santeros dropped their petition in the wastebasket. She didn't even bother to read it."

Sandy looked down at his slate and flipped a page. Crow couldn't quite see what he was reading. "Yeah, well. There's always France. I think they'll be willing to help out." Sandy held up the slate: *French for Americans.*

"You gotta be kidding me."

"Not at all. I need the refresher—it wasn't my best subject at Harvard. I've always been an admirer of French civilization," Sandy said. "The philosophy, the painting, the women, the food. The cheese, the mushrooms, the snails. You know. So I thought they'd really be the logical ones to lead the world into the next Renaissance."

After a moment, Crow said, "You backed up the database, didn't you? How'd you get it off the ship?"

"I'm gonna give it to the French. They'd ask me nicer."

"The French? You motherfucker," Crow said.

Sandy said, "You want to get out now? This is going to be a tiresome ride and I've got some serious reading to do."

A long silence. Crow didn't move. Then, "What do you want?"

"A pardon from the President," Sandy said. "I'll let her cover her ass. You know, 'We let the trial go on, because we wanted to make a point about discipline. But there are extenuating circumstances, he's very young and a little dumb, had a good service record' . . . blah blah blah."

"We can talk about that," Crow said.

"And I want an apology. I thought about requiring her resignation, because, you know, she's quite the serious asshole. But . . . I guess anyone else would be just as bad."

"No way she would quit," Crow said. "Or apologize."

"You could be wrong about that. If word got out about the stakes involved—the whole future of American technological leadership—I believe the House and Senate might be willing to listen. They don't like her much, anyway. I think she might resign rather than face impeachment."

"Word wouldn't get out," Crow said. "You'll be amazed at how secure our prison system can be, when it wants to be. When was the last time you heard a political statement from Ramon Roarty?" Roarty had conceived and planned the Houston Flash; he was now serving a life sentence at Leavenworth.

"I believe the French ambassador might be asking for permission to visit me in Leavenworth," Sandy said. "To check on rumors of inhumane treatment of prisoners."

"A request that would be denied."

"Amidst vast embarrassment. To say nothing of rather pointed inquiries from the Chinese." Sandy looked thoughtfully through the bars of his cage at the low ceiling of the van. "Maybe I should spread the wealth around. Let the French have the science stuff . . . they're no good with tech anyway . . . and give the alien technology stuff . . . to who? The Brazilians? They're really good with machinery."

For the first time in their entire acquaintance, Sandy saw a hint of surprise in Crow's eyes. "Now you are fucking with me. It's not the database? You've got a QSU?"

Sandy picked up the slate. "Hmmm, I need to work on my French for 'fuck.' That'll be important," he muttered. He read something on the slate. "And it's a little complicated. It'd be embarrassing to use the wrong version of the word. The French are so . . . intricate . . . in their sexual ways, don't you think?"

Another long silence, then, "I can get you the pardon."

"And the apology . . ."

"We'll work out something," Crow said.

"I have to insist on the apology," Sandy said. "A really abject one. Handwritten by herself. Signed. I'll promise to hold it privately until she's out of office. When she's out, though, I'm gonna use my grandpa's money to buy a mansion at Zuma Beach and I'll put the apology on the wall of the entrance hall. Gonna be so cool. But the pardon has to be public. Like right now."

"We'll work it out," Crow said again. "So. What did you do?"

"I won't give you the precise details until I'm walking around free," Sandy said.

"Just tell me. Or I'm getting out and the van can go on to Leavenworth. It's not the day camp you seem to imagine it is."

Sandy said, "You remember when I was fabbing the burn box and I had to do those measurements of the QSUs? Well, while Joe was busy building the circuits, I printed up a couple copies of the QSUs. I had my Red photos with perfect color-matching, and the precise scales, and when I finished . . . I mean, they were perfect. Then, when I was fitting the QSUs into the burn box, I switched a couple of them."

"Why'd you do that?"

"Because everybody was so worried about what would happen if the Chinese took the ship. It was an obvious possibility, so . . . why not? If everything worked out, I'd just retrieve them and turn them over to you."

"How'd you get them off the ship?"

"In my hand-camera case. Took the camera out, put the QSUs inside, sealed it up . . . and when we evacuated the Chinese from the *Odyssey*, took a minute to stick it on the far side of the ship with its Post-it pads. I was worried about the battery—that the lack of warmth would kill it. But then I remembered about the radiators. They put enough heat on parts of the hull that the hull actually was warmish, and that's all I needed. With just a little warmth seeping into the camera case, the battery would last for five years. When we got back . . ."

"You used your remote to unstick it. The camera case is in orbit."

"Yup. Saw it pop off the hull myself. It'll take you about a hundred years to find it, with all the other shit that's still floating around up there. What I'll keep to myself, until I get the apology, is exactly what time I let that puppy go. Got it right down to the tenth of a second. With that information, you could find it in an hour."

"Why'd you wait so long to tell me? Why this whole charade?"

"I think we needed it," Sandy said. "I think we needed the whole trial, all the theatrics, all the bullshit about doing research on the readers, all the *sincerity*, to convince the Chinese that we really didn't have anything, other than the raw science from the I/O. And that's mostly theory—that's gonna get out no matter what we do. Probably printed in *Nature & Science*. In fact, when I thought about it, publishing the science, even the little bit that we have, would set off a lot of research commotion, which would cover up the fact that we have all of it. For a while, anyway."

Crow nodded and said, "You're right. About all of it." He stood up, climbed out of the van, and said to the marshals, who were waiting on the sidewalk, "Let him out."

As the marshals came around, Sandy said, "You knew I'd been up to something. Why?"

"'Cause you once told me that you'd not only do what we want, you'd do what we need," Crow said. "I believed you. Plus, of course, that shit-eating grin that would pop onto your face, from time to time, during the trial. Santeros actually spotted it."

"Huh. Gotta work on that," Sandy said. "Uh, why are the marshals just . . . letting me go?"

"They're not exactly marshal-type marshals, if you take my meaning."

"Did you ever catch your spy?"

"Can't talk about that."

"Did you ever figure out how he was communicating with the Chinese?"

"No, never did."

"I read that Elroy Gorey died when the GPS went crazy on a twenty-wheeler, swerved across the road and killed him."

"A tragedy," Crow said. "We all felt terrible." Neither his voice nor his face showed the slightest inflection.

The marshals freed him and Sandy climbed out of the van. Crow handed him an envelope. On the outside it said simply: "The White House."

"What's this?"

"The pardon," Crow said. "I'll work on the apology. Listen, my car's right around the corner. You need a lift?"

EPILOGUE

2179
DEEP SPACE

The sun was the most brilliant star in the sky, but that was all that distinguished it from other stars. The white-hot pinprick shed barely as much light as the quarter moon did on Earth, three thousand AU away. It did little to illuminate the ship gliding through the inner Oort cloud.

Earth's first truly deep space mission had already satisfied two of its three mission objectives. The run out to the Oort cloud was the final field test of the technology critical to the interstellar vessel currently under construction in high Earth orbit. Long-duration antimatter containment and propulsion was a proven reality, and deep-space, self-contained life support a proven technology.

The ship's second objective had been to sample several primordial Oort cloud objects, comets yet to be born. It was science's first chance to study truly pristine material from the formation of the solar system and an excellent trial run for the remote-sensing and physical investigation procedures that would be integral to the interstellar ship's research.

The ship closed on its final objective.

Two service modules jetted out from the ship's air lock. Ever so carefully, mindful of four billion pairs of watching eyes back on Earth, they matched velocities with a vaguely egg-shaped module of antique design, human sized, encrusted with insectile appendages, ports, windows, and cameras. The main port was cracked. Crushed storage lockers and canisters surrounded the base of the egg.

There was a small hole in the egg's shell.

The two modern modules linked to the antique's grappling rings. Ever so gently, they shepherded it into the ship's air lock.

The lock closed.

The ship rotated until its nose pointed toward the sun.

Antimatter engines flared, immeasurably brighter than the distant pinpoint sun. In two years, the crew would be back on Earth, accompanied by Dr. Rebecca Johansson, the first voyager and the first casualty of the interstellar age, who was finally returning home.

AUTHORS' NOTE: THE SCIENCE BEHIND THE STORY

Dear Reader:

DON'T read this until you've read the novel, because you'll get a whole bunch of spoilers. Some people are fine with that. We know people who read the ends of mysteries first so they can find out whodunit and then enjoy the run-up. We're just warning you.

The science fiction author Greg Benford talks about "wantum mechanics." It's the totally made-up non-science that saves the crew in the last dozen minutes of a bad *Star Trek* episode. "Captain, if we invert the polarity of the phasers and couple them to the warp drive, we can produce a beam of the never-before-heard-of unbelievablon particles and render the enemy's fleet helpless."

That's one kind of thrill ride, and it's fun. But we wanted to write the kind of high-tech, hard-science thriller where you can't just make up stuff to solve your problem—where you have to deal with the real lemons that life hands you, to make your lemonade.

Such a problem is right where we started. One of us (John) had this idea for a novel. To give the story the right pacing, it needed spaceship technology that wouldn't take decades to build and could get to Saturn in less than six months. Even setting the story five decades from now, he didn't know how to do that without just making stuff up—wantum mechanics. So he reached out to the other of us and said, "Ctein, can you figure out how to make this work, because if you can, we might have ourselves a novel."

Cut to the finale. He did, and we did, and you just read it.

Here's some of the science behind the story:

The Big Problem is that space travel is hard. "Rocket science" became synonymous with "really hard" for good reasons. Getting anywhere fast is really, really hard. We couldn't come up with any way to meet the timetable we wanted with present-day technology, so the story is set half a century from now.

It is, in fact (well, in fiction) a fairly boring half century. For the sake of our story we decided that space travel won't make much more progress in the next four or five decades than it has in the last four or five. Science fiction is a game of what-if, not accurately predicting the future.

Still, if you'd told someone back in 1969, at the time of the first moon landing, that nearly half a century later humans wouldn't be doing anything outside of low Earth orbit, not even going back to the moon, they'd have thought you were crazy. It certainly wasn't what your typical science fiction author imagined for the next fifty years. Depressing as the thought is, our scenario may not be as implausible as we'd like to believe.

With fifty years' worth of steady and predictable technological advancements, we could pull off the science. That still doesn't make space travel easy. Space travel's hard because you need high velocities to get anywhere fast, and it's really hard to get high velocities. It takes appalling amounts of energy.

Typical solar system travel times are usually measured in years. The simplest low-velocity, long-duration trip from Earth to Saturn takes about seven years. It's called a "Hohmann transfer" and you can read about it in Wikipedia. That's way too slow for our story. Even then, it takes about as much additional velocity—seven kilometers per second (km/s)—to get yourself from high Earth orbit onto a trajectory that reaches Saturn, as it does to get into Earth orbit in the first place.

Once you get to Saturn, you'll need more delta-vee (rocket scientist shorthand for the change in velocity that you're making) to kill some of your initial velocity, so you'll put yourself in orbit about Saturn instead of flying on past. Then you'll need similar amounts of delta-vee to get you home again, and back into Earth orbit. That's why almost all the robotic probes we've sent out have been one-way missions; returning home means you need a lot more delta-vee at your disposal.

You might be thinking, well what's so tough about that? If it takes a total of twice as much velocity to get you to Saturn as it does to get into

Earth orbit, just make the rocket twice as big. Okay, maybe three times as big to account for getting into orbit around Saturn. And the same amount to get you back again. That doesn't seem that hard.

Unfortunately, that's not how it works. Now we're into proper rocket science, something called the "Tsiolkovsky rocket equation." Don't worry, no math here; you can get that from Wikipedia. The rocket equation ties together three things: the amount of delta-vee you want, the exhaust velocity of your rocket, and the mass ratio of your rocket.

What's "mass ratio"? That's just the ratio of what your rocket weighs fully loaded with reaction mass, divided by what it weighs when you've used up all that mass. That empty (or "dry") weight is everything that isn't fuel; it includes the empty tanks that held the fuel.

Exhaust velocity is the magic number. As long as the total delta-vee you want is less than your exhaust velocity, the amount of reaction mass you need isn't too bad. For example, a rocket that burns oxygen and hydrogen, one of the best chemical fuels you can use, has an exhaust velocity around 4 km/s. If you want to get a delta-vee of 2 km/s, the rocket equation says you need a mass ratio of about 1.7. That means you need to carry 0.7 tons of fuel for every ton of dry rocket you're trying to launch. If you want a delta-vee of 4 km/s, the ratio goes up to 2.7—1.7 tons of fuel for every ton of dry rocket. That's not hard to build.

If you want more velocity than that, it starts to get ugly quickly. Suppose you want a delta-vee of 8 km/s, enough to get you into Earth orbit? (In reality, it's a little harder than that, but we're simplifying for the sake of discussion.) You can think of that as being like getting 4 km/s twice. But, for that first 4 km/s, you're trying to push a rocket that is 2.7 times bigger, because it has to be carrying all that fuel to get the second 4 km/s. Your mass ratio winds up about 7.5. Only 13 percent of your ship is actually ship; 87 percent is fuel that you burn up.

It's awfully hard to build a rocket strong enough to survive flight that is 87 percent fuel. Tanks can only be made so lightweight, and there has to be a useful payload, like people or instruments. It's right on the edge of what our engineering is capable of.

Or a little beyond. No one has yet built a successful rocket that just launches from the earth straight into orbit (what's called "single stage to orbit"). Everything we build has stages, so we can throw away the really big and heavy fuel tanks as they get emptied.

In space, where you're not fighting gravity and you can use lower accelerations, you can build a lighter vehicle. Mass ratios of 10 or better are possible. But you've seen how the numbers multiply up. Even starting from Earth orbit, going to Saturn on a Hohmann transfer, entering Saturn orbit, leaving Saturn orbit, and returning to Earth? With our hydrogen-oxygen rocket, it's simply impossible. You're talking about mass ratios way over 100.

Besides, that's not fast enough! We need much, much higher velocities. We've got to stay within the laws of physics, so what can we change? The exhaust velocity. The higher that velocity, the faster our ship can go (for some particular mass ratio).

In our book, the Chinese are using tried-and-true technology, at least for fifty years from now. Nuclear thermal rockets can get much higher exhaust velocities than chemical rockets (see NERVA, Wikipedia). The *Celestial Odyssey* uses an exotic reactor design called a "lightbulb reactor" that no one's built yet but that engineers have designs for. If we needed them, we could have them in fifteen or twenty years. The Chinese ship pushes that technology to the limits of what engineers think we can do. It heats the exhaust to around 9000°C and it uses hydrogen for the reaction mass. It could use any gas as the reaction mass, because it's just heating it up in a reactor, not trying to burn it. Hydrogen is best because lighter atoms move faster than heavier ones at the same temperature, and hydrogen is as light as we can get. That gets the Chinese the highest exhaust velocity, 22 km/s, which is five times better than burning hydrogen and oxygen.

With that kind of exhaust velocity and a mass ratio of 7 or so, the Chinese can get from Earth to Saturn in around a year and a half. (How do we know that? Later.) It doesn't get them back, but Saturn's rings are water ice and the Chinese can break that down to get the hydrogen to refill their tanks.

Could such a spacecraft make it to Saturn in half a year? Not likely.

They'd need nearly three times the delta-vee, and the mass ratios would be hundreds to one. The Americans need something better. Enter the VASIMR engines. VASIMR stands for "Variable Specific Impulse Magnetoplasma Rocket." "Specific impulse" is how rocket scientists refer to exhaust velocity. We didn't make the VASIMR up. They're being tested on Earth, fairly small ones. Ours are a lot bigger, and a little better-performing, but it's fifty years from now. Building bigger and better VASIMRs doesn't look hard; powering them does, and we'll get back to that.

Becca's *Science Friday* interview in Chapter 21 explains why variable exhaust velocity is, in general, a good idea. The *Nixon* can get more thrust for the same amount of power, when the ship is fully laden, by keeping the exhaust velocity low. That consumes more reaction mass for the same delta-vee, but it gets the ship up to speed faster, shortening the trip time. As the ship gets lighter, it can get by with less thrust and still keep up the acceleration, so the Americans can run the exhaust velocity higher and make more efficient use of the remaining reaction mass.

We built a spreadsheet to let us play around with different velocity profiles. For a trip time of four to five months, we were able to get the ship down to a mass ratio of 10 with an exhaust velocity that varied from 35 up to 300 km/s. That's about half the mass ratio we could come up with for a fixed-specific-impulse ship of any remotely plausible design. Go, VASIMRs!

The reason the Americans' ship uses water instead of straight hydrogen is because it doesn't need to use straight hydrogen. The exhaust velocity that comes out of a VASIMR depends on the charge on the ion and its mass. Hydrogen produces the highest exhaust velocity. Strip off one electron and you're left with a charge of one and an atomic weight of one. Strip one electron off of oxygen and you've got a charge of one but an atomic weight of 16, so the electromagnetic fields in the VASIMR won't push it anywhere as fast. One of the ways the *Nixon* has to tailor its exhaust velocity is to tailor the mix of oxygen to hydrogen.

So how can the VASIMR keep up with a "lightbulb" ship? The lightbulb gets its initial velocity from one long burn—the rest of the trip it's in free fall, until the very end, when another burn will slow it down so it can go into orbit around Saturn. With a VASIMR, you simply don't turn it off. You're making a much more economical use of your reaction mass, and the accumulating thrust eventually adds up to much more velocity than is possible with a lightbulb.

VASIMRs have a problem, though. They're powered by electricity, lots of it. The only way we know of to generate so much power is a nuclear power plant.

Surprisingly, the reactor isn't the problem. Reactor cores can generate amazing amounts of thermal power. You have to get that heat out or the core melts down, but NASA figured out how to build a liquid-lithium-cooled core the size of a coffee can that would output 2.5 megawatts back in the 1970s. That's already as good, in terms of both watts per kilogram and watts per cubic centimeter, as what the *Nixon* needs. The two reactors in the *Nixon* are each four thousand times bigger . . . but they are not better.

The huge problem the *Nixon* faces is that only a little more than half of that heat can get converted into electricity that goes into thrust and is kicked out the back in the VASIMR exhaust. There are some fundamental thermodynamic principles that make it unlikely we'll ever be able to do much better than that. The rest of the heat, nine gigawatts or so, ends up being waste heat and has to be disposed of before everything melts down. That is the really, really hard problem in space.

There are only four ways to move heat around: convection, conduction, transport, or radiation. The first two can't get the heat off of the ship—in a vacuum, there's nothing to conduct heat away from the ship, nor is there gas circulation to convect it. You could transport it off, use it to heat up reaction mass and send it out a rocket nozzle. But that's just a nuclear thermal rocket like the Chinese have, and it's nowhere near efficient enough for the *Nixon*. It also requires infeasibly humongous amounts of heat-absorbing reaction mass; nine gigawatts is an awful lot of heat to be dumping off the ship, day in and day out for months and months.

We're left with radiation. Simple physics describes getting rid of heat by radiation (see "blackbody radiation," Wikipedia). At 80°F (27°C or 300 Kelvins) a two-sided radiator can dump about a kilowatt of heat (1 kW) per square meter into space. That's a lot by human standards, but it means the *Nixon* would need about nine square kilometers of radiator to get rid of all its waste heat—roughly the area of 1,700 American football fields. That would weigh far too much. Physics works in our favor, though. The amount of power you can radiate goes up as the fourth power of the Kelvin temperature. At 600°C (870K) that same square meter of radiator can dispose of 65 kW of heat. That takes the radiator down to a manageable size.

This requires running the whole power plant hotter, because the theoretical efficiency of the power plant is determined by the starting temperature vs. the final temperature (see "Carnot," Wikipedia). We've kicked the final temperature up nearly threefold, so the source temperature has to go up accordingly. That takes us out of the range of boiling water reactors and generators and into the world of pressurized liquid sodium, running at a red heat.

Is this insane? Definitely, by today's standards. We looked at power plant performance and benchmarks for the past century-plus, and extrapolated those trend lines forward fifty years. In half a century it doesn't seem so crazy.

What kind of radiator can run at 600°C? The only possible working fluid is molten metal, and that also works in our favor. Melting metals can absorb huge amounts of energy, far more than any other material. Aluminum, for example, melts a little higher than our working temperature, and melting 2.5 kilograms of it per second will suck up a megawatt of heat. Our imagined radiator alloy is a little better than pure aluminum, but not a whole lot. It's all plausible; we're still doing science and engineering, not wild imagining.

Some simple algebra and punching numbers on a four-function calculator tells us the size for the radiator sail, the speed of the sail ribbons, and the thickness of the ribbons. They are interrelated. The speed of the ribbons has to allow enough time for the semi-molten ribbons to completely solidify before they reach the collection beams. The amount of ribbon being extruded each second has to be sufficient to carry all the waste heat from the *Nixon*.

A minor bit of cleverness. That thin layer of solid cladding that's frozen onto the ribbon as it's extruded does three things for us. It roughens the surface, which improves the radiation characteristics (see emissivity). It keeps the ribbon a ribbon—molten metal has very fierce surface tension, and a thin liquid ribbon would otherwise break up into droplets almost immediately. Finally, it prevents evaporation of the metal. Typical metal vapor pressures are very low at 600°C, but you'd be talking about over a quarter kilometer of surface area and a year's time. You'd have to carry along considerable amounts of spare radiator metal to make up for evaporative losses. In space, it's waste not, want not.

So this is all pretty great: we have two ships that will fly more or less the way we need them to. What will those flights look like? That's orbital mechanics, and while the physics of that is high school–level Newton's laws stuff, the calculations are lengthy. They would've been impossible without personal computers.

We got lucky on one point. The starting date for the book was an arbitrary choice and the pacing up to the point where the ships launch was dictated by what would keep the story moving properly (and launch windows—the right alignment of the earth, sun, and Saturn). As it happened, we wound up in the easiest time frame for calculating orbits. None of the other planets came anywhere close to possible orbits for our spacecraft. All we had to deal with was the earth, sun, and Saturn.

We did the orbit simulations in a Windows program called Orbiter. That wound up consuming hundreds of hours of computer and personal time. Continuous-boost spacecraft like the *Nixon* are still exotic enough concepts that very few software packages can deal with them easily. Those programs are expensive and specialized, their normal clientele being major aerospace companies and research institutions.

Orbiter could very accurately calculate the motion of the spacecraft for each step along a trajectory, but those steps had to be carefully and manually specified. When the *Celestial Odyssey* was falling free, far from the gravitational influence of the earth or Saturn, a step could span months of simulated time (on the computer, that ran in minutes). We just needed the steps to be close enough together that we'd know where the Chinese were at any particular time in case that needed to be mentioned in the story. Entering or leaving orbit involved a lot more steps because the ship's trajectory was changing very quickly.

Simulating the *Nixon* was much harder. Except when Bad Things happened to it, it was never in free fall. The simulation steps had to be close enough together to accurately model the trajectory of a spacecraft that was always accelerating or decelerating. Spiraling out from Earth orbit took about fifty steps to simulate, similarly for the transit from Earth to Saturn. At each step, the thrust parameters were keyed in, the time interval specified, the step calculated, and the data—velocities and positions relative to the earth, sun, and Saturn—extracted and transferred to a spreadsheet. That spreadsheet also produced a plot for us showing the spacecraft's trajectory against the earth, sun, and Saturn. A different spreadsheet tracked energy budget—reaction-mass consumption, mass ratios, exhaust velocities, and accelerations.

We ran nearly a hundred such simulations as we developed the story. Some of those runs were dictated by plot changes as we developed the novel, but most were experiments designed to answer questions. How does the *Nixon*'s departure date affect the travel time? How long can the Chinese wait before chasing after the *Nixon*? What's the best way to get back to Saturn? What's the most efficient trajectory for a return to Earth?

Real rocket science. We think we did it pretty well.

It's not what's important, though, not really. You enjoying the story we told you, that's what matters.

Now it's time for a confession. There is one chunk of wantum mechanics in *Saturn Run*. We don't have the faintest clue how to make antimatter efficiently and in quantity. Antimatter's real, but physicists only know how to make it positron by positron, antiproton by antiproton. The price is currently many trillions of dollars per gram, and all the antimatter ever made amounts to a microscopic fraction of a gram. A way to make tons of it, in solid iron form? We totally faked that out of plausibly appropriate physics jargon. That shouldn't be a big surprise. If we knew how to do this, the Powers That Be wouldn't let us write about it freely. They probably wouldn't even let us walk around freely.

But the rest of it? Real science and real technology, extrapolated as realistically as we could.

(Oh, all right, we made up the aliens, too. But we didn't give them a magic star drive, okay?)

One last thing: Why did we call it the *Nixon*? Because we thought it was funny.

—JOHN SANDFORD AND CTEIN